The Immigration of
JOHN DUNN

Beverly Howard

iUniverse LLC
Bloomington

THE IMMIGRATION OF JOHN DUNN

iUniverse books may be ordered through booksellers or by contacting:

iUniverse LLC
1663 Liberty Drive
Bloomington, IN 47403
www.iuniverse.com
1-800-Authors (1-800-288-4677)

ISBN: 978-1-4917-2035-6 (sc)
ISBN: 978-1-4917-2036-3 (e)

Library of Congress Control Number: 2014900203

Printed in the United States of America.

iUniverse rev. date: 01/02/2014

Part One

IRELAND TO AMERICA

ONE

Ireland . . . it seemed a dream away. Like a mist that would soon lift and he would see the rolling hills and his family and the home where he worked as a stable hand. He would wake up and it would all be there. No, when he awoke he was still in a heavily wooded area in the cold biting rain, sleeping next to a big black slave and running from the law who believed him to be a horse thief! As he moved around trying not to awaken his companion and find a little more comfortable place to rest he drifted off to sleep and again the dream was of Ireland.

His earliest memories of his family included his Father. Father, Mother and two sisters and two brothers made up the group gathered around a large table in a tiny room. The room had hardly any other furnishings except a rocking chair and a bench on the far wall. Opposite the fireplace were two indentions in the otherwise square building that served as bedrooms, the parents in one and all the kids in the other. They were separated by curtains from the main room.

After grace the family was served some form of soup. It was made up mostly of greens and a little meat left from some scraps given to his mother from the place she worked as a housemaid. It wasn't very nourishing but at least it was warm. Warm was about the only thing they were. The Father looked around the table at the drawn little bodies and large eyes looking back. He knew they needed more but he had no more to give them. Just today he had lost his third job this year and they would have to move by next week and he had no place to take them.

The Father was born and raised a farmer, a share cropper, but when the government redid the land legislation his family farm fell to another Agent. The new agent immediately demanded more and more percentage of the crops until there was not enough left over for

1

the family to survive. Of course he offered to buy them out and did—at an unreasonably low price and they were permanently homeless. It only took them a few months of paying rent somewhere else and meager food to use up all the money that they had seen from the sale.

After the children went to bed (which was soon after eating because they could not afford to use the candles), the Father and Mother sat down and he told her that this was it. They would have to move to a city to find work. And again for the hundredth time he apologized to have brought her and the children to this state.

The next morning they told the children about the move and everyone starting gathering up their meager belongings and packing them into the wagon (that they had somehow managed to hold on to) hitching up the pair of horses that not only pulled the wagon but could help them earn a little money plowing a field if they could.

The Father loved the two horses as if they were fit for the carriage of the King! And little John had inherited this love of the pair. As they sat off John had crawled up on the back of one of the horses to ride as they began their trek to some city for some job.

They passed a few acquaintances that would only wave and some gave shouts of encouragement, knowing too well that they might be next to have to pack up and move. At least the weather had remained relatively warm and they made good time. Since the weather was good they camped on the side of a stream and ate a little left over bread. The kids played around the campfire for a while before a snuggling together in the wagon bed for sleep.

They passed several small villages and at some the Mother and Father did some work, enough to get a little groceries to feed the kids. But John could remember to this day always seeming to be hungry. And in some of the villages he would see stores that had such wondrous things. He especially liked to look in the windows of bakeries with their wonderful smell of the bread and other treats.

It took them about a week to get to the first large city. The Father had to spend a great deal of time giving out the new rules of how to live in the city; a whole list that of course included does not talk to strangers. Well, that would be everyone John thought.

They drove through the main street and since they had no money, out to the edge of town where they were surprised to find a wagon town. A wagon town was filled with other families like theirs unable to afford to live in the city squatted on the edge and lived in their wagons. There they would subsist until they were fortunate enough to get a job that had a place to live. Most had been there a long time as there were few jobs to be had. The local government had tried for years to run them off but there was so many that they just gave up. Oh, they would make a big show of telling them to move on . . . . especially when a new magistrate came, but soon as the show was over they mostly left them alone.

The children were delighted with the new place. All these other children to play with and since they were all in the same boat, so to speak, they had a lot in common. The girls when not helping their mother would sit around with other little girls and play with their dolls and dream of dressing up and going to a ball. Boys mostly gamboled around, chasing each other or some form of wrestling, and of course the older boys talked about girls. The lack of food and no permanent dwelling seemed not to bother the children.

But the lack of food weighed heavily on the parents all the time. Father found a job working at a livery, driving wagons to carry merchandise from the warehouses to the stores, and occasionally to drive rich people around in their carriages. Father hated carrying the pompous people around to be seen in the parks or to fancy parties. But he did not mind the wagon loads. A few days after he became gainfully employed he came home with great news. They were moving to town!! The man who owned the livery had been overly pleased with his work and had offered them a small loft above the livery. It was tiny with only three rooms, but it would be indoors out of the weather and would have a real hearth to cook on and keep them warm. At first it seemed like a great idea, but the children soon missed the out of doors and their friends.

In a few weeks Mother found a part time job as house maid two days a week and was lucky enough for it to be close enough so she could easily walk to work. The days that she was off were spent cleaning house, cooking and educating the children. Father and Mother had both been educated where they came from. Mother especially had had a lot of school. So they were taught to read and write from Mother. They were taught how to cipher from Father when he would come home at the end of the day. He was very interested in the boys especially knowing how to figure wages, and any type of ciphering that had to do with having a job.

They were not rich, but they were fed regularly and had a warm place to sleep. Sometimes Father and Mother would pack a lunch and they would all ride on the wagon out to the country and romp and fish. Father liked to fish and it was a real treat to eat fish that was not on their ordinary diet.

Tragedy struck the week after New Year of the next year! A run away wagon had plowed into Fathers carriage at a crossing of the roads. The people in the carriage were killed along with Father as the Carriage wheel had landed on him and one of the broken spokes had punctured his lungs!

The family lasted only a few months before the livery man told them that they had to find somewhere else to live. They moved back out to the outskirts of town. They had had to sell one of the horses to pay for the funeral. With one horse they couldn't do much. The boys tried to find work and sometimes would clean someone's yard or run a few errands from a rich persons cook, but it didn't keep them very fed. And Mother's job was too far away and she couldn't take the wagon or horse as the people she worked for had no place to stall them during the day.

One morning they arose to a series of barked orders and horses. The Constables were rousting everyone out to proclaim that the land they were on was being cleared out. The poor were not wanted here. They had a choice leave or go to the poor house! At least they had a wagon and horse so they packed up their few things and started off in the line with the others that were fortunate to be able to have a way to go. The others were marched off to the poor house in from of the guards.

Mother had no idea what to do or where to go. So they just continued along the road like the others. The next village John scoured around trying to find work. He did pick up one job of chopping wood and he gratefully took food for his work. Hurrying back to his family he shared what little there was of it. At twelve he realized that it was not enough and the rest of the kids were too little to help. Every day he would go out to find work. He found part time at a stable, mucking out stalls, he worked on some farm picking fruit or vegetables. But it was never enough and they were always cold and hungry.

His world changed in an instant, in the time it takes to react to an adrenalin rush. They had just entered a larger village and were proceeding down the main road. Mother decided to stop and buy a few things at a market nearby. The kids all climbed down and were hanging around the wagon when a commotion caught their attention and John's. Coming down the street was a large horse, with a wisp of a girl aboard. She was screaming and trying to control the horse. People were jumping to the side to avoid being run down. John was up in the back of the wagon loading what little Mother had bought when he saw the horse coming. Timing it just right he grabbed the bridle of the oncoming horse jerking him around nearly unseating the young lady. Then he jumped down and began assuring the horse and rider everything was going to be alright.

The young lady was helped down and John proceeded to walk the horse who still was very agitated. After a while he calmed down and John took him back to his owner. The girl thanked him and then popped back up into the saddle and was gone. The family finished their meager shopping and started back on the road to find a place to spend the night.

They had stopped when they heard a call and a rider approached them. The grown man on the horse appeared to be someone with land and money. You could always tell. They were well fed and clothes were cut to fit them. And as John always observed, he sat a well—bred horse. The man asked who had helped his daughter this morning and John was singled out. He thanked John and then quickly filled his hand with coins. John tried to refuse, but the man quickly mounted his horse and rode away. After he left John gave the money to his mother and when she saw how much it was, she nearly fainted! That night they were all happy around their little camp fire. At least they had money to eat for a while. The next day Mom had told them they were certain to find jobs and then some place to live. Wow! A place to live! John had almost forgotten they had actually lived someplace beside the wagon and cold ground to sleep.

A few days later their luck ran out again. They had moved closer to a larger village and were soon accosted by several men on horses. One said that he was the local solicitor and this area did not need any more people that had no means and were blight on the area. Could they produce papers saying that they were going to a job? Did they have a place to stay? Of course they had neither. They were then told to follow the troupe into town. They did as told and were carried before some kind of judge. Again the same questions about a job and a place to stay. Same answer "NO". The Judge then ordered the horse and wagon sold for their fine and they were herded off to the "workhouse".

John was soon to learn that the workhouse was a large building holding many families that were as destitute as they were. They were all entered into the book as to gender and age and overall health. They were given rules of conduct and Mother went over them with them and cried as she read where they could be split up as they found jobs for them. Smaller children would be sent out to homes that would provide for them. They did not know it but this might be their last night together. They went down to the dining hall and were given a soupy stuff with a little meat and vegetables and some day old bread. Mother kept telling them that it would be alright.

The next morning the Matron came around calling out names. All the children's names were called except John. When they lined up with the other children they tried to not cry and not seem afraid. They were then all marched up to the main room. Here they were divided by boys and girls and then by age. That put one sister and brother on one side and one sister and brother on the other. Baby sister was only 2 so she was then moved to the babies section.

John watched from a window he had climbed up to look in. Mother stood below the window to hear as John told her what was happening. The front doors opened and in walked about 20 people. Some couples, and some men representing their families. They walked up and down looking at the children. Then they went over to a book and wrote something. Then they left. One by one the children were called up to the desk and then taken out the front door. John and his Mother raced around the building to see what was happening. The babies and toddlers went first. Some went with the couples and some with the maids that the men had brought to see about them. Baby sister was about the 6th one to go. John started to go and get her, but was restrained by his Mother. She pulled him up to her and said, we can do nothing right now, but we will go get her.

Soon all the children had come out. Other sister cried out to John and Mother as she was led away. John turned and his Mother was gone. He started out to look for her when a large man approached him. He was looking for John Dunn. You are to go to work with the gentleman over there on the bay horse. He was not given time to see his Mother or gather his few belongings. He was lifted up behind the man and away they went.

TWO

The Man did not talk much. They seemed to travel for hours. Just a few stops for relief and drinks of water and a lunch that the man had in a small sack, made up most of the ride. The food was delicious and John ate hungrily. The man seeing his hunger gave him the rest of the food. They rode until after dark and John had fallen asleep holding on to the large man's back. He awoke when a large man lifted him down and carried him into a barn. He was carefully set down on a pile of hay and covered with a wonderful blanket. He was full and warm and slept the sleep of a small child.

This day and time John Dunn was twelve years old. But he was small because of the lack of food and looked more like 9 or ten. His clothes he had outgrown about a year ago and they were patched. He had no shoes or boots and had not had a haircut in quite a while. His hair was a sandy red and he had small freckles over the bridge of his nose. The cook observed all of this in one glance as the big man from the stables brought him before her in the kitchen early the next morning.

She then proceeded to make him wash and she tried to plaster the hair down but gave up. She then sat him down at the wooden table with benches and sat food in front of him. He really didn't know what to do next. He was wondering who all the people that were going to eat all this food. There were steaming hot biscuits, bacon and sausage, eggs, and red jam. A large glass of cold milk was sat by his plate. She then told him again to eat, that he couldn't stay here all day. She then proceeded to fill his plate and sat it in front of him. John then bowed his head and said a little prayer for all the food and hoped God had given his Mother and Sisters and Brothers as much food. The cook had to stop him several times and admonish him to slow down or he was going to be sick. She had sat down next to him and explained there was plenty more where this came from.

In a little while another house maid came in with some clothes and a pair of boots and a hat. She explained to the cook that the gentlemen had told her to bring them to the little one and they would have to do until someone went to town could buy ones that fit. Back in the barn, John put on the new to him clothes and thought that they were fit for a king. The boots were real leather and the hat although too big was quickly altered by Samuel affixing a string around the top and down the sides so that it didn't blow off. The sleeves of the shirt went clear down to his wrists and he would have to learn to turn them up when he was working to keep them clean. And along with all of this was a jacket!!!

Samuel, as John learned was the big man that had helped him from the stable and Flossy was the cook, and Hentley was the housemaid from the morning. Hentley was named so as her Dad was Henry and her Mother was Molley and they could not agree on a name. Other workers names he would learn as he was quickly put to work carrying wood and water, digging weeds in the side vegetable garden, and of course helping in the barn. There were a lot of horses in the barn and many more outside in paddocks and other pens. He also quickly learned which horses were stallions and not get close to their stall door, as they would lean out to bite him as he carried the feed and hay. And Samuel assured him they would eat him if he got close to them.

It only took a few days for John to become everyone's favorite around. He worked so hard and was so little, but he had a great laugh and was appreciative of everything around him. And with the three meals a day and lots of outdoor work, John grew, gangly arms and legs. And with each day he learned everything he could about everything he was involved in. The Dad had told him that the person that knew the most got the best jobs. So John decided to learn everything that he could. Sometimes this got him into trouble. His most used word was why. And "Why" would sometimes get him into trouble especially with Flossy. She would shoo him out the door and declare she had never heard why so much. His why extended to the barn where there was a lot of learning to do, but Samuel would just smile or laugh and answer as many of the whys as he could. Sometimes when he did not have an answer he would advise John to ask the Man.

The Man was the owner of this grand place and John was not about to speak or dare ask him anything. He was deathly afraid of him, even though the Man had not ever been anything but great to him. The Man gave him this great place to live and clothes like he had only seen in store windows and food . . . . as much as he could eat. So a few days later he was petrified when the Man was standing by the paddock as John haltered one of the mares for Samuel. And was even more so when the Man spoke to him.

"How are things going with you little one?" The Man called out. John did not know whether to speak or run. "Come over and let me have a look at you. You seemed to have cleaned up pretty good. And you seem to have a way with that little mare. Can you ride?"

"Uh, yessir. I can ride and I can drive a wagon. My Father had a wagon business and he taught me to ride and handle a wagon."

"Saddle up Kingdom for me and that little mare you have there and let's go for a ride."

"Who is going to ride the mare sir, so I know what saddle to put on her?"

"Well pick one about your size." John still did not understand that he was the one riding the mare. He took her in and picked out a saddle that he thought might fit someone his size and then Samuel helped him saddle Kingdom.

He then took both of them out to where the Man was still standing watching some colts play in the sunshine. He took Kingdom's reins and stepped into his saddle. "Well what are you waiting for?"

"I, sir, was waiting for the person who is going to ride this other horse sir." The Man chuckled and said, "John you are going to ride the mare get aboard."

John looked at him in great surprise but quickly swung into the saddle that seem to fit him like a glove. He had never had a saddle his size; he had only ridden the Dad's grown person saddle. He felt that he was on top of the world. He was riding a mare his size, in a saddle his size, and was going ridding with The Man. He must have died and gone to heaven. They rode around the house and barns and then set out over the fields. The Man seemed to know all the workers calling out to them by name. They smiled and waved back a sure sign that they knew him and were not afraid of him. Later they broke into a slow canter that eventually brought them to a small running stream. Here they stopped and cupped their hand into the clear water and drank. John found that he was hungry but didn't bring anything to eat. He turned to see The Man opening a bundle that he had brought with him. In it were cheese and bread and a wonderful tasting muffin. The Man gave John all of the muffins while they had shared the cheese and bread. When John tried to share the muffin, The Man assured him that Flossy told him that the muffin was for the little one.

They then moved on and after The Man had seen another field or two and spoken to several men who seemed to be the head one they turned back to the house. They had been gone quite a while and when they returned John had to hurry to do all his chores and after supper he fell into his bed and was soon sound asleep. He dreamed of riding with The Man and could almost believe that The Man had said we will have to do this again soon when he had handed Kingdom reins to John to put him and the mare away. But next morning John was sure that he had just dreamed the whole day.

John had been at the Manor for several months now and had a routine of sorts. He rose early to the sounds of Samuel quietly talking to the horses in the barn below where John lay in the hay. Many times he would roll over and peek over the edge and watch and sometimes would hear Samuel quietly singing some old folk song as he worked. John would then quickly dress and head down the ladder and run to the house to carry the wood in for the kitchen then make trips back and forth carrying the wood to each of the fireplaces up and downstairs of the big house.

He would quietly stir the coals from the night and place the new logs and get the fires started. His next chore was to run to the kitchen to see if they needed anything and hang around for his breakfast. Samuel would be there and they would sit next to each other while the cook and any other help sat around the table. Talk was mostly about other estates help, this one marrying that one, and who had a baby, and who got caught stealing etc. Then Flossy and Samuel would decide what they needed to do for that day.

One of John's favorite days was when Flossy and Samuel decided they needed to go to town for supplies. The first time that John went he was scared to death that they would put him back in the poor house. He told them he didn't want to go to town. Flossy got up real close to him and looked him in the eye and demanded that he tell her why. John began to cry like a baby and mumbled to her and Samuel that he was scared they would lock him up again. Samuel walked up and took him in a big bear hug and said that nobody was going to take him away from here. Did he not understand that he was part of the Manor now and The Man would not be happy if anything happened to him? Samuel then lifted him up on the wagon next to Flossy and the three of them set off for town. John also found out in a hurry that going for supplies was a several day trip. They drove all of that day down a little more than a cattle road until they joined up with a well travel road, where they could make better time. Samuel then clicked at the team and they started up to a sprightly trot that made their harnesses made sounds almost like a jingle. John like the sound of the horses' hooves and the jingling harnesses. He awoke later when Samuel shook him awake. He was embarrassed that he had fallen asleep. Flossy held the door and he and Samuel went inside a big room. It had tables and benches and a warm fireplace. They sat down and soon the proprietor came to take their order. Flossy ordered meat pies for all of them. They were not as good as Flossy's and Samuel and John were quick to tell her. After they ate Samuel paid for the dinner and two rooms. John felt like he was asleep soon as he fell on the bed. And he also felt like he had only been asleep a little while when Samuel said it was time to get up. They ate a quick breakfast and the innkeeper packed them a lunch and they were on their way again.

After a few hours they came to a bigger village. It had a sort of main road and along it were stores selling things. John could not believe some of the wonderful things that he saw in the windows. Flossy took him by the hand and they went into a big store that seemed to sell everything. She gave the merchant her list of supplies then took John over to the clothes and held up shirts and pants until she found the size she thought would fit him. She bought two shirts and two pants, and undergarments and socks. John was a little blushed when she held the undergarments up for measuring. Flossy then told the merchant they would be by early the next morning to load their supplies. They then scoured the street for Samuel. They found him almost at the edge of the town. John could not believe his eyes. There were these fancy painted wagons and dark skinned people all around doing wonderful things. There was a man that could swallow fire without getting burned. And there was one with his face painted that could juggle nearly anything. A little further along there was a group of people watching a man on a horse. He would lope around a circle and then stand up on the horses' back and jump around front to back and then did a handstand as the horse continued to circle. When he returned to the front of the crowd he did a somersault off the back of the horse and landed like a fairy on the ground without missing a beat! And John had not seen such fancy pants and shirts all the colors of the rainbow, even down to the small children. Samuel explained that they were gypsies and they traveled around doing their shows. John had seen Samuel put a few coins in a bucket near where they entered the camp and he realized that was how they got paid.

By the time they ate dinner and got rooms John was worn out again. They had to share a bedroom with another person but John slept with Samuel so that was alright until the other guy started to snore. John turned and turned finally he put his pillow over his head to get a little relief from the noise and fell asleep.

Early next morning after they made the harness store, they stopped at the merchants and loaded all the supplies on the wagon and tarped it down to keep the weather out of the food. Then the trip home was the reverse of their trip to get the supplies. Same stops, same road, same time to return. When they got to the Manor it was nearly dark, but they unloaded all the supplies, unhitched the wagon and bedded down the team before returning to the house for a bite and then John was back in his hayloft bed.

John stretched his legs under the cover, they ached sometimes and Samuel said that he was having growing pains. He believed it. The clothes that Flossy was always letting out seemed to shrink every time she washed them. As he lay there he thought of his family and wonder where they were and if they ever got back together. He missed them terribly but had learned to not let them be the center of what he was thinking about. Samuel had caught him a time or two over in a corner somewhere crying and had consoled him the best he could. Samuel understood the heart ache caused by being taken from your family. He had the same experience when he was about John's age and the same kind man that owned the Manor had taken him in. Many times Samuel would look at the boy when he was not looking and think back to the morning that The Man had stood up in the market and told the Constable that he would take the boy home with him and Samuel had been here since. That had been over 20 years ago.

John had decided after his last crying bout that the best he could do would be to learn all he could how to make a living and then when he had a little money he could go and get them.

He had been at the Manor for about 6 months when The Man asked if he would like to ride with him again. John quickly saddled Kingdom and the mare and off they went. They made nearly the same trip as before. The Man talked with the help and they saw the fields being planted, the trees being felled, and other various farms as they worked. As always The Man seemed to know everyone and ask about their families. At one stop The Man was told that old man Hunter had died so they quickly went to the house of his family. They were all in mourning. The Man went right in the small house, while John, out of respect, stood just at the door. The Man went straight up to the old woman by the fire and held her hand and told her how sorry he was. John then saw him take out his purse and draw out some coins and place them in her hand. He then spoke to some of the other family members and then he came out and they left. John did not talk as he could tell by the facial expression of The Man that he was sincerely touched by the death.

After a while The Man told John that old man Hunter had taught him to ride in the very stables where Samuel lived now. He had worked for his family for over 40 years and had just a few years back gotten arthritis so bad that he had to quit work. Some of his sons and daughters worked on the Manor now.

When they returned to the stables at the Manor, John heard The Man telling Samuel that old man Hunter had passed. He also added that Flossy and he needed to get some food together and take over to them. As John was coming out of the stables Samuel was hitching up the wagon. He told John to go in the kitchen and help Flossy to bring out the food. John thought that they had packed all the food in the kitchen. But Flossy assured him they had plenty to spare. Samuel motioned for John to jump up on the wagon and Samuel turned the wagon and team down the road. It was not far and it did not take them long to reach the house again. Only by now there was a lot more people. When Flossy and Samuel went inside John followed along this time. On the bed in the corner the old man Hunter was laid out. John had not seen many dead people besides his Dad and did not like it at all but he stiffened up and stood by Samuel as he said his goodbye. They then went back out begin bringing in the food that they had brought. Soon many women were there fixing the dinner. Flossy was right in there helping snapping beans and kneading dough for bread. Samuel and John went outside where the men had started a fire to cook a ham that they had brought. Soon the whole place seemed to smell so good that John was ashamed to be so hungry. And he couldn't figure out the whole thing. They were supposed to be gloomy and down-faced about the death and they were, but now everyone was visiting and eating and laughing like it was a reunion. Well he decided it was reunion of a sort. This was his first time to meet other kids his own age. There were several boys that he had seen on his ride and they were friendly and visited with him. They were curious how it was to live at the Manor. John quickly told them that he had all he could eat and everyone was real nice to him. They visited some more and John learned that most of them wanted to grow up and move to the city where they could make a lot of money. In John's memory all the city was pain and starvation.

But he didn't have the heart to dash their hopes. Samuel and Flossy discussed the usual grown-up things with the others way into the night. John was so tired and sleepy. Around him the other kids had just laid down anywhere and were already asleep when Samuel called him up and they went home. John slept most of the way home and Samuel had to wake him up to get him to go inside to his own bed.

THREE

The Man was a horse breeder. His horses were some of the finest anywhere around and John soon learned that men from many other countries came to the Manor to buy them. He soon heard many new languages and listened to many breeders talk about this stud horse or this sire and what races they and their get had won. He was a quick learner and soaked up all he could about the horses that he handled every day. He soon could nearly name all their names and their sires and dames, what races they had won and how much money they made. The money was staggering sums to him. He could not believe that horse racing could make so much money change hands.

His first real encounter with the world of racing was a bright day in spring when The Man told him to come with Samuel to the races. They were going to the next county over to the north. They left early that day, John on his mare, The Man on Kingdom, and Samuel on a big chestnut gelding leading a dark bay with stocking feet. The bay was called Lightning. They arrived in the middle of the afternoon and stabled the horses. The Man had lodging in a fancy Inn down the road. Samuel assured John they had to sleep with Lightning. And that they would take turns watching him during the night. John did not understand exactly what they were watching for but he quickly agreed. The Man brought their dinner and they ate hungrily in the barn near Lightning's stall. Samuel said he would stay up first and John quickly fell asleep on the hay nearby. He dreamed of riding Lightning across the meadows. He seemed to fly!

Then someone was shaking him. It was Samuel. "You stay awake now you hear?"

John sat down and leaned back on the door to Lightning's stall. John sat up and moved a little closer and stayed awake except for a few nodding offs the rest of the night. Early before sunrise, Samuel traded again and John got a few more winks before the sun came up. Soon The Man brought them breakfast and they were then busy getting Lightning fed and brushed down. Then he was led out to the paddock and walked and walked to get his muscles warm.

The race would be right after lunch. They ate on the way out of town. John was surprised to find lots of people in buggies and wagons, men and women and families. They had come out in the morning and brought their lunch and many had picnics spread on the ground. The race course was marked off and the starter was at one end. The Man spoke to lots of people as they went along. Everyone seemed to know him. Many of the men would comment on Lightning and some would run their hand over him expertly feeling his muscle structure. The women would admire his stocking feet. Good natured Lightning took it all in without getting upset.

John could not seem to take it all in. It was like a big party!! They passed by the starter and then on a ways away from all the people. The Man then gave Lightning to Samuel and then rejoined the men standing around in groups. John noticed that more than once money changed hands. Samuel laughed at him and then explained that they didn't run the horses for free, that the winner would make a lot of money today. He also explained that if Lightning won it would make him worth more money when they sold him. John's heart skipped a beat. Sell him! He had never realized that they might sell him. The only horses that he knew of that were sold were old and worn out or the owner needed the money. The Man sure didn't need the money. Wow! Raising horses to make money. That was a great idea!

When the race steward called the race Samuel took him over to the tiniest little man to mount up. John had not seen the tiny saddle in their stuff so he guessed right that the little man brought his own. Samuel explained that he was a jockey. Having a rider that was light weight gave the horse every advantage. The race would be lap and tap. The steward would simply line the horses up and shoot off a pistol and the race was on. It was a mile race around the course with yelling, screaming people all along the sides. It was enough to spook a horse and some of them did. But not Lightning. He ran like they were not even there! By the time he took the turn John found himself yelling for him. They ran around the crowd to the back stretch and John was amazed when Lightning came in ahead of all the horses by about a horse's length.

As he celebrated with Samuel, he took notice of money passing from hand to hand and then saw The Man collecting money also. John was that day hooked on having a race horse of his own. After the race people continued milling around visiting, bragging on how much they won or moping about how much they lost. Samuel and John did not have time to visit as they had to walk Lightning to cool him off and then rub him down. The Man came by to check on the horse and then sent Samuel and John back to town to put him in his stable. He told Samuel they would be spending another night and going home in the morning. John saw him give Samuel some money and then he returned to visit with the other gentlemen.

Samuel and John saddled their horses and leading Lightning slowly walked him back to town. In the stable they fed and watered him and bedded him down for the night. Then Samuel told John to watch the horse and he went and bought them supper and came back. John was really hungry as they had only had a few biscuits left over from breakfast. The food was nothing like Flossy's. It was mostly bread and cheese, and some kind of greasy meat but he was hungry.

Samuel had brought him some kind of cider that was really good. Samuel quickly told John to sleep first and it only took John a few minutes to snuggle down in the hay and be fast asleep.

The sun was up when he awoke the next day. Jumping up he looked around for Samuel.

The big man laughed when he saw his antics. "Did I sleep all night?" John said rubbing his eyes.

Samuel quickly assured him that it was alright. He had caught a few winks himself. But he was one that he claimed he slept with one eye open so it was not a problem. Later on John would try to sleep with one eye open but couldn't quite get the hang of it.

After the sun came up they fed and watered the horses to begin the trip home. Then when they had finished breakfast they saddled Kingdom, the little mare and Samuel's gelding and were ready to go home when The Man called for them. It was about mid-morning. He had finished his business and they started out. The Man told Samuel that it had been a "profitable race". Several of the gentlemen horse breeders were coming out to the Manor to see their other horses. As they traveled along, The Man told John about the breeding program. How he chose what stud to breed to what mare. Samuel and The Man had been breeding horses a long time. They could name each one and their parents and grandsires. John listened fascinated as they planned their program for the next few months. John was eager to learn everything he could. But it seemed like a lot to know just in your head. So John decided that when they returned to the Manor he was going to write it all down.

The next morning after their chores of seeing to the horses were finished, Samuel and John usually took a little break. This morning was no exception. They had followed the same routine ever since John had arrived there. As John sat on a bale of hay swinging his feet, Samuel could tell there was something on his mind. "And what may you be thinking of little one?"

"I was just trying to remember all the things you and The Man had talked about on the way home. I don't want to forget any of it about the horses. I have decided that when I grow up I am going to raise horses. And I am going to write down all their names and keep good records. I know how to write and cipher and I will learn everything I can." John did not see the smile that crossed Samuel's face. "The problem right now is remembering everything. If I had a writing pen and some paper I could start my books right away. So would you be able to buy me some when we go to town?"

They had not heard The Man walk right up to them from the barn door. "I don't think we have to go to town to get the writing materials. Come with me up to my study and I will see what I have you can use for your record book." The Man was curious to find out just how much education this young man had. So John followed him up to the study and The Man handed him a record book and pen and ink. Although The Man had all this information already entered, he thought it would be good for the little one to start his own book.

When John returned to the barn he was so excited. He made him a little desk with a board on a board and sat down to write. Samuel stood nearby munching on a straw of hay.

"I am going to start with Kingdom because he is the oldest right? "Yes, Kingdom is the oldest here now." So John wrote in nice lettering Kingdom. "Is that all of his name?"

Samuel said that he had a fancy name but he would have to ask The Man. "So what was Kingdom's sire and dam?" Samuel sat down nearby and began his story. "When I came here as a lad, the Manor only had one Stud horse name King's Pride. And we only had two mares. The Man was just a young lad too. The family lived in a big city and only came out here on holidays and summers. The Man learned to ride and when his family was killed in a fire he came here to live permanently. He did not want to rebuild the house in town. There was an overseer running the place then. When The Man came they couldn't get along so the overseer was dismissed. I remember him coming out to the barn and telling me that it was just him and me now. Well I didn't know anything but horses. So I told him he would just have to depend on someone else about the farming and such. Well The Man just wanted to raise horses and that was all he was interested in. But I convinced him that we could find someone for the other stuff.

That was when Flossy and her husband came to live here. Her husband made a find overseer and the farm did well. And even as I do say so the horse business has done well with me and The Man. You know I can't believe that was about 30 years ago."

John had a million questions but they had to go back to work. There were stalls to clean and horses to be brushed. And that one stud and two mares had multiplied to one of the largest horse farms in the country. And the barn that they worked and lived in was one of the best anywhere around. They had everything that they needed to pamper some of the best breeding stock.

A few days later when the work was done, John was back at his board. He had learned the sire and dam of nearly all the horses in the barns. Today he was going to start on the get (offspring) of the horses. He decided to make the legend in the form of a tree. Starting with the original stud and mares and then going out from there. He soon found that 30 years' worth of horse breeding took up lots of the book. So he began tearing out the pages and found a blank wall in the barn and began connecting the pages together. It was getting bigger and bigger! Of course some of the trees were cut short as the horses were sold to other horse breeders. Samuel couldn't remember all of them but the ones he knew they placed the name of the owner under the horse's name.

The next day John was hurrying around the corner of the barn with a halter that Samuel wanted, and ran right into The Man. He was standing in front of John's legend. "Did you do all of this?" "Yes, with Samuel recollections." The Man was very pleased with what he was seeing. He took up the pen and ink and began making more notations on the pages on the wall. He corrected a few things but mostly added horses and mares and then when Samuel came in they both began talking about this horse or that. They quickly had written all over the legend until it was a mess.

The Man looked down at little John's face and realized what they had done.

"Oh John, we are so sorry about your work. We just love these horses so much; I guess Samuel and I just carried away. I tell you what. Come up to the house I have something for you."

Flossy and the other help watched as Samuel, The Man and John marched across the yard and into the study. In one corner of the room stood a large flat wooden table with some mechanism that made it tilt up and down and it had a lamp right over head. Over to one side it had pen and ink. John's whole legend would have fit on it! John was doubly surprised when The Man took out a huge piece of paper the size of the table and attached it to it. Now you can go get your legend and repair it to this paper and it will be better than ever. John flew out of the house and quickly pulled his work sheets off the barn wall and ran back into the house. Without even taking time to ask if he could begin work he quickly spread his pages out on the floor and began thinking how to transfer them to the large sheet. He was so into his work he did not notice that The Man and Samuel had quietly left him there and gone about their business.

An hour or two later John had finally started on his new sheet. He didn't notice the time until Flossy came in and ask if he was coming to supper. Oh my! What about my chores and stuff. He stopped long enough to eat with Samuel and told him he was so sorry he had not done his work and he would not do it again! Samuel laughed when he told him it was ok. They would make time every day for him to work on his legend, but after his chores were finished.

So began the Manor's first Horse Tree by John Dunn. As he worked he learned each horse and its family and where it went and who owned it now. John found that when they went to the races he would recognize a horse when owners would say he is out of so and so or he is a get of so and so's horses. One race day it got him into a lot of trouble. Another of the stable lads from another horse farm was telling that his horse was out of a stud named Donagel. John told him that was not right and to his amazement the kid hit him in the mouth. John had never been in a fight before because he had been such a scrawny kid he would just run. But good food and exercise had made a muscular little man out of him and he returned the punch and the fight was on. It took a little while for Samuel and The Man pushed their way through the crowd that had gathered around the fight. Samuel pulled John up as The Man took hold of the other lad.

"Whoa! What is the problem here? "John was so embarrassed that The Man had seen him acting like a beast.

"He claimed that Donagel's get is their Rainy. I told him he was not and he then hit me. And I am sorry to say I seemed to have hit him back a few times." The crowd had dispersed and the other lad has scurried away. "I am not sorry that you hit him." The Man said. "He comes from a bad horse barn. But we must be very wary of people like him. He will want to get back at you. He is a bully and you will have to watch out for him. By the way are you ok?"

Samuel and The Man were a lot easier on John than Flossy was when they returned home. She was mad that he had torn his shirt besides getting all dirty in front of company and then she was mad because he had busted his lip. She didn't know whether to lick him or hug him. All of the help at the Manor had adopted John and they often did not know what to do about him. But they knew that he was theirs and they would not have anyone beating up on their little John.

A few days later The Man caught John again at work at his table. The Man asked how the work was going and John happily told him it was nearly finished. He had started on a second sheet of paper to continue the lineage as it happened. The Man had brought one of the carpenters from the Manor into the room with him. He told the man to measure the sheets of paper. He told him that he wanted them framed with a glass front, but where they could be opened to continue writing on them. John could not believe his ears! His legend was going to get framed suitable for hanging on a wall. The Man asked him out to the hall by the study.

"What do you think of hanging the legend here on this wall? So when buyers come in they will be able to study it?" John could hardly whisper "Oh that would be great."

The Man asked if there was anything that he could give him for all his hard work on the Legend. John quickly asked if he could read some of the books in the library. The Man laughed and told him he could read them all if he was a mind too. All that anyone else besides him did was dust them. So that very day John chose a couple of books and carried them back to the barn with him. While choosing his books John noticed a book on the new colony of America. He quickly took it and began to read from front to back. Samuel had to call him to supper several times before he could put it down. He could not imagine a land with so much prosperity as the book foretold.

FOUR

The morning after the legend has been hung up in the hall with all the help watching and a glass of cider passed around for everyone to toast the legend, The Man was again out in the barn. John was measuring out feed in the buckets for the different horses. Except for The Man and a few others on the Manor reading and writing were not things they had had available to them.

Samuel could read a little but did very little ciphering. The Man wanted to know how John could keep up with what feed was mixed with what for each horse.

"I cheat you see. I have them all written down, the names of the feed and the amount, see here on the wall." On the wall was each horses names and underneath in the same neat handwriting was the recipe for their individual horses feed.

"If it changes I just rub the old out and add the new things."

"Can you figure out how much of each kind of feed we have to have each day?"

"Sure sometimes now I help Samuel figure how much we need when we go to the feed store. And how long it will last so we will know when to go to town again. That way we don't run out. And sometimes we can decide when to go to town to get the best prices by using my ciphering."

As The Man made his way back to the house he smiled as he thought about the little horse lad that could read and cipher and make horse legends and take care of the horses at the same time. He realized he was no regular lad, especially from this part of the world. Samuel and he had discussed John before about how bright he was and how he was a natural horseman.

John loved the stable of horses. He loved the smell of leather and the distinct odor of the horse. He had learned to ride well from Samuel and the mere fact that he had different horses to ride every day. He learned each horses gait and how they liked to be handled. He now knew each name and lineage of each foal. He would ride one and lead three or four for exercise every morning. Samuel rode along with the same string. The horses were fat and shiny in the spring as their winter coats had been shed through hours of brushing. The new baby colts were born in January and by March were running and playing together in the paddocks. John would stand at the fence and watch them come up to him and then snort and run away. Samuel had said that they would start haltering and handling them next week. He could hardly wait.

Flossy had told him just today that they would have to buy bigger clothes again when they went to town as his pants were too short and his sleeves had to be cut off as the cuff was too little for his growing arms. He had had another birthday and was now a 16 year old "little man" as Flossy and Samuel called him.

The following day Samuel told John to pick out one of the foals to begin working with. He stood at the fence for a while then walked up and haltered the mare and led her into a smaller pen. The colt he had picked was about the color of John's hair and its mane and tail were flaxen nearly white. He then led the mare and colt down a very narrow set of pens. He then lean over and placed a pony halter with a lead rope on the colt. When Samuel let them out again into the pen the colt was dragging the lead rope. They would put it on the colt every morning and then take it off later in the day. All day long the colt would feel the lead rope pull on his head as he or his dam would step on it and make him jerk his head up and stop. After a few days John would get the colt in the chute again and start rubbing and petting and talking to him. At first the colt was afraid and tried to shy away. He would try kicking the chute sides and one time tried to bite the rope. But after a few days and with some cut up apples for treats, he got used to John and would sometimes nicker and come to the fence when he saw John. He also started looking in John's pockets for his apple pieces. Soon John was able to walk right up to the colt. The colt had to learn to be tied to the post. This he did not like at all. Then John began the hard work of trying to hold the lead rope and pull the colt to him and walk with him. At first the colt did everything he could think of to get away. He bucked and jumped around. He would turn away and not look at John. But with quiet patience and the apple pieces he soon learned to lead and John was taking him along with him when he exercised the other horses.

John had five colts of different colors and dispositions to do the same with. It was trying work pulling on their lead ropes all day. But Samuel and John in a few weeks had all the colts halter broke and in another month or so they would be weaned from their mothers. Unknown to John, The Man was watching all of his hard work and was very pleased with his "little man".

When "Red" as John called the first colt he had picked out was nearly a year old his real training began. And John's also. They had a real connection by now but riding would be a different thing all together. Samuel told him the day before that they would have to start getting the colts ready to be broke to ride in the morning. First order of business was to separate them from their mares.

It nearly broke John's heart to hear the colts call out to their mares as the mares were being moved to a far pasture so the colts could not see them. The colts had already begun eating solid feed along with their mother's milk. John rubbed their noses and tried to comfort them. For about a week the colts would run up and down the fence looking for their mothers. But then Samuel and John had to get busy with preparing them to carry a saddle and a man on their back. When they were haltered they then were taught to work on a long line. This was simply a halter with a long lead rope. The colt was taught to walk then trot around John or Samuel. Then they would learn to go the other way. And most important they were taught to stop and come to as the long line was taken up and they would end up near the one working with them. With John they learned quickly that included the treat he would have in his pockets. The first days were spent with a saddle blanket being eased on to the back of the colt. Some would look scared eyed but would stand while it sat on its back. Others would jerk away and jump and buck. But day after day the blanket was eased on to their backs as Samuel and John talked quietly to them assuring them that it would not hurt them. Each colt took a different amount of time. After the blanket they would start with the saddle. Same results some would stand now and some still had a fit. But after a while most were saddled and then led for days around the round pen. They were then put on the long line with the saddle on. These days were challenging as on the long line they would buck and snort and do all kinds of contortions and John and Samuel would laugh at their antics.

John went to bed most of these days soon after Flossy fed them their dinner. He was sore all over from the colts pulling, pushing and yanking on his arms and shoulders. They stomped on his boots and bit him when he was not looking. But he loved every minute of it. He could not wait to get up in the morning and see what they had to challenge him with. Especially Red! Samuel said that he was spoiling him, but had to admit that Red caught on to every lesson faster than many of the other colts. And that was saying a lot as there was twenty-two colts this year. The orders for horses from the Manor had grown and grown. They were now well known and The Man sold them for lots of money so it was a win—win situation. Samuel knew that any of them might be the stakes winner and they were careful to see that all of them remained healthy through all the rigorous training. And The Man had watched his colts learn their lessons, even taking the long rope with some to just enjoy their company. He loved the horses as much as Samuel and John. He also watched John as he learned along with the colts. He was impressed with how gentle John was with the horses, never asking more than he thought they were ready for.

After a few weeks the hard work really started. The colts had to learn to have a person on their backs. They started with putting a sack of feed on when they saddled the colts. That way they would feel an extra weight on their back. Some did not like this either and some just took it in stride. Poor John was not prepared for Red to be one of the ones that did not like the extra weight! He jumped and snorted and bucked trying to throw it off. Samuel and The Man were on the fence and laughed a lot. After the saddle and weight were removed John told Red while he was brushing him down, how he had embarrassed him in front of the others. And tomorrow they were going to work twice as hard and he better clean up his act!

The next day they put the sack on the saddle over and over, and over and over Red threw it off. John was exhausted. He called out to Samuel to come help him. Samuel picked up the sack of feed and started to lift it on to the saddle. Red would stand for you to put the sack on but then throw it off like it was a game. John told Samuel to not put the sack on he had another idea. He slipped a rope rein through the halter and turned to Samuel. "Give me a hand up."

This meant that he wanted Samuel entwine his hands and he would put his boot in his hands and jump up on Red's saddle. When he was lying across the saddle Red just stood there, shaking and trying to figure out what John was doing. John continued to talk to him and assure him that it was him on his back not that ugly sack of feed. Samuel took the rope rein and slowly led Red around with John still lying across the saddle. When they stopped John carefully eased himself off to the ground and stroked his neck and head. Samuel had never seen this done and he thought it was a great idea. They would try it on some of the other colts. Unknown to the both of them, The Man saw the connection that had been formed between the kid and the colt and he smiled. After a few more days of riding around lying over the saddle, John one day slid his foot over the saddle and staying low to the mane of Red, let Samuel walk them round and round. Later in the week they would gradually go back to the long line and work with John aboard. Red would sometimes balk or stop and not go and some days he actually bowed up and tried to jump around, but didn't buck. Then they worked in the rope rein while they were on the long line. Red learned that when John pulled on the rope rein he was to stop. Soon they took off the long line and Red learned to go when John put pressure on his sides with his legs or a quick little nudge with his boots. It had been over six weeks and the colts were coming along well. John had to remember that there were 21 other colts to work with. He just wanted to make Red a great horse.

But Samuel and he had all the colts broke to ride and then they all had to be exercised every day. It was demanding and trying work. They couldn't ride all of them every day so they had to devise a schedule so they all got worked during the week. And of course John had to have the scheduled written on the wall in the barn. He had each colts name on the head of a column and where it was in its training. Some learned as fast as Red and some were much slower. but they all had been ridden in a few weeks.

John put a lead rope on the halter in addition to the rope reins, when they would let John on their backs comfortably. Samuel would then mount one of the grown horses and hold the lead rope up so the colt was next to him and they then would take the colt out of the pen to learn to lead and get used to the big horse. Soon they would walk, trot and lope along next to Samuel's horse. Most enjoyed getting out and stretching their legs. Again it all took a lot of time. They could only work three or four colts a day due to the fact they still had all the other work to do in and around the stable.

One of these mornings it was Red's day to go out "snubbed up" to the big horse. The Man was watching from the fence. He had stood well when John mounted the saddle and didn't seem to mind Samuel and his big gelding. They had just started out of the pen when a big rooster jumped out of the way of the horses' hooves. He squawked and ran with both wings spread out. This of course scared Red to death and he soon threw John off his back. John felt a great pain in his arm. Soon as he hit the ground and was trying to get up The Man was there helping him get up. Samuel had put Red back in the pen and tied up his horse. When they ask if he was alright he tried to say that he was but they could tell the arm was hurting really bad. Samuel get the buggy we are going to Doc O'Brian's, I think the arm is broken. It was not far but every rut the wheels hit seemed to jerk the arm. John was in pain. Sure enough it was broken and it was put in a thing called a cast. The Doc put two pieces of board on each side of his arm and wrapped it solid from his elbow to this hand. He then gave him some medicine that tasted awful. He didn't remember much of the ride back. Since he could not climb the ladder to the loft, they made him a bed on the floor of the stable and took turns along with fussy Flossy checking on him. John just kept asking if Red was alright.

FIVE

Since he could not do much with a broken arm John just kinda wondered around. This is when he noticed all the activity in the house. What is the fuss? Flossy and Samuel in unison said the buyers are coming! What? The first buyers for the colts are coming and will stay with us a few days. So we have to get the Manor all spruced up and ready for them. Samuel had gone outside and hitched up the mules. Flossy came out, all ready for a shopping trip. John just stood there watching. "Well are you going or not?" Samuel asked. "I have to get my things."

John quickly stuffed a clean shirt in his sack and climbed into the back of the wagon. After they had gone a few miles he wished he had stayed home. The jostling and bouncing of the wagon made his arm hurt, but of course he said nothing. Samuel at the next stop asked him if he wanted to ride on the seat with them for a while. Flossy moved to the center of the wagon seat and when John was up on the outside Samuel moved forward again. The wagon seat was much better than the back of the wagon, but he knew that Flossy was a little cramped, but she did not complain.

When they came into the town they were going to buy their supplies, the first order of business was clothes. That is the reason that they had made sure John came along. The Man had told them to get him several changes of clothes and good ones. He did not want the buyers seeing a rag a muffin from the streets. And Samuel even bought a new set of shirt and pants. John before now had only bought one set of clothes and was amazed when Flossy told the merchants they would take four shirts and four pants and underthings for John. They then went to the boot maker and he had a pair of boots that just fit; so he was given a new shiny pair of boots. A new hat finished off his wardrobe. He couldn't wait to get the new clothes on! "You will not wear these to work in Samuel told him. They are your traveling pants."

As John was young and healed fast, a month is all it took for the arm to heal. He found it a little stiff when the wooden cast came off, but it worked just fine. He quickly was back working with the colts. Since it was his left arm he could use the right just fine to lead and work with the colts. One of his first orders of business when he went back to work was to take Red to see the chickens! When they got near the chicken pen, some of the hens were out pecking around for their morning food. He did not see the devil rooster but knew he was somewhere around. Red seemed to tolerate the hens as they drifted near and around him, clucking to each other as they moved along. John did not see the rooster until he was on him. He had come around the hen house off his blind side. It jumped on one of his legs digging his spur in the side of his leg. John let out a yep and Red spooked. Samuel had looked out the barn door and all he saw were Red and John running toward him with the Rooster still attached to John's leg. His spur had gotten caught in John's britches and couldn't get off and John couldn't get him off. Samuel knew he needed to help them but couldn't for laughing. Another laugh had joined him in the person of The Man. Finally they were able to untangle the rooster and get Red calmed down. John was so embarrassed! When all the confusion settled down, The Man quietly suggested that they leave the poor rooster alone and they would be alright. Little did he know that later that rooster incident would be a deciding factor in Red and John's lives.

The buyers started coming a few days later. John did not realize that it took so many people for one man to come look at the colts. Beside the main man there was his driver, his manservant, and sometimes his overseer. And lo and behold sometimes he brought his family and they all had to have maids and helpers. And all those people had to be fed and taken care of. Flossy was in a fuss all the time. She barely had time to cook for John and Samuel. And a few times he knew for certain that they had left overs. The Man had had her hire extra help in the house and John found several new house maids running around too. It also meant more work for him, keeping the firewood at every fireplace, and running any kind of errand Flossy needed. He soon learn that Samuel did not go to the house at this time except for meals, because Flossy would catch you and put you to work doing something for her.

Samuel had spent the last few weeks coaching John how to show off the horses to the prospective buyers. If they still had colts that tried to kick, they would try to keep him turned away from the buyers. Some buyers wanted to touch and feel the horses. Some would want to lift up their feet. Some brought their overseers and they went over the colts very carefully to see if they were sound. They would check their teeth to see their age. They would look at their eyes.

Some of the buyers never came to the barn. That amazed John. They came ate the food and enjoyed being out of the city and some bought horses and some did not. Each time as the horde, as John called them left, they would sit around the kitchen table, Samuel, Flossy, John and the maids and laugh and talk about the visitors. The inside people would tell Samuel and John all about what had happened in the house and likewise tales would be told about what went on in the barn. It was always a few days later when The Man would let them know if they had made a sale or not.

Very few times did the buyer take the colts with them. Most wanted them to be older and handled more. So they just picked out the one that they wanted, paid for it, and then either sent their overseer back weeks later to pick it up or Samuel and John took it to them. The first one they had to deliver was John's first trip to another Manor.

It was several days trip to take the colt. It also involved going through the town where they bought supplies, so they took the wagon to deliver the colt and then bring the supplies back.

Samuel had John make a list, Flossy telling him what food stuffs to buy, and Samuel adding the feed and The Man even added a few things. They left just at daylight after one of Flossy's good breakfasts. The mules were soon hitched. Samuel and John had their few belongings and their food Flossy had packed for them under the wagon seat. John was surprised when he saw Samuel put a gun under the seat also. But he did not ask any questions. The colt and another gelding were safely tied to the back of the wagon. Samuel had told John that the colt would go along easier with another older horse along. The trip took three days traveling. Two nights they slept in the wagon and ate at their campfire. The third night they had a bath in a small village and put on clean clothes. Samuel didn't want to be seen looking bad. John had also put on better clothes. It was about noon when they rode up through a stand of trees and there the rock house stood. It looked like a castle that John had seen in a storybook.

Samuel circled around the back and they pulled up in front of a rock building that matched the house. When they went inside it was a fancy stable. The foreman came striding out to meet them. He quickly went over and took the colt from the wagon and then disappeared again into the recesses of the barn. In a few minutes the owner came out of the house and greeted them. He thanked them for bringing the colt. He gave Samuel a piece of paper showing they had received the colt. He then turned and went back into the house. Samuel and John stood around for a few minutes and then Samuel said let's go. They climbed back into the wagon and left. John wanted to know why they did not get a welcome or at least water the mules, but by the look on Samuel's face he didn't dare ask.

They had ridden several miles before they came to a stream running by the road. Here Samuel stopped and watered the mules and the gelding. John was getting hungry. Having three good meals a day and treats were making a sorry hand out of him he thought. It had only been a few hours since he had eaten but he was starving. And he used to go for days without. But he tried not to remember those days much. In fact he hardly thought about them at all. That starving life seemed a long way off and more like a bad dream. Sometimes he did think of his family but as he grew older he just worried about himself.

Samuel continued the rest of the day seeming to hurry the mules. They found a good place to camp at nightfall and by daylight Samuel already had them on their way. At the next inn they ate a little food and fed the mules and horse and continued on. They next day they arrived at the town to get the supplies and Samuel seemed to relax a little. It took most of the day getting the supplies and the wagon loaded and they started out. They camped that night and the next and then made it home just at dark the next day. John asked why they did not stay in the inns like when Flossy went with them to town and was told Samuel just like sleeping out better.

It was a few days later that Samuel and John were taking a break that John got up the nerve to ask about the other Manor that they had visited.

"Those people at the place we took the colt were not very nice were they?" Samuel's forehead wrinkled into a frown. John had never seen that look on Samuel's face before. He hoped he never saw it again.

"The Man should not sell the colts to that man. I worked for The Duke one season and his hands and he are mean to the colts and everyone else. I quit them when a poor stable boy brought The Duke the wrong horse to ride one day. The Duke struck the boy with his riding whip over and over until the boy could not even move to get away. Then the other hands drug him into the stable and threw him in a corner. They did not even check to see if he was dead or not. During the night I went over to him and helped him get up and I put him on a horse and I had saddled me one. We rode most of the night. We then let the horses go, knowing that they would go home. We then walked for days, hiding when we heard anyone. When the moon was up we slept during the day and then covered ground during the night. I bought food and begged some for the boy. He mended and in a few days we were close to where some of his family lived and we parted company. I wandered around the country for a few weeks during odd jobs and sleeping in the woods. In one of the towns I heard they were having race day. I went out to see the races. That was the first time I had seen The Man. The other stable hands were talking about him needing help in his barn. Most of them were not going to go live all the way out here. So I mustered up enough courage to ask him for a job and I have been here ever since. I told The Man what had happened at the other place and why I had left there. He said that it sounded like I had done the right thing."

Samuel continued, "The first time that The Duke came to the ranch to buy colts he saw me. He acted like he had never seen me before. I guess he figured that I had told The Man what had happened and he didn't want to talk about it. That is why I always stay away from him as much as I can. The Man asked me last week if I minded taking the colt. If it was a problem he could make The Duke send someone to get him. I told him that we could handle it. When we got back the other night The Man wanted to know how things were and I told him that I didn't stay around for supper and he laughed."

"The Duke only has dregs working for him and they neglect the horses. When The Duke does not win he fires the people and gets some more. So they have help coming and going and so they do not have anyone who knows the horses or cares about them. You have to know your horses to be able to take care of them. Nobody wants to work for him. And you young man will stay a long way away from any of them. In the next few weeks we will take some of the sold colts to their new homes and you will be able to see some more horse farms like ours and you will meet some real horsemen. But for now you have to see about your own horses here."

When several of the buyers wanted to buy Red, John would hold his breath until he heard The Man say that he was not for sale. The Red had grown tall and had muscular legs. Now when John rode him he was always pulling on his reins wanting to gallop. And so gallop across the fields they would go. John could feel the power under him and the wind in his hair. Sometimes his hat would come off and just be staying on with the string holding it on. John felt they could fly. Sometimes the workers in the field would see them and would call out or wave their hats in the air at him. Then one day after they had had a good run he returned to the stable to see The Man standing there. He looked a little mad. John reined in and quickly took his saddle off and started walking Red to cool him off. The Man joined him as they walked along.

"Have you ever heard of blowing out a horse?" The Man asked. "No." John did not know what that was.

"If you let a young horse run too much he will blow out his stamina and will not be any use for anything. You must be very careful. Too much right now will hurt him and his chances at being a champion. And I hear you have been running around the fields like a mad man. If you make one wrong turn going that speed you will break his leg or ankle and we will have to put him down. So you will only gallop him on the meadow where we have plowed the course and no place else. You may take him out into the fields but only at a trot or walk. And do not let me see you bring him in that hot again. You will have cooled him off before you come back to this barn."

John hung his head and apologized. The Man patted him on his shoulder and said, "You will learn and so will Red."

Samuel grinned at him later when he came in the barn. "So you got your first lecture from The Man today huh? Well listen to everything that he tells you, he knows a lot of stuff. And he knows a lot about horses."

SIX

The summer went by fast. Samuel, Flossy, Hentley and John would some afternoons pack a lunch and go down to the little stream that ran through the farm. They would spread out a blanket and Flossy would put out the food and they would have a good time eating and visiting. Hentley had been gone to visit her family for a few days and she all kinds of news to tell. Samuel and John told about their trip to take the colt. They heard a horse coming and turned around to see The Man standing over them.

"Is this what I pay you all for? Going off to picnic with my wagon and my food and not inviting me?"

John was a little taken back until all the others laughed and The Man sat right down and helped himself. Samuel and Flossy treated him just like one of them and he had some gossip about some family to tell and they all laughed at his jokes. It was nearly dark when they got back to the house. Samuel and John put the mules and wagon away while Flossy and Hentley carried in the picnic baskets. It had been a good day John thought. But the picnic had reminded him of picnics that he had had with his family. He wondered where they were and were they all right. He had convinced himself that they all had the good fortune to be picked up just like him and things were alright. Then he thought, what if they had gone to someone like The Duke and had gotten beaten like the stable boy. He would ask Samuel about that in the morning. The next morning John and Samuel were riding some of the two year olds. Samuel could tell something was bothering the young man.

"What's eating you John?"

"I think I need to go try to find my family. I don't know where they went or if they are all right. Would you think that The Man would let me do that and then come back?"

Samuel pulled his horse up and looked at him. "What happens when you find them and they are not all right? What can you do for them? Where would you go look? They will not have records where they went. Just as no one knows that you are here except that book The Man signed saying that he was giving you a job. They could have been passed from place to place all these years."

John decided that he had to look for them.

"Ok." Samuel said. "We will see what we can do." Later in the day when The Man came out to the barn, John saw Samuel talking earnestly to him. Then they both came over to talk to John.

"Samuel says that you want to go try to find your family. Since all the colts are going good and we have extra help now that the harvest is in. I think that this would be a good time for you to go. And I think we can spare Samuel to go with you." John shook The Man's hand (he was too big to hug now) and told him he would be back soon and would never forget what he had done for him.

At supper Samuel announced to Flossy and Hentley that they would be going to try and find John's family. John looked at him in surprise. "The Man told me to accompany the lad so he would be sure and come back." They all laughed. Later when John saw The Man out for his nightly walk he thanked him mightily for sending Samuel to help him. The Man told him that no thanks were necessary. He had earned it with all the work he had done around The Manor.

"Just don't get your hopes up too high. There is a chance they are all gone."

It was a few days later that Samuel and John would start their trip to search for his family. They had to make sure everything would be taken care of while they were gone. John had made lists all over the barn wall and The Man had chuckled to himself as he walked by and read them. John had no idea that most of the other workers were unable to read a bit.

The wind was blowing but had the wisp of spring when they started out in late March. Flossy had overdone herself in making up supplies, bedding and utensils for them to cook out of. She was well aware that Samuel did not stay at many inns when traveling and figure this would be no different. The Man had given Samuel money for the trip and wished them well.

"If you were to run out of money go to the Solicitor in Crownhill and he will help you. I believe that you should be able to do a goodly search by the end of the month, but use your best judgment on the time."

It took them two days to return to the village that housed the poor. It was the same trip that had brought John to The Manor those years before. It was abandoned and weeds grew up in the steps as John and Samuel surveyed it. So they went to the closest house and inquired about it. They were told that all the people were put out and then they closed it. They believed that the village headsman would be the best to tell them anything about it. With the directions in hand they were soon standing in front of a nice place with Wurthom the gate in faded red letters. The same gate squeaked when they opened it and proceeded to the door. Before they could knock an elderly gentleman with white hair and a cane opened the door. "I heard that gate squeak. I keep thinking I will oil it but then I would not know when someone was coming up. What can I do for you?" "Are you the Headsman of the village?" "Yes, but it doesn't pay much and all I hear are gripes. "We are here about the poor house that is closed down. Can you tell us where the people went? "Excuse my manners. Come in and sit down. How about some tea?"

He went into another room and they could hear him putting a kettle of water on the hearth. They had followed him in and so they all sat at a table nearby.

"The poor house has been closed for several years. Some high and mighty over in Commission decided that it was a waste of money and they were all put out as servants and then they closed it. And the awful stories that I heard about those people. Some were beaten, some starved, and some never even made it to where they were sent, they were so poorly when they started out." John wanted to cry or shout in anger he couldn't decide which so he just sat in silence. Samuel had watched his reaction closely and knew this was eating at the lad's insides.

Samuel then asked the Headsman if there were any records as to where each of the poor people went.

"Oh yes! I have it here somewhere. When they came to close it they wanted an accounting of all the people. I just couldn't give it to them. I hid it and still have it. But what do you want with it?" "The lad here lived there a while with his family before being given out. He never saw them again. So we are on a trip to see if we can find them."

The Headsman shook his head. "That is the reason that I hid the book. I just knew that someday someone would need those names. Or I was hoping that they would." He rose from his chair and poured Samuel and John tea. He then gave them bread and some wonderful red jelly to put on it. He explained the neighbor lady made it for him since he had no wife. John thought he was going to burst. The book! The book! He wanted to look at the book. He was too young to realize that the Headsman had few visitors and was very pleased to have them here. Finally after rummaging around in another room he returned with a ledger book. In it were the names, dates the people arrived, the dates they left and where they had gone. John was amazed as was Samuel who was looking over with him, at how many were noted down as dead and the date. As John searched the approximate dates that he and The Man had figured out before they left, he was encouraged to find fewer deaths. Suddenly his hand stopped and he let out a little cry. There was his Mother's name and under it all of the children including John! John had never forgotten the morning that they lined all the children up and were given away. He also remembered his mother telling him that someday they would all be together again. He started to tear up and Samuel put his big arm around him for a while. Samuel then told him. "We are bound to find some of them."

After the Headsman had furnished him with writing material John quickly copied down each of the names and where they had gone.

Baby Ann		Carlton House
Rebecca	3yrs old	Carlton House
Henry	5 yrs old	Wilmarland
George	8 yrs old	Castilone
Sally Mae	9 yrs old	Hinderwater
John	11 yrs old	The Manor
Mrs. Dunn	34 yrs old?	

John was about half though the list when he realized the list was in his Mother's handwriting. This just about did him in. He lovingly ran his fingers across the writings. When he had finished he ask the Headsman why there was no placement name by his Mother's name.

"Son some of the people just left and we don't know where they went."

John felt like someone had stabbed him in his chest. How was he to find his mother?

He also had noticed that the age his Mother had put on the page was a year off from what he knew was his birth year. As John looked at the page he soon realized that this had been written nearly 5 years ago. Most of the kids would not even know him if he could find them.

Samuel and John took their leave after assuring the Headsman that they were fine with their sleeping and traveling arrangements. They didn't go far until they found a nice place to camp.

In fact it appeared to be a poplar camping place and during the evening several other families and a wagon master carrying freight stopped for the night there. He came over and visited with John and Samuel before they all turned in for the night. When it was light Samuel found John sitting on the back of the wagon going over the list.

"Where do you think we start?" John asked him.

Samuel had been thinking about the Mother. "Maybe someone around here knew where she went. They might even know her. So he suggested to John that they start asking around in the village if anyone knew of her."

They had not gotten far when they found an old woman puttering in her flowers.

"Did you know my Mother Susan Dunn? She might have come here about 5 years ago looking for work."

The old woman shaded her eyes from the sun. "Who wants to know?"

"I am her son John and I have come looking for her and my brothers and sisters."

"How do I know that you are her son? I know that she had a scar on the top of her right hand."

The old woman walked over and sat on a bench near the front door. "She came here in the night. She said that she was running away from the poor house. She too was on a journey to find you kids. She spent the night and I fed her, she was so starved. I told her that she should stay a few days and eat up and get some strength but she said she had to go. So I packed her a bundle of groceries and she left the next day. I never saw her again."

The old woman stood up and took something out of her pocket. She left this in case anyone would come looking for her. She held out a bracelet. John immediately recognized it as one his Aunt had sent her many years ago at Christmastime. He took it and held it close to his chest.

"This was my mother's." On impulse he grabbed the old woman and gave her a big hug.

Then he was hurrying Samuel to the wagon so they could get going. Samuel climbing onto the wagon seat but just sat there. John said," Let's go."

"Soon as you tell me where to go I will go."

John realized he didn't know where to go either. He hurried back to the old woman.

"Did she say where she was going?

The old woman replied "Yes she had a list of where each of the children had gone. She was going to go to each of the places on the list."

John took out his list and asked whether she knew where Hinderwater was?

"No never heard of it." John then went down the list and the old woman continued to nod her head no.

"Go find an innkeeper somewhere they might know where some of these are if they pass by there."

So Samuel and John were off to find the nearest Innkeeper. His list included Carlton House, Hinderwater, Wilmarland, and Castilone. It was many days and many innkeepers before they had any luck. They had gone into an inn on a rainy night. They had decided to see if they could spend the night in the barn with the horses. The innkeeper was very agreeable for a few coins in his hand. They then sat down and order a scant supper and began eating. They had asked the innkeeper if he knew any of the names of where the children had gone but he did not know any of them. They decided that after they ate they might ask some of the other patrons if they knew them. While they were eating they heard a loud exchange going on farther down the room near the door. One burly man was shouting to another that he knew for certain that the fight had taken place over by Castilone. Something to do with a ship that had come in and the argument had carried over to the stables at Castilone. John started up at once, but wise Samuel put out his hand and eased him back into his chair.

"We will wait a while to ask. We don't know what the fighting was all about." So they sat finishing their meal and drinks. When the innkeeper came around late to take up their plates, Samuel asked him who the burly man was.

"Ole John? He speaks loud and looks rough but is as nice an old guy you would find. He used to be a seaman but an accident several years ago brought him to shore. He still goes down to the docks some days and sits and watches the ships come in. Then in a few days he will wander back this way."

"Do you think he would join us for a pint? "I will ask him." Soon Ole John as he was called, lumbered over and sat down. Samuel pushed him a pint of ale and introduced John and his self. "We are looking for a place called Castilone. Can you direct us there?"

"Why would you want to go to Castilone? It is a run-down old place with the old man not able to take care of it anymore and none of his hands worth anything."

"We are looking for" Samuel kicked John under the table Samuel then said, "We are sent by our manager to see the man." Ole John had seen Samuel stop the boy but kept it to himself. But it did get his curiosity up. "I might be going down that way tomorrow if you would like to ride along."

The next morning they started out. Ole John could not but notice that the horses that Samuel and John rode were not your run of the mill workers horses. But he didn't say anything. They spent two more nights on the road and the old seaman did not mind when they slept out. The next day when they awoke they could smell the salt air and the horses even were perkier than usual. As they rode along Ole John told them about some of his adventures at sea. John thought they were great stories and wished for pen and paper to write them down. Late in the evening they saw the waves crashing on the rocks. They were up above on a slight cliff and the roar was deafening. They followed along for another few miles. John could hardly watch where he was going, he was so entranced by the waves and the noise. They soon came upon a beach and saw men mending nets near their boats. One or two called out to the old seaman. After visiting with each group

42

they would continue along. About sunset they could see tall ships and John held his breath. "They are so big!"

"Yes they be pretty big". Ole John laughed.

The docks were bordered by a road that ran alongside. On the opposite side of the road a town had grown up. Buildings were built with adjoining walls and the string of them seemed to go for a mile. Each little door led to some form of business. Most of them were two stories with the owner and maybe a family lived upstairs. People were bustling everywhere. There were workers from the boats unloading every kind of things. Men in dress clothes and Ladies in fine dresses strolled along. When the sun set the taverns were filled with noisy music and laughter. The lights from the doors spreading out into the road. Ole John had handily found them a stable and made arrangements for them to sleep there, as all the inns were full. The big ships had just come in the day before and every bed was filled with sailors from all over the world. Samuel took John to look around for a short trip as Ole John had quickly gone off to visit old friends. When Samuel turned back to their stable John started to protest he was not tired. But Samuel quickly whispered that when there are this many people, there are thieves and we need to watch our horses. So reluctantly John returned to the stable. But when they climbed up into the hay loft the door to stack the hay looked out on the bay and the street below. So he was happy to sit in his crow's nest and watch all the action below.

He noticed there were lots of fights! And lots of fancy ladies in clothes not like the ones the ladies had worn that he had seen during the day. They were loud colors and they had lots of paint on their faces. There were all kinds of people. The short people with the slanted eyes fascinated him. They looked so tiny compared to some of the dock hands that stood over six feet tall. Then there was the really black men. John had never seen anyone so shiny black. He quickly noticed that they did not interact with the others but stayed apart by themselves.

They did not see Ole John when they got up the next day, so they set out to find him. Again the town was lively as an ant hill. People scurrying everywhere. Samuel found an open market and they bought bread and cheese and sat down on some wood planks to eat them. Some children were running and playing with a folded up rag they threw to one another. John soon realized that he had not played ball since he had left the poor house. Samuel too caught the look on his face and thought about the small little boy they had raised at The Manor. He had not ever thought to play with him. It made him sad.

After they had eaten they again began their search for Ole John. They soon found him sitting outside of a roadside cafe with others like him talking over old times. When he saw them coming he stood up and called out. When they approached him introduced him to a couple of captains and some more old seamen. Wow! John thought, a real sea Captain. Both had blue coats and bright yellow buttons and some kind of pins on their chests. They must be very important! The one smoking a pipe smiled and asked John if he was ready to come go to sea and sail out to see the world.

"Oh, no", John answered. "I have never been on a boat."

"We will just have to do something about that." He hauled himself up and taking John by the shoulder they all marched over the dock and proceeded up a gangway up into the big ship. John was showed around by a first mate to every nook and cranny. John could not believe that the ship could hold so much stuff. He then took him to the Captains quarters where the Captain fed them a delicious lunch of mostly things John had never eaten; great fruits and fish that he could not even pronounce their names.

After a while Samuel thanked the captain for the lunch and tour, but that they had business back on land. After getting directions, Samuel and John set out for Castilone. It was easy to find since it was the only place down a deserted lane that had soon turned off the main road. The lane was lined with some kind of trees and John could tell at one time was a pretty ride. The large house was in the same dark neglected state. There was no one to take their horses when they rode up. Actually they both looked at each other and then tied their horses to a nearby tree. The steps were worn and they had to watch where they walked to the door. It seemed to not have been opened in a long time. John knocked timidly and when there was no answer Samuel took a turn banging quite hard on the door facing.

The door opened a crack and a frail, white-headed lady looked out at them. "What do you want?"

"We are looking for a boy taken from the poor house about 5 years ago and came here."

The door opened a little wider.

"What do you want with him?" John answered that he was his brother, George. And he was looking for him and the rest of his family that had been separated at the poor house. "Didn't stay long. Ran away."

"Ran away where?" John asked.

"Don't know. Just was not here when we got up a few weeks after he came here."

"Why did he leave?" Samuel looked right at the old woman. "I guess because he got thrashed for not doing his chores."

"Did he have any other acquaintances while he was here?"

"Not that I know of."

The old woman did not offer anything else so John and Samuel thanked her. They mounted up and rode back to town. Soon as they rode into the town proper there was Ole John.

He was told what had happened and he just shook his head.

"Anyplace else we might look? If he did chores he might have come to town for supplies. Let's ask around at the mercantile stores."

The first one did not know George, but he said that the old woman did not trade with him. He told them to try O'Keefe's down the next row. At O'Keefe's they had to wait as the proprietor waited on other customers. Then he came over.

"What can I do for you?"

They explained that they were looking for a George Dunn that would have come to Castilone about 5 years ago. They thought he might have come in with some of the help there for supplies.

"I was not here five years ago but the owner is in the back. He might can help you."

They were shown into a room just past the bags of flour. Sitting at an old desk was a large man with the biggest nose John had ever seen. But he smiled when they called out and asked them into his office. It was quite crowded with Ole John, Samuel, John and himself.

John stated their business and the man quickly told them he remember the kid. When he described him John knew right away that this was his brother.

"Poor little soul!"

"What is he dead?" John asked.

"Oh no. But he might have been better off. He would come in with that Cotton girl and he would be all bruised up. When I asked the Cotton girl just said that he was awful clumsy."

"Where is he now?" Samuel spoke up. He was getting madder by the minute. He did not hold with anyone beating up on a child.

"Let me see. I heard something about that."

The merchant rubbed his chin and then spoke quickly.

"I remember. He came here just as I was closing one night. Again he had been beaten pretty bad. He wanted to know where to go since he was running away and had no idea where to run to. I ask about his family and he told the same story as you all, that he had been put out from the poor house and he didn't know where or if any of you were alive. About that time an old Captain from the Vermeil came in. When he saw the boy he immediately asked him if he would like to sail on a big ship. He could use a cabin boy."

George had turned to me and I told him, "If you took the job the bunch at Castilone would not be able to find you. The old sea captain had had me gather up a few clothes for him and away they went. And I have not seen them since. I know that the Vermeil has been in port a few times but I haven't seen the boy." John pleaded with the merchant that if it came in again he would inquire about George. John also quickly borrowed pen and paper and wrote a note.

George Dunn

I am looking for you. I live at The Manor upland.

Your brother,

John Dunn

He left the note and they went out to the street. It was nearly dark so they decided to stay another night. They ate at a local tavern, then said goodbye to Ole John. They made their way back to the stable and took care of their horses and made their bed in the hay. Again John sat and looked out the hay opening at the bay and all the ships anchored there. Just think, George has sailed to some other country on one of those big ships. He prayed and hoped that George would someday sail back and find his note. The next morning he crossed off Castilone from his list.

The next morning the search began again. Going from store and tavern along the row, John showed his list to everyone he could. All he got was lots of nodding no's. The last place was a barber shop. The men inside did not know the place but thought that the Constable might know. He traveled quite a bit. They were directed to a larger house up the hill from the docks.

John was nearly out of breath when they came upon a nice house with a white fence all around it. An older lady was sitting in a rocker by the door. Samuel introduced himself then John and explained what they were doing. The Constable is out but will be back soon. She had raised herself up and turned to the door.

"Don't just stand there come in."

She continued to the back of the house where a cook was making something that smelled wonderful. The lady motioned them into chairs around a table and the cook brought them a pitcher of cool drink and just seconds more the most wonderful smell came in with the cookies on a plate. John felt like he could have eaten the whole platter. But he only took two and ate them quietly. The Lady then asked the cook if she knew anything about a George Dunn that had run away from Castilone.

"No but all I hear about that place is awful."

There was tramping of feet and the Constable came in. He nodded at the visitors and took off his coat and joined them at the table. The Lady quickly told him what their business was. He smiled and told them he would try to help them.

"Where are you going?" They told him who they were and who they were trying to find. John named off his list.

The Constable took John's list and studied it.

"I think I know sort of where Carlton House is. But it is quite a ways from here. And Hinderwater is down the coast quite a ways off also." He did not recognize the other names. He went into his study just off the front room and came back with a crudely drawn map. He went over it with the two travelers and then also added some names on the back of John's list of people that he was acquainted with in both areas that might be able to help them in their search.

He then told them that he had become involved with George Dunn's escape. When George had run away, the old lady had sent another maid down to him to demand that he find George and send him back. When he went to inquire around the docks he was told the same story that the kid was beaten regularly. He soon found the Vermeil Captain and told him he had to give the boy back. The

Captain swore he did not have him. And let the Constable search the ship. He did not find George Dunn. The next day as the Vermeil weighed anchor, the Constable happened to be on the dock watching, when he noticed a small lad standing next to the Captain as they slid away from the dock. The Captain tipped his hat to the Constable and the Constable waved in return.

The old Constable chuckled to himself. "You see gentlemen; I do not have any authority on the high seas! So I do know that the Captain is a good man and I am sure that George Dunn is doing well, where ever he is." John was so happy! He wanted to get up and hug the Constable.

So with map in hand they returned to their horses. Again Samuel just sat there.

"Let's get going." John said. Samuel answered," I am soon as you tell me where we are going."

John studied the map and then decided to go to Hinderwater first. Although still along the coast Hinderwater would be several days ride from where they were. Samuel decided that they had better stop at the merchants for some supplies. While they had been around the docks they had been able to get their laundry done by some Chinese laundry. John had carefully stowed the clean clothes in his saddle bags to have when they arrived at Hinderwater.

As they started their trip they followed a road that meandered across the cliffs above the water. The crashing waves occasionally made his horse a little skittish. At times the road carried them away from the coastline and then back again. As dark approached they started looking for a campsite. The area was completely devoid of any trees. Since the horses had been fed well for several days at the livery they did not have to be hobbled to graze. But there was little campfire as the wind off the bay blew it around. But they were finally able to get a little supper fixed and ate. The ground they found was damp and they spent a miserable night of it. Soon as it was light they ate a little left over bread and cheese and were on their way. They had met a few travelers going the opposite way from them, but only a couple going the same way they were. These they had passed and were soon out of sight of them. When they had gone another couple of days they stopped one of the travelers and ask about Hinderwater.

"It be another day's ride and then about half a day away from the water." One of the travelers told them. John hated to think about another night on the hard ground but that is what it was. After asking someone else they made a turn and started away from the coast.

After a few hours they started down into some meadows and thank God a few trees! Although the road was not heavily traveled they made good time and about midafternoon they came down off a hill into one of the prettiest valleys John had seen. It was green and had a stream running right through it. The horses drank thirstily of the clear water. Off to the North they saw what looked like a house so they turned and headed that way. This was not a castle but just a large farmhouse. It had two stories and a porch across the front. The gate in the fence squeaked as they walked up to the porch. They were aware they had been seen as a curtain in one of the front rooms had been snatched shut. John knocked on the door and called out.

A large woman wearing a white apron came to the door. "What do you want?"

John asked for the head of the house.

"I am the head of the house," said the woman not making a move to ask them in.

"I am John Dunn and I am looking for my family. They were all given out from a poorhouse a few years ago and I was informed that Sallie Mae had been sent here. Do you know her?"

The lady's face softened and she moved aside and motioned John and Samuel to come in.

They entered a front room that was very neat and had good solid furniture in a pretty dark wood. She offered them a seat and then went to get them something to drink. Little people seemed to appear around every corner, eyes taking in the visitors. But none came in the room. The woman returned with cool drinks and pastries. John and Samuel tried to act civilized but they had not eaten since daylight and they were hungry.

When he finished his drink John again ask him about Sallie Mae.

"She was here a few years back. And we liked her a lot. Then one day she received a letter from her mother saying that someone was coming to fetch her to take her to her Aunt Beatrice's. And sure enough a couple of days later a coach and driver came and took her away. And we never heard from her again."

"Where did she go? We never knew. But I do have the letter."

She went over to a small desk in the corner of the room. She brought the letter to John. He recognized his Mother's handwriting. And it did say someone was coming to get her to take her to Aunt Beatrice's. Beatrice was his Mother's sister and had married well and John had always been told they lived a long way off. But if they lived a long way off why would they just send a carriage and a driver?

This seemed like another dead end, but it was comforting to know that his sister and his mother were being seen about. It was getting late in the evening when the woman said would they like to stay for supper and they could sleep in the barn. When they were invited into the dining room it was a big table. Two men sat on the side with several children on both sides of the table. John did not count them all but he was impressed that it was a lot.

The woman noticed his looking around and said. "I don't have much, but when I heard the poor house was closing I just went over there and got all the kids that I could take care. Mostly the ones that had not been chosen by the other people. We farm here and sell peat. So soon as they get bigger they help around. The little ones feed the chickens and work the garden. The big boys take care of the animals and farm. And I just try to keep us together. For the big jobs we have labor come from town and neighbors help out." As John looked around the children were all smiles.

Again John said a silent prayer that his other siblings had found a family like this one. The next morning they decided to try the next place on their list. The woman did not know where Wilmarland or Carlton House was but she assured them that when they returned to the main road there would be an inn just a few miles down the road. When they were saddled and saying their goodbyes the woman brought them a lunch wrapped in a cloth. John started to refuse the food, but a stern look from Samuel changed his mind. He thanked her mightily and then waved at all the children as they rode away.

"We should have not taken the food. Those kids needed it."

"I know," said Samuel," but her feelings would have been hurt had you not taken it." As they rode along John thought about the woman that had taken in all the children. To himself he said if I had money I would take in all the poor children too.

As the woman had said it was only about a day and a half to the inn. They arrived late one evening. They stabled and fed their horses and then went inside to eat and ask around. After the woman's cooking the food was pretty bad but John had learned to eat knowing it might be a long time until you ate again. The Tavern owner tried to get them to stay in a room but Samuel quickly said that they would sleep in the stable with their horses. The Tavern owner did not know either of the places that John was looking for. And when other travelers came in no one seemed to know these places either.

When they went to bed down, Samuel was talking to the kid that took care of the horses. "Have you ever had a really nice carriage come by here with a young lady in the back? It would have been a couple of years ago." About that time another man appeared in the door of the barn.

"Who wants to know about a fine carriage? Are you planning on robbing them on the road?" Samuel quickly explained to the man that they were not ruffians and that they were looking for John's family and thought that the girl in the carriage might be his sister. They told the story again and added that they had no idea where to go to look for the carriage. The man had taken his hat off and scratched his head.

"Seems like I do remember a fancy carriage because we had not seen one in a long time. So when they went in to eat we opened the door and the inside smelled of leather seats and it had royal red curtains."

"Did you get to know the name of the people that it belonged to?"

"No, but I know that it went North from here."

John and Samuel thanked the man. The next morning they set off again headed North.

It had been a month since they had left The Manor. It was now coming on fall and the weather was turning colder at night, but the days were still warming up.

Samuel pulled up next to John and said, "Young feller we had better set us a time for this traveling. We do not want to get caught in the winter looking around. Before bad weather sets in we better be back at The Manor. Then next summer we can look some more." So they decided that they would be out one more week and then they would turn back.

The next person that helped them in their quest was a tinker. He was riding along the same road as John and Samuel and they struck up a conversation as they rode along. Samuel first broached the subject of Carlton House.

The tinker spoke quickly. "There used to be a big family at the Carlton House but I think they have moved on. Someone said they had gone to Australia. When we get to their turn off I will show you but I am going on straight." A couple of miles farther the old tinker pointed to their left as the road made a sharp right turn. So Samuel and John thanked him and turned to their left. The tinker had said it would be about a days ride and so after spending another night on the ground, the next afternoon found them at a nice quiet meadow and then sat back from the road a white large house. They rode up and tied their horses. As they made their way to the front door a quiet voice came from the side of the house.

"Ain't nobody here. They are all gone. Left last year for the land down under. Australia I believe they call it." John walked closer to the man and asked if they had adopted a couple of small children a few years back. The man said, "Yes they had gone to the poor house and got them a couple of little ones a few years back."

"Why did they go to Australia?

"Only the son and his wife went. The old gentleman and his wife had died and they just decided to go."

"Do you have any way to get in touch with them?"

"No since I don't read I guess they didn't care to write. They said I could stay here long as I wanted to as I had no place to go. Becky and the little Susie were the names of the babies they brought home with them. See they couldn't have any children. The kids were well mannered and the son and his wife adored them."

John and Samuel thanked the man and left. As they rode along John decided it was not meant to be that he find any of them. He told Samuel he was ready to go back to the Manor.

"We have not looked at every place on the list." Big Samuel had turned around to face John.

"I guess I have given up on this deal." John said and turned away so Samuel couldn't see his tears.

SEVEN

The next morning they began the month long trip back to the Manor. It was fall by now and the weather was not good. It began to rain the second day out and even though they both had slickers that covered all their clothes it was still cold. Nights were miserable on the wet ground and John was so depressed. After the first week the sun finally came out and going was a little faster and better. They passed many of the same inns that they had gone to on their hunt. They continued to tell everyone that they spoke to that they were trying to find John's family. Samuel said maybe word would get back to some of them that way.

The day that they reached The Manor they could see it a few miles away. John was glad to be home. Wow! he had just thought of The Manor. And he supposed that he was right. It had become home and The Man, Samuel, and Flossy had become his family. And he was proud to have all of them. They were both pretty dirty when they road into the stables. But first they tended to their horses and the Samuel suggested that they get a bath in the spring nearby. With new clothes in hand they quickly bathed, as the water was cold, and put on clean clothes. Then they presented themselves to the house. Flossy, of course, already knew they were there and had a meal fixed for them. They had just sat down when The Man, who had seen them come in from his study window, came in and sat down to hear all about their trip. He seemed genuinely sorry that they had been unable to find any of John's family. He said maybe next time. He then told them about what had been going on here while they were gone. He had sold some more of the colts and the harvest had started well. He then left them to finish their meal. He would have like to have stayed and listened to all of their adventure but knew that it was not his place to stay there. Sometimes he envied them getting to sit by the fire and just have company. None of them could know how lonely he really was.

The next day Samuel and John were up early getting back into the routine of caring for the horses. Red smelled John and quickly was at the fence railing for his carrot treat.

"Oh you didn't forget me huh? "Later he would take him for a ride John decided. He was mucking out the stalls when The Man called to him and Samuel.

One of the colts was bought by a man in America and we have to ship him next spring when we can find a ship to send him on. I believe that you call him Red, John. John's heart nearly failed him. Not Red! Not his Red! What did I think that he would stay here forever? He wasn't half listening when he heard The Man asking him if he would take Red to America.

"I need someone I can trust to sail with him and then you will have the return fare to come back. It will take a couple of months of sailing to get there." John's head was spinning. He knew he really had no choice in the matter after how good The Man had been to him. He was able to stutter out that he would be happy to take Red to America. Inside John's heart was breaking. He had not found his family, his favorite horse was sold to someone he didn't even know in America of all places and now he had to sail in a big ship with the horse He guessed if his brother could sail he could too.

After The Man left Samuel pounded on John's back. "Going to America! Wish I was young enough to go with you."

"Can't you come? John asked.

"Who is going to take care of all these horses if I go with you? You saw how neglected things were when we came back." Samuel grinned to himself. He really wished he could go with the young one but he knew he could not. It was not very neglected as John had seen. Things just were not up to Samuel's standards but none of the horses seemed the worse for wear.

The next day The Man called John into his office and handed him a pamphlet.

"Take this and read it, it will give you a little history of America and we will see what else we can find for your travels."

After his work was done that evening John readily opened the little book and started reading. He could not imagine going to a country where there was red savages that killed people! He read of the pilgrims He then read of the revolution when the little band of Americans had thrown out the British army. He read of the new things like turkeys and tobacco.

A few days later, The Man brought John a map. The map had marks showing where the ships sailed and where they would usually make port. It showed that the ships sailed south from England to Africa and then sailed across to some islands and then up the coast to America.

The Man then was gone a few days. When he returned he announced that he had booked passage for Red and John on the ship, the Arbella, and they would sail on or about the 1ˢᵗ of April of the next year. The Man also had brought John more material to read. And John absorbed it all. He learned that he would sail from Bristol. He also learned that England exported manufactured wares and imported from America sugar, tobacco, rice, coffee, naval stores and dyestuffs. The Man said that it would a long voyage and when John got to America he was to rest up before coming back.

The Man said, "You need to look around at this new country so you can come back and tell us all about it."

The next day John found Samuel boarding up Red's stall. He had nailed the window shut and was not putting boards up all around even up to the ceiling. It would only be a few slits of light entering the stall. Samuel explained to John that Red would ride in the belly of the ship and he would not have very much light and he had to become used to it. You will bring him in here a little at a time and extend the time until you get ready to sail. He will then be used to you taking him in and the dark. We will also teach him to wear the sling that they will lift him up onto the deck of the ship and then down into the hold.

So the next few weeks were spent going into and out of the dark stall. Red at first of course did not like it but soon would go readily as long as John was there to comfort him with a soothing voice and gentle rubbings. The Man had seen the sling he would wear so they spent most of the day with him helping them construct one. Red was almost crazy eye at the contraption. But with a lot of coaxing from all three of them it was rigged up on him. He got away from The Man who was holding his halter and tried to buck the thing off but after a while settled down. Every day he looked wild eye at them all, but slowly did not run away from the sling. The last problem was to figure out how to teach him to be off the ground without throwing a fit, which might hurt him or the ship's crew when they tried to tug on the ropes to get him over the hold hole.

One day John was riding him along the river that ran through the property when across a narrow stretch of it, he saw a cliff and had a brain storm. He loped back to the barn and found Samuel. He explained that he believed they could construct something on the top of the cliff and let the horse down off the cliff. What a wild idea they both thought. But The Man had heard them and decided they could give it a try. Days were spent drawing a design that would basically be a seesaw type of affair. They would have a large beam with a fulcrum in the middle and weights on the other end that way they could slowly let the horse down. John also realized that Red would also be learning to be over some water at the same time. The whole thing had wheels so they could push it out over the water far enough to get him away from the cliff and not hurt himself.

Over the next few weeks John and Samuel saw more of The Man than they ever had. He was at the barn working on the seesaw. He had had some classes in Engineering and found it wonderful to be out using his hands. They soon finished the contraption as they called it. They then spent the next few days putting Red in the harness and taking him out. He soon learned to stand still as the harness was attached to the contraption. One day The Man said let's see if we can lift him up off the ground. They then began placing sacks of feed on the other ends box. When they exceeded Red's weight his front feet came up first and then his back. Just a little before he didn't like it. They quickly took some feed sacks off and let him back down. Another thing to do for days until he didn't mind too badly.

One thing in John and the others favor was that since Red had been a young colt, John and Red had swam in the river on hot days. Red seemed to love the water. Even now they would sometimes go down to the river and take a swim.

When they thought Red was ready they decided it was the day to try it out. With some help from some of the other hands and the mules they pulled it upriver and across to the cliffs.

When they had it in place John quickly volunteered to get in the harness and try it out. He handily was raised up and then pushed out over the cliff. As they removed the bags of feed he was lowered farther and farther down until his feet touched the water. Then at the same time they all realized they hadn't figure out how to get him undone. So they pulled the contraption back and pulled him up again.

Leaving the contraption there they went back to the barn. The Man and Samuel worked the rest of the afternoon trying different ideas to get the horse undone after they got him in the water. It would not be a problem on the boat as they would be setting him down on a hard surface. But here in their experiment there would be no one in the water to get him loose.

John then said, "I will ride down with him. And take him loose."

"What if you get tangled up in the harness or something?" The Man looked at Samuel with a worried look. Samuel told John he didn't think that was a very good idea. And they continued working on other ideas, which none of them worked. Finally The Man looked over at John and Red and said ok we will try it.

"But if anything goes wrong you jump off and away from him so he is not thrashing around on you in the water."

The next day John rode Red over to the river and let him smell the contraption and then they went down river and went for a swim in the cool water. This continued until Red was very comfortable with the contraption and the water. Then a few days were spent with Samuel and The Man there to help practicing getting the harness and sling on and off.

It was a full two weeks before the grand day. Flossy had packed a picnic lunch and off they all went to see the horse lifted down the cliff. They had considered using another horse but that would not have taught Red anything and he was the one going to have to wear the thing.

Red was put in the sling and then the contraption was eased up behind him. John climbed up on his back. As they put enough weight on the other end of the contraption Red slowly was raised off the ground. He struggled a little and John spoke to him in a quiet voice. Slowly they moved the contraption over the cliff and put large rocks on the wheels to keep them from going any farther. Red looked around a little wild eyed but did not struggle. They quickly lowered him and John in to the water and John released the rope holding them. They quickly splashed into the water and were off swimming downstream.

He could hear Samuel and the rest shouting encouragement to them both. It was decided that since the experiment had gone so well that they should not try their luck anymore. Something might happen to spook the horse and right now he seemed alright with the whole thing. So Red, John, and the rest of the group with the mule pulling the contraption headed back home.

Late at night when John went to bed he still thought about his family and wondered where they were. He also thought about the trip ahead and sometimes it was a fearful thing. He had never traveled by himself more less gone on a long adventure across the ocean with the responsibility of another man's horse!

The Man had thought about the trip also and the next time they needed supplies from the town, he suggested that John make the trip on his own and take care of getting the supplies. So the next day John started out with the wagon and mules. He had money secreted on his person and Samuel also showed him a hidey place on the wagon. So if they got everything off of him he and the mules and wagon would still be ok. It was a lonely feeling going off without Flossy and Samuel but also gave him great pride to know that he was being considered a grown man to go and get what they needed. The trip was uneventful and John made it back in good time with all the items on Samuel and Flossy's lists. Behind his back both were grinning with parental pride at his accomplishment. Samuel and Flossy were both apprehensive about his going with the horse, but knew he had to go. They had tried without appearing too protective to tell him everything they could about being on a long journey even though neither had been anywhere to amount to anything. John had tolerated the extra advice as he understood they were just trying to help him prepare for his trip.

It had been a mild winter and the days went by quickly. Before John knew it April 1 was only a couple of weeks away. The closer the time came the more Samuel, Flossy, and even The Man spent time reminding John what to do about this and when to do this and how to do this. Sometimes they repeated themselves on the same day and sometimes they all told him the same thing the same day. But he had stored all the advice he could as he felt he would at some time need all of it and more.

EIGHT

About ten days before they were to sail, The Man came down to the stable and told Samuel and John to pack up as they would start out that morning for the coast. Unknown to The Man they had been packed for a week trying not to forget anything. The Man had brought him a trunk to hold his clothes. The trunk had a place on one side to hang up his clothes and the other side was little pockets to pack everything else. He also had a pack for his back to hold things and of course Flossy had packed a couple of boxes of food. She was really afraid he would starve before they got to America. Samuel and John filled the back of the wagon with feed and a couple of horse blankets for Red. Extra halters, reins and other rigging were also packed. Then they loaded the trunk and food boxes. Flossy tried to not cry as they sent him off but he got a few tears when she hugged him up.

And then they were away. Samuel driving the wagon, The Man on Kingdom, and John on Red. At first they were going to lead Red, and then decided that if he got a little tired on the trip might be good for him. It took them about five days to reach the coast. They had followed the same route Samuel and John had looking for his family. They reached Karney Bay and as before it was bustling with commerce. John quickly looked for the ship that might hold his brother but with no luck. They found an inn and The Man ask about the ship, Arbella. We are expecting her any day now the Innkeeper told them. So they got their rooms, Samuel and John in one and The Man in an adjoining one. They made arrangements for the mules, Kingdom and Red in the stable owned by the same innkeeper. It was late afternoon when they arrived and so they ate their supper and soon retired to their rooms. Although he was tired, John was unable to sleep. Samuel heard him tossing and turning and in the dark asked if he was alright. John said that he was ok, just anxious about the trip. He said that he hoped that he would not disappoint the Man and Samuel. Samuel assured him that he thought he would do just fine. He then told John to be sure and come back. You might get over there and find a good looking honey and just stay there. Probably will not even worry about ole' Samuel and The Man. He chuckled and John tried to assure him that would not be the case. After a while they were both sound asleep. John dreaming about some good looking honey in America.

The next day they were walking down the docks when someone shouted out to them. It was the old captain that had befriended them before. He at once wanted to know how they were and what they were about. John straightened up tall and said,

"I am sailing to America to deliver a blooded horse for The Man."

"Well blow me down!!" The old captain was clapping John on the back. "That will be quite a trip! And carrying a blooded horse! The Man must think a lot of you."

"I guess so," John modestly answered.

"You will be going soon. I hear the Arbella is only a few days out."

The Man had joined them. "That is what the shipmaster told me this very morning. John you better get Red out and ride every day until the ship comes in."

So John would ride Red everyday down the coastline. They saw lots of birds, and lots they didn't know what they were. There were fishermen everywhere and they would go down and watch them take the fish out of the nets for the market. Other days the same men would be on the shore sewing the holes in the nets so they would be ready to go out again. At first Red would not get close to the water and the men and the fish. They smelled funny and Red didn't know about them. But after a few days he would follow John right up to the fishermen and let some of them pet him. They also would ride on the beach and Red got used to the sound of the surf and the water running up on his feet. He only tried the salty water once. He had put his nose down in it and John laughed as Red tried to cough and sling his head to get rid of it.

One day when they came back to the dock from their ride, there she sat out in the harbor. The Arbella was here! A lump formed in John's throat and he felt like he could hardly breathe.

Maybe he didn't want to take Red to America! Maybe he was too scared! He wanted to ride Red back to The Manor and wake up and it all be a dream! But no, there was Samuel and The Man waiting for him. He quickly turned into the stable and unsaddled Red and brushed him down. Anything to use up time. John believed that Samuel would be able to see the fear he was feeling.

So he went about his business in good manner and found that the beating of his heart had settled down. He put Red up and fed him and then stepped out on the dock to see his ship that was going to take him across an ocean and to America.

The Man had already met the Captain O'Leary and they were taken by a small boat over to the ship. They climbed a rope ladder up the side and were soon shown around the ship. It was huge! It was like a floating town to John. He was shown his small stateroom where he would live. It was small with a bed and a small table and chair with a few storage bins. The captain then called for a lantern and they descended into the belly of the ship. The captain explained where the cargo would be stored, and then they came upon a stall made just like the one at The Manor.

"We had the stall constructed to the specifications that you sent sir. I hope it meets your approval. For the first few weeks the other end of this area will remain empty so you should be able to exercise the horse in there. Later it will eventually fill up with cargo but you shall still be able to walk him up and down each day. He doesn't kick does he? Some of the walkways may get a little crowded and I wouldn't want one of my men getting kicked."

"No he doesn't kick." John assured the Captain. "When we are in port we can open these side windows and let some light and air in."

He showed them the windows high up on the sides. "When sailing they will be closed and most of the time it will be dark in here. Can the horse handle that?" John told him how they had been putting him in the dark stall getting him used to not having light.

The Man asked when they would sail. "We plan to leave on April 4. Since we got here a day or two late, the crew needs a few days on land before we start out again. We will board the horse the day before we sail to see how he handles getting on board and let him spend one night with the ship rocking. If we feel like he can't handle it I will have to return him to you. We can't have a horse kicking out the sides of our ship and drowning all of us." He was serious but he smiled at John and quickly told him that he thought he had done a good job of getting Red ready to sail.

Good to his word the Captain two days later told The Man they would board Red the following morning. The dock seemed to come to a standstill when John brought the beautiful stallion down to the place they would lift him onto the ship. Many had never seen such a magnificent horse and others were just curious how they would put him on a ship from the dock. Samuel and John took their time getting the harness and sling on Red. Red looked around at all the people and started getting a little wild eyed, but John rubbed his neck and assured him everything would be just like at home. Slowly a long beam extended out over the dock and a dock hand connected the hook to the top of the sling. And before John knew it Red was up and away and John had to run up the ramp to be there when he was lowered into the hole. Racing down the stairs leading the two decks down John got there just as Red's feet hit the flooring. The below deck hand quickly undid the hook and it was out the hole and back on the dock to pick up other cargo. The deck hand told John he needed to get Red into his stall so he would not get hit by the loading of the rest of the cargo. He assured him he could leave the door open for air and light. So into the stall that would be home for the next eight to ten weeks went the adventurer and the horse.

It wasn't long before Samuel and The Man came to check on their progress. Red had settled down and was drinking the cool water that John had brought him. The Man was very proud of Red and John. He was looking ahead to the commerce that this trip would bring to The Manor. If all went well and he could prove to others that he could ship horses safely, no telling where the horses might be sent and the money that he could make. The Captain also came by and told John that he was not sure that they would get him on board but they had and good so far. Later John shut the stall and they all went out to eat supper. At the Inn many people came up to talk about loading the horse and trip they were taking. They stayed up pretty late and John went on board to check on Red and he seemed to be fine. Going back to their room, Samuel asked how the horse was and then they both went to sleep.

The next day saw the Arbella finish loading all her cargo and John could not believe the barrels of food and water that was loaded. While the loading was going on the other deck hand were scrubbing every inch of the ship. His stateroom was scrubbed shiny and everything was clean, even sheets and towels! When he went to his room the next day a deck hand appeared and asked him where he wanted his trunk. "I guess in here" John said. The hand brought it and then could see that it took up most of the room. Why don't you unpack what you need in here and the rest I will put down by the horse and you can get it as you need it." So John quickly took out some clothes and his books and maps that The Man had sent with him. He started to take out Red's papers and sale receipts but decided to leave them hidden in the lining of the trunk. The Deck hand came down a little while late and carried it away. Later John went below to check on Red and there was the trunk right by his stall as agreed. Since the loading was complete, John took Red out of his stall and they walked down narrow aisles between the cargo. It was a pretty good walk all the way down and back. Red's stall was a little off center toward the front of the ship.

Red was as curious as John about all the stuff that had been loaded. They could smell fish and other things they did not recognize. The fish smell made Red blow a little but by the time they had made their way past it and back he hardly paid any attention. Past where Red's stall was there was large area with nothing in it. So there was room for them to work at a walk on a short line. Later when a deck hand came down John ask what the empty room was for and he was simply told that they would get more cargo at another port.

The Captain told all of them at supper that they would sail at first light. The Man suggested that John go aboard tonight and then he would be ready the next morning. Sure enough the dawn brought a lot of scurrying feet and yelling. He went out on the deck and the deck hands were all hurrying about. He ran down and checked on Red and when he felt the ship shudder he ran up on the deck and to the rail. Sure enough The Man and Samuel were on the dock. The Man took off his hat and waved it to John. And Samuel saluted him. Wow! What a send off! The Arbella slid away from the dock and soon they were out in the bay and out to sea. They had not been gone long when John could no longer see The Man and Samuel. All of a sudden he felt very alone, and immediately went below to see Red. He hugged his neck and did not realize that all the tears were coming out in a tidal wave. He told himself he had to get it together. He had to get Red to

America and then get back and he needed to do a good job of it. So he sucked up his crying and decided to find out all he could about sailing this ship.

The ship had three large beams going straight up with four main sails on each beam. The sails graduated from large on the bottom to smallest on the top. There was a triangular sail in the front and back of the ship and rigging or ropes everywhere. John stumbled over quite a few the next few days until he soon learned that there was a path through them intentionally kept free by the deck hands. John also learned to keep out of the deck hands way as they would push him aside to get to their work. They were not rude just seemed always in a hurry. For a few days they followed the coast line, staying out in deep water but John would get a glimpse of land every so often. The Man had given him a small telescope and John had followed along on his maps. He had studied hard with The Man before the trip to learn to judge distance by the stars and he was allowed in to see the Captain's large maps to see their progress. The Captain also gladly answered the hundreds of questions John had about the ship and the voyage. He could see the lad had a head for knowledge and he got to where he would even test John on his information. So they would spend a great deal talking on the trip. The Captain had sailed almost everywhere and had a lot of knowledge to give John. And he found John a great listener soaking up everything like a sponge.

There were two other passengers on the trip with John. Mr. Cavanaugh and Mr. Kildown had boarded with John. Mr. Cavanaugh was the older of the two. He was a merchant and some of the cargo was his, going to America. Mr. Kildown was a lawyer and was going to America to seek his fortune. Having been born the middle son of the family he had a choice of the army or navy or strike out on his own; the oldest son having inherited all the family holdings. He had just finished law school and was eager to be out on his own. He had a little trouble associating with John, a hired hand, but noticed that John had nice clothes and spoke well at table. His curiosity was aroused and did not believe John's story that he was just taking a horse to America for The Man. He soon convinced himself that John was somebody and he was just travelling like a hired hand. So on the voyage he decided to find out exactly who this gentleman was and why he was traveling like a commoner.

Mr. Cavanaugh on the other hand spent most of his days simply walking or reading a book. He talked when addressed and not much else. He did not seem very interested in what the rest of the people around him were doing. He ate meals with the others and then would excuse himself and go off by himself.

The first few days went well for John, but soon as they left the shelter of the land side and sailed out into deep water John became sea sick. He thought by the second day he was going to die and by the third day hoped he would. In between hanging over the rail throwing up what seemed to be all his innards he would race down and feed and water Red. After a few pats, he would be back outside in the air and hanging over the rail. Several of the deck hands that came by would encourage him that it would soon go away. He felt awful until that afternoon found Mr. Kildown on the fore deck and learned that he too had been sea sick. So John did not feel so bad. He later ask one of the deckhands why they did not get sick. He had told him that sometimes they did, but mostly after a few voyages they were not sick anymore. The fact that they did get sick usually told the Captain whether they were real seamen or not.

True to the deckhand's word, the next day John was able to keep a little food and water down and by the next day was back almost to his regular routine of taking care of Red. After several days of not being out of his stall, Red was ready for his walk up and down the aisles in the hole. John was still weak from the seasickness but they made a goodly circle before putting Red back in his stall. And each day as John got stronger they were able to do more. John still wondered what was going in the big area in the front of the hole.

Red traveled like a seasoned veteran. The deckhands had told him that if the horse became sick to give him some vinegar. But either John was too sick to see it or it didn't happen, he never saw Red get seasick. When John cleaned out the stall he would shovel the mess into a bucket that he would carry up on deck and empty over the side. Some days this would take several trips and John would get very dirty. So he would do this chore early in the morning and then take a bath and wash his clothes. That way he did not offend any of his traveling companions. His bath would consist of a deckhand splashing him with a bucket of water, his soap down and then another bucket of water. He then washed his clothes out and hung them on the line designated as the clothes line.

He could not say the same of his companions. They did not bathe very often and certainly did not wash their clothes. So by the end of the second week John did not like being around them in the closed in areas too much, especially the older gentleman. John wondered if he was ever going to clean himself up. That question was answered in another 10 days.

John awoke with a start when he heard the hand yelling land ahoy. He quickly dressed and ran topside. They were sailing into one of the prettiest bays he had ever seen. As he they approached the city, the town all looked like it was white. The buildings were flat topped and he could see narrow passageways running between them. As with all the docks they would put in at, this one had a pier that they soon had the gangway down to and everyone was informed that they would be several days here taking on supplies and water. Some of the deckhands went down the gangplank with John and some stayed working on the ship. He soon learned they would take turns having "shore leave". John walked up and down the wharf, looking into the shops and in one shop he saw Mr. Cavanaugh getting a shave and waved to him. The sign also said baths so John realized that Mr. Cavanaugh had taken this trip before and knew he could clean up here.

Mr. Kildown had ask John if he wanted to go with him but John said he couldn't stay long because of the horse and Mr. Kildown had gone on his way. In one of the shops John bought Flossy and Hensley real pretty head coverings for Church. In another shop he bought Samuel a new pipe and in still another he found The Man a nautical book. He then found a place to send the parcel to The Manor.

After he had gone back aboard and tended to exercising Red he came up on deck. The Captain saw him and invited him to go ashore and eat supper with him. John accepted and they started out. But they soon passed by the dock area and headed up one of the narrow passageways to a pretty little house partway up the hill. The Captain turned in and knocked on the door. The family opened the door and happily brought John in with them. There was a man and wife and four little children. One little boy quickly perched on John's lap. The woman tried to move him but John told her he was fine. John listened while the Captain gave them news of their families he had visited at another stop a few months back. He also told them he had packages for them on the ship that they could come get the next day. The Captain then surprised them with the story of Red's arrival and loading on the ship. The little one in John's lap immediately demanded to see this magnificent horse. And John readily agreed. So after a wonderful meal they made plans to come aboard at a set time the next day. While walking back to the ship, John asked why they had not carried the packages when they went.

"Because this way the little ones get to come see the ship and your magnificent horse." the old captain replied.

John rose early and exercised Red extra time. He didn't want him to be too excited with company coming to see him. He was rewarded. The whole family soon came down the stairs and stood to see the horse. Red allowed the youngsters to pet his neck and especially let the little one stay very close. The Captain then invited them all up on deck for some lunch. John put Red back in his stall and joined them. They wanted to know all about his trip. He explained how he was a stable hand and the colt had been sold to a buyer in American and he had the job of delivering him to his new owner. After they had left John ask about the family, since they seemed so close to the Captain. The Captain explained they were not his family but the family of a seaman that had drown off his ship many years ago. Since then they had become his family. The Captain also added that he had no family. He had gone to sea as a young lad and although there had been several chances, he didn't feel getting married would be fair to the bride since he would be gone all the time. John then told the Captain about his brother that had gone to sea and that he wondered where he was. The Captain told him to write down his name and where he was from and he would ask around as he sailed out.

That evening John soon wrote his brother's name and where they were from on a sheet of paper and presented it to the Captain. And said a little prayer that someone had met him or knew of him.

NINE

The next day the Captain watched as the crew who had had the day before off, as they began loading the cargo hole again with supplies. John made his way into town and also picked up some supplies, including fresh fruit and canned meats. He also indulged in some more writing paper and supplies and while at the store he saw some colored pencils and paper and decided to take those and see if he could draw a little. He had also written to The Manor telling everyone how the trip was going and how well Red was doing. These letters he mailed while ashore. When he returned to the ship he went to check on Red. By this time he was usually not bothered by the noise of the banging of the supplies into the hole and the men hollering as the ship was loaded.

But again he noticed that the front of the hole was not filled with anything. He was glad as it gave Red room to move around more than just up and down the aisles. After a few days out to sea though the empty part of the hole began to have hammering and some hands were building some kind of shelving along all the sides of the walls and then some free standing in the middle.

John could not figure out what they would need all that shelving for. He was soon to find out.

The next week they sailed out into deep water but this time John was only mildly sick and just the first day out. They then one afternoon late the Captain said he better see about his horse well as they were heading into a storm later that night. He showed John how to look on the horizon for the signs of the impending storm. John asked why they couldn't just sail around it or just stop and let it go by. The Captain laughed as he explained that the storm would be all along that part of the ocean and they could not sail around it. No they would just have to "weather" it out. John then saw all the hands scurrying to secure everything with ropes and put things down in the hole that was usually on the deck. He went down and sure enough Red had sensed the change in the weather and was rocking back and forth at his stall gate. John got him out and walked him up and down the aisle hoping to at least make him a little tired. When they reached the hole and Red saw the shelving he snorted and pulled back away. John just thought he was buggered about the new things in his exercise pen. Finally he took him back and put him up with extra feed and water and told him that he would come back later.

When he came up to the deck it had started to slightly rain. They sky had turned dark in the east and you could see just a sliver of the sunset in the west. John went below and joined the others at their supper. Mr. Cavanaugh asked John, "Is this your first storm?"

"Yes," John answered. The Captain then joined them and carefully explained to his passengers that it would be better if they did not go out on deck until the storm passed. He then asked John about the horse and John told him he was ok for now.

"When the ship starts rocking and that water starts hitting the side of the ship, he might get a little frightened." The Captain reminded John.

When John went down to check on Red after supper, a deckhand by the door to the stairs reminded him that all the hatches were closed and he needed his lantern to go down there tonight even though it was not completely dark. So John returned to his cabin and got his lantern and decided to take his blanket. He might need to spend the night with Red. By the time he returned to Red's stall the ship was rocking and the rain could be heard pounding on the ship. He also noticed some water was leaking down where they were. But he assumed that was to be expected. A little later John began to hear the wind roaring. Red was walking up and down in his stall. John stayed right by his gate and Red would come up for a neck rub and then pace some more. Finally they both settled down as the roar and rain continued battering the ship about. Red seemed to decide that this was just some more awful stuff he was having to endure on the trip. John didn't realize that he had gone to sleep until he awoke to the sound of the deckhands opening the hatches and letting the sun shine in the hole's openings. Red nickered at him as if to say get up and feed me.

John did and then quickly made his way with his lantern and blanket to his berth. There he washed up and went to breakfast. His traveling mates were discussing how they could not sleep with all the rocking and rolling the ship was doing in the storm. John grinned to himself, because he had slept like a log. Later as he was up on the deck with the Captain he asked him about the movement of the ship. The Captain said that it was worse farther up you went out of the water. So he had slept well since he was down in the water and not bounced around as much as the others.

That day the world seemed so calm and the ship was washed like a new one. Everything was shiny and clean. The deck hands had taken the time to do their laundry and it was hanging out everywhere! The hands were also in a jolly mood. He heard them laughing and telling tales as they worked. Some were about the time they went through some storm and how it had come out.

They acted like the storm was a thing that happened all the time. When John asked one he told him that they were in that part of the ocean that the storms were many. And that they would see many more when they started across the ocean. They sailed for a couple more weeks before they saw some islands. These they sailed around and through. Some he could see people on the shores and some looked completely deserted. They had sandy beaches up a ways and then seemed to be covered with trees. Some had pointed mountains in the middles. A few more days and they were to make their last stop before starting across the ocean.

They put in the night before and early the next morning John was in the group ready to go ashore when the gangplank was lowered. As he started down he heard the Captain call him. He hurried back up to the deck. The Captain in a serious tone told him he was not to go ashore here. It was not safe.

"But Mr. Cavanaugh just went ashore ahead of me."

"Yes, but he has business here and comes here often. You and Mr. Kildown will not be going ashore here." The stern look on the Captain's face told John that he meant it: they were not going ashore here.

John spent part of the morning with Red walking up and down the aisles. Since they were anchored off, the ship did not rock much so Red was more sure footed as they walked up and down. After Red's rub down, John returned to the deck to watch the going-ons on the dock.

As with the other stops they had made the deck hands were scuttling up and down the gangplank with supplies and the others were using the draw lines to load fresh water and barrels of salted meat and fish. John noticed that they were taking on more supplies than at the other docks. He also noticed Mr. Cavanaugh in a conversation with a gentleman that had arrived in a carriage. They had exchanged a packet that Mr. Cavanaugh handed to the man. They then shook hands and the man entered the carriage and drove away. Mr. Cavanaugh then came up the gangplank to the Captain. He told him that the cargo would be ready to board in the morning. The Captain just nodded and continued to watch his men work. John wanted desperately to ask what the cargo was but could tell by both men that was not a good thing to do. He also thought it strange that Mr. Cavanaugh did not eat or get a bath or shave ashore as he had done at the other ports. Mr. Cavanaugh asked the Captain how the weather looked so far. The Captain said that this time of year you never knew.

"But the next few days looked pretty good. We are in for some rough weather before we cross ole' Lanta. She will try very hard to throw us out and many a ship has not made it. But this will be our 12ᵗʰ trip so we know a little about her tricks."

John's eyes got a little bigger the longer the Captain talked about the bad storm last time and the time they nearly sunk off the islands. Nobody had told him he might drown. Of course he knew they were going to cross an ocean, but how big could an ocean be. He had never known anyone that had crossed one so he really didn't know too much about it. It looked big on the map but he thought it can't be that bad.

The next morning while John was exercising Red he heard a commotion up top. He quickly put Red in his stall and headed up the stairs. He ran to the railing and could not believe his eyes.

In a line snaking its way down the dock road was all these black people shuffling along. There were men along the sides keeping them moving. As they got nearer, John could see that they were tied together with a rope around their necks and then a little rope space and then the next one was tied on. Their legs were hobbled like horses. There were all kinds. From old men to young children that ran along beside their mothers. Some of the young men were pitch black and had muscles like John had never seen. And they were very tall. They all just had some kind of clothing, but they were mostly just around their middle and none that he saw had any shoes.

Now John had read about slavery in some of The Man's books but had never really thought too much about it. He also just realized that this was Mr. Cavanaugh's cargo and the packet that he had given the gentlemen on the dock was his payment. When the Captain saw John on the rail he called him over to him. "Go and stand on the front and do not come down until I tell you."

John ran to the front of the ship where he was told. He could still see everything that was going on. He sat down on a keg and waited. There was some kind of trouble near the back of the line still on the dock and he saw one of the guards lash out with a buggy whip on one of the slaves. Then the line started moving again. Soon they were all in lock step and made their way up the gangplank. They were then herded down the stairs and then they were all gone. And it was then that John realized that the shelves that he had seen built in the hole were for these people. But he also realized that the shelves were for people about his size. He didn't know how those big people would fit in them.

Soon the Captain looked over at him and told him he could come with him. They headed down the stairs and the Captain told John to check on his horse as he checked on the slaves. Red was a little nervous with the new company and he knew it was a distinct new smell. Thankfully they were on the other end of the hole so Red would not have to interact with them. While John was giving Red a little more feed, the Captain came by and commented on what a good job that John and the Red were doing. He then said that He was sorry that John had to travel with the slaves but he just hauled what he was told to haul. He did not like it but he had no choice if he was going to make a living. The Captain then told John to stay away from the other end of the hole.

"You will not like what you see and the men guarding them are not very nice. And I would not discuss the slaves with Mr. Cavanaugh . . ." He then turned and walked up the stairs.

They usually sailed at first light but today soon as the slaves were aboard the Captain had the crew up the anchor and undo the ropes that held them and they were out to sea again. That night when John went to feed and check on Red he could hear the slaves moving about and many were crying out. He didn't like hearing it and did not stay long. When he went in to supper everyone was talking and carrying on conversations like the slaves were not even on the ship. John had a million questions about them but would have to wait and ask the Captain when they were alone again. That night John had a bad dream. He dreamed he was the one with the rope on his neck that the guard was whipping with the buggy whip. He awoke all in a sweat. He got up from his berth and looked out his port hole that was open to let in a little breeze. He drank a little water from his glass and then settled back down but it was a long time before he went back to sleep.

For days John's routine remained the same. He would get up, wash and eat breakfast at the Captain's table. Each day he waited for someone to mention the "cargo", but none ever did.

He would then hurry down to take care of Red feeding, watering, cleaning his stall and exercising him. Only now when they went down the aisles they did not go completely down the end of the ship. It was if a chalk line had been drawn across some boards and they did not cross it. The guards evidently took turns checking on the slaves and they would pass sometimes in the aisle but they were not friendly. So John and Red just passed and then went on their way. It was several days out to sea when John went down one morning and found one of the guards near Red's stall.

"What are you doing here?" John wanted to know. The Guard said that he had just been looking at the fine horse. "You do not have the right to be anywhere around him. Get away!"

John did not know where all the bravado he had just shown came from. He weighed in at about 160 pounds and the guard was a giant. The guard came towards him threateningly and told him he went where he wanted and no stable hand was going to tell him what to do. About that time the Captain stepped down off the stairs. Quickly sizing up what was going on here, he told the guard to get away. The guard glared at John and moved on down the hole. The Captain then told John to come upstairs. They went up on the front deck. "I am sorry that happened. I will see that they are not allowed anywhere near you or your horse again. I will speak to Mr. Cavanaugh about this."

John saw the guard one or two times again on the trip. One time he was heading down the stairs when the guard started up. The guard moved back down the stairs and made a low bow as John went past. Otherwise all the others left him alone.

Days turned into weeks on the ole' Lanta. Several storms had come over them but the ship made it through fine. They were out about 6 weeks when the "big" one hit. John had seen enough of them to know what it was on the horizon. He had gone early and taken care of Red and was back on the deck with the Captain.

"She will blow in tonight. I don't like to looks of her. Have you already seen about your horse?"

"Yes I am done down below. And the hands were already batting down the hatches. We are good I think. What about the slaves?"

"Boy, must I remind you that the slaves are not our business. Mr. Cavanaugh and his goons will take care of the slaves; what care they will get. You really must try to forget they are there. You just worry about you and your horse."

The wind picked up first. John was still on the deck when the sprinkles started. He went below and had his supper and by the time they had finished the hard rain had started. They weaved along taking their plates to the sink. John again as he had done every time, thanked the cook for his meal. The old cook smiled and told John he was just doing his job. Missing teeth shown in that smile and John felt like he had found a friend. The storm lasted three long days. John stayed in his room having learned that they were not opening the stairs to go to the hole until the weather cleared. John wondered about the slaves, who was feeding them or taking them water? The fourth day the sun came out and John was told by the Captain to go up by the wheelhouse. John climbed the short set of steps and sat down on a barrel. He heard shouting and when the stair door opened the guards were pulling the slaves one at a time out on the deck. They only brought about ten at a time. The slaves shielded their eyes as they had been in nearly total darkness all this time. The guards lined them up and proceeded to pour water over them. They were then sent back down the stairs dripping wet and the next group brought up and the same water thrown on them. This seemed to go on for hours. John thought he counted 12 groups. That would mean about 120 slaves were in that little place in the hole. A few of the bigger men tried to struggle with going back down but were beaten. Strangely the mothers were able to shush the children and not much crying went on. After all of them were doused, John would not call it a wash, the deck then went back to work like nothing had gone on.

After supper a few nights later, John was on deck and saw the cook sitting on a stack of ropes. John sat down nearby.

"Something bothering you lad?" The cook lit his pipe and blew out a few puffs of smoke.

"Aren't slaves people?" John asked.

"Some say they are wild animals that look like us."

"Where do they come from?"

The old cook moved around on his seat and said, "They come from a place called Africa. The Slavers, the people who hunt them, go into the Africa country and catch them just like a rabbit and tie them up and then bring them to the coast and wait for a ship to come take them."

"Where are they going?"

"These will be going to America just like you and your horse."

"And what will they do then?"

"They will be sold either all to one gentleman or in the open market. They sell them just like livestock. And that is how Mr. Cavanaugh makes his money by buying and selling his "cargo"."

"Do you feed them like you feed the hands?"

"No, the guards feed them some kind of gruel once a day like feeding your horse. I believe they feed them once a day."

The old cook then eased out of his seat, stretched his back, and gave John the same advice the Captain had given him. "Just stay away from them and you will be alright." And then he took his bucket and went below.

John sat on the deck until it was pure dark. He didn't want to go below. Later he had moved over to a big coil of the tie off rope and had lain down to look at the stars. The next morning when the sun was up several of the deck hands were standing over him. John shielded his eyes with his hand and the hands began to laugh.

"Did you have too much to drink little one? Why did you sleep out here?" John scrambled up and asked the time. "Oh most of the morning is gone." the sailor replied.

John hurried below and entered the kitchen. The cook smiled and said, "We missed you at breakfast, but I have a little left over sit down."

The cook laughed when John told him that he had slept all night in the coil of the rope. John ate his meal and then went down to see Red.

John had noticed that as the voyage went on the more the smell from the other end of the hole turned into pure stench. Of course, he realized that there were a lot of people in that little space and except for the weekly water bucket over their heads they had no way to wash. When he went down the aisle to exercise Red he always turned way before the front of the hole. The guards were not friendly and he wanted nothing to do with them. They seemed rough and vulgar to John. Even though John had been raised without money, his mother had always stressed good manners and cleanliness. These rogues did seem to have either quality. After he had put Red up one day he needed some vinegar to put in Red's water. The night had been pretty rough seas and Red seemed not to feel well. While searching for the vinegar, where the cook had told him it was, John passed by the divider between the middle hole and where the slaves were kept. He saw the vinegar about halfway down the divider. When he reached down to get a gallon jug his sight was presented with a slit in the boards of the divider. He could see right in the front where the slaves were. He nearly fainted. Those people were packed in that place like sardines. Some were up but many were just squashed onto the shelves as John had called them. Some were crying and moaning and they all looked so sick. And the stench was terrific. John heard the tromp of boots and quickly grabbed the vinegar and started back down the aisle. One of the guards yelled and wanted to know what he was doing on this side of the hole. John showed him the jar of vinegar and quickly went back to Red's stall. After putting a little vinegar in the horses' water John went upside to find the Captain. He was up on the wheel deck looking through his glass. John quickly went up to him and said

"Did you know that those people are sick below?"

"Yes, they nearly always get sick. Many of them will die before we get to where they are going."

"Why are they not doing anything about them?"

"John they are not our problem. And so do not bother yourself about them. They are Mr. Cavanaugh's business not ours. And you will not discuss them with him. Do you understand?"

John could tell be the look on the Captain's countenance that he meant every word he was saying.

"Do you understand John?"

"Yessir."

John had been keeping a diary of his trip. So he took out his papers and pen and began to write about what he had seen and felt about the slaves. Later he heard them pass going up to get their bucket of wash. Then he heard them on the stairs as they passed back into their hole. A dark, dank and stinking hole is what John called it in his diary.

Every day he had to hold himself back from speaking to Mr. Cavanaugh. He also observed that Mr. Cavanaugh never went to check on his "cargo". He continued to eat three meals a day, walk on deck or sit on a deck chair and read. He was still cordial to John and talked to him about the world and his horse just like there was nothing happening down in that hole.

They had been out on the ocean about three weeks when the Captain called him into his cabin. "Look at the map John. We should be at our half-way mark this very evening."

John watched as the Captain plotted their course from his notes he had taken the night before with the stars. On the map it still seemed a long way to go. The Captain turned to John and told him what a good job he was doing with the horse.

"I was down there yesterday and he looks like he is traveling well."

"Did you see the slaves?"

"Yes."

"Can't you do something to help them?"

"No, they do not belong to me."

"They don't belong to anyone they are not livestock."

"Some people would disagree with you John. When you get to America you will find that they are not treated very well. You best learn to not mix in any of the slave owners business or you will get into real trouble."

"What will happen to the ones that make it?"

"Many are already sold and will go to their owners soon as we get there. The others will be sold on the open market."

John had gone with Samuel and The Man to livestock sales but had no idea the people would be sold the same way. He was learning a lot in a short time. And some things he was learning he did not like. And this was the second time the Captain had had this conversation with him. So he tried very hard not to think about it. But when he went below the stink was everywhere now and he and Red hurried with their exercise because the smell bothered Red as much as it did John. But John knew he had to keep Reds legs exercised so he diligently walked the small aisle up and down, but only on the side without the slaves. So it was a short walk turn around and then a short walk back and it was tiring. Red and he would be glad to see the open spaces again. John could just imagine Red and him galloping along some beach with the ocean spray in their faces!

The next weeks were repeats of the ones before. About every week they would have a storm and the hatches had to be closed and Red and the slaves were in the dark for days. Then the sun would return and everything would be good for a few days. During the storm more "cargo" would die and when the sun came out they would unceremoniously be thrown overboard. When they came up on deck now to have the bucket of water tossed on them there were fewer and they all were very thin and there was a lost look in their eyes.

A few days later the Captain spoke to John. "You can begin a lookout in the next few days we should start seeing some islands." And sure enough the very next morning when John came up from exercising Red he heard the deck hand that was up in the crow's nest call out "land ahoy" and looking the way he was pointing John could just barely make out a dark form on the horizon.

"Is that land?"

"Yes, that is some small Islands we will sail around."

"Will we stop on some of them?"

"Yes, we have one stop for water and then we will continue on."

The Island to stop at was two days later. They sailed into a beautiful bay and some of the deck hands put down the little boats. As they scrambled aboard one turned to John and said,

"Aren't you coming?"

John turned to get permission from the Captain and saw a big grin on his face. He repeated the deckhand. "Aren't you going?" John scrambled down the rope ladder over the side and joined the hands in the little boats. They rowed quickly to the beach. There they all took buckets and started inland.

"Have you been here before?"

One of the older ones laughed and said, "yes many times."

And they knew exactly where to go and found a small water fall with a wonderful pond it was flowing into. They each filled their buckets and started back to the boats that had two barrels each on them. This back and forth took most of the morning. When the deckhand went back for their last trip, they all stripped off and jumped into the pool. Some had brought a little soap and they not only washed themselves but washed their pants and shirts. They laughed and had a great time. Then they dressed in the wet clothes and filled their last buckets. They returned to the boat and filled the barrels and rowed back to the ship. The barrels were then partially emptied by sending up water by the buckets full. When they thought they could manage, they roped the barrels and with lots of hand pulled the remaining barrel of water onto the ship. Water had been rationed for several weeks and the Captain and others enjoyed a cup of clean fresh water.

John and the deckhands that had gone ashore changed into dry clothes and hung their washing on the rope lines. John decided that having his hair really washed was next to heaven. After that day with the hands, John joined them more often in the evenings to listen to stories they had to tell. Some of them had been out to sea for years. But some were as "green" as John, when they sailed as it was their first trip. They also listened excitedly as the old sailors told their tales.

The next day they passed several more small islands. Mr. Cavanaugh had come out more to the railing and was watching the passing islands. He still had never mentioned the "cargo". Mr. Kildown also had taken to coming on the deck more. They were delighted the next morning when the Captain called a meeting of the deckhands. They hands all gathered together on the deck as the Captain stood a couple of steps up toward the steering deck.

"Tomorrow we will land at Point Venagus. No hands will be allowed to go ashore until all the cargo that is stopping here has been unloaded. Also remember that you are not to discuss what cargo that we carry to anyone. It is no one's business but ours what we carry. You younger lads will do good to watch how the older hands handle themselves ashore. We will work in shifts so there will be some hands on the ship at all times. We will post when we will sail again. It will be a few days. If you are not on board when we sail that is your problem. We will not wait on you."

"Mr. Candleson, put us to shore." Mr. Candleson was head of the deckhands and the ship under the Captain. He smiled and started barking out orders to get the ship up snug to the dock so they could start unloading. The big ship eased into the dock and the big ropes were tied off. John stood at the railing watching all the people that had come out to see the ship. The gangplank was let down and Mr. Cavanaugh was the first one off. Mr. Kildown followed. The Captain came up next to John.

"Are you not going shore?"

"Yes but not just yet. I have to see to Red."

"No, you should just wait until late the afternoon to do that. The "cargo" is getting unloaded here and then the hole will be washed down. Then you can see about Red. So you have today off to go and look around."

"Ok!" John raced down to his cabin and took out a few tokens and went ashore. But before he had gone far he could hear the crying and the guards yelling and the chains clanking as the "cargo" was led down the gangplank. Nearby a couple of gentlemen shook their heads.

"Damn Slave ships! If they would refuse to bring them we could get rid of the practice."

"But Henry, who would do all the work in the fields? Who would clean our houses and mind our kids?"

"You are right but the way they look when they get here is inhuman I think."

John looked back at the group of slaves now on shore huddling together. They had lost about a third of what number had come on board. His attention was drawn to a man standing on a box.

"We will be selling this fine lot tomorrow at four o'clock at the holding pens."

He then led the possession down the street. John followed a short distance behind. He could not help himself. He had to see what happened to them.

The slaves were held in a pen with a tall pole fence around it. John could peek through a crack in the poles. They were then separated. Men to one pen and women and children in another. John saw several talking to each other through the fence. He supposed they were family. The guards then brought in tubs and told them to wash their clothes (such as clothes they had) in the tubs. They all stripped down naked and washed their clothes. They were then marched a few at a time and allowed to wash themselves in the ocean. The guards had called out that the boss wanted them to look good so they would bring more money.

John was shooed away from the fence then by a guard and hurried back to the market area. In the market he saw a lot of foods he didn't know what they were. He bought and tasted some great hairy fruit and ate some kind of meat wrapped in flat bread. After he ate started serious shopping. He bought some more trinkets for his friends back at The Manor. Buying the gifts made him homesick a little but he told himself he was nearly through his journey. Then that made him sad because he would have to say goodbye to Red.

Red! Oh my. He had let most of the afternoon go by and Red had not been fed! He raced back to the ship. When he scurried down the stairs he noticed that there was a different smell to the hole. Running down to where the slaves were he was amazed. All the shelves were torn down and the lumber stacked. The hole smelled like vinegar and all the windows and doors were wide open. There was the faint smell of smoke lingering there also. He would have to ask about that as he had not seen a fire anywhere.

Today Red could go the length of the ship and they did several times at a brisk trot. One trip Red stopped and looked out one of the windows. He seemed to be breathing in the fresh air.

"It's ok boy. Soon you will be off this ship and able to run like the wind again."

One of the younger deckhands came along as John was putting Red back into his stable.

"Want to come ashore with us?"

"Sure." There were three of them and John. They made the market and ate again. They sat around for a while or laid on some of the bundles on the dock. It was good to be on land. They then decided to go down the beach and have a swim. Stripping off their clothes they dashed into the water. They were like silly kids again. Splashing and yelling, and ducking. It was a fun afternoon.

They went back to the ship and changed clothes to some clean ones and then went out to see the town at night. They found an inn that was not too crowded. Here they ordered something to drink and ate again. John took his first sip of brew and nearly threw up. The others laughed at him. The girl waiting on them quietly brought him some lemonade and made the others stop making fun of him. After a while they wandered back out on the street. Some ladies of the night came by but they sent them on their way. John remember Samuel telling him about them so he knew to stay away from them. They decided to sleep on the beach instead of returning to the ship. They had not been lying long when they began it itch. It was sand fleas. They quickly jumped up and into the ocean again washing the fleas out of their hair and clothes. They then returned to the ship and shed their clothes and hung them out and put on dry ones and went to sleep on the deck.

They next morning John was awakened by the deckhands. "Get up and out of the way we have work to do."

John quickly scurried below like a rat and the cook smiled as he handed him some breakfast.

"Hard night in the town?"

"No, we got in some sand fleas."

The Cook laughed. "You are learning a lot on this trip!"

After John fed and exercised Red he hurried back on the deck. The loading of more real cargo in big barrels and crates had started. The pulleys squealed and moaned with the loading.

The cook came by and asked John if he would go with him to help carry his supplies back to the ship. They soon entered the market. The cook would look the food over and then would start bickering with the seller over the price. Sometimes the cook would start to walk away and then the seller would give in to whatever price the cook wanted. They soon had several baskets full of vegetables and spices. The cook had made arrangements for another man to bring him beef and goats to be slaughtered the next day. They then went into a tobacco store where the cook bought some cigars for the Captain and pipe tobacco. He then went into an apothecary shop and bought a few medicines. Then they carried all their supplies back to the ship.

Then it dawned on John. He was about to miss the auction!

TEN

He ran down the gangplank and down the street to the holding pen. Sure enough the auction had just begun. A slender young black girl was being handed upon a small platform. She was petrified! The Auctioneer stood by a table and was telling the crowd that the great deals that were going to make today were brought to them from Africa by the great trader Mr. Cavanaugh of the continent who is here with us today. Let's all give him a hand! John saw him at another table nearby and watched as he stood and took off his hat to the crowd.

Then the auctioneer was now beginning the real sale. He extolled all the virtues of the young girl. She was an excellent cook, house maid etc. It was all John could do to keep from laughing. Cook and maid. She had never even seen a house more less worked in one. Then when the bidding started he looked around at the buyers and was amazed to see that most of them were not much different from The Man. They were dressed well and as the sale went on they all seemed to have plenty of money. Some had brought their wives, but they stood at a distance. When one came up that looked like a house worker, John noticed that the men would look back at the wife and he saw them nod yes or no a time or two. The big blacks headed for the fields brought the most money. But strange to John some of the younger boys brought good money too. They were all gone over like you would a fine horse. The buyers even checked their teeth and some ran their hands over their legs to see if they had any deformities. By then end of the evening all of the slaves were sold. Many were dragged off screaming to other members of their families that had been sold to other plantation owners. No one seemed to notice or care when a child was taken from their mother or husband and wife were separated. It certainly seemed just like a livestock sale to John. When it was all over,

John saw the auctioneer and Mr. Cavanaugh dividing up the money. Many of the new owners went by and shook hands with them and congratulated them on a good sale. Mr. Cavanaugh looked over and saw John standing there. He motioned him over.

"How would you like to eat supper with me?"

"Great but I don't have much money. I usually just go back to the ship and the cook feeds me."

"Well young man, I just had a good sale day and I believe I can afford a nice supper for the three of us."

"Three?"

"Yes, here comes our great captain that got all my cargo here and made the sale possible. We will reward him also."

The Captain joined them and they walked past all the pubs and inns and turned to the inward side of the island. The walked a few blocks and then turned into a small alley. About half a block down there was a faint sign. Here they entered a quiet, very fancy decorated place. It had tables for dining and a three piece band played in the background. Everyone seemed to know the Captain and Mr. Cavanaugh. There were many of the buyers from the sale there and they also visited with them. They were shown a table across the room from where they came in and soon a waiter came with a paper called a "menu". John had never seen a menu before. And was very surprised when he looked at it, it was in French. Wow! I can actually read most of this! One of the books that he had borrowed from The Man was a book teaching French. John thought to himself. The Captain asked if John needed any help with the menu. John said, "I think I can get most of it." And he did. He ordered fish and some kind of vegetables and fruits. When it came they all laughed. He had ordered nearly everything on the menu. But heartily he ate and the Captain and Mr. Cavanaugh helped him with the rest. He was so stuffed. The Captain took pity on him and said, "Let's get back to the ship. I have work to do tomorrow to get us sailing again."

Mr. Cavanaugh wished them a good night and informed them he had taken a room there and would see them off when they made sail.

As they walked back to the ship John asked about Mr. Cavanaugh. "Is he not going with us?"

"Oh, no! He will stay here until we come back next month and we will pick him up and he will sail with us back to Europe."

"Uh how often does he bring the Cargo here?"

"Usually just once a year. You saw him. He makes a lot of money when he sells the Cargo. I make some too but I told him this was my last trip to bring the Cargo. I don't like it and don't think selling the Cargo is the way to make a living. I make good money carrying regular goods and that is all that I need. The Cargo trip was for me to make enough money to buy a small house and farm to retire to in a few years."

They had come up the gangplank and the cook was out taking in some of the cool air.

"Would you and the young lad want something to eat?"

John spoke up. "Not me, I have had enough for the rest of the trip. Or at least until breakfast." They all laughed. Soon as John lay down he was sound asleep. And it was early light before he was awakened by the deckhands going to work. They had all been called back to ship during the night and they were back to work. Some did not look like they had slept much and some were definitely still hung over but on ship and at work they were.

ELEVEN

Breakfast over; John turned his attention again to Red. They sailed two days later after the ship had been restocked and loaded. So John and Red went back to their routine again. Exercise, feed, clean out the stall, brushing to keep his coat clean and lots of TLC. John realized that every day they were closer to being parted and begin spending more and more time with Red.

They were now sailing along the southern tip of Florida. Most days they were able to see some land and on clear days they would see some cities especially at night. But the Captain did not put ashore at any of these. He explained to John that they would next see a state called Georgia and that would not be their stop either. They were headed to a place called Charlestown. It would several more days. John's heart nearly stopped. Charlestown! That is where John had to hand over his beloved horse. The Captain saw the look on John's face. "Remember Son, delivering this fine horse was entrusted to you by The Man. And deliver him you will do. And then we will sail back to your family reunion." This did make John feel better while. The Man had treated him like a man when he sent him on this journey and John would do the best he could for him. Then he would go below and bury his face in Red's neck and cry like a baby!

The days raced by and before John knew it the Captain said they would sail into Charlestown the next day! John had Red out of his stall nearly all day. He even missed lunch so when dinnertime came he was very hungry.

The cook shook his head and said. "You are going to have a hard time letting go of that horse."

"Yes" John said. "But I have a responsibility to hand him over to his new owner. I have many more just like him waiting for me to train when I get home."

"Spoken like a grown man. I believe you have done quite a bit of growing up on this trip." He patted John on the back as he passed by going around the table. "And we are proud of you."

TWELVE

There was quite a crowd at the docks in Charlestown. The Ship was among a group of the tall whites that sailed the oceans. The Captain with a great deal of confidence sailed into the bay and then to the dock. The gangplank was lowered and pure emotion took John over. He raced down the stairs and grabbed a handful of Red's mane and held on tight. But it was not long before a deck hand appeared on the stairs and called out to John. "The Cap says that the horse unloads first then the rest of the cargo. So get your things together to strap him in as before."

Red was very patient while John again secured the sling on his body. He lead him down the aisle to just below the hole opening. It soon opened and great bright light flooded in. At first John and Red could not see much but then their eyes adjusted and they could see the blue sky above. Again the pulleys were attached to the sling. John reassured Red when he moved around a little. When his feet left the ground John again called out to him to keep him steady. John then turned and raced back to his cabin. He had packed a small bag the night before not knowing where he had to go to take the horse. As he came up on the deck he could see Red being set down on the pier. He raced over and with help they had the big stallion loose from the sling. Red looked around and walked with a funny walk. John realized that it had been months since he had seen the outside and had been able to move around a great deal. The crowd gathered on the dock stood back and made a lane for John to lead the beautiful horse out to the road. He heard a lot of murmurs wondering what horse was this. Many gentlemen put out their hands to touch the magnificent animal.

As soon as he was able John led Red away down the street away from the docks and the crowd. He had not gone long until he found a livery that he could board Red until he could deliver him. Leaving Red there, John quickly found a store and bought new clothes and then had a bath and shave. Since it was lunch time, he ate before going to find the Judge Evans that he was to introduce himself to and present his papers for himself and the horse. Judge Evans was to give him directions to where to deliver Red. Off to the corner of the main street John found the Court House and entered. Reading a list on a board near the door he found Judge Evans office was located on the second floor. He hurried up the steps and soon found the right door with the name on the window.

Inside the office, Judge Evans sat at a large dark wood desk looking over a stack of papers. John stood quietly inside the door and waited to be acknowledged.

"What do you want?"

"I have just arrived and I am to present my papers and my horse's papers to you. And to receive instructions where to deliver him."

"Oh, you are the horseman bringing Lord Davidson his stallion from Europe. Well do you have the horse ashore?"

"Yes, I have him in a livery waiting for me to come get him and take him to his new home."

"Ok give me your papers." John stepped forward and presented the packet he had protected across the Atlantic and through several great storms.

The Judge looked them over and then gave them back. "Ok. In the morning meet me outside here and I will have a man who can show you how to get to Lord Davidson's Plantation. At mid-morning will be about right."

"Thank you sir. I will be here on time."

With a nod of his head the Judge dismissed John and went back to studying the papers on his desk.

John raced down the street and turned up the block to the livery. He had all the rest of the day with Red. He would take him out and let him get his land legs again. He stopped on the way and bought a lunch for himself and then stopped in a market and bought apples for Red. Turning in the livery big doors, Red heard him and stuck his head over the divided stable door. John quickly saddled him up and they were out and down the coast line. Red was restless and it was not long before they were loping along with the waves spraying on them.

The big stallion's muscles gleamed in the sunlight. After going quite a distant they stopped in a little cove with white bluffs.

John ate his lunch and fed Red the apples he had brought for him. Then they turned back toward town. It was nearly dark when John put Red in his stall and fed him and then spent a great deal of brushing him. He was finally driven out by the livery man wanting to lock up for the night. John returned to the ship. When he climbed up the gangplank he could see the light from the Captain's pipe. "Did you get the horse ashore ok?"

"Yes, he is in a livery in town. I took him out for a run on the beach today. He needed to stretch his legs. We leave tomorrow to deliver him to his new home."

"You have plenty of time we will not sail for a couple of weeks."

"The Judge said the plantation is about a days ride so I should be back in plenty of time.

"Good night then and a good trip tomorrow."

John awoke early and ate breakfast with the cook. Then he took the bundle of food the cook insisted that he take with him. Hurrying down the gangplank he was off to the livery. He fed Red and when he was finished he paid the livery bill and they were off downtown to meet their guide. The Judge was standing out in the street when he came to the Court House. Joining him were two rough looking men, but John figured that if the Judge was sending them they were all right.

"These two men here will take you to Lord Davidson's. It will take you about a day and a half so you will have to spend one day on the way. I have here you a pack with a blanket and some food." Wishing John good day he walked back into the Court House. The men turned and started down the street.

"Names Will and Jack."

"I am known by John. John Dunn and the horse is named Red."

"He is about one of the prettiest horses I have ever seen. I know that the Lord raises horses but this beats them all. He must have wanted him pretty bad to pay a lot of money to have him shipped over here."

"I guess so although I was not privy to the amount paid for him."

They had continued down a well-worn dirt road. They would stop and rest at some of the running streams that ran along parallel to the road. There were quite a few other travelers on the road so John assumed that it was a well-used way to go for the area. They saw all different types of conveyance. There were wagons with families that did not look like they had much money and then there was the grand carriage that had a man riding on the back and the driver of the team on the front. It also had four men in matching clothes riding along with them. They all slowed to look at the young man and the grand stallion. Many called out to John what a beautiful horse.

That night they made a fire, cooked and at their supper and made their beds on the ground. John was thankful for the blanket as the night turned a little cool. The next morning was bright and dry. They were worrying about a rain but it did not come. Red was fed and after a breakfast of the left over bread and cheese they were on their way. A few miles down the road the men took a turn to the South off the main road. This road was not as well traveled and some places were nearly dark where the tress intermingled across the road and swamp ivy hung on the branches. It gave John a creepy feeling. But in a little while they would ride out of the dark and back into the sunlight. They had not gone far when the men stopped and stepped down from their horses. Just thinking this was a welcome break, John did the same. He got down and tied Red to a tree. He then walked away from the others to relieve himself. When he returned the men had drawn their guns and were pointing them at him.

"What's this?" John asked.

"We have decided to have this horse for ourselves."

"You can't do that. You were hired to take me to the Lord Davidson Plantation. The Judge even said that you were dependable men. You can't take the horse."

"These guns and the Judge say we can and we will. He will pay us a lot of money for the horse. You can take your blanket and food and we will take the horse."

One of the men proceeded to untie the blanket and throw it at John along with his sack of food. They then mounted their horses and leading Red they loped off down the road. John grabbed up his things and started running after them. But it was soon evident he could not keep up with the horses. He sat down on the side of the road. He considered going back to the town. But if the men were really working for the Judge he would just deny that he had ever seen John. We he would show them his papers. Oh God his papers were in the saddle bags, along with his money, his passport, everything. He had nothing but the clothes, the blanket and the little food that was left. And he did not know where he was or where to go.

He decided the best idea was to continue down the road hoping that it led to the Plantation and he could explain to Lord Davidson about the men and the Judge.

Night came on and he ate the little food and rolled up in his blanket and didn't even start a fire. He was so discouraged he didn't even want to live. But he reasoned he had to live to go get Red away from those awful people.

The sun was up when he awoke. His stomach rumbled from lack of food and water. So John decided that finding water would be a good idea. Cutting through the woods, it was not long before he found a running stream. He bellied down and cupped his hands and drank long drinks of water. He hoped that Red had gotten a drink or two by now. When he rose up he was in the hands of the blackest man he had ever seen. He immediately reminded John of the ones on the ship. The man had hand me down clothes that we several sizes too big and he was bare footed.

"Who are you?"

"I am John Dunn and someone has stolen my horse and I am trying to find him to get him back."

John then proceeded to tell the man his story of coming on the ocean ship and how he had gotten in with the men that had taken the horse. He also advised him that he was needing to get to Lord Davidson's Plantation and tell him what had happened. The black man stood back from John.

"Your horse wouldn't be a big stallion that came in yesterday would it. With stocking feet?"

"Yes have you seen him?"

"He is at the Lord Davidson's Plantation. And I have been taking care of him. He is a fine looking animal. Lord Davidson says that he is going to win a lot of money on him at the Derby."

John could not figure out why the Lord would steal his own horse. This seemed like a lot of unsavory people he was dealing with. And he had to decide now what to do immediately.

"What is your name?"

"Franklin"

"So Franklin you go to work tomorrow to take care of my horse?"

"Yes sir."

Franklin looked down at the red headed stranger. "I don't think your Man is going to get any money for this horse. I think they will just knock you in the head and that will be that. And I don't think that Lord Davidson is going to want to see you, I think those mean mans were supposed to killed you already."

"I don't know what to do. The Man should either get his horse back or get his money that Lord Davidson was supposed to give to me on delivery."

"You have another choice. Just leave, go back to the ship, and go home and tell The Man what happened to the horse."

John scanned the black Franklin's face. "Why are you warning me away from Lord Davidson?"

"He is a mean man just like the two that you had your run in with. He is a slaver and he has some pirate friends. They trade all kinds of things that you can't get anywhere else and they get good prices for it."

John looked toward the heavens and prayed. "God you have to help me figure this one out."

Franklin smiled when he saw the prayer go up to God. "I think youngster the best thing you could do is get your horse back and then high tail it away from here. Then up north somewhere you could catch a ship back to where you com' from."

"Just how do you expect me to do that? Walk up to Lord Davidson and say you have my horse and I am taking him back."

"No I don't rightly think that would work. So I guess you have to steal him back. And I can help you do that in the night tomorrow. It will be Saturday night and the hands all go to town to get drunk. I am the only one left at the stables on Sat night. So after they is all gone I will call you in and help you get the horse. Then you will have all night to get as far away as possible. I will feed him good this day and then he won't need feed for at least a couple of days. I can get you some food too."

So the plan to steal the horse back was in place. During the night John wondered why he trusted the Franklin man. What would keep him from telling the Lord the story and get him caught. For some reason he felt he could trust the man.

The next day John stayed hid. Franklin had told him where to come to and when to come. When it was good and dark John ventured out through the woods. At the appointed time and place Franklin stepped out from the trees leading Red.

"I thought I was to come to the barn and get him."

"I decided that you do not know this country like I do. I wouldn't want you to be out here going around in circles and come back to me. So I have decided to go with you."

He chuckled as he said. "I mean they hang people for stealing horses or slaves so it doesn't matter which you are doing. So now we have to go. We only have a few hours to daylight and we need to be a long way away from here."

He lifted a pack on to his back and then handed one to John. He grinned as he told him that he knew the cook and she didn't mind helping a friend out.

Unknown to John, Franklin was not all black. He was half Cherokee Indian and when they started out John had some trouble staying up with his steady trot. But John soon learned to get into the rhythm of Franklins progress and they covered a lot of territory by morning. They then had to be more careful of where they went. They would hide out in the woods until it was clear and then rush across a clearing into more brush. This went on all day only stopping to get a drink and water the horse.

John had wanted to ride Red. But Franklin told him that it would be better if he didn't. If you are up on the horse you will draw more attention through the woods. If others just see the horse and you are hid on the other side, they just think it is a wild horse loose in the country.

When the sun got high in the sky, John was so tired and hot and just wanted to lie down. But Franklin did not let up and he didn't seem to lessen his pace. Red had no trouble keeping up and so John had to dig deep into his being to keep going.

The next night they ate and Franklin said they would rest for a little while. They did not light a fire and just ate their food cold, but hungry as John was he didn't care. Franklin said that he would watch and John rolled up in his blanket and was soon asleep. It didn't seem long until Franklin woke him and told him to get ready to go.

"Did you sleep?"

"No I don't need much sleep."

"I can watch and you sleep." John offered.

"No I don't think that is a good idea. We will try to get to the ferry early and with luck no one will be there to see us."

"I have no money for the ferry." John said.

Franklin smiled. "I had a little put back from some odd jobs I done so I brought it. But maybe we won't need it."

Sure enough the ferry was riding up close to the bank, tied off. No one was around so Franklin quickly got Red and John on board and then cast off the lines and pushed them off with a pole. The ferry glided across and they were soon on dry land again. Franklin quickly shoved the ferry back out into the stream. He told John that the ferrymen would just think some kids let it loose for a prank.

Two more days brought them to a small town. Franklin suggested that John go into the town and he would wait out with Red. They decided on what supplies that they needed and Franklin shared the money they had with John. John was reluctant to leave Red, but like Franklin said John would not cause anyone to take second look. But the big stallion would cause a lot of questions.

John walked the couple of miles to the town. He quickly went into the general store and bought the few supplies that they needed. He then turned down a side street to stay out of sight as much as possible. Then he slipped away back into the woods by a different route and then came back to where Franklin and Red were. They were soon back on their route to get as far away as possible. The next day they stumbled upon a campsite by accident. They neither one had seen any sign of anyone around. The camper was rolled up in his blanket when they came up on him. He rolled over and came up with a pistol in his hand. Franklin and John together called out

"Hold it we are not trying to grab you."

"Who the hell are you two and what are you doing with that high blooded horse?"

The man quickly sized up the situation. The black was a slave and the young man had the horse. "Come on in. I want to hear this story."

They sat down as he stirred up the fire. The man quickly made some breakfast of meat and bread. As he cooked John explained the most unlikely story he had ever heard in his life. But the youngster told it with such brevity he began to believe the story. The runaway slave was not uncommon these days, what with the mean masters that they had and the bad way they were treated and how they had come together at one time. He didn't quite buy the story of the boy being just a stable hand though. For one thing when he spoke it had education behind it and his boots were hand made of European leather. This was not an ordinary stable hand.

"My name is Michael Collins. I am currently out of work and have been just kinda wondering around trying to find my way. I am from this country and darn if I know why but I feel like floating along with the two of you and can help you on your way. I had heard of some of Lord Davidson's dealings and over the years have had some run in with them. They are a bad lot. And if they are tracking you the more miles we keep between us and them the better. What do you think of that?"

John looked over at Franklin and all he got was shrugged shoulders. "I guess we could use some more help if those guys decided to jump us and you have a gun something that we do not have."

Part Two

CHARLESTOWN TO INDIANA INDIAN TERRITORY

ONE

So early in the morning the new group started out. Mike would tell Franklin which direction that they needed to go and Franklin again would set the pace. Although Mike looked a bit older, he had no trouble keeping up. And John by now had learned to keep up. They stayed on this pace for another week before they decided to take a rest. During that week some days they would travel during the day and sometimes at night, but always skipping around any populated areas. After this week Michael turned them northwest and soon they came to a cabin.

"Do we know these People?"

"Yes this is my home and there is no one here but us."

"We didn't know that you had a home."

"You didn't ask."

Red was delighted to be in a stall with feed and water. And John found the hayloft a wonderful place to sleep. And sleep he did. Like a dead person. It was full light when he awoke.

He looked out the hayloft door down at the pens and was surprised to see Franklin had Red out and was exercising him on a long line. The Red acted like he had known Franklin's hand forever.

John was tempted to crawl back into his blanket, when Michael called out from the cabin door.

"Are you going to eat breakfast or wait for supper?"

"I am coming." John scampered down the ladder and off to the cabin for some more great breakfast.

Franklin joined them and while they were eating he ask Michael if they were safe here.

"Yes, I rarely have company here. In fact I am going to leave you both here. I need to take care of some business in a nearby town. I will stock up on more supplies and be back the day after tomorrow. If anyone shows up that you do not trust head due north and I will find you."

He took a wagon and headed off to town. John and Franklin kept a close eye on the horse and the road to see if anyone was coming. No one came and as he had said Michael came the next day. He had the wagon loaded with supplies and when ask he had told the store man that he was going to hunt for gold. They all laughed. Then Michael got a serious look on his face.

"I have not known each of you long but I have enough for us to get by. We will use the money to buy us another place when we feel the time is right. But we must get moving. There was a handbill at the store offering a reward for the horse so people will be out looking for him."

They rested the rest of that day but daybreak found them on the loaded wagon with Red tied on the back and they started out north and sometimes a little west. The wagon was slow but sure beat walking. A few days later they came upon a tinker in a covered wagon. Michael asked him if he had any canvas with him.

"Yes but it is only a piece not enough to cover your wagon."

"We will take it." And Michael bought the canvas and some string.

A few miles away they stopped and Michael explained the canvas. "I think we need to cover this horse up a little." So they cut and sewed a cover for the horse. Franklin then scooped up hands full of dirt and mud and rubbed it all on the horse and canvas.

"He looks a lot worse now."

"Yes I think he does too." John agreed. Even with the horse covered up he still looked like a good horse so when the three would be coming up to a town, John, Franklin and Red would skirt the town and meet Mike on the other side. He had soon become Mike not Michael to the other two. So this way they put a lot of days and miles between them and the ocean and Lord Davidson. But at night when he was still John would wonder if he had done the right thing. He prayed that he had. But now he was running across a country he knew nothing about their ways with a runaway slave and some would say a horse thief. The slave and the horse thing were both probably hanging offenses here. When he figured out how he would get word to The

Man and ask him what he should do. He couldn't board a ship with no papers and no money.

They moved on each day north and west. Mike said that Franklin would be safer the farther north that they got him and it was not likely that Lord Davidson's bunch would hunt them very far. A few days later found them near a stream where they decided was a good place to stop for the night. Franklin had found a good place secluded from the road and so that night they could have a small fire for their dinner cooking. Red was fed his little bit of oats and then tied out to graze. John helped Franklin gather up some wood and Mike got some pork belly cut up with some potatoes and onions. And they took the time to boil some beans. John and Franklin took time to take a bath and wash their clothes in the stream and hang them on some bushes to dry. John decided that he must be hungry because it sure smelled good. When it was done and Mike had called them to fill their plates John noticed that Franklin seemed to eat with relish also. Then it dawned on all of them that they had not stopped for any lunch. After supper Mike took his turn at a bath and laundry.

Later with their bellies full they all three fell sound asleep. The last few days they had discontinued their taking turns to stay up and watch. All of them came up in a hurry though when they heard something that sounded like moaning coming from the other side of the stream. After they had listened for a few minutes, Franklin chuckled and said, "I be right back."

Mike and John exchanged wondering glances as Franklin headed off across the stream and up the other bank. They could hear some talking but couldn't understand what was being said. Soon Franklin returned still very happy.

"Those are some of my folks. Runaway slaves like me. They are going to the north to join up with the underground railroad they sezs."

"How many are there?" Mike asked.

"Only five. Three men, a woman and a young boy."

"We can't take on that many people. We don't have enough supplies."

Franklin looked at them both and then said, "I wuz thinking about joining up with them. They believe that if we can get to some of those railroad people we can go north and be free. I believe that I need to take that chance. Us coming up on them like we did seems to be some kind of sign. And if I can't get to be freed up there somewhere I will try to find an Indian tribe that will take me." Franklin had mentioned before how some tribes would not take him because he was so black. They were superstitious about him.

John had only known Franklin a few weeks but had built up a real affection for him. "We hate to see you go and can never pay you back for helping me get my horse. But I wish you well and maybe we will meet up again somewhere."

The next morning at daybreak, Franklin rolled up his blanket. Took a few bites of breakfast and when he stood up to leave Mike had put together a little sack of supplies. Franklin started to protest when Mike told him that there was some little candies in the bottom for the kid.

Hugs were given all around and Franklin quickly disappeared across the stream and joined up with his new companions.

TWO

Mike could tell that John would miss the big black. They had bonded he knew. So he quickly broke camp and they were soon on the trail again, Mike, John and Red this time.

"We need to find someone in the next town to help us know where we might be going and maybe get a map of some kind. He looked over at John and smiled. "I don't think we can keep going on forever. We might run into another ocean or fall off the face of the earth."

Both laughed at Mike's idea. It felt good to laugh. They had not had many times to do that and most of the time they had traveled very quietly to not draw attention to themselves or the horse. But this morning seemed to be a turning point to their future whatever and wherever that might be.

When they came to the next town, John and Red again went around and Mike went down to the town. He drove in his wagon like always. He went to the general store and bought the supplies that they would need for the next few days. He didn't have to buy as much for two and for three so he indulged in extra blankets and a few apples for the horse. He then started out of town. He heard some loud talking and music farther up the street. When he pulled along next to the noise he knew it was a drink selling place. He decided that he might just have a drink.

He parked the wagon and tied off the lead horse. The saloon as it was called was not very full. He went up to the bar and ordered his drink. He drank it slowly as he would only allow himself one drink. He then turned to look around at the clientele at the tables. There were some cowboys playing cards and a few old men just sitting around swapping stories. Over in a corner he saw the person that he was looking for. And when he got close and he smelled him he knew he had found the right one.

"May I sit with you?"

"Why there are a lot of empty tables around?"

"I just thought I would talk to what looks like the smartest woodsman in the bunch."

The smelly large man with a full beard motioned to a chair and Mike sat down.

"I am traveling to maybe find my fortune. I have pulled up stakes and am heading west.

I need someone to guide me."

"I ain't no guide."

"I pay good money and keep you well fed."

"Where are you going?"

"I don't rightly know but I know that the next leg of my travels is going to lead me across those mountains that I can see in the distance and I need someone to help get me over or through them."

"Those mountains now I know them. They are where I trap through the winter. I just came down and sold my hides. Got a good price for them too."

"So what do you do until it gets cold again and the hides set?"

"Usually just sit around here and spend all my money then I have to go make some more."

"This way you can travel with us and make some money and still end up back up in the mountains by the time the first snowfall.'

"Who is us?"

"Oh just a young lad and me."

"Why didn't he come with you?"

"He doesn't like coming to town much."

The two of them talked some more and then decided on terms for him to guide them. They then went out and down the street a ways to the livery where the mountain man had his mule and his supplies stored. The mountain man packed his things on the mules back and then covered all of it with a canvas tied on with ropes. Then he started out walking down the road. Mike called out to him to join him in the wagon.

"I don't like riding much. And I walk a pretty good clip so try to stay up." Mike was surprised at the pace the mountain man set out on.

And he was more surprised that he could keep it up all day with just a few short rests.

At the edge of the woods outside of town the mountain man stopped and waited as John and Red came out to them. He quickly sized up the blooded horse, but said nothing. Mike introduced him to John and the mountain man said that his name was Ebenezer McWilliams. Everyone just calls me Eb. After a short rest they were on the road again. The sun was high in the sky when Eb stopped and they had a little bite to eat.

"Yessir we will get to the foot of those mountains in about a week. Then the climb will start. There is a wagon trail but it is not very good so we will see how far we can take the wagon."

They continued the rest of the day taking them ever closer to the mountains. John could not imagine them up close as they already looked huge to him. He had never seen real mountains before not like these.

For some reason John was unusually tired that night and soon as he had seen to Red he rolled up in his blankets and was soon fast asleep. While he slept he began dreaming. For some reason he had a hold on Red's halter and one of the original bad guys had the other side. Then later on he dreamed he was about to be hung from a tree for horse stealing. He cried out for Mike to help him. Mike and Eb were soon at his side shaking him. He looked up into both of their faces.

"You were having a bad dream. Wake up and sit up." Mike looked at him up close.

"Are you awake?"

"Yes I am awake. I dreamed the bad guys had a hold of Red and then they were fixing to hang me by a rope in a tree when you woke me up."

"Uh is there something I need to know here about you two and the blooded horse?" Eb said.

"Yes I guess there is." Mike said. "You see this lad has a tale to tell you that will be hard to swallow but I guarantee it is all the truth."

John started at the beginning of his Father dying and losing his family. He then told about The Man and Samuel and how he was elected to bring Red to America. He told them all about the trip and the "cargo" and the auction. He then recounted the bad men and how

Franklin helped him get the horse back. And then they met Mike and now Eb. Eb sat back against a log.

"So that is what is causing the nightmares about hanging. Well, let me tell you that is not going to happen if Mike or I have anything to do with it. It sounds like you just got your horse back and there was no stealing to it. Now I suspect you better get some sleep we have a long haul tomorrow and then in a few days we will meet those mountains." John snuggled back into his blanket and with Eb snoring next to him felt safe enough to sleep again this time without the nightmares.

They always started out at daybreak. And today was no exception. They had gone about half a day when Eb called a halt and came back to the wagon. "John, you best saddle that horse and get on his back."

"What's up?" Mike asked.

"Indians. They have been tracking us for about half the morning. I guess they have seen the horse. I have an idea how to flush them out and get rid of them."

John had saddled and jump up when Eb told them to continue on. He tied his mule to the wagon and then slipped in the woods. Soon the Indians were riding closer and closer. Mike had managed to put his pistol on the wagon seat just under the blanket he was sitting on. John kept Red on the off side from the Indians. Then the lead Indian rode out in from of the wagon causing Mike to have to stop. The other Indians circled around them. They talked and pointed at the horse. About that time there was a blood curdling yell coming right at them. It even made John and Red very nervous. The Indians moved back away from the wagon and about that time Eb stepped into the opening. The Indians shrank back farther. Then the leader broke into a big smile.

"What you doing ole' Ed?" The leader talked in perfectly good English.

"I am trying to scare the Hell out of you."

"You nearly did and the white boy on the horse I thought was going to faint."

"These are my traveling friends and you stay away from them and the boy's horse that you are eyeing. And spread the word that I will gladly scalp anyone of you no good injuns that tries."

The Indian leader had gotten down off his horse and walked up and gave Eb and big bear hug. He then shook hand with Mike. John had come down off Red and the Indian shook with him also. He then turned to the other Indians and with some kind of Indian talk and hand motions to John and the horse, seemed to be telling them what Eb had said. The others laughed too with the leader. Eb then told Mike and John that this was "Talking Wolf". He then explained that he had gone to the church school and learned to speak English and could read, write and cipher. But he then returned to his tribe and would someday be a Chief. John wondered if this was one of Franklin's tribes but was too scared to ask. He would ask Eb later.

The Indians made themselves a fire nearby and spent the night with John and Mike and Eb. They followed along about a week. Then one morning when John awoke they were gone. Their fire was covered with dirt and there were not hoof prints anywhere. It was like they were never there. Eb laughed at John looking for signs of them.

"Did they just disappear? I can't find any sign that they were ever here. Why didn't they say goodbye or something?"

"They do not say goodbye except to people dying. Otherwise they believe they will see you again. They will pass the word that we are not to be bothered and we will have safe passage for over the mountain."

"Where did they go?" John had to know where they went.

"They were a hunting party. They will kill meat and then take it back to their village. They live about 50 miles north of here."

During their stay, John had noticed that Mike had very little to do with the Indians. John had spent every spare minute talking and listening to Talking Wolf. He was fascinated with him.

Talking Wolf let him see his bow and arrows. John also touched the beaded vest that he wore.

He felt the soft leather of his breeches and moccasins. And Talking Wolf listened as John told him he had come across the ocean with the horse.

"He is a fine horse. You must keep him close to you or someone will steal him. He will sire many good colts for you."

After the Indians left and John realized that Mike had had nothing to do with them he asked him about it. Mike explained that when he was about 8 years old Indians had attacked his family and killed all but him and his little sister. They were then sent to live with the Indians until a Priest came along and got them back. They were then raised by the Nuns at the Church near the reservation. Mike was never very comfortable around them since. But he did not hate them. He understood that they felt like someone was taking away their land and livelihood. And if it was to happen to him he would fight too he thought.

John found that the days following the departure of Talking Wolf were sort of lonely. Although he had grown very fond of Eb and Mike, they were not the best talkers in the world. In fact the very next day he realize how much he missed his talks with Talking Wolf and the things he was teaching him about his surroundings. He had realized that by the end of that day, he bet that no one had said more than 20 words all day. So that night around the campfire he was determined to have Eb and Mike talk about something, anything.

"So tell me about this deal about slavery. What gives anyone the right to own a slave?

Eb spoke first. "I guess they feel like the pay good money for them and have a bill of sale so I guess they think they own them."

Mike chimed in. "They need the slaves to work the plantations or they would not have any crops."

"But why don't they just pay them like other workers?"

"There are not any other workers to pay. Have you seen any "other workers" around here?" Mike said as he stroked the fire.

"How do they do their work in Europe?" Eb asked John.

"They have landowners like here. But then the work is done by sharecroppers or by day workers. Sharecroppers live and work on the land. At the harvest they are given part of the harvest for their labor. Some day workers live on the owners land or have a little piece of their own land and get paid by the day or with goods and food. They are free to harvest their own piece of land and keep the fruits of their labor. But they are all free to come and go as they please."

"What if you don't have any land or job? What do they do?" Eb kept on.

John was glad it was evening and Eb and Mike couldn't see the frown come upon his face. "If you have no means of support, they put you in a place called a poor house. A poor house is where you all live with charity from the government or a church. You are fed very little and you just have the clothes on your back. At some time they have a meeting where people come and get you to come home with them to work. That is how I came to work for The Man. They called us all out in from of the large building where we lived. People came up to a table and signed in with their names and what kind of person they would take home with them. Some were families wanting little ones. That is where my younger siblings went. Some wanted young girls for maids. Older women would be hired as cooks. And none of them had a choice. Everyone was basically in jail until someone came to get them out of there. Some could be "rescued" by a family member. After I had been with The Man and Samuel for a while we went looking for my family but never found them. Maybe I will look for them again when I get back."

The evening darkness hid the look between Eb and Mike also. They were pretty sure that the big Stallion and the boy were never going back across the ocean. All they could try to do was keep them safe until they could get them far enough away that no one would care who or where they came from.

The next day brought them climbing into small hills and the road was becoming less traveled. Eb told them that they had better get all the supplies they could at the next town as it would be the last one until they climbed over ole' Appalachi. So the next morning they were coming into a small town. John started to hang back with Red. Mike said that he thought it was time they took the horse and boy to town with them and see what the reaction was. They could always cut and run if they needed to. They decided on a story about the horse and headed into town. It wasn't much of a town. At the edge was a small house that might have been the school house on one side and a church. Eb laughed at the idea of a church being all the way out here.

"Wonder how many go to it?"

Farther along was a general store, blacksmith shop and a saloon. Eb tied his mule in front of the saloon and went inside. John and Mike had stopped at the general store and tied up the wagon team and Red. John started to stay behind with Red. "Come on in and act like it's the most natural thing in the world to leave that horse outside."

Mike had made a list the night before and gave it to the clerk who started filling it. Some of the things on the list were canned beans and peaches, flour and sugar, molasses in a can. The clerk then told Mike they had just butchered a hog and they had some of it for sale. Mike took him up immediately. Although they had not gone hungry, Eb, Mike and John had soon learned that they were not the hunters that

Talking Wolf and his group were. They had kept them in deer and wild turkey while they traveled with them. Since they had left it had gone to back to beans and biscuits pretty quick. Mike told John to pick out a couple of shirts and pants and they both bought a heavier coat like Eb told them to. They also bought each one new socks. After they finished loading the wagon they edged on down to the saloon. John could tell Mike was torn about going in the saloon. So he quickly offered to go in and get Ed.

It was very dark in the saloon, the only windows being in the front of the building. A stairs led away from the end of the bar. Eb sat at a table near the front of the building. John nodded to him and turned to go back outside. Eb stood up and followed him out. A dirty cowboy watched out the window as they started down the street. John was riding Red, Mike in the wagon and they were following Eb and the mule.

"I wonder about those three" the cowboy said to no one in particular. "They certainly don't seem to match up much. And wonder where they got that blooded horse. You can tell he is something even though they have tried to make him look bad."

Eb had had a strange feeling of someone's eyes on them as they left the town. He hadn't lived as long as he had by not being observant of the people around him. When they had gone a ways away from the town he circled and they were nearly back where they came from that morning. Then he struck off to the North again. John rode up beside him.

"Why are we making this wide circle?" John ask as he pulled Red up beside the walking Eb.

"So whoever it is that is wondering about us thinks we are going the other direction."

"Who was wondering about us?"

"I didn't ask him his name."

"You know which one in the saloon?"

"I don't know but my gut tells me we better be on the lookout the next few days."

That night when they made camp it was decided that they would take turns again staying up and keeping watch. They had gotten out of the habit when they had ridden with the Indians.

The cowboy didn't sneak in until about 1:00 in the morning. John and Mike were sleeping and Eb was keeping watch. Eb had moved away from the fire and into the woods near the horses. The cowboy didn't even know that he was there until the big bear hug surrounded his body until he could hardly breathe. Eb drug him into the light of the fire. John and Mike both jumped up and Mike went for his gun. The cowboy grasp for air when Eb let go of him. He was down on all fours trying to get enough air in his lungs to breathe.

"You had better start talking now." Eb told him. "Especially why you did not call out to the camp and came sneaking in here like a snake on his belly. What do you want with us?"

The cowboy had finally got some air. "I thought I might like to see that fine horse up close."

Eb said. "We can arrange for you to see up close, like tied to him and drug about a mile up close to his back hooves." The cowboy's eyes were about to pop out. He was really scared. "But on the other hand if you have changed your mind about seeing him up close we could just tie you to a tree and the next fellows that we come up on ask them to cut you lose when they come this way."

"You are not going to just leave me here?" the wide-eyed cowboy stuttered.

"Why not? You came in here to steal what was not yours. I could never stand a thief and especially a horse thief. I should have let you get your hands on him and then I could have just hung you and been in my legal rights to do so."

"Oh Lord! Just let me go and I will never look at someone else's horse again. I promise."

"Well," Eb said. "I guess that since this has just been a bad dream and you never saw us or the horse I might let you live. But I am still tying you to a tree. It will take you about the rest of the night and tomorrow to work your way loose and that should be enough time for us to be on our way minding our own business."

"Oh yessir. It was just a bad dream and I never saw you ever, ever."

Since it was breaking dawn Mike fixed breakfast and they loaded up and set out. Good to his word Eb tied the cowboy to a tree and left him there. As they put more miles between them and the tied up cowboy, John wanted to know if he was loose yet. Later he asked Eb again.

"Is he loose yet?" Eb told John, "He might and he might not be loose yet. But I hope he is because there were bear tracks at that stream we just crossed." John then worried the rest of the day about the cowboy.

That night John wondered aloud. "Will he come looking for us again?" Eb chuckled. "I don't know but if he does I will kill him next time not just hug him."

Wow! John had never thought about killing anyone. I mean really killing someone. He had felt better knowing that Mike had a gun but just thought about it as like a stick 'em up thing and then get away, not really kill someone. But he was pretty sure that Eb meant that he would kill the cowboy if he came around again.

The road they had traveled on now for about a month was becoming more of two trails running along together. John soon found it easier to walk than to ride in the wagon as it bumped along the tracks. They were seeing a lot more wildlife now that they were not around any people. At the last stream, Eb had shown him a beaver's dam and then a little farther down they had seen the beaver himself gnawing on a tree. When he had cut it off at the ground he drug it out into the water and disappeared. When he came up he did not have the branch. When he came up he saw them watching him. He made a loud smack on the top of the water with his tail and a couple of other beavers that they had not seen quickly dove in the water and were gone out of sight. Eb explained that the house they had built had a place that was above the water level where they could go and be safe and not drown. Later in the year they would raise their babies in the place.

"If you hunt for beaver hides why are you not getting these?" John asked.

"It is the wrong time of year. When the weather is warm and you take the hide the fur will slip off. Like it is shedding. But after a few freezes in the winter the fur will stick solid to the hide and that is when you hunt the beaver." Mike called them to supper and while they were eating they could hear the beaver falling some more branches and a few slaps on the water.

THREE

The next morning Mike decided to walk and let John handle the wagon and team. John had driven a few times with Mike on the seat with but not by himself. He was a little unsure of his ability. Just pull up if you want them to stop Mike told him. Mike then start off and soon caught up with Eb and they walked along visiting. John wondered what they were talking about. He took his job very serious. He watched carefully to see that the horse walked where the wagon wheels would fall right in the ruts cut out by the travelers that had come before them. He also learned that if he didn't watch what he was doing and the wheels got over to the side of the track and then fell back down in the track it nearly jarred his teeth out. And it always made Eb and Mike look back to see how he was doing. Mike saw that he was learning more each day about being a woodsman. Mike had been intrigued with how fast John had learned everything that Eb and he had tried to teach him. He was always a happy lad and willing to work hard. Mike was very happy that he had decided to come on this adventure. He had been just kinda wasting away back at his farm and needed this new life to get him going.

Eb too had decided that he was glad to be guiding again. He was getting fat and lazy during the time between the trapping and selling of his furs. This was good for him also to have company. He had led a solitary for a long time and at first couldn't join in most of the visiting that Mike and John did during the day and at night around the fire. But to his surprise he soon caught the bug and started telling some of his adventures. And Mike and John were good listeners. During the days he found himself teaching young John everything he could about the outdoors that he had lived in all his life. He taught him the name of the plants and which ones you could use for medicines and which ones to eat and more importantly which ones not to eat. He taught him how to make traps to catch their dinner. These would include rabbits, fox, and sometimes a quail or two. And of course they fished, but John seemed to know instinctively how to catch a fish. Eb also taught John how to read a track, what made it and how old it was and where it was going. At the last town Eb had purchased a rifle and taught John how to use it.

Then the day came that Eb handed John the rifle and told him that they were out of meat and it was time he learned to supply it for the group.

"Get going ahead of us. Continue North and a little west and we will meet up with you tonight."

"What if I get lost?"

"Then we will have to come find you."

"Ok then I guess I am off."

John had made a few trips to town while still at The Manor, but it was nothing like this. Those trips were made in the wagon going down a worn trail and people along to ask directions if you needed them. Although he was nearly a grown man, John suddenly realized he had never been completely by himself with as big a responsibility of finding food for himself and his friends. He shook his shoulders and readjusted the pack on his back and taking a firm grip on his rifle started out.

"Hoy there!" Eb called out. "You hunt in front of us not where we have already scared the game off. That way you can just wait for us to catch up and help you if you kill something big like a big deer or bear. And you will have to get off the wagon track to find anything."

So John turned and started off the direction that Eb had pointed out to him. He followed the wagon track around the next bend and then started off on what appeared to be a deer track. He walked most of the morning, mostly just trying to keep from falling down from all the branches and stuff on the ground, the tree limbs trying to choke him, and mostly just trying to see whatever thing was out there before it saw him and did him in. He must have checked his rifle a dozen times to make sure it was working properly. He stopped when he thought it was midday and ate a little of his biscuits that he had brought with him. He drank a few sips of his canteen.

While he sat there he thought how proud Samuel would be of him; out in the wilderness on a trek to find food for his camp. He was startled by a sound he heard in the distance. He jumped up and made for it and before he knew what it was he could see it was Eb and Mike in the wagon. They had caught up with him while he was eating and reminiscing. He quickly turned back into the woods and started hurrying to be ahead of them. Then he remember some of the wood lore that Talking Wolf had told him. First he had to become the prey. He had to think like him. That meant he had to walk quietly and not make sounds or smells that would spook the deer. So he began trying to walk like Talking Wolf and the braves. After a while he was doing a lot better and to his astonishment right before him was a rabbit. It hopped behind a big tree right in front of it. He took down his rifle from its shoulder strap and then remembered that Talking Wolf said it was easy to just knock a rabbit in the head and save your bullets. So he shouldered his rifle he picked up a fallen limb and tiptoed around the tree. And he then hit the rabbit. His first kill! He had learned to like rabbit when Mike fixed it. He quickly gutted the rabbit and tying it to his pack set off to find another meal for them.

He soon came to a stream and laid down his pack. While quenching his thirst by drinking water from his cupped hands he saw the fish. Many big ones! He eased on back to his pack and quickly made him a hook and line. He found a small sapling nearby and tied the string to the end of it. Making his way back he threw the hook into the water. It just floated down stream and no fish took any notice of it. So back to his pack for a little piece of hardtack. This he placed on the hook and threw again. Still just floating along with the little current. But then whap! And he was fighting to keep from falling into the water. He ran backwards and pulled the fish out of the water on the land. It was the biggest catfish he had ever seen. Again he caught another and another. When he had a little piece of rope full of the fish he realized that it was getting late.

Looking up at the sky and the setting sun he figured where he thought that the wagon might be. Sure enough in a while he could see the campfire. He walked quietly into camp hardly making a sound. Mike had his back turned to him and when John spoke he jumped. John laughed and Eb coming from tending to the horse laughed. "What are you trying to do? Take ten years off my life coming up on me like that. I might have shot you!"

"We have supper old man!" John held up the small rabbit.

"Is that all you got for all day?" Eb had come up on him.

"Yes but I have a few fish too." Holding up the stringer of fish John saw the look on his proud friends faces.

"Let's get them cleaned and fried. This will be a feast tonight."

The fish were cleaned and dipped in corn meal and fried in a big skillet. They had lived on hardtack for a few days and the fish was a great treat! Eb made John tell him nearly every step that he took for the day and told him a few more stories. Some John missed as he fell asleep there by the campfire. When he awoke someone had spread his blanket over him and he just turned over and slept some more. No nightmares tonight. He was plain tuckered out.

The next day Eb came out of the woods and told John that he had seen a good recent deer track. "Get your gun and see if you can find him this time." John quickly got his pack and the rifle and going where Eb had seen the freshest tracks, he soon was on the deer trail. He soon noticed that the track was actually tracks. One set was a big hoof and there were others smaller. Remembering what Talking Wolf had said he knew that the bigger one would be the buck so he planned to turn off when the big hoof turned and not follow the smaller ones. He was so busy watching the tracks that he was only about 30 yards from a clearing before looking up and staring right at the buck. He slowly but quickly slid the rifle off his shoulder and taking aim he shot right behind the shoulder as he had been taught by Eb. The deer jumped straight up and then fell to the ground. The other does made quite a racket as they ran into the woods.

John ran over to the buck on the ground. Taking his knife from his belt he slit his throat so he would bleed out and then started "cleaning" him. Deer have a musk bag between their hind legs that if it is not severed from the body whole everywhere the fluid touches ruins the meat. John carefully slit the hide open and removed the musk bags. He then drug the carcass over to a tree and with his rope tied him high up enough that his front legs were dangling barely touching the ground. Then John proceeded to split the carcass down the belly letting the innards fall out on the ground. Talking Wolf said that Mother Earth would use the innards to feed other smaller animals and she thanks you for leaving them. After cleaning out all he could, John took the carcass down and making a makeshift skid he started back to the camp. He passed another small creek on his way and stopped to clean himself and the inside of the carcass. He then reposition it on the two sticks that made up his slide and started back toward the wagon trail.

He was ahead of the wagon when he came out into the open ground near the wagon track. But he could hear the two men talking and was tickled when they saw him and rode up alongside him. He had left the sled near the edge of the clearing and made a motion with his hands like he had not gotten anything. Little did he know that his rifle shot had carried a long way and the two seasoned hunters had heard it. But when John turned and drug out the carcass they both acted very surprised. They looked at each other and smiled knowing that each of them were eat up inside with emotion at their little lad killing his first dear. They made a big deal out of the skinning and cutting up of the deer. After it had been salted and wrapped tightly they loaded it on the wagon. John thought they would build a fire and eat some right then. But to his surprise Mike turned to him and said we are burning daylight lets go. And go they went and the wagon trail was good for most of that day so they made good time. Eb had told Mike that they could stop at a good stream of water the next day and cook the meat so it would last longer. So that night they ate a little of the meat and by afternoon the next day they had come to a larger stream and they had pulled under some trees and built camp. Mike soon made some drying racks out of small willow branches he then cooked strips of the meat in a skillet and then hung them on the racks to cure and dry out. He shook some salt over them. John then had a new job of keeping the crows that had come up to steal the meat, shooed off. Mike said that they would have to watch during the night too as the other bigger beast would come calling to get the meat as the smell was all over the forest now.

A little before dark a bigger beast was drawn to the smell also. But it walked on two legs.

"Hello the Camp came to call." Mike eased over to sit down by his gun and Eb had slid over to the tree where his rifle was leaning. John called for the visitor to enter as that was the way in the woods he had learned. Into the haze of the setting sun stepped a big man dressed in buckskin and carrying his own gun.

"Mind if I join the camp?"

"No come on in."

He stepped closer to the fire and squatted just like Talking Wolf.

"Where you headed?" Eb ask a mite quickly. "I am going over the mountains. It is getting too crowded on this side. I figure I can make my way and have had pretty good luck staying out of the way of the Indians. I am good with my hands and think I might be able to get a cabin up before the snow starts. I don't need a big one just making for myself. What about you all?"

"We are going over the mountains too." Mike told him. "We are I guess doing about the same thing you are."

"I saw the horse." The stranger said and his smile should two front teeth missing.

"I had seen the posters back in Handertown. But that has been a few weeks past, so I think you are about in the clear. That old man must want him bad; he had upped the reward to $5000.00. So you better be careful."

John nearly died. This old buckskin man was sitting here telling them all about Red. He wonder why Eb didn't just shoot him and then they could just throw him in a hole. But then John noticed something else, Eb was laying down his rifle, but Mike remained by his pistol.

"You seem to think you know our story so what is yours?"

The man looked down into the fire. "I am wanted for killing a man. I had been out hunting for a couple of days and when I got back home I found him in bed with my wife. So I just killed him. They took me to jail and was going to hang me. The night before the hanging the judge came during the night and let me out. He said that no one man should have to hang for another man's lust."

"He just let you out like that?" Mike asked.

"Yes. He just came in with the keys and said for me to lit out and never come back that way. So I went by my cabin got what I needed for the trip and here I am. I have a couple of horses out a ways I would like to bring in a little closer if you don't mind my staying. I seen a couple of bear tracks coming in a few miles back and they will have smelled the cooking meat by now. In fact if I was you I would pack up right now and use the last of the daylight to move on farther down away from here or they are going to be all over us this night."

Eb and Mike decided that they would stay put but we would be up and guard through the night. The meat was taken down and wrapped up and put in a small empty barrel they had brought. Then they settled down for the night. Eb took the first watch. Henry, the new man offered, but Eb seemed to be watching him as much as the bears. John brought the horses right into camp and tied them to the wagon. Sleeping nearby John heard Red snort and stomp. He was quickly up and so was Mike. Eb was nowhere to be seen. Then they heard running and shooting. John started to go but Mike held him back. "Best we stay here we don't know the lay of the land right now out there." Soon Henry and Eb both came into camp quite winded. But then they were slapping each other on the back and laughing so hard they could hardly tell their tale.

During the night Eb had seen Henry ease quietly out of his bedroll and taking his gun he had gone out into the night. Eb had quickly followed to see what he was up to. As the two of them was watching each other a big brown bear had come along heading straight for camp. They both forgot about each other and aimed at the bear. Both shooting at the bear that was directly between them. If either one had missed they would have killed the other. The two had gutted the bear in the woods and drug the rest of him near camp and hung him in a tree to keep as many varmints out of him as they could.

So another day was spent cutting up and curing meat and another night spent before they started out again. In the meantime Mike and Eb had asked Henry Roberts if he would like to join them going over the mountain. Another hunter and help if they needed it from the Indians were welcome. The next few days were mostly the same. The wagon trail was getting rougher and less traveled. They had passed only one cabin in the last three days and no one was there. The stream that they had camped along the side of had cooler water. John did not linger in the water as he had done in the past. He had taken the time to wash all his clothes while they were cooking the meat so he felt really good about being cleaner. Mike also was a clean person. He could not say the same about Eb. They often had to tell him that he smelled. He would just laugh but would wash the next stop they had with water.

John rode or exercised Red each day. He did not want him to forget that he was broke to ride not a wild horse. He had taken to the trip like he had been out in the wilderness all his life. He had learned to not spook at every sound he heard. Since they were climbing in altitude each day, John noticed that Red's coat was getting thicker. The long trip had toughened up his muscles and his neck had broadened considerably. Red, along with John, had aged on the trip.

John could not believe that they had been on the trip for nearly six months. He understand that he had lived through a traumatic time and had been very lucky to find Mike and Eb and now Henry to help him on his journey. In the back of his mind he still considered that he might make his way back to The Manor and The Man and explain his predicament, but it was not in the front of his mind. Everyday had become a day of keeping moving and living each day as it came. And he found each day he learned more and more about his wilderness world around him. Since he had no mirror, he did not realize that he, like Red, had grown bigger and more muscular as they had gone along. His hair had grown long and he used a piece of broken harness to tie it back in a ponytail. He also had grown a beard. Not many of his people would recognize him anymore. But he still thought of himself as a teenager. On the trip he had gotten a year older and the others had helped him celebrate by having an extra portion of meat that night. Henry had given him his only gift, a sharp hunting knife that he had produced from his pack. Assuring John that the he had another one, he grinned widely when John gave him a hug in appreciation.

FOUR

Mike had been keeping a small journal on their trip. He announced to the group that this evening marked their seventh month on the trip. Eb then started planning their next month's trip. He said that they would take the wagon as far as the trail was available. At some point he told them they would have to abandon it and they would have to pack everything on the horses and on their backs. Then their upward climb would be the hardest time. They had to hurry as much as possible pushing hard to get over the mountain before the big snow falls started.

So the next day they started stopping only for short breaks and ate on the road and only stopping at night to rest. Since Red had never carried a pack, Eb showed John how to start packing small portions on Red's back so he would eventually carry his full load. The older wagon horses and the mules had all been trained to carry packs. As the days went on the climbing became steeper and the wagon bounced along over big rocks and at a few places the track barely could fit alongside the edge of the mountain.

It was about a week when Eb decided that it was time to abandon the wagon. So the next morning they spent about half a day dividing up the supplies and loading each horse and mule. Each man took some supplies in his pack and his knife and guns. John wished for a gun of his own now but they had not seen anyone to trade for one. But he felt better with the knife that Henry had given him. Eb carefully had each man take enough supplies for himself so if they were to get separated they could survive until they found each other again.

He also reminded them that through the mountain pass they might encounter Indians.

"I know many of them so let me always do the talking and hopefully we will not have any trouble, but you never know." Eb also made each man's pack have his coat that they had bought. Although John didn't think they needed it yet he did as he was told. But he would have rather just let Red carry the cumbersome thing. Red smelled of most of the supplies as they were tied and packed on his back, but by now he did not object to the extra weight.

Increasingly the next days found the wagon trail becoming a trail just wide enough for a man and horse to go along. John was not fond of the places that the trail was just a cut out on the side of the mountain and looked off the edge way down to a rocky fall. He quickly learned to not look at the edge but stay next to the mountain side itself. It added to his discomfort when one of the mules slipped and he could hear the rocks falling and falling down the cliff. But the sure footed mule did not fall and did not seem to care about the falling rocks. Eb had been over the mountains before and knew where to go to find a wide place for them to build camp for the nights. It still was not like camping near a stream and wide open plains. Red did not eat much as there was little grass and they had long ago run out of grain. Beginning to worry, John ask Eb how much longer they had to climb and he said only a few more days but they would soon come to a sort of table top that would be a place to let the horses and mules grazed for a day. And sure enough a couple of days later they came out on a flat plain type of area. From the top of it you could see the mountains for miles. Red and the others quickly set to work filling their bellies. Mike took the time to cook a good meal with biscuits, meat and beans. They all ate well and then lay down to sleep. There had not been much wood for the fire and during the night John noticed that he was getting colder. But he went back to sleep after kicking up the fire some more. When he did that he noticed that Eb had taken his big coat off his pack and covered up with it. Another lesson learned.

The next morning each horse and mule was repacked and each man repacked his back pack with supplies and they started out again. They had not gone far when they came to a roaring sound. Red's ears stood up and he stopped for a while. With John's encouragement he came on and John understood why he had stopped. Right in front of them was a huge water fall! He had never seen so much water in all of his life. They all just stood and watched it falling for hundreds of feet down the side of the mountain. Thank goodness they did not have to go across that. Eb said that they would travel miles upstream to a place where they could safely cross. They continued along the side but not too close to the river. Eb explained that the water would soon freeze and this would all be a frozen lake but for now it was still running. And in the spring the fall would nearly double in size from the melting snow and ice. They traveled up river until Eb decided on a camp site. The horse were hobbled and camp made. They had been climbing in elevation all day and until they stopped they did not realize how tired they were. The air was harder to breathe. That night Eb decided that they would spend a day or two here to get them more acclimatized to the air. He told them that night around the fire that the next few days would be the hardest. They would walk slower and have a harder time breathing in the high altitude. But by the end of the week they should be climbing out on the other side of the mountains.

The next couple of days the animals ate their fill and drank heavily from the river. And the men rested and repacked their packs. Eb told them to take some of it off and put on the pack animals as they were going to have a harder time climbing the next couple of days. Daylight the next day found them packing the animals and then by mid-morning they were climbing again. At least some of this climb was a little wider and John did not feel like he was going to fall off the side.

Later in the afternoon they passed a carcass of some horse or mule. It had been dead a long time. John did not like looking at it. It reminded him of the chances they were taking with Red. No worry about himself but for his horse. The path lead them up and around the mountain side. The climbing was slow and they stopped to rest many times. That night they rested with only a little fire and they slept sort of sitting up on big rocks as there was little place to lie down and stretch out. The next day during the morning it started to snow. Not a big snow but snow that was cold and wet. It snowed the rest of the afternoon and John was surprised when Eb turned off from the path and struck out across a piece of rocky land. It landed at the mouth of a big cave. They all could fit in it and the animals also. They quickly gathered wood and built a fire. Mike started supper while Eb stood at the mouth of the cave. "Will it last long?" John had come up behind him to look out. "I don't think so. But it might snow the rest of the night. We will have to be very careful tomorrow as the rocky climb will be wet and slick."

And it did snow the rest of the night. In the morning Eb decided that they should try to push on so they packed and started out. He was right about wet and slick. The animals remain sure footed but John slipped down lots of times and felt he was black and blue all over. The next morning after the sleep on the rocks he felt like ever muscle in his body was screaming with pain. He pulled himself up and began his part of the work. As they climbed the next day he started feeling worse. Eb had started watching him and had spoken to Mike about him. They topped out that day and could see down the other side of the mountain. Eb did not let them linger long. He gave them new instructions on how to stay out of the way of the animals so they did not slid down on them. They had to remember that they were still in the high altitude and would still travel slowly and would have to find shelter on the way as it looked like more snow coming.

They took shelter in another cave the next day. The snow had started. And John was definitely sick. The men recognized that he had a cold. He was freezing one minute and burning up the next. They piled their blankets on him and washed his face with melted snow. John tossed and turned. The trip was put on hold as the three men worried about their little man. Three days later he awoke and seemed on the mend again. They made him eat and drink and then decided that they would continue the next day. The climb down on the west side of the mountains had more level areas and their climb down was easier than the climb up on the other side. They had made John ride on Red for the next couple of days for him to get his strength back. They were thankful that he was young and healthy and soon was walking again and a few days later he was back to carrying his pack. The snow continued to fall and they continued to be wet and cold. But they could tell that they were losing altitude and it was becoming easier to breathe and walk. There were places that the horses and mules could dig with their hooves and find some green weeds to eat.

It was over ten days before the sun came out without any snow. They camped alongside a running stream that had begun to freeze along the bank. With the sun they took the time to repack their packs and hang some of their clothes out to dry and air out. They had not bathed in a couple of weeks or so and they smelled and did the clothes but the water was too cold and Eb told them not to wash any clothes as they would never dry. That night they stayed up later talking. The days before they all had been so exhausted that they just ate and fell asleep. They all felt that the worst was over and according to Eb it was.

During the night John and the others were awaken by a screaming. It made the hair on John's arms stand straight up. He had never heard such a horrible sound. Eb laughed at them all and then explained that it was a mountain lion. They would now have to start keeping a watch on the animals as the mountain lion was hunting. They decided and each one took a turn staying up a few hours watching near the animals. John drew the early morning watch. He settled down with his back against a tree with Eb's rifle in his lap and Red and the others nearby. It was a moon light night and it was almost like day time. But John was alert and watching every shadow that moved during his watch. He did not see anything and soon the camp was up and getting breakfast.

"Did you see the lion?" Eb asked as he drank his coffee.

"No I didn't see anything and the animals did not start."

"He was here but not too close. There are tracks all around us. Come let me show you the track."

Eb showed John the big cat paw print in the wet ground. It was a little ways out but he had certainly been there.

"Why did he not come any closer?"

"He probably smelled you and saw the fire. But he will continue to follow until we are out of his country. And he will be looking for any chance to jump on us. So we will have to be on the watch on the ledges especially hanging out above us. He will hunt day and night so we will have to keep the animals in the middle of us not at the back as before."

The next day the men took turns with the lead and the pack animals in the middle and usually Eb in the back. It was the third day out that John got his first look at him. Eb and John were leading the group when Eb put out his arm and stopped John. He slowly pointed to a large overhang of rock on the left side of the trail. The big cat stood looking down at the group seeming not to be the least bit afraid.

"Do we shoot him?" John was excited at the thought of killing his first lion.

"No, but I am going to fire to try and scare him off. If he then continues to hang around we will have to put him down. If he goes off we will let him go." Eb then fired a shot on the rock nearby the mountain line. He quickly disappeared into the rocks above and then out of sight. John thought he was one of the most magnificent animals he had ever seen and was glad they let him go his way. But he also was very scared of him at the same time. They did not see him again. Nor did they see any more tracks. Eb explained that he had his own territory and rarely traveled out of it.

That afternoon it began to rain. Although this side of the mountain was not as many cliffs to navigate around it still had a lot of rock slides and steep slopes to get down. And then the rain started washing out what little trail there was. The horses began slipping and sliding and sending more rocks and dirt down the trail ruining it that much more.

The first clearing that they came to Eb pulled his mule over. "Boys I believe we should try to get some dry firewood while we can and make a camp until this blows over."

So they quickly all ran under some of the bigger timber and they gathered wood and started a fire. It spit and sputtered from the rain that manage to come down through the tall pines but it soon caught. John helped Henry unpack the horses and Mike hunkered down to fix some supper. Eb soon had them gathering small saplings and they soon had a nice lean—to built near the fire. They had covered the top as well as they could with other limbs but of course it still leaked but not as bad as standing out in the open rain. John could see Red shaking some of it off him and felt sorry for him. He knew that he had toughened up on this trip. When they started out all he had ever known was a warm and dry stable. Now he had crossed an ocean in a ship, raced for his life, trudged over the mountains in the snow and now stood hoof deep in wet soggy ground. John smiled and under his breathe told him how proud he was of him. Some night like tonight John could almost believe that Red was his horse, but then he remembered that he wasn't and would become quite sad. But he was still determined to take him home or least to where ever The Man wanted him taken.

The food was good tonight and they were hungry even though they had only gone about half what they usually did. When John went out to check on the horses, when the rain let up, he brought in more wood to try and keep it going through the night. They then all snuggled next to each other in the lean-to and kept each other warm during the night.

Eb was the first one up. John felt him stir and knew that he would be calling them soon.

Yes he was calling them! "Get up! Those gal darn Injuns done stole our animals. Every gal darn one of them. Here is the tracks so they come after the rain let up." They all scrambled up and out of the lean-to. John nearly died. Red was gone!

"What are we going to do? How do we get my horse back?" John shouted over the rain.

"Your horse! What about the rest of us?" Eb glared at John.

"Oh I meant all the animals Eb. I didn't mean nothing about just one."

Henry had already started packing up the supplies into bundles. Each man would now have to carry what his pack animal was carrying before. Since they were a little light now on supplies not having stocked up in a while they soon all had a decent pack on their backs. With no discussion and no breakfast they all started out following right behind Eb. They all figured that if anyone could track an Injun it would be Eb. The day went long and Eb did not stop but short periods for drinks and a little rest. Mike had kept out some hardtack and biscuits and they ate them as they trudged along. The tracks remained running in front of them like the Injuns didn't care if they tracked them or not. Eb said there was about eight or ten of them—a hunting party probably. That night after dark they finally fell down on the ground next to their packs and slept the sleep of pure exhaustion. Eb had warned no fire until they saw the Injuns so it was cold camp. Daylight he had them going again. He had already been out scouting before they were up and found where they had crossed a small stream and turned west. It was the middle of the morning when Eb in the lead stopped dead in his tracks. They all hurry around him. Now that the ground was dryer Eb could read the track better.

"They had a good hunt. They are all carrying more than their weight on their horse with them. It is making a deeper track. They are not stopping today to rest so I believe they are coming near their main camp." Eb spoke quietly.

About sundown of another night of just meat and biscuits Eb sat up. "Do you hear them?" he again spoke softly to the rest of the bunch. John and the others listened with concentration but heard nothing, thinking that the old man was having a dream. "No listen. They are in their camp and they are having a welcoming party. You all stay here and I will go see what I can see."

He was not gone long. "Sure enough they are dancing and drinking, celebrating the return of the hunters, and the good luck with the horses."

"What are we going to do now? We can't jump a whole passel of Injuns with the four of us." Mike looked hard at Eb. "Not the four of us." Eb said. "Just John."

Eb turned to John who had just turned pale and tried to faint. "Me jump the Injuns?"

"Didn't you tell us that you could ride the Red without any saddle or bridle?" Sure but in a padlock and every gate closed."

"It will be the same thing. You will just sneak in there and get on Red then start a ruckus that will scare the rest of those beasts and then let Red run like hell. We will all run along until we catch ours and then we will meet up later on. Me and Henry will go a different direction than you and Mike; you follow the Red's lead. You fellows only take a little pack and your weapons. John you have your knife with you?"

"Yessir but aren't the Injuns going to come after me?"

"Yes I guess that they will but if you make enough confusion they won't be able to catch their horses either for a while. And if Red is as fast as I think he is you will be well away before they can catch you on their nags. When you get out of camp turn due East when the sun comes up. In a couple of days you will come to old settler's cabin. If he is there tell him I sent you and stay there. We will all circle around and end up there." He then turned to the two older men and explained to them where the settler's cabin was and then they all crept as close as they all dare. Eb turned to John.

"Go on son. And God go with you. Remember that The Red will take care of you soon as he knows you are on him. Just give him his head. And for God's sake hang on."

John crawled most of the way to the place the horses were tied to a long rope. He could not believe there was not one watching them.

Red was about half way down. So as John crept along he cut the others loose and then cut the main rope. He then let Red smell him and he jumped up on his back and hanging on to his long red mane he started to booger the other horse. He knew he was to make a commotion but when he tries to yell nothing came out. But the horse instinctively knew that they were loose and when John encouraged them with Red the run started. And of course it wasn't five minutes until the Injuns started also. But the more they ran the more the horses ran. And like he was told, John just gave Red his head. And he led the pack and like all horse herds the others followed. When he went by a stand of trees on the east side some forms seemed to appear out of the woods and soon he was joined by Henry and Mike. They were there on their horses and Eb was on a strange one but he had a strong hold on his mule's rope. It was funny to see Eb on a horse with the mule pulling along, as he had walked the rest of the way. When they hit the stream that they had crossed a little while back Eb took the lead and away into the night they all went. John kept his head low so Red would not run him under a limb. It was not long until all they could hear were their horses blowing and Eb let up to a slow lope. They continued on until daybreak. "Darn I hate that we lost our supplies. But we can get some more I guess." They had stopped for a rest. Eb said that the cabin was just about another days ride and then they would be ok. For as he knew the Injuns did not come this way much. And their horse would wander back toward the camp after he had run them off.

The next morning they made hackamores out of the rope left from the night before and sort of a rein for each rider. Then they headed east like Eb had said and by lunch they could see a cabin down in a small valley. Smoke curled out of the chimney. Wow! Maybe they could get something to eat John thought. He was awful hungry!

"Hello you old geezer!" Eb called out to the man with the pipe sitting on the porch.

"Hello yourself old Ebeneezer! Where'd you come from? Why are you over the mountain? Some fool injun will surely scalp you."

After he stood and looked at the sweating horses he asked. "And are you trying to run these horses into the ground?"

Eb had dismounted and when he walked up they embraced like two old women.

The old geezer, as Eb called him, told John and the rest of them to get the horses into the barn and fed and he would see if he could round up some grub. So they quickly bedded the horses down in the barn and joined Eb and his friend in the house.

"This here is little John, Mike and Henry, my traveling companions. This here is Marshall Dixon. Marsh we have always called him. We met a long time ago over the big mountains where we just came." John asked if he could help with the food and quickly started peeling potatoes. He was hungry and wanted to get the food going before the old stories started. He might starve to death before they quit. He had heard Eb when he got going.

Coffee was soon boiling, biscuits were in the dutch oven, some meat was searing across the fire and the potatoes were frying in the skillet. The smell was wonderful!

Marsh then settled down at the head of the table and the others gathered round.

"OK how far back are the Injuns and when can I expect them to come see me?"

"How did you know Injuns were chasing us?"

"What else would be bringing you in here like bats out of hell? With horses 'bout rode plumb down and all of you worn out and hungry. You sure haven't stopped to make a camp the last night or so."

"To tell the truth Marsh, we are horse thieves, running like hell from their owners." Eb replied. Marsh started to laugh.

John jumped in. "No, it's the truth! I snuck in an injun camp and stole my horse and the others here's animals and I jumped on Red's back and let out. A ways down the rest grabbed their mounts and the mules and we have been running ever since."

Marsh looked at John very seriously. "Let me get this straight. You crawled into an injun camp on your belly, stole that big bred horse and the others on the rope line and got clean away? I don't see an arrow sticking out any of your body!"

John did not realize that Marsh was making fun of his adventure. "You see, Red can run very fast and I just let him have his head and the others just followed. But I could hear the Injuns behind me running for a while on foot and yelling but they soon gave up and went back."

Henry could hold it no longer. He burst out with a haw and the others joined in.

John then looked around the room at his friends and the fun they were having with his story.

"That is how it happened!"

As the others laughed, Marsh got the food together and sat plates all around. And he had a surprise for them all—milk. Good cold cow milk! He had gone out the back and retrieved it from the cooler on the back porch. Now John had not had milk for weeks and it was as good as drinking honey! He even helped himself to seconds on milk and everything. Marsh turned to Eb at his side. "How do you feed that growing monster?"

"As long as you feed him regular he doesn't quite eat as much at a setting. But we have like he said been not camping for a couple of days and I guess he was plumb running on empty."

"How do you keep the milk cold?" John asked between gulps. "Come out back and I will show you." Marsh signaled for him to follow. The cabin sat right by a small fast running stream. Marsh had diverted a tributary across the yard and through the back porch by lining a ditch with flat rocks. And then it continued on back across the yard and back into the stream.

"That way it don't ever clog up. And it stays cold all year. But sometimes we turn it off by damning it up in the dark winter cause it will freeze. It is cold enough to just keep it out here on the porch."

Eb had joined them. "Where did you get the cow? I don't member you having a cow."

"Ha! I bought it off of a family going west last year. I didn't really want it and they had little ones but they insisted after staying here and eating off me for about a week. I have no idea what they did after that. They had no money to speak of but they were going on."

John felt bad then about drinking so much milk that belonged to a family that had to give it away. But come morning he didn't have any trouble drinking a couple of cups again.

After supper they had sat around and told the whole story again. John started out with the bringing of Red to America. As each person entered the story they would take over the telling, with a few interruptions by the others. The story ended here at his house.

"Do you think they are following you Eb?

"I don't know. If they are, they are a day or two behind us, whenever they rounded up all those old nags of theirs."

"That is a permanent camp for them; they had been there a while." Marsh replied. "They have never bothered me here but they will know that you have been here what with all the tracks around the in yard."

"Then we best be gone at daylight then. Are you going to be ok here or do you need to clear out with us for a few days?"

"Oh I have traded a little with them and they don't bother me."

"Ok, early in the morning we will be on our way and we sure appreciate the kindness." Mike spoke up. "We have money to pay for all the food that John ate."

"Oh no I have plenty and it is good to see a lad eat like a horse every once in a while. Have some more milk John if you want it." John was red as a beet in embarrassment. "At least I am a good horse thief!" They all settled down again on the floor for the night. It seemed only a little while before Mike was rousting him out. "Come on horse thief we have to get an early start."

FIVE

Henry already had the horses out at the edge of the woods and Eb was dragging a big leafy limb all around the yard trying to blot out their tracks. Marsh had packed them some grub in a salt sack and handed it up to John. "You might try to share some of that with your friends." He stood back and laughed. Eb dragged the limb a little ways into the woods and Henry quickly took off the trail and into the woods.

They had planned all along to hang to the side of the mountains until they were farther north and so this they did. There was plenty of game and water and they made good time. And about the second week out from Marsh's place they rode into a small town. John guessed it was a town, it had a mercantile store and on the side of that was a saloon all run by the same man. They had a barn in the back for a livery of sorts. John put Red in one of the stalls, fed and watered him. The others just turned their horses out in a corral next to the barn. Red nickered for the others but the guys decided it was best until they saw who the patrons of this little town were. They had come too far for someone to steal Red now. And the truth be told, they were all really tired from the last few days. They also decided not to go in together. So Mike and John paired off and Henry and Eb went the other way.

First order of business was to buy some clothes. The ones they had on were plenty ragged. Although how John had been able to keep up with his boots that The Man had sent him off with he will never know. That was the only piece of clothing that wasn't filthy and hanging torn off his body. So Mike and he proceed to the store and each bought two suits of shirt, pants, underwear and socks. Just the thought of socks made John smile. They told the proprietor they would be back in a day or two for supplies. They carried their clothes with them to the back of the saloon for a bath, haircut and shave. On the way they passed the

other two friends but did not acknowledge them. They were bellied up
to the bar having a beer.

When they came out you would not have recognized either one of
them. Mike had told John that he still cleaned up pretty good. He had
better watch out. There were not many nice looking young fellows in
this part of the woods and the girls would be all over him. John had
looked at a couple of girls along the way but knew there was no place
for one in his life until he figured out what he was going to do.

What he was going to do and what he had planned on doing
seemed to be getting farther and farther apart. He had planned to get
back to the coast, find a ship, and go back home. And try as he might
to explain to The Man and Samuel what had happened here. But they
were further away than they had ever been now from the coast and
John did not know how to strike out on his own without his group.

"Thinking pretty hard there." Mike looked right at him. "Just
thinking that I am a long way from where I planned to be on this trip.
After the horse thievery I thought we would just go a short way and
then head north and return to the coast. There I would be able to get
word home and The Man would find a way to get me and the horse
back across the water. I don't think that is going to happen now or the
Good Lord would have already sent me back that way. So I am trying
to figure out what our next plan is."

"I have been thinking about that too." Mike said. They were sitting
to one side of the saloon eating a meal cooked by the same lady that
had provided their bath. She looked like she needed the bath, but they
were hungry and the food was hot. "I think we head back west and
find us a nice little place and settle down. We can catch us some wild
horses and breed them to your horse and sell them. I know how to
farm so we can raise our food and feed. The others can come too if
they want. Henry I think would stay, Eb might have to go back to
trapping. We might be too tame for him."

While they had been busy eating and talking Henry and Eb had
taken their turns with the bath and new clothes. Henry's face was
smooth as baby skin. But Eb had resisted the shave, but his beard was
trimmed and they both looked great! They had decided there was no
danger here so they join the other two to eat. "We are just trying to
figure out what to do next." Mike started. I am for finding a place to

settle down on. I am a farmer and John wants to raise horses with his stallion. What do you both think you want to do from here?"

Henry turned to Eb and said, "We were both thinking about the same thing. Now Eb says he doesn't know how he will act when it is time to go chasing the furs but for the summer he is for hanging out with you all. And I have no place to go and I am pretty good with my hands so I think I will be able to help get you and house and barn up when we find the place."

"What we need is a map so we know where we are and where government is giving out land grants. And that will take a bigger town than this. We will have to find out where to go for this information."

"We will ask the mercantile man when we get the supplies." Mike answered. "If we all get our own land grant we can get four times the land and have it all together as one piece if that is alright with everyone." Henry added. Everyone nodded in agreement and then finished eating their meal.

The next order of business was tack for their horses. There were two old saddles to be bought and some leather to make hackamores the other would have to wait. When they ask about a wagon and old guy said that about a mile out of town a smithy sometimes had fixed up one for sale. Leaving their supplies at the store they rode out to see the smithy. He was banging on an anvil.

"Hi sir, we are hearing that you sometimes have a wagon to sell. We abandoned ours on the other side of the mountains. Do you have one?"

"I have one but it is pretty old. But it is cheap. And I have the harnesses for the team that the old boy that died left."

He dug around in the back of his shed and came out with a set of harnesses and reins. Two of the horses were soon hitched up to the wagon and Mike and Eb climbed aboard. They had tied Eb's mule to the back of the wagon and Henry and John had taken the saddles for their horses. They returned to the store and loaded their supplies. The store keeper in reply to their questions told them to head north and east again and in about three days they should come to Pineville Junction. He said it was a quite large town, with a church, school and three saloons. Real people lived there in houses bigger than his store. He had gone there once several years ago.

So with spirits raised again the group sat out on their next leg of whatever they were chasing or in John's case, running from. Just as the store keeper had told them, it took about four days to get to Pineville Junction. It was so progressive that it had a sign at the edge of town with Pineville Junction painted on it in bright white paint. And again as told, they passed what must be the Church and next to it the school. On the other side of the street there were several houses with picket fences. Then they saw the boardwalk begin and there was a doctor shingle, a lawyer, and then the large mercantile store. The saloons and boarding houses were then placed farther down the road and back from road. Next to the mercantile store was a hotel. A hotel! Can you imagine! John had not seen one in so long it could have been a dream.

Henry was first to speak. "Have we died and gone to heaven? I haven't seen this fancy of a little town in my life."

Mike ever the observant one said. "Where are all the people?"

John and the others looked around. They were riding down a road with no one on it. No one on the boardwalk and as John turned all around, no one in sight. It was creepy.

Deciding that this part of town was too spooky for him, Henry continued on down the road to the saloon part of town. Here there were a few cowboys sitting around and they could hear voices inside. Tying their horses to the hitchin' post they stepped into the saloon. It was very ordinary and built like most they had been in. On one side was a long Bar and on the other part was table and chairs. They took a table and looked around. No one seemed to pay them much attention. After a friendly bar keep brought them drinks, Henry ask him why the town was so dead down the road. "Oh it is Sunday. They don't believe in being anywhere but in Church on Sunday."

"All of them?"

"All of them. They will stay inside that Church all day."

"But we didn't even hear anyone." John added.

"Silent prayer."

"Silent prayer?" Mike questioned him. "Yeah, silent prayer all day. No one talks on the Sunday." Henry just shook his head. The idea of not talking at all, all one day, was beyond his understanding.

John spoke up then. "We are looking for a government map for land grants."

"Going to trying homesteading? Or just planning on being fodder for the injuns?"

Laughing he told them that the lawyer would be their best bet, but he was in Church. But after dark he would be wandering down this way. They were welcome to hang around until then.

He added then as an afterthought. "Most of the men will be wandering down this way after dark. If you want to camp instead of the hotel or here, there is a nice stand of trees about a mile north of here with a stream."

"That is what we think we will do and come back later." Mike spoke up.

So they left town and soon found the stream and decided on a camping spot on the bank. Since they were not running or chasing it felt good to be able to just camp when and where they wanted and hang around for a while. Mike soon had food cooking and the others took care of the horses. Eb decided to repack the supplies in case it rained and soon had it rearranged to suit himself and had it all tarped down. With their bellies full they all made them a pallet with their blankets and slept all afternoon, something they had not done in months. They could actually breathe safely.

When it was about dark they walked back to town, leaving the horses tied off. They had decided that was safer here. When they entered the saloon it was a different place. There were more men and the tables were full of card players and many whiskey bottles were out with shot glasses. John didn't understand how they could be so pious during the day and go back to whatever that same night. But here they were. When they got to the bar, the bartender motioned to a large man in the corner. "There is your lawyer next to the wall."

They decided that Mike would take care of the lawyering talking since he had the most schooling. Mike walked up to the lawyer. "I hear that you are a man of the bar."

"Yes I am what can I do for you?"

"I am needing a map that show government grants for land west of here."

"Ha! All that is west of here is wilderness and injuns. You need to stay here and find some land close by where you will have help if they come after us. We are trying to build a great community here with

Christian families and education." The Bar Keep failed to tell them that the lawyer was the Preacher.

"Do you have a map?"

"Why yes! In my office down the street. If you will come by my office first thing in the morning I will be happy to show it to you. It is the very map that I used to come out here and establish this town myself."

"Ok, we will be in there tomorrow."

"Are you staying in the Hotel? It is mine also and it is a fine place to stay even if I say so."

"No we are camped outside of town." Mike eased back over to the bar with the others.

Eb spoke quickly. "We have found out some more about Mr. Lawyer. He let them put up this saloon but they can't rent out the rooms except to the girls that work here. That way everyone has to stay in his hotel."

After a few more drinks the group decided to call it a night and rode back to their camp. Since they had eaten in the town they made no fire, just rolled up in their bedrolls and were soon fast asleep. Then the screaming started. It seemed to come to them closer and closer up the stream they had camped on. They were all soon pulling on their boots and shirts and coats. John immediately ran to check on Red and soon had the other horses quieted. By the time they were up and about the screaming had stopped.

"What should we do?" John asked looking around at each of the others.

"We don't know what it was. Maybe it was just an old mountain lion."

Henry said. "No it weren't no lion I ever heard." Ed said as he scratched at his beard. "It sounded like a woman. Wonder what she was screaming at?"

"It came from between us and town. I am sure we will find out in the morning." Mike said.

They all lay back down but didn't get much more sleep. Dawn found them mostly all except Eb already up building a fire and starting some breakfast. Mike had biscuits soon baking in the dutch oven and bacon and beans in another pot. John made the coffee and they all sat around sipping it because it was so hot.

"Wonder why coffee has to be so hot?" John asked. "If it isn't it don't taste good. I can't stand cold coffee." Mike answered. They woke Henry and they all enjoyed breakfast. It had been awhile since they could safely just sit around the fire and enjoy the morning. It didn't last long.

"Riders coming." Henry slid his carbine out of his saddle he was sitting near. The others also got nearer to their sidearms. The riders pulled up their mounts right next to the camp sending dirt onto the fire. "Which one of you was with Mary Belle Harthorne last night?" asked the man in the lead. "Who is Mary Belle Harthorne?" John was the first to speak.

"You know good and well that Mary Bell is the preacher's daughter."

Another man chimed in. "No, I don't believe we have had the pleasure of meeting the Preacher's daughter." Eb said.

"One of you did and molested her right down here on this here creek last night. She came in to her house all her clothes tore and screaming like a lion." Ed had eased up to a standing position.

"We heard the screaming during this early morning but just thought it was a lion. But it was not one of us. We have all been together ever since we got here and no one has been with any woman."

"We were told to bring one of you in, so I guess it will be all of you," Eb turned to Mike and Mike just shrugged his shoulders. "We haven't done anything so I guess we might as well go in and get this cleared up."

The men stayed by as they broke camp and packed their mules and saddled their horses. It was without saying they were all ready to leave this strange place. They were soon back in town and went straight to the sheriff's office. The sheriff named Pearce and the Preacher were there to meet them.

"Sheriff arrest the one of these men that molested my daughter during the night. He came in her room and took her right out of her bed and carried her down to the creek and he needs to be hung right now." The Preacher shouted, red faced at them.

"Ok boys, which one of you was out with Mary Bell last night?" The Sheriff looked at each one in turn. "None of us." Mike spoke up for them all

"It had to be one of you cause she said the person had a camp on the river."

"I am sure there are others camped along the river besides us." Eb joined in.

"One of you is staying in jail until we find the person who did this. So who is it going to be?" The Sheriff had pulled his gun out of his holster and was just holding it out in front of him.

They all looked at each other trying to figure out what they were going to do. Mike then stepped down off his horse.

"I guess I will be the one to stay. You boys go on and find out who did this and get me out of here as soon as you can."

John did not like leaving Mike there. But the look on Eb and Henry's faces told him not to say anything.

"I believe that you boys need to just go back out and camp where you were, that way we can find you if we want you." The Sheriff called out as they stepped off the boardwalk.

So the three of them went back to their camp and made the fire again. It was a while before Eb spoke. John had tried to get the both of them to talk to him on the ride back but neither answered any of his questions.

Now Eb spoke. "What do you think Henry? That little gal got a boyfriend that got carried away or did some one really take her out of her bed."

"It seems to me that the story would sound right if she sneaked out of that bed and out in the night to meet someone. But maybe met the wrong one and decided she better finger one of us seeing that we were not from here and couldn't get her into any more trouble with her papa."

They had not been there long until a lone rider came up the stream and was in camp before they could warn them off. It was a girl with wild dark ringlets and skin the color of silk.

She rode right into camp and announced, "I am Mary Bell Harthorne and I am the one that caused you all the trouble in town. Please accept my apology."

"If that is who you are you need to go to town and we will get our friend who is innocent out of jail." Eb announced. "I can't do that." she replied.

"Why can't you?"

"It was not a boyfriend that was after me last night."

"Who or what was it then?"

"It was the preacher." They were all struck dumb as it soaked in what she was telling them.

She sat up straighter in the saddle and began telling her tale.

"He adopted me when I was small. My parents were killed by the Indians near here and his wife and him took me in. She died a couple of years ago of the consumption and it has just been him and me in that big house. I knew that he was looking at me lately and I had been careful to lock my door at night. Then I went out to relieve myself and he caught me coming back to the house. He was hugging and kissing on me and touching me where he should not. (She had turned her head away while she was telling the story). So I screamed and ran into the woods. He was yelling that I was his and he would do as he pleased with me. God had given me to him and I was his. I hid the rest of the night and snuck back into the house this morning after I had seen him leave. I ran into the house and packed my clothes and I am leaving. But I know that he will try to follow and drag me back. I have run off before and he always finds me and takes me back and no one helps me."

"Ok, let's go tell the Sheriff and we will get him thrown in jail and our friend out." Eb started to the horses.

"That will never happen. The Sheriff and everyone else there belongs to the Preacher one way or the other." She said matter of factly.

Eb then told her, "We have to get our friend out so you just tell them some other side busters name and let us get on our way."

"And what about me? He will just take me home and beat me and have his way. I cannot go back there."

"Where were you planning on going from here?" Henry stepped up.

"I thought I would ride to Granberry. It is about two days ride from here and get a stage back east somewhere. I am educated and should be able to get a job as a governess to some kids somewhere or teach school. I just have to get away from here."

The three of them stood around a while then Henry spoke. "John you take the pack animals and Red and the girl and ride like Hell to this Granberry place. Get her on a stage and out of here. We will get Mike out one way or the other and meet you there."

"If we are not there in two days head west," Eb had joined the conversation. "Go to a place called Herald Hollow. It will be about a week's ride west and then wait for us. When you get to the Hollow tell them that ole' Eb sent you. They will take you in."

Henry always the practical one said, "Do you have any money?"

"A little."

"Ok then be on your way. You know that the country side is looking for this gal."

John climbed on Red and took the reins of the pack mules and the two of them set off north at a fast trot. They soon climbed back into the side of the mountain to stay off the beaten trails. Mary Belle soon told him to let her have one of the pack mules lead. She deftly wrapped it around her saddle horn and they sat out again. It was easier going with each one having one animal to lead. As they rode John told her that if someone found them she was to let the pack mule go and ride off and he would try to detain whoever came on them. He did not tell her that Henry had slipped a pistol in John's saddle bag and a few shells.

"Try not to use that unless you have to." Henry advised.

"I won't." John promised.

As they were riding as quickly as they could they did not do much talking. They stopped at a few streams for the horses and them to drink.

"You don't talk much." the woman started.

"You aren't much to be talking to." John said and bent down to get a cool drink of water from the clear running stream.

"What do you mean?"

"I don't buy your story. I think you were out with someone you weren't supposed to be with and got caught. And you had the opportunity to get away with your lies and took it."

"I don't like you John Dunn!"

"I don't care much if you do or not." John had started back to Red. "My friends are back there may be getting put in jail with Mike or getting shot over your mess." She looked down at her saddle horn.

"Your right. I was out with my fellow and we got caught and I was so mad that I made up the story to get the Preacher in trouble."

"I ought to leave you here right now and high tail it back to town and tell them your lies.

But I won't. But I have no idea why." John swung into the saddle and turned away from her.

They rode into the night. By then Mary Belle was complaining she was so tired. John turned around to see her nearly slide off her saddle.

"OK we will stop, but only for a little while."

Mary Bell took a blanket off her saddle and lay down and was quickly sound asleep.

John only let her sleep a couple of hours and then made her get back on her horse. They rode all the next day and then the next morning found them a few miles out of Granberry. They had asked directions from a family in a wagon they had come up on.

As Mary Belle came up next to Red he said, "This is where we part company. Good luck. Give me the mule lead."

"Aren't you going to take me into town and get me on the stage?"

"No, I am leaving you right now." He took the mule lead and turned away.

"You are not much of a gentleman," she yelled at his back."

John turned and yelled at her, "You aren't much of a lady either."

Then Red and the mules just vanished into the woods, like they had never been there.

"Belle straightened in her saddle. "I don't need you anyway." She then trotted down the road to her new life."

SIX

John and the mules had learned a few lessons from Eb, Mike and Henry. He quickly backtracked a few miles and then headed west. He could only think about his friends. And friends they had become and he could not bear to think anything bad would happen to them. He stayed off the main trails but had to stay close enough to find his way. He kept riding west and a little north as Eb had told him. Since they had left the big mountains, the country had flattened out some and was mostly hills and valleys with lots of trees. He did not know the names of all of them but he soon could tell the difference one from the other. He wished for a book from The Man's library to tell him what they all were. He had only seen a couple of old mountain men and only one had shared his campfire one night. When John awoke he was gone. John realized that he was an honest man or he would have taken every horse and mule and packs that he had. He said a little prayer of thanks to the Lord and decided not to be so trusting in the future.

As he rode along he spent most of his time worrying about his friends. Did they get out or were all of them in jail now? He was deep in thought and when he looked up he was surrounded by Indians. How stupid could he be? They motioned and he followed. He did not recognize any of their signs on their clothes or faces. I hope they are friendly he prayed.

They rode the rest of the day and into the night, arriving at their camp after dark. He was motioned to get down from Red. Then they unpacked his packs and unsaddled his horse and the mules and led them away. He started to protest but decided this was not the time. They were still communicating with sign language, some of which John had learned from Talking Wolf. They were surprised when he signed a little and they laughed.

Soon he was directed to a campfire where an old Indian woman gave him some kind of soup and some dried meat to eat. There was some kind of watery liquid to drink that was almost like peach cider and maybe it was John decided. After he ate he was given his blankets and left by the fire. The Indians all went to their tepees and didn't leave any guard on him. I will just get my horse and go John thought.

So he waited for what he felt was a sufficient amount of time and rose up and started to walk toward the way they had carried Red. He had only gone a few steps when he stumbled and his legs were too wobbly for him to continue. So he crawled back to his blanket and seemed to pass out. The next morning found him staring up at several Indian children who were looking him over and giggling. He sat up but nearly passed out again with the worst hangover he had ever had. He had to hold his head with both hands to keep it on. The kids kept giggling and pointing until an adult Indian Brave pushed them aside and sent them away. He looked down at John and just shook his head. He bent over and tied John's hands together. And then left. The children came back later to touch him but not any ugly stuff. They had never seen a white person before. They were not sure if he was man or animal.

John stayed this way for about a week. He would walk over and see Red grazing with the other horses, and much to John's surprise bred a few. The Indians would have a bred bunch of colts in the spring. One other night John decided to try and slip away but the same brave that had tied his hands walked out of the darkness and carefully put him back by his fire. John was fed good and had plenty of water. Once another brave took him down to the river and with motions made John know that he stunk and so he bathed in the river. When he came out of the water there were clean buckskin clothes for him to wear and his old ones were gone. Later he would get them back cleaned and folded neatly. Unknown to him the young squaw that took his dirty ones and washed them was made fun of for days. John learned that these were a fun loving people. They laughed a lot and the kids were just like kids when he was growing up. They had some kind of games they played with sticks and the young boys were always playing "war". He supposed with a white man.

The fifth day there he saw a young brave come loping in and go to the large tent on the side. He went inside and then came out with the Chief. John supposed that he was the Chief as he had more head feathers and was old. They walked over to John and John struggled to his feet.

The young brave in clear English said, "We will take you to town and you will be traded for one of ours that they have in the iron house. We will ride at daybreak. If you try to get away we will kill you. And then they all walked away and life returned to the same as before."

Sure enough the next morning just as the sun came up John was put on Red and two braves joined the first one and they were off. It was almost noon when they reached a town. It was mostly just like all the others that John and the others had passed through with the exception that this was a fort. A military fort. With soldiers and a high fence built around it. The town had grown up around it. They passed a saloon, mercantile and a school and Church and then entered the stockade into the center of the Fort. Around the perimeter of the Fort were buildings with different uses. There was storage for food and supplies. A place for guns and ammo and tack for their horses and mules, and a blacksmith shop across from it. One side had a row of pens for horses and mules. Straight in front was one whole wall that was barracks and in the center was a main building. The Indians drug him down off Red and into the main building.

Military men in fancy uniforms were waiting in the main room. One came forward and introduced himself as Lt. Carlton Stone. Lt. Stone then ask the Indians to untie John's hands.

This done John shook the Lt.'s hand. The Indian then ask Stone for his brave in the lockup.

Lt. Stone told one of his men to go and get the brave.

"Have you been treated well?" Lt Stone ask John.

"Yes they have not bothered me."

"And did you get to bring your horse?"

"Yes I thought that was . . ." Lt Stone butted in. "Good that is what we ask for."

The brave brought in was filthy and stunk. Even his own made faces with their expressions of disgust.

"This is our bargain and here he is. But I do not want him in the town again buying whiskey and getting drunk. Next time I will not be able to give him back." Lt. Stone told the braves.

Nodding in agreement they took their brave and quickly left. Red was left tied to the hitchin' post as John quickly went to the door and checked. Now, John had ridden in clean and clothed with clean new buckskin that made the military men leery of him. The Lt. especially wanted to know how he was so clean and had new clothes.

"The Indians are very clean people and they said that I stunk so I was bathed and new clothes were provided. I was fed well and no one bothered me while I was there."

"Do you know these Indians?" Stone asked.

"No sir never saw them before."

"Where did you get the big Red horse you came in on? Steal it somewhere?"

So here we go again John thought. "It's a long story and I am really tired can I rest somewhere for a while and can I have some liniment for my wrists where they were tied."

"Sure Sgt Main take this man, what was your name?" "John Dunn"

"Take John Dunn and find him some quarters and let him rest."

After John had left the Lt. and the Captain Miles Cork exchanged glances. They then went into Lt. Stone office. "Where do you think he got that blooded horse?" The Lt. spoke first.

"No telling but he probably doesn't have any papers for him." Captain Cork answered.

"Send a runner to Memphis asking if he is wanted or something. Something here doesn't add up. First he is treated well by those savages and then rides in here like he is somebody on a horse he would never have the money for. No sir, I don't believe a word of it. But it will be entertaining to hear his story."

Even though John had been treated well, after that first night of sleeping off his drink he had not closed his eyes much so when he was shown to a cot he fell in it and slept like a log the rest of the day. When the Lt. asked about him all he heard was he is sound asleep. Even though John was dressed from head to his boots in Indian buckskin, there was no mistaking him for a brave. His hair had bleached out some but still was a sandy red color. He was tanned from all the traveling and muscled up considerably.

After a meal with the other soldiers John went back to the Lt.'s office to tell his tale once more. As he told the whole story he could tell by the looks on the Lt. and Capt.'s faces, they didn't believe a word of it. And John was thinking that I wouldn't have either had anyone told it to me.

"You just rest up a few days here with us and maybe your friends will catch up to you."

John spent the next few days just eating and sleeping. They had let him keep his cot and he ate in the mess with the soldiers. The sergeant of the company kept trying to get John to join the army with them. During the day the soldiers would practice riding in formation and drilling even on foot. Then about once a week they would ride out to scout for Indian trouble. As far as John could see the only Indian trouble they had they stirred up themselves. He made a trip or two into town to look around. Since the army was feeding him he did not spend his money at the saloon or eating place. He did buy himself some sticks of candy one day in the mercantile store.

He had been at the Fort for about two weeks. Worrying himself sick over his friends and wondering about Mary Belle if she got on a stage east. He had just walked out into the courtyard when the Lt. called to him from his office.

"Hey, John. Come in we need to talk to you."

John walked into his office and there sat the Capt.

"When you first came here and told us the story about the bred horse we didn't believe you and we now know why. I sent a note out to see if you were wanted or anything and sure enough we got the letter back today. It says here that you are wanted for horse thieving, slave stealing and one place says that you abducted a young lady and carried her off. And John, her Daddy a preacher?"

"Now these stories and your story all match except they seem to be on opposite sides of the fence. Where is the young lady now?"

"She was left at the edge of Granberry to get on a stage east. I then came this way. That was about a week before I got here. And she was caught with her boyfriend and her clothes and wild hair was from the Preacher beating her. She had to get away from there and I guess the boyfriend was too afraid of the Preacher to take her away. The Preacher fingered us as the ones that had spent the night with her. The deputy that came to our camp believed us but said the Preacher said he had to bring us in. So the rest of my group went to town. That is when they put Mike in jail.

I took Mary Belle to Granberry and came here like I told you before."

The Lt. had also sent inquiries about the town that John said all this happened at. His reply had come in the same mail. It backed up John's story. The town was run by the Preacher and his friend had been in jail. During the night after the friends had gone back to town they had broken Mike out of jail by pulling out the window of the jail wall and they were on the run. The town folks were scared of the Preacher and would do anything to keep him happy. They had trailed the "outlaws" for several days but then lost them somewhere back on the mountain. The Preacher and the others had returned to town but wanted posters were enclosed in the mailing.

The Lt. handed John the letter and the posters. John turned pale.

"Oh no! Now my friends are in trouble and not of their own making. What a mess! If that darn gal had told the truth none of this would have happened."

"Well, it did happen and now I have to deal with it since you are here. John Dunn I am putting you under house arrest. That means that you can't leave here without getting into trouble with me. You can go to town and here in the Fort until I decide what to do with you. I figure that it will be about two weeks before your friends will arrive here, and then we will see what will happen. If you try to leave the area we will hunt you down and you will be put in the stockade and I will send word to these people that want you to come get you. Do you understand?"

"Yes sir. I am not going anywhere like you said." The Sergeant laughed when he arrived back at the barracks. "You are still alive I see. I should have told you that the Lt. is a fair man and we have served with him for a long time. He will do right by you, but don't cross him. He will bring the whip down on you."

So John spent his days like before just sort of wandering around. He began visiting the blacksmith where he found his making things with the hot hammered iron fascinating. About the third day of his hanging on at the shop the blacksmith ask him to hand him some iron. This turned into a daily thing of John helping him out. He would show up early and light the fire and set out the tools the "smithy" needed. He would help clean up at the end of the day. The Smithy was a large man. And from hammering the iron everyday he had muscles on his arms the likes John had never seen. But he was also a quiet and gentle man. When he worked with horses, fitting their hooves with new shoes he was gentle handling them and they seem to understand and stood for him. Most of the time but a few times they would get one that evidently had had a bad experience with having their hooves trimmed and they would have to rig a rope to hold his foot to keep him from kicking them.

One day when they were not particularly busy, the Smithy told John to fetch Red. This he did. Now John had pulled Red's shoes a long time ago and not having any tools and no knowledge of how to use them, Red's feet were not in good shape. The Smithy quickly went to work first cleaning out the frog of the hoof and then filing off the overgrown hooves. He then measured a horse shoe and began working on making a pair of shoes to fit his big feet. Red was a little scared of the big man, but he had had shoes put on since he was a colt and did not resist much. And John stood at his head speaking softly to assure him that everything would be alright. When the shoes were on, John held out all the money he had, which was not much, to pay the Smithy.

"Keep your money. The work you have done around here helping me is pay enough.

Today we have some real work to do. We are going to fix a wagon wheel. And you can start by making some of the spokes." John was excited about finally being able to see if he could wield the big hammer. After several bad tries that the Smithy patiently redid, he finally got one spoke straight enough to be put on the wheel. "Ok now that you can do it I need you to make about fifteen of them from that pile of cast off over in the corner. That way I will have some made up ahead of time."

So John spent the next few days working over the fire. He would melt the cast off material and then mold it in the molds that the Smithy already had made. Then he would take the spoke out of the mold and heat it and hammer it to a correct size and would file off all the edges to make them all the same. He found that he was finishing work, eating supper and falling into the bed really tired. But he slept like a log and the waiting was not as hard.

SEVEN

During the night about two weeks later the Sergeant woke him up.

"You have company in town. The old miner and your other friends were asking about you in the saloon tonight. I didn't say anything to them and neither did my buddies cause we didn't know if you wanted them to know you were here or not. They are camped about a mile south of here. What do you want to do? Do you want some of us to ride out with you? They are pretty wild looking ones."

John was pulling on his pants and boots as he talked.

"Oh yes I want to see them. And thank you for everything but I will be fine." He grabbed up what little things he had and ran for the stables. He quickly saddled Red and walked out of the fort and then jumping into the saddle he was away to see his friends. It did not take him but about half an hour to see the camp fire. He circled to make sure it was them and then called out.

He rode into the camp and was quickly pulled off Red by Mike and given a big hug. The others gathered round patting and all talking at the same time. After they had unsaddled Red and tethered him with the other horses, they sat down around the fire to catch up on the last few weeks apart.

John started with, "How did you all get out of the Preacher mess?" They all begin to laugh. Then Henry started. "We rode in to town and went to the Sheriff's office to check on Mike. Only we were told that Mike was not there."

"Where was he?"

"They had let him loose the day before and they didn't know where he was." So we started looking for him. We found him alright; at the saloon drunker than a skunk. He couldn't tell us what happened but the bar keep came over and told us. The bar keep said that the day after they put him in jail the Preacher was ranting and raving about hanging him up. Then the circuit judge showed up unexpectedly and said there would be a trial. So the next day they were gathering in the saloon that had been cleared out for the occasion. Of course everyone in town was there. They were seated in all the chairs that had been lined up like a courtroom. There was people all along the railing upstairs and even kids were sitting on the steps to the second floor. Some had never seen so much excitement in their lives. Three tables had been put up at the front, one for the judge and one for the defendant and the other for the sheriff. The Judge gaveled the room into order. It took several banging with the gavel and some shouting but soon the room got quiet.

The Judge then told them that the court was in session. It was the state against Mike, for breaking the law, for molesting Mary Belle. He then told the Sheriff to give the particulars of the case. The Sheriff said, "Give what sir?"

"Oh, Sheriff tell us what happened."

"Oh, okay. The Preacher came in my office all riled up yelling that someone had molested Mary Belle and he wanted someone arrested for it. He said it must have been those new men that were camping down by the creek because that is where he found her."

"Preacher you can have your say."

"It was way past dark and Mary Bell did not come home so I went to look for her.

I found her in the woods behind our house with all her dress tore and her hair all in a mess with leaves and grass in it. And she was crying and begging me to take her home and get the ones that did this to her. After I had put her to bed I saddled my horse and came straight to town and went to the Sheriff's office. He got a posse together and they went out and got that man (pointing to Mike) and brought him in."

The old Judge had been a judge a long time and he felt something was not right in all of this. So he asked for one of the posse to come forward and testify. "Did you go out to these fellers camp?"

"Yes I did."

"Did they know anything about someone bothering this young lady?"

"Yes they did. They said that right after dark they heard some screaming and at first thought it was a mountain lion. Then their old trapper said it didn't sound like any cat he had ever heard. Then they decided it was a girl screaming. But by the time they made up their minds to go see about it, it stopped. And not knowing the country they did not venture out in the woods."

"What else did they say?" The judge had leaned down on the table and looked right at him.

"They claimed that they had all been there together all night and none of them even knew the Preacher's daughter. So we told them they had to come to town and we would get this straightened out."

"And did they come to town willingly?"

"Yes sir! They rode along with us and came right on into town."

"And what happened next?"

"We took them to the Sheriff and the Preacher was there all screaming and yelling that we should just string them up right there. Then he could not tell the Sheriff which one if the men it was, so one of them volunteered to stay until it was straightened out. The others were told to go back to camp and stay there until we could figure this mess out. So we put this one here in jail and the others went back to camp like they was told."

The Judge then was looking all around the courtroom. He then turned to the Preacher and asked, "Where is your daughter?"

"Uh, I don't rightly know."

"What do you mean you don't rightly know?"

"When I went in to get her this morning she wasn't there. And many of her clothes were gone. I guess she left when I came to town. I am sure she has gone to a friend's house because she can't handle all the talk about here that is going around."

The crowd then started talking and the Judge had to gavel again to get it quiet again.

"Is that all you have to say Sheriff?" the judge turned to the other table.

"I guess so."

"Ok defendant, come up here and sit in this chair and tell me what you know about all this." Mike took off his hat and ran his fingers through his hair and then took the chair next to the Judge's table.

"We were just sitting around camp having eaten our vittles for the night, when we heard this awful screaming down the creek we were camping by. Eb told us that it wasn't a cat sounded like a person. By the time we decided to go see about it the sound stopped. Since we were not from here we didn't know what to do. So we just settled back down. We decided that we would have a look around when the sun came up. It was a while before the posse and the Sheriff came riding in all stirred up about the Preacher's daughter. We tried to explain to them we did not have anything to do with any of this and we were wondering ourselves what to do about the screaming that we had heard. And then we came to town like the posse man said and you know the rest."

The courtroom became very loud with all the people talking and yelling that he was a liar.

After banging the gavel again for order, the Judge looked around the room and said, "Does anyone else have anything to say in this manner?"

Henry stood up. The Judge motioned to him to come to the front of the room and take the chair. The Judge said to him, you are a big one aren't you? "Yes sir, "Henry replied.

"Now tell us what else you know about this mess."

Eb had eased down the aisle and was standing near Mike's chair. The Judge noticed him and asked him what he wanted. Eb said that he also was there and was another witness for Mike.

"Ok take a seat, give him a chair somebody, and we will get to you next."

So that taken care of the Judge turned back to Henry.

"Ok big feller give us your story on this."

"Most of what you already heard is about like it happened. We left Mike in jail and we went back to our camp."

The Preacher jumped up and interrupted by yelling, "What do we want to know about what they did when they went back to camp. We have the man and I say we string him up."

The Judge's face was very angry when he turned to the Preacher.

"If you interrupt my court again I will hold you in contempt and you will be in jail. Now sit down and shut up." The Preacher sat back down but everyone could tell he was not used to being told what to do. The Judge again turned to Henry.

"Now man what does your going back to camp have to do with anything?"

"We had just made our fire back up and were sitting around discussing what we should do about Mike when this horse came right into camp with a young woman we had never seen before on him. She was all agitated and her hair was all over the place. She told us right away that she was Mary Belle Hawthorne and we had to help her get away from the Preacher.

The Preacher jumped up again out of his chair. He was yelling that it was all lies and he had not done anything wrong. Judge after telling the Preacher again to sit down, then ask Henry to continue.

"She said that indeed it was her screaming, but she was trying to get away from the Preacher that he was the one trying to molest her." When Henry said that, the Preacher jumped up again and made for the door. The Judge told one of the deputies to not let him out. And he was dragged back to his chair and pushed back down in it. Again he banged his gun butt on the table like a gavel and yell for everyone to shut up.

Then he nodded to Henry to continue.

"She said that he had tried before and she had to lock and put something against her door at night she was so afraid of him."

"So where is she now?"

"We didn't know what to do. We had already figured out that this Preacher as he calls himself runs this town and the Sheriff so it wouldn't do us any good to come in here and complain and we were afraid to bring her in her for him to get his hands on her again. She said that she wanted to go to the next town and get on a train back East. So amongst us we decided that John would take the girl to the train and we would come back in here and figure out how to get Mike out of this mess. So far as we know she went and got on the train and we are to meet up with John farther west."

The Judge said that he would take some time to make his ruling. So court was adjourned, but when the Preacher and the Sheriff got up to leave, the Judge called the Sheriff over and told him to arrest the Preacher and throw him in jail.

"Everyone went to eat. We got some food and took it to Mike and we sat in the jail with him just waiting." Henry turned to John.

"Soon one of the deputies came in to get Mike and told us the Judge was back in the courtroom."

When everyone had settled down again and the Judge had called the room to order, he began to talk.

"I have made a careful study of this case. And according to the law there has not been any law broken because the young lady did not come in and make a complaint. Most of the testimony here today is each ones account of what happened. I don't even know if that John kid ran off with Mary Belle or not. But according to the law Mike is not guilty of anything. And as to the Preacher, I believe that the citizens of this town would be better served if they ran him out of town and told him not to come back! Court is adjourned!"

And the gavel came down and we all hooped and hollered.

"We had packed up camp that morning so soon as we could get through the crowd we lit out of there and we have been looking for you ever since. And since you had all the packs we have had pretty poor camping with no supplies!!" Eb explained.

"I will go get them right now!" And John did.

He rode quickly back to the fort and gathered the mules and packs and came right back to the camp. He had stopped by the mess and the cook had given him some left overs and they all ate and just kept smiling at each other. It was great to be back together again. Then John had to tell them that he was in house arrest for the horse stealing. Well that did it. They quickly packed the mules, killed the camp fire and headed out. Outlaws again!

EIGHT

John could not remember them even discussing going back and trying to convince the military at the Fort that he was innocent. Mainly because they all knew that he had no evidence to show that the horse was his and he had no money, no letter from The Man, no birth certificate showing that he was from overseas . . . . nothing. The friends did not even stop worry about their own part in this escape. They just acted. Soon as they were packed they followed Eb into the creek they were camped by. Staying in the creek they headed north after many miles the creek took an eastern turn and Eb turned west and up out of the creek. They continued west for several more hours. Although they had traveled down out of the big mountains, there were still smaller mountains and this is where Eb headed. These mountains did not have a tree line. The trees continue up to the top of the mountains. This would give them a lot of cover as they continued west.

It was the middle of the next morning before the Lt. became aware that John Dunn had not come into the fort for the night. He sent several soldiers into the town and other looked around the fort. They all had the same story. No John Dunn anywhere. That was when he learned that John's friends were camped on the nearby creek the night before. And he had no trouble figuring out that is where John was. So he sent the Sgt. out to get John. He was soon back with the news that the camp was cold for several hours and they were gone. No tracks . . . . nothing. The men and the Sgt. had ridden both sides of the creek for several miles and found no tracks. They turned back to the fort. The Lt. was livid when they came back and said they were gone. "Are you telling me that four horses and two pack mules left no tracks? What is wrong with you people?"

He then called out his Captain and told him to get a group together and he expected him to have John Dunn and his co-conspirators back at the fort by the end of the day. So Captain Cork, one Indian tracker and 16 troopers set out to find John Dunn.

John and the group had only stopped long enough to rest and take a little food and water and then continued to ride. Eb was still leading the front and Henry bringing up the rear with John and Mike in the middle leading the pack mules. Eb knew that with the mules in the middle the horse tracks would mess the track enough to maybe cover up the mule print. Mule shoes are bigger and a different oval than a horse and are easily tracked by a good tracker. They stopped the next night and slept for a couple of hours and then continue up the mountain. They continued this for the next couple of days.

The Captain and his troop were doing the same only nearly a day behind. The tracker had met John Dunn and thought he was a true man as he called him. He slowed the troops the best he could, knowing that he was giving John a little time but not much, he didn't want to lose his job.

Then on the fourth day again some Indians unknowingly intervened in John Dunn's life. John and the men had crawled out on an outcropping to see if they could see the troops below them. They were not hard to spot. They rode in a formation and stirred up quite a bit of dust. Henry was the first to see the hunting party coming up on the troop's left. The Indians had seen the troops and were just trailing along parallel to them. There was about twice as many Indians as there were troops. As Mike and the rest of the bunch watched the Indians did a strange thing. They turned toward the soldiers and ran right at them. The troops were strung out in a line, riding two abreast and the Indians ran right into them. Causing a lot of confusion and separating the troops from each other and the Captain. The Indians did not attack anyone they just ran on through and of course the Capt. quickly got the troops back in formation and away they raced after the Indians. The last John saw of them was some dust way in the distance across the canyon. Eb soon took advantage of this incident. Jumping in their saddles away they went in the opposite direction. They were pretty sure that the troops would not come back looking for them. Although they rode another night and cold food, they felt good enough the next day to stop and make a small camp with a fire and cooked some deer meat off a deer that Henry had shot that afternoon.

Discussion was about the surprise of the Indians showing up. John wanted to know what they all thought happened when the troops lit out after them. Eb soon spoke up.

"I figure that that little band led those troops right into a big bunch of Indians and I don't think any of them went home tonight."

John thought about that and was very sorry for the troops even though they had been chasing him just the day before. "Should we have gone to help them?"

Eb said, "If we had we would all be dead just like them. The troops will never get the Indians until they start to think like one and act like one."

That night they took turns keeping watch. It felt really good to sleep on their bedrolls and not in a saddle. In fact Mike took the last watch and the sun was up in the sky when he finally kicked them awake. He already had breakfast cooked and it smelled so good. It was biscuits and deer meat and hot coffee. While they were all finishing up their food, the conversation turned to what they were going to do now. The map that they had gotten from the Preacher of homesteads was no good to them now. They were a long way from that area anymore. John told them that he didn't know for sure but he thought they had just been chased out of the last fort on the western frontier as it was known. So from now on they were on their own.

And Henry laughed and said, "We don't even know who owns this country now. It might not even be part of the United States."

Mike spoke up, "I don't care what country it is. I think we ride about another week and then find us our own homestead."

Everyone agreed and so they pack up and headed out to find their own homestead. Still heading north and west they rode into the country that would someday be Indiana. It was just about a week when they rode over a small hill and looked down into a big wide valley. When they rode down into the flat country, a big wide stream was running through the whole valley. Mike stopped and stood up in his saddle.

"What do you all think? Isn't this the right place for us?" They all agreed and rode on up into the other end of the valley and made them a camp.

The next morning they gathered around Mike as he looked over the map the Preacher had given them. He had just discovered that it showed the outposts and forts even in country that was Indian lands. He had decided that another Fort was about three days ride north east of where they were. In discussion around the fire last night they had decided that they needed some tools if they were going to try to build some kind of shelter before winter set in. And since they had traveled quite a distance north they knew they would have snow and ice so shelters for them and the animals had to get built. Soon as they decided on what they needed Eb volunteered to be the one to go to town. He wisely had insisted that they keep all their hides they had saved from the animals they had killed on the trip. So they packed all the hides on the mule and Eb started off. No one would suspect an old trapper to have anything to do with John, they hoped. While he was gone they would hunt and fish and try to get some meat salted down for the winter also. It was now July and they knew they didn't have much time. They had one small ax and they cut large saplings with it and used some of the vines that they found growing to soon build a small pen for the animals and at least a lean to for them to get under. As they hunted game Mike would make jerky out of it. They could smell it for quite a ways and hoped he didn't get eaten by a bear or something.

It took Eb better part of a week to get to the Fort. He straggled in trying his best to look bad. And he did smell since he had purposely not bathed in four days. His first stop was the saloon for a drink. He then asked about a store and was sent to the mercantile a few more doors down. He rode on down and went inside.

"I have a few hides to sell."

The owner looked at him and to get rid of him because he stunk he agreed to barter for them. He would tell him how much he would give him for the hides and he could use that for credit at the store. They went out and the owner gave him a price. And Eb was delighted as it was more than they usually received for them. So he then went back into the store and started on the list that Mike and the others had sent him. He was able to get two axes and then some salt, beans, flour, sugar, and coffee. While he was in the store he heard baby chickens.

"You have baby chickens?"

"Yes, I have four left in the back. And old woman brought them in for trade. I buy eggs from here so I took the chicks."

"How much?" Eb asked.

"How much for what? The Chicks?"

"You can have them. I am tired of listening to them. I will even throw in the little cage if you can carry it. I will be glad to get rid of the stinking things." As he spoke he was thinking *and get rid of you, you smell as bad as the chicks.*

As Eb was leaving the store he saw some vegetable seeds. "Do I have enough for some of those seeds?"

"Yes take you some." So Eb took some corn and bean seeds.

Then Eb packed the mule with the supplies and after he had mounted his horse the owner handed him the small cage with four little chicks in it. Eb smiled to himself as he rode out of town. He then realized that he must have lost his mind. Did he think he was going to settle down with those four coyotes he had running with? He had never had a permanent home since he was a teenager. His dad had died and he had moved on to make one less mouth for his mother to feed. He heard a few years ago that she had passed but had no idea about any of his siblings. But having a home might not be too bad. It would be a place to come back to when he was not trapping. And he had four chickens. He had never owned anything but a mule and he grinned as he stuck on of his fingers through the cage and one came up to peck on him. At night he sat the cage on the ground where the little chicks could find seeds in the grass to eat. One day he caught them some grasshoppers and another day a grub. When he lay down to sleep he put the cage right next to him with his wrap over the cage to keep them warm.

While Eb had been gone the others had been hunting. One day when Henry and John returned to camp with a big deer, they saw Mike walking up and down and then turning and walking another direction.

"Maybe he has lost something," John said.

Henry said, "Looks like he has lost something all right, his mind."

They rode up to camp and called out to Mike, who came down from where he was and told them excitedly that he had been planning the house. "Come and see."

They went a ways away and up a little from the creek. "I figured that when the snow melts that this creek will get a lot bigger so we had better build up a ways. He had marked off the house with rocks from the creek. He had made a large room and then two smaller rooms.

"There are four of us. Can't we each have our own room?" Henry asked.

"Of course! The other two will be upstairs.

"A two story house?"

"Yes. Look here is the kitchen and the fireplace". And he continued to walk and show them where everything was. He was so excited! Then he took them outside to some more rocks a little ways away. "And here is the barn and a corral." They were very impressed and liked the way he had it laid out.

They then skinned the deer and Mike started cooking the meat. "I will sure be glad to see ole Eb. Maybe we can have something besides meat to eat. "Oh that reminds me. I found some plums today while you were gone." He took them over to see plums boiling a pan on the fire.

"When we get the bread made we can have something sweet. Eb better get here soon. That is the last of the flour."

The bread always smelled good when it cooked. When it was done the three of them had bread, meat and the wonderful plums. Henry smeared the plums and juice all over his bread. When he looked up John and Mike were laughing. He had plum juice all in his beard. It felt good to laugh; they hadn't had time to do much of it.

It was two more days before they heard Eb coming, He was singing and as they neared the other horses the mules began braying. They gathered around him and stood silent as they realized he had something in a little cage. "Well, don't just stand there take this cage." John stepped up and took the little cage with the fuzzy yellow chicks in it. "These are too little to eat."

"They are not for eating. They are for eggs and raising some more chickens you fool."

Henry and Mike took the pack mule and started unpacking the supplies. John then put the little chicks down by the fire and took the mule and Eb's unsaddled horse out to graze with the rest of the horses.

"Whoa! said Mike. "What is this corn seed and beans? Are we becoming farmers? I thought we were going to raise horses and cows."

"I thought we might want something else to eat," Eb shot back. Eb then settled down by the fire and Mike handed him a plate of meat and plums. "Where did you get these?"

"I found them down by the south end of the creek. And there are lots more. If we had any jars we could have put some up for the winter, but that is another time."

"While you were in town did you hear anything about us?" John quickly wanted to know.

"No one said much of anything. I just got what I needed and got the Hell out of there!"

That night they slept again out in the open around the campfire. Eb and the chicks were under his blanket. The next morning Eb was taken on the tour of the new house and barn. He laughed aloud. They all looked at him.

"Do we all remember how to live in a house?" They others joined him in a laugh. And then they all patted each other on the back. It felt good to be together today.

The rest of the day they started cutting more saplings for the horse pen. They had decided that since they didn't have a lot of time, they would build the barn first and live in it while they built the house. The next day they started falling larger trees for the walls of the barn. They notched the ends of the logs so they would fit snug together at the corners. It took them the better part of two weeks working from dawn to dusk to get the walls up. Since they had no help they had to make the roof beams one at a time and using the horses to help pull they put them up one at a time. After they were up smaller logs were laid cross them for the roof. Mike made brought mud from the creek bed and they packed it into the cracks all around and on the roof. Then they covered the roof with sod from around the valley floor. The barn had one large opening in the loft area and a big door on each end of the lower floor. One of the doors faced toward where the house would be and the other would go out into a pen for the animals.

Inside they made a couple of stalls on each side and one area for all their saddles and tack. Eb was smelling the wind one day and he told them that winter was coming. He told them that they had better put the house off until the next spring or get what they could built but he didn't think they would get it finished before the first snow fall. He also suggested that they go out and cut some grass and store it up in the loft for the horses to eat when winter came. They had found a valley just over a small hill that was waist deep in grass. So the next day they started cutting grass with their hunting knives. They then left it a few days to dry out. When they went back they would cut a bundle and then John would come along and tie it with vines they had found near the Plums. They would then put them on a contraption they had fashioned out of two poles and dragged it behind one of the mules. They then took it back and stacked it in the loft of the barn. John would stand in the opening and they would tie it on a rope and John would pull it up. After about a week they had the barn loft nearly full.

They then turned their attention to meat for the winter in earnest. They hunted, salted the meat, and buried the hides to cure. While they were busy working, the chicks were busy growing. They fed themselves on bugs and seeds around the barn. At night they roosted on one of the beams of the loft. In the morning one started crowing just about dawn. So they had one rooster!

Since they had no jars, Mike took to picking the plums, cooking them and then setting them out and drying them. He then packed them in deer hide.

John and Mike had chosen to sleep in the loft on some of the grass hay. Eb and Henry slept on the bottom floor. The rooster had crowed several times when John stood up and looked out the loft door. He couldn't believe his eyes.

He called to Mike, "Come quick!"

At the other end of the creek just where the bend turned right and continued on its way was a herd of horses! John counted about 20! Mike and he stood in wonderment. Then they heard Red. And about that time they saw him. A magnificent black stallion. He came down to get a drink but had spooked when Red made his noise. He quickly came to the front of the herd and then shook his mane. He then turned and galloped away taking all his mares with him. Eb and Henry had been looking at them from the door below.

"Wow, I guess that answers where we are going to get our mares from for our herd." Mike said.

"Yes but I don't think he is going to just give them to us." Eb added.

NINE

Days passed and turned into weeks. Every day the wind was a little cooler. Although the logs were cut for most of the house, it would not get finished until next spring. So they decided to make the barn as warm and comfortable as they could. They closed in one of the stalls with a second wall inside to keep some of the cold out. The chickens were already up and pecking away in the barn and outside. They had a permanent chicken coop that they slept in during the night. Eb was sure to put it in the barn before he went to bed.

The next day as they stopped to rest, Eb told Mike that he thought they should get busy and go to town and claim their homestead with some legal papers.

"That sounds like a good idea, but we have no survey." Mike stated.

"We need to do something that shows this is our land here." Eb continued.

So it was decided that Eb and Mike would make a trip to town. The town now had a name, Rockwood. As before, it took a little over two days travel to get there. After they had wet their whistles at the saloon, they crossed the street to a lawyer's office. The lawyer was a man named Whittenburg, Joseph P. Whittenburg to be exact. Barrister Whitten burg was a short fat man. Mike decided he was round as a ball. But he was friendly and shook hands with each of the men in turn. They introduced themselves and sat down.

"We need to know how to make a legal claim on some land that we are homesteading three days ride southeast of here." Mike opened the conversation.

"That is Indian Territory and there are no claims to be made on it," replied Barrister Whittenburg.

"We know that, we just want some kind of paper that says that when it is not Indian Territory it is ours. And so others can't come squat on it in the meantime." Eb put in.

"Do you have a survey?" the lawyer asked.

"No but we put together this map the best we could." Mike spread their made up map on the desk. The Barrister looked over the map.

"This is a fairly good map. I can draw you up a paper that says that this map is a true picture of your country. But I tell you again that until that is part of the country it is not worth the paper it is written on." The barrister had stood up to look at the map.

"How long will it take you to write the paper?" Eb wanted to know.

"I can do it right now if you are not in a hurry." The lawyer stood back and looked at the pair.

"We have some errands to run so we will come back after lunch. Is that enough time?" Mike had also stood up.

"Yes that will be fine,." the lawyer said. Mike shook the lawyer's hand.

So Mike and Eb returned to the street and began looking around. Their list for supplies was small as their money was small at this point. They walked over to the mercantile store and started purchasing supplies. While they were there, a very tiny old woman came in and ordered her supplies. The merchant smiled and reminded the little lady that she would have to wait until the next day for Samuel to come unload her wagon for her.

"That is a hell of a note. Come in and spend good money and can't get the load unloaded."

Eb, always being ahead of everyone else, said "Can we be of assistance mam?"

"I need to hire someone to come home with me and put these supplies and stuff in the barn. Do you need a job?"

"Sure how far is it to your house?"

"Oh just a mile out of town." The little lady looked Eb up and down.

Eb looked over the head of the little lady and Mike nodded. They were soon out the door. Mike had Eb's horse and Eb had crawled up on the buckboard with the little lady.

"You can ride your own horse. I have been driving these mules since I was about 10 so I don't need any help now. And you stink anyway."

"Yes mam."

Eb hurried down and got his horse and they were away. She was correct; it only took them a little while to get to one of the prettiest places you had ever seen. All clean and every board painted. They quickly helped her with the things that went into the house and then they turned the wagon toward the barn. Soon as they drove up she was already opening the barn doors and they drove in. The barn was twice the size of the one they had built. All on one side was horse stalls and in them some of the best blooded horses they had seen since Red. Others were running out in the sun, exercises their long legs and their coats shown in the sun.

"Wow you sure have some fine horses here." Mike was the first to speak.

"Yes we brought the first pair with us on a ship from the old country many years ago. My man long since died and the old Stallion about a year ago. And there is no one to take my mares now so I guess the horse raising is over." The little lady looked longingly out to the mountains.

"Is there anything else we can do for you?" Eb asked. "No here is your money." She handed them some coins out of her pocket.

"Thank you for all the help. If you come back this way, come by and see me. I don't get many visitors these days."

Mike and Eb thanked her and then were on their way back to Rockwood. They were both thinking about the herd of mares and Red.

Eb said "I didn't mean to cut you off, but I thought if we wanted to introduce her to Red the best thing would be to just clean him up and just come by for a visit. And then we will see if she sees anything in him."

The Barrister had their paper all filled out. It told of the map and the dimensions as close as they could guess and named all four, Mike, Eb, Henry and John as owners. He had also made a copy for each of them. They paid him most of the money they had earned that morning. Back on the street they could hear an auctioneer down the street. They walked down to watch the sale. There were quite a few people gathered around. They were not smiling. Mike turned to an elderly man next to him.

"What is going on here?" Mike asked the nearest person.

"These people have been here a long time, but they just couldn't make it. And nearly everything they make here will go for back taxes." Was the reply from the old man with the pipe.

"Who are the couple?" Mike asked again.

The old man motioned and said "Over there, the white haired man and the big woman."

The auctioneer was taking a break when Mike approached the couple.

"Where are you planning on going from here?"

"We have no place to go." The man spoke in broken English. "We would work and my wife is a good cook but there is no jobs for us." Mike looked at Eb and Eb just smiled.

"We have jobs for you and a place for you to live. Go tell that auctioneer that the rest of the stuff is not for sale. Let the county have the country for the taxes. Get you money and come with us."

So Gertie and Joseph Berkhalter climbed in their wagon with all their stuff, along with a milk cow, a sow and 7 pigs, and one old mangy dog and they set out with Mike and Eb.

As they traveled along, Jo, as he wanted to called, told of them coming to America with a Lord from England and his family. When they got too old to work for them, they had been given money and told to go find their own way. So they had come west and found this place and bought their land. But since they were too old to farm or raise anything soon their money had to go to buy food and they had run out. Jo was not exaggerating when he said that Gertie was a good cook. Even with just the little ingredients that they had on the trail the food was great! They had told her about the plums and she proudly told them she had the jars to put them up in and many more. Some neighbor woman had died and left them to her.

The next day Eb turned in his saddle and ask Mike, "Where are they going to live?"

"We will have to make them a small cabin off the barn someway.

"And what will we pay them with?"

"I have already talked to Jo. He said that they are happy to have a place to live and food to eat so until we get some money together they want no wages. They are just happy to have a job and he smiled as he said they are happy to have a family again."

Mike laughed when they rode up to the barn the next day. The look on Henry and John's faces was priceless. But they knew not to ask any questions. Mike presented Gertie and Jo to them and introduced each man in return. Gertie gave each one a big hug. John especially turned red.

Then she turned to look around and said. "Where is the house?"

"We got here late and there is not one yet." Mike explained. "But we decided on the trail that we would add a cabin to one side of the barn for you and Jo."

Mike then proceeded to tell the others their story and how they came home with them.

There was squawking in the barn and the pigs had to be run out of the barn, as they were chasing the chickens. The new members of the group were shown around the barn and arrangements in another stable was made for Jo and Gertie until a cabin could be made for them. Gertie fixed the best supper they thought they had ever tasted. John soon was exchanging his trip experiences with them. Seems that they had about the same rough weather as he did coming over on the ship. But they did not come with a load of slaves.

That night they cooped up the chickens, put the pigs and milk cow in their stalls and all fell asleep. The next morning they awoke with the sound of Jo milking the cow. Gertie already had meat frying on the fire and biscuits made. The men jokingly told Mike that since he was no longer the cook he would have to start making a hand. After they ate, Jo helped them decide on how to use one side of the barn for a wall and then add three more for their cabin. Mike had envisioned a one room cabin. But Jo and the others soon had it one large room and two smaller ones on the side. One for a bed and the other to store groceries and supplies to get them out of the barn. Since they had learned from building the barn the cabin went up quickly. They already had the logs cut for the house so they soon had them stripped and notched and the sides went up quickly. The roof was easier too since it was just a slant off the side of the barn. They had left a hole in it for the chimney. Jo said that he could work with rock so they had gone into the hills and brought back enough rock for a large fireplace and chimney. As the others finished the building, Jo, with Gertie making the paste from mud made a sturdy and well-built fireplace and chimney. He told them that it would take several days to dry and then they would try it and see if it worked.

In the meantime the meals were great! John especially enjoyed the milk. Henry had made a trap looking thing that Gertie could put the milk in the stream near the house to keep it cool. They had decided to divert the stream to run through the house like the one they had seen before.

After they finished the cabin and Gertie and Jo moved into the cabin, the men decided to start on the house anyway. The weather was getting colder but the men were determined now to get a house up. Or part of one anyway. Gertie reminded them that the first thing was a cellar had to be dug to keep the food cold in the winter so they dug the cellar and then built the house around it. Soon the sides were up and the roof on. Jo made them a fireplace in the big room. There was lots of things needed doing to finish it but it was good enough that they moved in. When they got the money it would have real windows but for now they were covered with shutters that Jo built. He assured them they would need to be covered with tarp before the first snowfall. Each man had a room but only had their blankets. John said the he would sleep in the barn until he got a bed. The floor was too hard and the hay made a great bed. And of course unknown to the others he had slept in the hay most of his life at The Manor. It was only a few nights later that he was joined by the others; they had decided too that the hay was softer.

With all the building and moving Mike and Eb had completely forgot to tell the others about the tiny little lady and the mares. But one evening sitting around the fire they remembered as they were telling of their trip to Rockwood. They were sitting around drinking some of Gertie's great coffee. They were talking about the mares and the ole stallion. They had seen them just at sunset the night before drinking at the same place at the end of the valley. Mike suddenly sat up, "We forgot to tell you about the little old lady we met on our trip. We needed some money so we hired on to help her load her wagon and take her supplies to her place a few miles out of Rockwood. When we got there she had some of the finest brood mares we had ever seen. She told us that she had lost her husband and her stallion so she was just stuck with these mares."

"And she didn't want to breed them to some wild something over here. Although I believe that if she had seen the ole black stallion she might have changed her mind." Eb jumped in. "So we thought she ought to see Red and maybe you could make some kind of deal on the colts.

We thought if you cleaned him up real good we would go by there on our way back to Rockwood and see her. She invited us anytime. But we haven't told her about Red. We thought we would just let you, John, ride up on him and see if she sees anything in him she might like."

The others just sat there. John could not believe what they were telling him. There was a chance there were blooded mares here!

"Do we need to go before someone else comes along?" John asked.

"No there isn't anyone else around she had told us. She had put up posters and asked around and all she got was mustang half-bred horses." Mike told him.

"We don't need supplies for another week or so," Gertie spoke up.

"I guess we need to get to work," Mike said and they all followed him outside.

TEN

They were working everyday on the house in a hurry now. Once they had started it seemed they had to finish it before winter. They roof was on and after they caulked it with the mud they covered the whole thing with branches for warmth and to try and keep some of the rain and wind out. When they could afford a saw they had decided that they would try and make some real shingles for it. But this would have to do until next spring.

Inside the floors were laid and Henry had made some great cabinets for the kitchen. Mike had diverted part of the stream to run across the back porch in the trough that Jo had made out of rock. The water running through there was a pleasant sound and kept the food cold and kept the varmints out of the food. Eb built a smoke house and they all helped in smoking the meat that they hunted for. After the meat was smoked Gertie covered the pieces up in the salt sacks. And it was hung in the cellar.

In the evenings Eb had started working on his traps for the winter. He had been able to trade for some in Rockwood and Jo had brought a few. It was not near enough but would do until he could sell some hides and buy some more. He had seen plenty of sign in the valley just beyond them and the weather was turning colder everyday so the hides should set soon and the trapping could start. John had been helping him and was eager to go with him to set them out.

The first snowfall happened during the night and John couldn't get enough of it when he awoke the next morning. It was so white and made everything so clean looking. The horses seemed to get some of the excitement too as when John turned them out in the padlock they ran and bucked and seemed to know that it was a change. A few days later Eb announced that there was ice on the river so it would not be long before they could start trapping.

The house was nearly finished. Today they had made frames for beds and each one was different and suited that particular man; some longer than others. They had enough tarp left over that Henry stuffed it with hay and sewed it up and he had his first mattress. And that night he slept first in the new house. The rest continued to sleep in the barn.

The next day they set to work making a table and chairs. Again Henry knew how to put the legs on and how to make the rungs of the chairs fit in holes they made in the chair legs. The supplies from Gertie's cabin were hauled over to the big house and she told them where to put them in the supply closet. The meat now hung in the cellar along with the vegetables that had been put up jars. The little old lady had supplied them with a couple of more boxes when they came so Gertie had been busy making plum jelly that week.

They were all awaken early one morning with Henry yelling his head off back of the house away from the barn. They all scrambled into their clothes and took off running. They were just in time to see a big black bear running into the woods and Henry running after yelling like an Indian.

"He had been trying to get into the back porch." Henry said. "We will have to make the door a little stronger I think." Eb quickly said, "We need that bear hide. It will bring us a good deal of barter money."

So the bear hunt was on. As soon as they ate breakfast, John and Eb saddled up and took their guns and what little ammo they had and Eb started tracking the bear. The tracks away from the house were easy to see but the bear soon climbed into some rocks and Eb had a hard time finding his print again.

"He will be back to the house." Eb said. And they headed back toward the house. "We will have to be sure that every animal is safely inside now every night until we get him. Eb told the others. When they arrived back at the house the others had reinforced the back door.

The next day Gertie had them all digging potatoes and chopping the corn. They cut the ears off the stalks and Gertie tied them together and hung them in the supply closet. They then used the stalks to feed the pigs and horses. Beans were picked and boiled before being put in the jars and the lids sealed. The house had a wonderful smell for days when she cooked the plums and made the jelly.

John was the first to hear them. Some little squealing that he had not heard. When he lay on his belly and looked down from the loft there they were. The sow had had little ones during the night and it seemed they were everywhere. John woke the others and they all stared down at them. "She sure had a passel of them didn't she?" John spoke in wonderment. They eased themselves down the ladder as they had no idea how possessive the sow might be of the little ones. But she didn't seem to mind when John bent down and picked one of the pink wiggly things up. The piglet looked John right in the eye as if to say "Who are you picking me up like that?" John giggled to himself. He like the piglet and soon realized it was the runt or smallest of all the others. A small pen over in a corner was soon made for the little pigs and the sow; even with that they seemed to get out everywhere. For days they were underfoot, so they gave up on the pen. But every evening it was a chore to find them all and get them in the barn so old big black bear wouldn't get them.

Things seemed to be going fine, then one morning Eb said, "We have to go for supplies. Bad weather is coming and we don't know when we will get back to town. "So everyone but Henry decided to go. But first they had to get together whatever they had to barter with and they pooled all the little money that each one had. They felt bad when Gertie brought out her little stash of coins. But she declared she was part of this family now and they let her add them to the little pile of money. They decided to visit the little ole woman first and then go to Rockwood.

Jo soon had the mules hitched to the wagon and helped Gertie onto the seat. The others had put everything they had to barter in the back. Gertie was carrying some vegetables and eggs and they had several deer hides and had decided to try and sell some extra chairs they had made.

The day before John had taken Red down to the water and washed him all over until he shown in the sun. That night he cleaned his saddle real good. The next day he put on his best pants and his extra shirt that didn't yet have any holes in it. He noticed that everyone had cleaned up and put on their best. Even at that though they were a motley lot. They sure needed some way to make some money for clothes.

The wind got up during the day and it threatened rain. The blankets were not much as they slept by the fire. Gertie and Jo huddled together in the wagon. John was getting old enough to wonder about him ever having a wife and family. Didn't seem like anytime soon. He had absolutely nothing, not even a good name right now to give anyone, even if she would have him. Whoever she was.

Gertie and Jo and Eb had turned and gone into Rockwood. Mike and John continued on to the little ole ladies house. They arrived about noon time. She was out in her yard with a bucket watering some flowers in her yard. She sat the bucket down and eased over to the porch. Mike quickly realized the shotgun was probably in reach now. So he called out.

"Hello the house. It is us the ones who helped you unload the wagon a few weeks ago. You said we could come by so we have."

A wonderful smile lit up the wrinkled old face and she called for them to step down. But not before she was at John and Red's side like a flash. He didn't know how she could move that fast. John stepped down beside her as she ran her brown, wrinkly hand over Red's hip. She circled him and then opened his mouth to see how old he was. Before John could call out she lifted up one of Red's front feet and taking a piece of metal out of her pocket clean out his hoof.

Then she turned to John.

"Lizzy Farnsworth is my name. Where did you get this blooded horse? Steal it?"

"Oh no mam, he is mine, well I think he is mine." John was stuttering like he was an imbecile. Mike had tied his horse to the rail and come around.

"How are you Ms. Farnsworth?"

She then eyed him and recognized him from before. "Come in and maybe you can get your story straight about the horse."

They pulled off their boots at the door behind Ms. Lizzy who had taken hers off. They then entered the house on stocking feet. An old sheepdog raised himself up from the fireplace and came forward for a pat and then returned to his place.

"He is deaf and blind in one eye. So he ain't any good for anything. But he hangs around. So tell me about the stallion you are riding."

So John had to tell the tale again. It now seemed a long time ago that he had rode across the ocean and all the troubles they had. While he told his story she made lunch and every once in a while would mutter something but did not interrupt until he was finished.

Then she turned to Mike. 'Is all that so?'

"'Yes mam."

"'Ok I believe you." Then she sat the table and they had a nice lunch.

"Ok so since I have the blooded mares and you have that fine stallion I guess you came here to make some kind of arrangement with me after your friend here had been here." Lizzie spoke as she poured coffee for all of them.

"I thought you might like to see Red." Mike told her.

"I am happy to see your Red. And I am happy to say I would like to make an arrangement with you. I need a stallion and you seem to need mares so what can we do about that?"

John was at a loss. He didn't know how to answer.

"Speak up lad or we will never get anywhere and I have other business to tend to."

John looked at Mike who was grinning from ear to ear.

"I guess we could breed my stallion to your mares and have colts."

"And how would we pay each other?" Lizzie grinned as she looked right at John.

"How about I take some of the colts in payment." John spoke almost in a whisper.

"And what about the years after that. I am still without stallion since the colts would be kin to my mares."

"Then how about we make a yearly deal. I come down here once a year and breed your mares and then when the colts come I take some of them back." John had pushed his chair back from the table.

"Ok that sounds like a good deal to me. We will start now." So out to the padlock they gathered the mares and one by one they were bred to the stallion. It was dark when the last one was bred.

"So next time you come to town you bring your stallion so if any of the mares didn't stick this time we will try again." Lizzie reminded John.

"That we will do," John said. They returned to the house. The little Ms. Farnsworth took out a piece of paper and wrote their agreement on it and they both signed. She then made herself a copy and they signed that. And then she turned to Mike.

"I will pay you wages for helping today with the horses" and she took some money out of her pocket and paid him. Then she took out some more. "That is for John's new shirt. I will take it out on our trade next time." And as much as John wanted to go to town he didn't rightly know what to do about Red.

"And put that stallion in the far stall and take that bay mare to town. You can pick Red up tomorrow. If your story is right and I believe you, you don't need to take a chance taking that horse to this town. If anyone comes by I will tell them that I bought him somewhere."

"We will be back tomorrow. If you will give us your list I will pick up supplies for you too." Mike told her. "If that is the case take the wagon and I will make the list."

So it was dark when they entered Rockwood. Henry saw them coming down the road.

"We didn't need another wagon. Where are the horses?" They told them their story. He then showed them where they had camped right outside of town.

Next morning they filled Ms. Farnsworth's list and then bartered for their needs.

The Mercantile man then drew Mike aside and told him that if they were helping Ms. Farnsworth he would extend them some credit if they needed it for the winter as long as they promised to bring him their hides in the spring. Mike stepped back on the porch and talked to the others. They agreed since they had no money. But Eb was wise enough to say that the hides only covered the bill and they would be free to sell the others to anyone else. The old merchant saw a man who had barter before and sadly agreed. He thought he would hoodwink them into selling all their furs for just a little grub. But he didn't get too because Eb was too smart. So Gertie went back into the store and bought several things that she had not bought before because they did not have enough money. She bought material for new shirts and a few more blankets and sewing thread along with more canned beans and peaches. She also got another two cases of jars. While she was not looking John had sneaked a pretty scarf he had found in the pile.

When they were repacking the wagon the next morning for the long trip John brought the scarf out and gave it to Gertie. She started to cry. And then hugged him until he was losing his breath. "I never had a scarf so beautiful!"

"We have never had food so good." Henry chimed in.

ELEVEN

So they all, like a little parade rode back out to Ms. Farnsworth's. When they got there, they started unloading the wagon.

"Stop!" She came out of the house. "I have decided on a different arrangement."

John looked at Mike and Mike just shrugged his shoulders. "Come in the house."

So they all went into the house. She didn't take her boots off this time so they didn't either.

They all sat down. It felt like they were children and had been caught in the cookie jar.

"I am getting old and have no family. You all have a stallion and I only have mares.

I have no one to see about me here. So I propose that I go home with you. We can run our horses and I have some cattle to gather. I shall sell this place and put my money with you all."

Eb was sitting there with his mouth open. This had started out as him guiding these first two across the mountain. Then we picked up Henry. And then Gertie and Jo. And now they were going to take on this cantankerous old lady that might fall over dead on the trip home.

She had continued, "We can take all this furniture that you need and all the tack and tools. I have another old wagon behind the barn that has a cover. I already have a buyer and can get my money soon as I go to town." She then turned and went out to the barn.

Mike was the first to speak. "What does everyone think?" No one spoke. What were they to say? Eb was the first to get up. "I guess I will go see about the old wagon with the cover." Smiles broke out all around.

Mike said, "I guess I will go with her to town so she won't get swindled." Gertie and Jo said they would begin packing.

So Mike went to town with Ms. Farnsworth and the others started packing. In town Ms. Farnsworth's lawyer eyed Mike suspiciously but did not refuse to begin the paper work for the selling of her property. Then to Mike's surprise they headed down the street and walked into the Saloon. Over in one corner a large man in a dirty Stetson hat was playing cards.

Ms. Farnsworth walked right up to the table and said, "Carlisle I need to talk to you right now!"

The other people at the table quickly stepped away from the table.

"Want to sit down Lizzy?"

"No come to the lawyer's office right now." So with a lot of onlookers the three of them returned to the lawyer's office. Lizzy and Carlisle took the chairs across from the lawyer's desk and Mike started to leave when the lawyer said, "We will need a witness to all of this."

So Mike took a chair close to the door. Lawyer Burke then began.

To Mr. Carlisle Woods

Ms. Lizzy Farnsworth hereby declares her intention of taking you up on your offer to buy her property and all buildings attached hereto.

This does not include any livestock, furniture or any other property in the barn and surrounding area. It also precludes you from coming to said property until one week from today. One week from today the property will be cleared of all tangibles afore mentioned and you may take possession on that date. On that date you will deposit in Rockwood First National Bank a sum of (the lawyer then showed Mr. Carlisle the amount) and then can come here and take possession of the deed to the land.

The Lawyer then asked Mr. Carlisle if that was the agreement that he had presented to Ms. Farnsworth before. "Yes, but I assumed that the agreement we had was for the mares also."

The Lawyer repeated, "No, there is no livestock included in the sale."

"Then it should be for less money."

Lizzy then spoke for the first time. "The offer is for the land and buildings and if you don't sign and give me my money today or I will go to Mr. Davis and he will own the land."

Mike just sat watching the chain of events unfolding in from of him. The Lawyer then said, "Lizzy we had decided on a week from today to give you time to get you things moved."

"I am changing it until tomorrow. I want my money in the bank tomorrow and the papers signed today or I go see Mr. Davis." There was a loud sigh from Carlisle, but Mike saw a slight upturn to his mouth like a small smile. "Ok let me have the papers and I will go put the money in the bank right now." As he signed the papers and then handed them to Lizzy to sign, he asked,

"Where are you going with all this money?"

"No where you will have any business being around. And for the money it will remain in the bank until I decide what to do with it. Are we through here?"

"Yes, I will file the papers in the court right now." The lawyer stood up.

Mike stood and opened the door and followed Lizzy out on to the wooden sidewalk.

"As much as I would like to be at the place helping I want to make sure my money gets into that bank." She nodded at the bank across the street. She then headed that way.

She went through the bank and toward the office in the back. She then turned and motioned to Mike to follow.

"Why do I have to keep asking you to keep up?" So they went into the bank and Mike was introduced to Mr. Davis.

"Today I am expecting a large deposit. We are going to the hotel and when the deposit is made sent someone around to tell me."

"Ok. Ms. Farnsworth," the banker nodded. She then turned and went to the teller window and took out some money. Mike then followed her to the hotel. She then turned to him and handed him some bills.

"Please go buy some new clothes and get a bath and shave. Then we will have something to eat."

Doing as he was told Mike went to the mercantile and bought a new shirt and pants and underclothes. He then went to the bathe house and barbershop. When he returned to the hotel he looked like a new man. He was handsome to begin with, but the long hair and beard and many days on the trail had taken its place in wrinkles and dark tan.

While they were eating Lizzy ask Mike what else they needed.

"We need nails if there are any. And we could use some wire. And if Gertie could have some plain ticking she could make us some mattresses for our bed and we could quit sleeping in the barn."

When he had said all this, he blushed and quickly said, "I am sorry I didn't mean to go on and on. We really don't need anything we can get by on what we have."

"We will send the boy back in for the rest of the supplies," she answered without missing a beat. They did go back by the mercantile and she bought the things that he had mentioned. She also bought some ammunition and a couple of shotguns. The merchant did not say a word about what she bought. Over the years he had become accustomed to the tiny lady buying strange stuff so since she was a good customer he said nothing. He was surprised when she said that a young man would be in to get the stuff later.

Ms. Lizzy's place was not but a few miles from town so it was middle of the afternoon when they rode back. Everywhere she looked they had taken things out and had them sorted as to where they would go. Mike quickly found John and was fixing to send him back to town to get the other stuff.

"Go on that mare over there and go to the blacksmithy and see if he has another wagon and team for all this darn stuff. Here I will write a note to him." Lizzie sat down to write on the back of the wagon.

So off John went to town to get the other supplies and another wagon and team. Then Ms. Lizzy started getting the stuff that was there gone through. She quickly built a fire out in the middle of the road. She then started throwing things she did not want on the fire. As she went through the things she would tell whomever that was nearest where it came from and why she didn't want it. So after a while it was a pretty big fire. Mike had to suggest that she take a break on the porch and Gertie got her some lemonade from the kitchen. A few things Gertie had grabbed up and Lizzy let her have them. Before sundown the pile had been gone through and the fire was burning down.

John returned with a wagon and two mules and the extra supplies. He gave Lizzy the bill from the blacksmithy and she smiled. The blacksmith was an old friend of hers and her husband and he had given her the wagon and team for no cost.

Gertie had supper ready and they ate and all fell to sleep in the barn. The next morning all was spent loading the things to carry on the wagons and the livestock let out of the pens and headed for their valley. Jo led the wagons, with Gertie taking the second team and Lizzy driving the last. The others pushed the mares and livestock behind them. There were about 40 mares, 25 cows and a bull, and three goats. On one side of Lizzy's wagon were cages with chickens and in the back a small place for the old dog. No one saw Lizzy take a short peek back at what had been her home for years or the little trickle of tears that rolled down the weathered face. But then a broad smile covered all the other and she began to whistle a happy tune.

It took them an extra day to get back and Henry was ready to come looking for them. Was he surprised when three wagons and a herd of livestock came into his sight. He had his horse saddled so he rode out to meet them. The first one he came up on was Eb.

Eb said, "Just don't ask." So he rode on until he found Mike.

"It is a long story, but we now have another partner and our horse herd and some cows and Eb has some more chickens."

It was nearly dark when they got all the livestock in the pens and gathered in the house. Gertie had wanted to start supper and Lizzy jumped up to help. Soon they had the meal cooked and they sat down to eat. Lizzy gave Henry a long look and then prayed before beginning the meal. She prayed, "Thank you lord for this day and this food. Thank you for my new partners and their friendship. Thank you for everything you have given us. Amen." Everyone entered their own amen and then they ate and all fell into bed. They had moved Lizzy's bed into one of the bedrooms and she fell sound asleep in her new place.

The next day found everyone busy. Gertie sorting her supplies and getting them stored. The men were busy with the livestock and separating the horses and mules into padlocks. Lizzy just seemed to be wandering around, when Gertie saw her out a window. When Henry came by the house for a drink she told him that they should include Lizzy with their doings with the livestock.

"Oh, I am not used to having a woman helping at the barn."

"I know but that is where she is most comfortable so find her something to do."

In a little while Lizzy was back in the house rummaging through some of her sacks of things. She soon came up with a black bound book and a pencil. These she quickly took with her to the barn. When she got there she showed John the names of all the mares and their foals. John was amazed at the number of horses she had raised over the years.

"We need to write down the name of the mare and a description of what she looks like until we can get used to which is which." Lizzy told him. So with Lizzy's help, John made a separate page of each of the mares. He even drew pictures of the mares and their coloring and markings. Then on the other side of the page he had made a lineage of each of her breedings and the foals that she had. He had proudly included the dates they were bred to Red.

The next day they presented each of the mares to Red. If they were bred they would have nothing to do with him. So these were separated from the others. The ones that were not bred were bred again. Red was turned out in the big pen with the mares and soon as it was evident that one was bred, she was moved to the other pens. Soon all the mares were bred and their enterprise was on its way. A new pen had to be built on the other side of the barn for Red. He still wanted to hang out with the ladies as Lizzy put it. So he had to be moved. With pens for the milk cows, pigs, mules and donkeys, and the chicken pen between them Red began to settle back down.

Soon as the mares were taken care of the men fell in to adding on to the house for Lizzy to have a separate place and they decided to add on to Gertie's cabin also. They quickly finished another room on Gertie and Jo's cabin. Then logs were cut and hauled and in a couple of weeks Lizzy had one large room with a fireplace and a smaller room for her bedroom. The larger room had a door leading into the main room of the original house so Lizzy could come and go without having to get out into the weather.

One day Gertie and Lizzy were in the kitchen having a good laugh. They had seen one of the men (they never would tell which one) rushing to the woods pulling down his pants. That day they decided to build an "outhouse". It seemed to take a long time deciding where to put it but finally a decision was made. Now an "outhouse" is simply a deep hole in the ground with a small building built over it, with a floor and with holes in a board across it for the "seat" that was placed over a hole that went to the pit . . . But when it came winter and it was freezing cold it was as nice a place as a person could want.

And winter was coming. The next day a new layer of fine snow had fallen during the night. Not much and it had melted by mid-morning but it was a reminder that everything they needed to do better get done soon.

As the men sat down for breakfast they went over the many things still left to do to get ready for bad weather. Since they had so many mares and not enough barns, they decided to build wind breaks on one side of the paddocks. That would at least give a little buffer from the wind and blowing snow. So they spent a few days cutting and binding small trees to the north side of the paddocks. It wasn't near what they would need but it would be better than nothing. On the opposite side of the barn to the south they built more open stalls. If the mares all decided to foal at once, they would all be needed. John was well aware that some mares gave no sign of birth and you would just come out to the paddock the next day and there would be new babies. And since these were older mares they probably would not need any help, but you never knew what would be needed.

The creek running through the valley began to freeze around the banks. The snow came more often now and they had to slush around in the muddy pens to do their work.

Gertie had finished putting up all the vegetables that she could for the winter. She had dug the last of the potatoes and pulled the last of the onions that morning. She hung the onions from the rafters of the storage closet. The potatoes were taken down into the cellar to stay cold and dry. When she came up from the cellar, she took time to look around at all her handiwork. There were rows and rows of jars of vegetables. The plum jelly looked rather festive in its red jars.

Lizzy announced that Thanksgiving was three days away. The rest just grinned because they had had it about three weeks ago. But they didn't tell. Eb said he would go and try to get a turkey and the others left grinning from ear to ear. It was left to Gertie to tell Lizzy about the turkeys a few weeks ago. Eb had come in with two turkeys and they had plucked them and cooked them and declared it thanksgiving since none of them had a calendar. But now was the real thing and Lizzy made a big deal out of hanging up the calendar she had brought. She also reminded them that if Thanksgiving was three days away that meant Christmas was soon on its way!

TWELVE

Lizzy turned when she heard Gertie come through the front door. Going out she saw that Gertie had the turkey all cleaned by Eb and was basting it up to put on the spit to cook. She had rubbed the insides with the plum juice and with Lizzy's help they ran the rod through the turkey from top to bottom and then hung it back over the coals. Lizzy then attached a handle to the rod and they would take turns all day turning the turkey so it would cook all over.

Then they cleaned and put green beans in a pot to cook. Roasting ears of corn were cleaned to be added to the coals later to cook. Then they made a pumpkin pie with a pumpkin from the little garden that Eb had started months ago. His little garden had grown a lot since Gertie and Jo showed up. They both seemed to have "green thumbs". They had brought plants and seedlings when they came and all of it survived the trip and replanting. A cake made with sugary icing came next. It was going to be a Thanksgiving feast!

The men had been out all day doing their usual things. Henry had been busy working in his tool shed on a surprise, as he called it. John had exercised Red and checked on the mares. Some were already putting on a little bit of a belly. Jo and Eb decided to get more wood cut for the winter. And Mike, well, they didn't rightly know where Mike was but they were sure he was busy.

They didn't have a boss so each man just saw something that needed to be done and did it. They had kept their work up really well that way. Each of them had a certain skill and the others deferred to that one when they did anything. And all of them, without him knowing, tried to do extra work so Jo did not have as much to do. Although he never complained, they had seen him rub his hands and his back when he had worked too long. All of them had grown very attached to Gertie and Jo over the months and tried to make their lives as good as it could be with them.

Even Eb had commented that he was glad he thought to bring them here!

And Jo and Gertie thanked God every night for bringing them here. They loved the men and wasn't Lizzy a treat! They would always wonder what would have happened to them if they had been left with nothing, like was going to happen when Mike stepped in and brought them here.

Gertie had had two boys but they both died a few days after they were born. So these men were the sons she never had and she loved taking care of them.

Although John had never heard from anyone at The Manor, he had faithfully sent letters, about once a month when anyone went for supplies, but no answer came. He couldn't decide if they were mad at him or the letters just never got to them. In his latest one he had described how they had come from being just four men to a whole family now. How they had brought Lizzy and the mares and they were expecting foals in the spring and how good a cook Gertie was, and all about their buildings and land. He also added he missed them and hoped someday they could all see each other again. In his latest one he had asked Samuel if they had heard anything from his real family. His family was always in the back of his mind. It had been so long now and so much time had passed that he could hardly remember what they looked like, not that they would look like that now. The brothers and sisters would be grown now and some might even have families of their own.

Thanksgiving Day dawned clear but cold. Even though it was a holiday the milking and feeding had to be done anyway. Soon as breakfast was cleared away and cleaned up, Lizzy sat the table with some of her real china she had packed and brought with here. Gertie clapped her hands in delight to see such a service! They had real napkins and glasses to drink out of instead of tin cups. When it was near lunch the Turkey took its royal place at the head of the table on a real silver platter. When the men came in, Henry said, "Whoa, we must be in the wrong house!"

After all had settled down, Lizzy asked them to hold hands and she prayed for all the things they had to be thankful for. And then they ate until they were all stuffed. The men all went to the barn and soon all were taking a nap something they hardly ever did. John had climbed into the loft and like the others slept, content with his life and happy with his companions and especially happy with the wonderful meal.

Henry too was filled with thanksgiving for all his good fortune here. He was so happy to have a home again and people who did not judge him for his past but for what he was now. He turned over in the hay and slept easy.

Eb sat up thinking about the cold weather setting the hides. Soon maybe even before Christmas he would start his trap line. He had already been out scouting his places for the traps, by watching the tracks and signs. Although he enjoyed this settled living, the trap line called to him and he was ready to get going. And he was glad he would then be able to add some money to the till to help everyone else out. Eb had never taken credit that he had been the one to get them safely here to begin with, and blushed when he was reminded.

Supper bell called them all up again. They quickly did the evening chores and then went back to the house for great "left overs", that were just as good as lunch had been. They sat around for a while, but soon they all said good night and we out to their beds in the barn, Gertie and Jo to their cabin and Lizzy to her little corner. It had really been a Thanksgiving Day for all of them.

A few days later John, while riding Red along the creek, remembered his last Christmas at The Manor. All the good food smells and the decorations hanging everywhere. He decided that they would have a grand Christmas here too. He knew what things you needed so he secretly started getting things together. He found some berries a few weeks later when he was riding Red in the woods. He filled his saddle bag with as many as he could stuff in it. He then took them back to the barn and as the days went by he strung them on a string. The others had gotten the spirit also. Henry carved several little figurines to hang on the tree. Days before Christmas Eb and Mike had brought in a large tree and made the stand for it to stand up in the large room. Greenery was brought in and Lizzy hummed as she hung it around the fireplace and the door.

It was getting a lot colder. Lizzy wished for windows that didn't let in the cold air. At least her side of the house was on the south and she didn't get as much bad cold as the rest of it. She smiled to herself as she looked out one of the shutters. She had dreaded spending another holiday alone. She remembered the old days when she was young and the big house filled with the smells of Christmas. There was the grand staircase that they would run down to find presents all under the tree that had been left the night before by some Santa. Those relatives would be shocked to see her now, in her pants and shirt and moccasin boots. They would not even recognize me.

She had tried to keep in touch for a while, but when no correspondence came from them she just quit. That did not keep her from wondering about her older sister and were her parents still alive.

They had been so disappointed when she announced that she was coming west with her husband.

At least they had not disowned her exactly. Her father had outfitted them with their new wagon and team and her mother had helped her pack all the pretty things she had for her dowry. The day that they left her father had come up and hugged her and handed her an envelope. In it was letters of credit for money at any bank if and when she needed them, and to get back home when she decided to return. She still had the envelope and bad as some years had been it had never been used. As she was thinking about all of this, Lizzy went over and opened a different trunk than the one that had the pretty dishes in it. When she opened the lid there lay several of the prettiest dresses anyone here had ever seen. She picked the first one up and holding it up to her danced around the room. Then she decided. She would sew on it and make it fit to this old woman and wear it for Christmas. She also decided that with some of the material from another one she could make Gertie a new dress. She wanted to start tonight, but it was already dark and they tried not to use up any more candles than they needed to. So she tucked the dressed back into the trunk and after getting into bed, pulled up the many blankets and then giggled to herself like a school girl about the surprise they would get on Christmas!

In the morning Lizzy could not get enough done fast enough so she could go to her room and begin on the dresses. After lunch Gertie usually went to her own little cabin for a rest and didn't come back until time to fix supper. So after she had left, Lizzy hurried into her rooms. Closing the door she quickly took the pale yellow dress she wanted to wear out of the trunk and tried it on. Since she had no mirror she had to just adjust as it felt like it needed it. Several tucks and the hem taken up it fit quite nicely. She then took out a blue lacey dress and cutting off some of the hem she inserted that material in the sides hoping she could make it big enough for Gertie. Gertie was a little on the round side but she had hugged her that day just to get an idea of the size to make it. When she heard Gertie come in to start the evening meal, she quickly stuffed the dresses back into the trunk and went out to help.

The next day John came rushing in and called for Lizzy to come. Gertie and Lizzy went running out of the house. John pointed down the valley. There was the old black stallion and his mares watering at the end of valley just as they had been before. Lizzy clapped her hands and said, "Isn't he magnificent?"

"Yes, I believe that he is not a wild horse like the others but a blooded horse that someway has gotten away and became wild out here."

"Can we get any closer?"

"No soon as we saddle up he runs away. Some day we hope to catch him, but right now through the winter his mares need him to help them find enough food. We will take some hay down and leave it for them after they are gone."

Although they had had some snow already it was not staying and had not begun to pile up.

It was Eb that decided at breakfast that they had better make one more trip to town to get enough supplies for the rest of the winter. He could feel in his bones that winter was going to get a lot worse and they needed supplies. He also chuckled to himself as he also thought they might need to buy a few Christmas gifts!

So it was decided that Eb and Henry would go for the supplies the next day. During this day they got the wagon stocked with some food and a tarp in case the snow started on them on the way. Each person had taken one of them aside and given them a little money and instructions on what to buy for presents. Eb laughed when he heard Lizzy's request, but he took her money and added it to the others that had told him what to buy. Gertie had made him a list of food supplies and as always ask for some more jars. She also had on the list some material and the lengths that she needed. The next morning they hitched up the mules and they all stood out in front of the barn as Henry led them out on his horse. They waved goodbye and then all went back to being busy at something. John had again written to The Man and sent his letter with Eb to be mailed in the town. Lizzy had sent a letter to her lawyer and had smiled when she handed it to Eb.

Everyone was by now used to Gertie doing her work in the big house and then retiring to her own cabin that was twice as big now. It had not taken the men long to extend her little room into a large room allowing for a sitting area separate from the kitchen and dining area. It too had a large fireplace in one end. Gertie would do her work fast as she could as she was busy making something for each of the men and Lizzy for Christmas. Lizzy had given her a rug out of her big house and it covered all the area in front of the new fireplace. Henry had made her rocking chairs and a bench seat. She had made a couple of pillows stuffed with rags that matched the curtain in the window. As she sat in her rocker and looked around she was very happy with her little home and the wonderful friends they lived with. She smiled as she remembered the day that they were invited to come out here to the wilderness after their home was sold for taxes. She had her doubts and wonder if they would even live to get here, but it had turned to be a great move. And Lizzy was a wonderful little ole lady.

Some chores had to be done every day. There was milking the cows, feeding the chickens and livestock and always chopping wood. It seemed to John that it took a lot of wood chopping to keep Gertie and Lizzy's fires going. John and Mike after they finished feeding started out to cut some more logs. They were still determined to build the house into a two story with more bedrooms in the second story. They had about half of the logs for the frame cut and should the weather hold they might get the rest cut by the end of the week. They had not gone far into the woods when Mike who was in the lead motioned for John to be quiet and still. When John looked to where he was pointing, he could see the black bear digging at the base of a large tree.

He had his back to them and they were downwind from him so he was unaware of them.

Mike slowly took his rifle off his shoulder strap and knelt down. Taking careful aim he pulled the trigger and the bear took a few steps before it collapsed. Being very careful, they approached to see if he was indeed dead. Mike had reloaded his gun and poked the bear, but no response, his aim had been true. He had shot him in the neck and Eb would be very pleased that he had not ruined the hide. Using their knives they soon had his throat cut and let him "bleed out". They then quickly began gutting him. After they had cleaned him out or "field dressed" him, John went back to the barn and brought one of the pack mules to carry the bear back to the barn. Mike was careful to dig a hole and bury the guts, hoping it would not draw too many wild animals close to the house. Everyone came out to see the bear when they returned to the barn. With all the help they soon had the hide off and the meat cut up. The hide was tacked to the side of the barn to dry and the meat hung up with the other meat in the cellar. It was nearly dark when all of it was taken care of. Gertie had fried up some of the bear meat. It had a wild taste and was plenty greasy, but with biscuits it wasn't too bad. And the men were happy that the bear would not be eating some of their livestock this winter.

Except for the cold nights, Eb and Henry's trip was relatively uneventful. It took them the usual three days to reach Rockwood. As usual their first stop was the saloon. They selected a table in a corner and ordered a meal. The food was not near as good as Gertie's. They laughed as they discussed their good cook. The saloon was filled with the usual collection of pioneer men. Some were dressed in their good clothes and others were trappers and farmers in their work clothes.

They paid Eb and Henry no notice; they were used to all kinds of men in the area. They were mostly talking about the Indian situation and the Uniforms, as they called them, inability to do anything about the raids. Henry heard about the burning of several homesteads to the north of the Rockwood. It made him and Eb very nervous for their friends. Although they lived south of Rockwood they did not know how stirred up the Indians were. They soon learned that the government was trying to get the families that had settled the area to go back across a line that the government had designated as Indian's land. They were not having much luck getting anyone to go back; mostly because most of the settlers had nothing to go back to. They had given up all they had to move west and were not giving up their homesteads. After making camp near the edge of town, Eb and Henry were soon joined by several other families camping for the night. Around the campfires the same talk was about the government trying to get them to go back. They were all in favor of pushing on and building their futures. Some thought they could "tame" the Indians and some vowed to just shoot all that they found. Eb and Henry were torn with the talk, after having met good Indians and then the savage ones. They had no good advice to give either side of the argument.

The next morning they did their shopping. The Mercantile owner remembered them and asked how they were. He was tickled with some of the items on the list.

"Got you a woman now?" he asked.

"No, we have the same one that this blasted town turned out of their house for taxes last year." Henry told him.

"Ole Gertie and Jo? We were wondering where they had gone. I remember her, she was a good cook."

Soon the supplies were loaded and the wagon tarped down. They had to drive by the camp ground when they left and they called out well wishes to some of the ones they had talked to the night before. And then they were on their way. It started to snow after lunch the next day and by nightfall it was getting heavier. Since they had no dry wood Eb and Mike ate cold food. After taking care of the mules and the horse they crawled under the tarp on the wagon and were soon sound asleep. The braying of the mules in the morning woke them to a winter wonderland. It had evidently snowed all night. The mules were digging in the snow trying to find some winter grass to eat. Mike gave them some hay they had brought and then they decided to skip breakfast and be on their way. Afternoon found them facing the crossing of a stream that was already frozen near the banks. The mules did not want to get in the cold water, but with Eb using his whip and Henry at their heads pulling, they soon eased into the water. It was not that deep and they soon had the wagon out on the other side. They had to make a decision as night neared. They could continue in the dark as it was not far to the house or wait until the next day. Eb said that the mules knew where to go and they should just continue. The moon gave them some light, but they did not need it as the mules made short work of getting them home. Of course everyone had gone to bed but as they entered the barn yard one of the mules decided to bray, announcing their arrival! Soon they were all dressed and out to see the friends. The wagon was pulled into the barn to be unloaded when it got light. John then joined the others who were listening to Eb and Henry tell them all about their trip. They neither one mentioned the Indian uprisings up north. They had decided to just tell Mike and John and see what they thought they should be preparing for.

Lizzy and Gertie were not the only ones preparing gifts for Christmas. John made Lizzy a new bridle with silver Conchos on the head band. Of course they were not real silver but some metal that he had found in one of the stores way back when and had brought along with him. Gertie's present was a set of new spoons made out of wood that he whittled. Eb made each one a new pair of gloves. He had learned to sew the fingers from an old Indian he had spent some time with one winter. Henry made each one a chair and Lizzy a bedside table. Mike just wandered around not able to come up with anything for them as he had no skills or crafts. Then one day when walking along the stream he looked down and saw some colorful rocks in the stream bed. Scooping them up he decided what he could do for Christmas and soon had his pockets full.

Jo too had a time trying to find something for gifts. He had little imagination and when they lived near town he simply went in and bought whatever the mercantile man suggested. So Christmas Eve came and he still had no presents for the tree. He decided late in the evening to go for a walk. He walked along the stream and then out to the tree line and had started back to the house when he saw it. It was bedded down and being very quiet. At first he thought it was a fawn and he was going to pass it by as he felt the doe had left it there and didn't want it to get up. But as he got a little closer he realized it was not a fawn. Taking a piece of tie string out of his pocket he eased it over the little head and with little tugging led it back behind their cabin. He decided that this would be his gift to everyone.

Christmas morning was soft and white. A new snow had fallen over night and it did look like a winter wonderland. Everyone had gathered in the house for breakfast and then they were going to open their presents that were scattered under the tree. Jo could hardly wait for his turn, but intentionally waited until last. Gertie loved her new dress from Lizzy. All the men told her how much they appreciated the new shirts. John handed out his hackamores and then Lizzy's bridle with the Conchos. She teared up and had to turn away and sniff. Lizzy had bought all of the men new bandanas and she had candy for everyone. They had eaten breakfast on their new chairs and Henry had brought in Lizzy's new bedside table. Mike had made Gertie and Lizzy necklaces made out of the stones he found in the riverbed. He also had made each man a catch all to put by their bed to put their money in. And everyone got gloves from Eb. After all these were passed around and admired, Gertie looked at Jo.

"And sir what have you for us for Christmas?" She thought he didn't have anything. She had tried to get him to give Eb money when they went to town for a gift but he refused.

"Well I have a wonderful gift from the Magi. It came last evening. But we have to go out to the barn to see it."

So they all put on boots and coats and followed Jo, grinning from ear to ear.

He led them all down the barn to the last stall. He eased the stall gate open and invited everyone in to see their gift. Lizzy fell to her knees and took the little head in her arms. The baby colt nuzzled her hair for a minute then pulled away. The filly was a dark bay with four stocking feet.

Her head was dainty and you had no trouble seeing the black stallion in her.

"Where did you get her? And where is her mare?" John was first to speak.

Jo then told them that he found it walking. He then told them that there was a bloody place nearby but the mare was gone. "I guess a bear or something drug it off."

"What is big enough to drag off a horse?" Mike asked. They all looked at each other.

"Indians!" Eb spoke what they all thought.

"Yes, there were tracks of a travois leading away down the valley away from the little one. I have no idea why they didn't take the little one unless it had run away and then come back. The Indians must be getting awfully hungry to eat a horse. But I had heard that they would when one died. But I have never heard of them killing one to eat it." Jo informed them. "We could have tracked them yesterday but the new snow has covered all their tracks this morning."

Mike was next. "We knew they were here somewhere so now I guess we will have to see where they call home; and if we can see if they are friendly or not."

Gertie then called them back into the house and they all gathered around the tree. Lizzy had taken her Bible out and she read again the story of the birth of baby Jesus. She then told them that in her family they all took a turn telling what they had to be thankful for this year. So each in turn told what they were thankful for. Nearly all of them repeated the fact that they were thankful for their little family and their health. Chores were an abbreviated thing that morning. Just milking and feeding. Then they were back to the big house for turkey and dressing, beans and corn, and for dessert sweet potato pie. Mike said that he was stuffed and they all agreed.

THIRTEEN

After lunch they all drifted away to their own rooms and most took a well-deserved nap. All except Lizzy who had snuck off to the barn and returned to the baby colt's stall. She had carried it a bucket of milk. She first got it to suck the milk off her fingers and then as it got used to that, she slowly put her fingers down in the milk bucket so the colt was sucking her fingers under the milk. A few days of this and the colt would quickly learn that the bucket meant milk and he would drink his fill. Colts take to people quickly, so this one was no different. Since it was a Christmas present they decided to call it the Magi. Of course in just a few weeks Magi was in to everything in the barn. Just like with small children, a lot of things had to be hung higher up especially leather things, as he like to chew on things just like a puppy. He was let out of his stall more and more to roam around in the barnyard. He soon was poking his nose into everything and checking it all out. One of his biggest smelling errors was clothes that Gertie had hung on the clothes line. After he had smelled them he got his head and ears tangled up with the clothes line and managed to pull the whole thing down. Then it scared him so he was trying to get away from it and then had it strung out all over the barnyard and then into the barn. There it got tangled up with some tools that made an awful racket. Wild-eyed and scared to death he had started out the barn door again when one of the tools got stuck in the barn door and when he was discovered he was completely covered with the clothes and tangled in the rope. It took them all several minutes to get him untangled. Gertie was not happy about the clothes having to be rewashed and some discarded as they were ruined. But she laughed as heartily as the others when they found him.

He never got over the episode. Even as a grown horse he could not be coaxed to ride close to a clothes line especially if it had clothes on it.

Since Magi was loose he was petted and talked to by all as they went about their chores. He was like a large puppy to them. If someone went off to gather wood in the wagon he would trot along as if he was helping. When they cut hay he was in the fields with them. If someone was working in the barn he would mosey in to see what they were doing. Consequently with all the people touching and petting him he had no fear. He would let them pick up all four feet and they could rub him anywhere on his body. John made him a small halter and soon he was leading. He was a big bone strong colt. And he grew fast. With plenty to eat and lots of water his bones were strong and he was going to be a tall fellow. Since he was born in the winter his baby hair was replaced by winter hair to keep him warm. This made him look and feel like a wooly bear. Any of the people could call him and he would nicker and go to find who was calling him. He was put up every night in his stall and he would bed down and sometimes before John was through with his chores in the barn, Magi was sound asleep as he could hear him snoring. Many times John would tiptoe over to look over the stall gate and just stand watching him sleep. He really was Magi and John knew he was part of their horse herd's future.

Lizzy too spent a great deal of time with the young colt. But the others did not know that Magi reminded her of one of her first horses she had back when she was just a girl. Her Father had given him to her for her birthday and she had called him Spirit. Spirit was her hers, and hers alone. She would saddle him up and ride like the wind through the pastures, waving wildly at the workers in the field. They would stop and wave back. The old foreman would take his hat off and wipe his forehead and shake his head. He said that she should have been born a boy the way she carried on with that horse. Lizzy would come in from the barn all dusty and smelly and old Merny would shoo her up to her room to get her in a bath and a dress before her mother could see or smell her. Lizzy remembered hating to wear dresses and stockings and shoes. Especially shoes! Her boots were so comfortable and her shoes hurt everywhere they touched her feet.

But then she would be presented to her mother and they would sit down at the long table for their meals; Father at the one end and Mother on the other and the children along the sides. Lizzy always sat by her Father, that way when she was about to spout off about something from the barn or farm her Father could touch her on the arm and smile and she knew that was not something to talk about at the table. Lizzy was fond of her two brothers and her sister but not close. Even as a child she was a loner and preferred to be outside seeing what was going on while her sisters were in the house learning to cook, clean and do needlework. Lizzy's mother had demanded that Lizzy learn to do embroidery, but after a couple of weeks it was such a mess that her Mother gave up and she was not made to do it anymore. She did learn to sew a little and to cook as she liked the cook and it was like a game to her.

Although Lizzy was not very big she had a big heart and took on any task that someone larger than her would do. She had learned to stand on a nearby stump and throw her saddle on Spirit herself instead of having a stable hand saddle him for her, like her sisters did. She would ride with the sisters and some of their friends out to the woods for picnics, but didn't take part in much of the conversation about cities and books. As she grew into her teens, her mother and her sisters insisted that she start going to parties and wearing more dresses. She was aware that when she looked into the mirror that she looked ok and many young men came around. Their house with three eligible beautiful and wealthy girls was the place to gather and there were always young people around. Lizzy just couldn't get into the flow of things. She didn't like sitting around flirting and talking about who was wearing what or who was going where. She found it very boring. Her Mother clucked at her constantly to get over being a tomboy and begin thinking about a husband and family. She didn't really want to think about either of those. She still just wanted to think about horses; until He came with his Father to buy a horse. His name was James Franklin Farnsworth. He had jet black hair and the bluest eyes she had ever seen. She had been out on Spirit and when she came into the stables and dismounted they were walking from the house to the barn. She quickly tried to straighten herself out and do something with her hair that seemed to be all over the place. When her Father saw her he frowned a little then decided a warm smile would help the situation. He was thinking my wife is going to kill me over this. The introductions were made and since her Father had not dismissed her she tagged along with the three to look at several of the colts born this year. The elder Mr. Farnsworth ran his hands over each one and took his time looking at each one from each side.

While he was at his business, Franklin leaned over to Lizzy and asked her which one she would choose or did she have a favorite. Lizzy blushed and started to answer when she saw her Father glance at her. She quickly answered "They are all well-bred and any would make you good stock."

Her Father smiled and nodded then turned back to Mr. Farnsworth. He quickly made his decision and made the deal to buy three of the colts. He said that he would send a representative around in a couple of weeks to pick up the colts.

After they had left, Lizzy's Father walked with her to the house. Her Mother was standing in the parlor when they came in and she did not look happy. "First young lady you should have come to the house not stayed at the barn when men were discussing business. You had no place there. Secondly don't be getting any ideas about Franklin Farnsworth. They have money but it is money made from business and they do not have any background. He is not on our list of possible husbands for you."

"What list?" Lizzy quickly asked.

"I made a list a few months ago of eligible bachelors that were suitable for you girls. They all have old family backgrounds and old money. And they are the only ones that your Father will allow to come courting at this house. Now go to your room and cleanup for dinner and come back looking like a young lady." Lizzy turned to her Father for help but he only shrugged his shoulders so she ran from the room and up the stairs.

It was a couple of weeks to the day when Franklin Farnsworth and two other men came to receive the colts. Lizzy had watched out the window for them to come. They had corresponded with her Father when they would be here. She quickly came down the stairs in a dress and her Father smiled when she joined them in the parlor. Her Mother was also there. Her Father introduced the two new men and then turned to Franklin

"I believe you remember my daughter Lizzy from the other time that you were here."

"Yes I remember her." He took her hand and looked right into her eyes. Lizzy thought she was going to faint.

Her Father came back to the house later by himself. He said that they had left with the colts. Lizzy was so disappointed. She thought they would at least come back in. She then went out on the porch and was surprised to see Franklin coming up the steps.

"I thought I would visit for a minute before we left. I wanted to talk to you."

They sat on the porch. Lizzy knew that her Mother was inside simmering. You did not sit on the porch by yourself with a young man without him first asking permission to do so.

"I know we are not supposed to be out here by ourselves but before I go inside and ask your parents if I can come see you, I wanted to know if you wanted to see me again."

Lizzy really knew she was going to faint this time. "Oh yes, I would like that very much."

Franklin then got up and went inside the house. He was there only a short time and he returned. She had stood up and he stopped only for a short time.

"Your mother regrets that I will not be able to come see you."

"That can't be right!" Lizzy exclaimed

"That is what she said. "Franklin handed her a small piece of paper. "Here is my address if you ever get to town."

"I will see you again," Lizzy promised him.

She was in tears when he rode away. Then she turned and ran into the parlor.

"Why did you tell him not to come back to see me?" She demanded.

"Now Lizzy, your Mother had already told you that he was not one of the ones we have chosen for you."

"Since when do you get to choose whom I see or not?"

"We do because we are your parents." And when Lizzy started to protest again, he dismissed her and told her to go to her room. And go to her room she did. She lay on the bed and cried until she thought she would die. When she was summoned to dinner she refused to come down.

An hour later there was a knock on her door and her Mother came in to sit next to here on the bed. "When you are older you will understand how things work. Until then you will begin going to the parties the other girls have been going to and I will discuss the list of young men that we feel you can have come call on you. And even then some of the sons of better families will not suit for us." When Lizzy started to protest again, her Mother told her that the problem was not open for discussion.

The next few weeks were filled with party after party as it was "the season". It was at the seventh week of Lizzy's dressing up and being totally bored with the whole thing they had gone to the Roman's House. The girls had been whisked upstairs to get ready for the party. Lizzy with the help of the maids was soon laced into her underclothes and when she could hardly breathe the dress was lowered over her head. All the dresses had been quickly pressed when they arrived by the servants and looked like they had never traveled in a buggy for miles in a trunk. When they had their hair done and their gowns on they were sent down to the ballroom to be looked over like buying cattle Lizzy thought to herself.

She was standing over in a corner to herself when she saw him come in the room. He was dressed up like all the others but he still stood out. Lizzy did not know whether to acknowledge him or not. Her Mother had been watching them like a hawk. She had no choice as he had turned and saw her and came over to talk to her. Sneaking a look toward her Mother she was happy to see that her back was turned and she was visiting with a group of other mothers also there to check out the possible husbands for their daughters.

"How are you?" He smiled.

"I am fine. I enjoyed our visit and talking about the horses when you were there."

"Yes you seem to know a lot about them."

"I would spend all day long with them if I could."

"As dressed up as you are today I dare say you have not been to the stables today."

His grin was infectious and Lizzy had no trouble smiling back. Then it happened. Her Mother saw them. It was like a thunderstorm had overtaken them. Here her Mother came!

"Oh, hello Mr. Farnsworth. I didn't know you were acquainted with the Romans."

It was a question more than a statement. She was trying to find out how he weaseled an invitation to this ball.

"Our families go back a long way. I even went to college with one of his sons, Adam."

"Oh! Mother looked amazed. You went to college?"

"Yes and graduated an engineer." Franklin was enjoying bantering with Lizzy's Mother. But he knew better than to push his luck so he excused himself and drifted across the room.

"How did he get in here?" Mother demanded of Lizzy.

"I have no idea. I did not have anything to do with the list of guests."

"What were you doing talking to him? I have told you that he is not for you. Now get out of the corner and go try to visit with some of the boys on the list."

Obediently, Lizzy moved around the room. She talked to a few people that she knew and then caught his eyes on here again. She smiled and then continued across the room and our on the veranda. He was there almost instantly.

"I thought I would never get to talk to you alone. I didn't want to make it hard on you with your Mother. I am not on the list I gather."

"You know about the list?"

"Oh yes. Everyone knows about the list. In fact I probably can name nearly every young man on your Mother's list. I am glad that I got this opportunity to talk to you. I might have missed you before I left."

"Left? Where are you going? Lizzy's heart sank.

"Out west. I have decided to take my inheritance and make my way out west. And you will have to come see me as I am going to raise horses wherever I land."

"When are you leaving?"

"In a couple of weeks. I have to get all my papers in hand and buy wagons and supplies. I am going to join a wagon train in about three weeks." He then bent down and kissed Lizzy right on the mouth. "That is to remember me by." He then started to walk away but Lizzy caught him by the sleeve.

"You are going to think me very forward Mr. Farnsworth, but I want you to know that you are the only man on my list and I am going west with you. That is if you would like me to."

Franklin stood there in silence. "Your Mother would never let you go out West especially with me."

"It is not her decision."

"You would be disinherited I am sure."

"I don't need her money."

"No we will have enough money. But they are your family."

"Well you will just have to be my family. Lizzy squeezed his arm next to her.

"When are you going home from here?" He asked.

"Tomorrow. Ok, I will come to your house tomorrow and ask your Father for you. He will say no because of your Mother."

"Then what will we do?" he smiled.

"I will then just run away with you when you leave."

"Will they come after us?" he asked.

"I don't think so."

"We will see. If it doesn't work out we will find a way to get you on the wagon train."

They traveled home the next day. They were all exhausted so everyone but Lizzy took a nap after lunch. She was too excited waiting for Franklin to come. It was dark when she left the stables and started to the house. She had decided he had changed his mind and was not coming. As she walked along she was soon joined by someone who took her hand and there was Franklin!

"I decided that they will never let us go so we have to just go. I will make all the arrangements. You need to secretly pack anything you need but very little and manage to get it out of the house somewhere. I will come back in a couple of weeks just like this and we will go away. I hate doing that but I love you and I do not want your parents telling me I can't marry you."

"I love you too. And I will do as you say about packing." When he took her in his arms this time she was thrilled to return his kiss.

The next few days for Lizzy were miserable for Lizzy. Time seemed to pass like an old woman. But she had started getting things that they would need together. Since she had her own room she was able to pack a few boxes and stow them under the bed. The maid she had was young like her and she decided that she needed some help. So the next day she explained to the maid what she was doing and with paying her off got her assistance. The maid was not a live-in so she came to the house each day from her father's farm nearby. So it was no trouble to let her take a little bundle of things home with her each day. Since she was young like Lizzy she thought the whole affair was very romantic and would do whatever she could to help out. So each day when she walked home she had a little bundle of things that Lizzy was taking. Some of the things were very practical, sewing things, first aid things and medicine. Then she started on the clothes. Taking one dress was her limit! She would bundle a pair of riding breeches and shirt together and away they went. This went on for days.

Then one evening she was sitting on the porch when a whistle alerted her that He was there.

She quickly joined him at the stable and he had news.

"The wagon train has been made and we are to leave in two days. Can you get to town in two days?"

"Sure all I have to do is ride my horse from here and join you."

"I have decided that we have to ride for a few days and then join the wagon train. They would catch us soon on the wagon so I have hired a driver and we will join them about a week from now. I have received your things from your maid. She came into town yesterday and had them packed in boxes for you. They are already on the wagon. And surprise! She is going with us. I knew you would need some help on the way and in your new home so she said yes. But it will be easy for her to join the wagon train, and she will ride with the driver I hired."

Lizzy could hardly breathe. She was really going to marry Franklin and she was going out west and raise horses! The next day was horrible. Lizzy thought it would never end. She did everything she could to make the day go faster. The maid, Sarah, was there and they whispered and gave each other looks of conspiracy all day long. Sarah was to go to town the next day and get her stuff on the wagon and she had a note for Lizzy to give her Mother saying that she was not coming back to work.

Lizzy just left the note on her Father's desk the next morning. She did not want to try and explain about Sarah leaving. She did not leave her own note. Afraid that they would not get away. She then went out and saddled her horse and mounted. She had told the cook she was going to be out all day so she had packed her a large lunch. In fact when she started off one of the stable hands gave her a saddle bag and it was full of food. He grinned as he gave it to her and told her to be careful on her journey. So they all knew!

Franklin had been watching on the road for her. He had a pack mule and they took off through the woods. He said that the mule track would help them not be the ones they were looking for. We have to get as far away as we can today. So they road until way in the night. Since Lizzy was used to riding she was able to keep up easily. Late in the night they stopped for a rest near a stream. They watered their horses and they grazed and Lizzy and Frank as she now called him lay down in their blankets and slept. But not for long. Soon as the sun was up they ate a cold breakfast and away they went again. They traveled like this for three days. They were by now exhausted. They came to a small town and decided it was safe to go in for some supplies. They had a bath in a stream the night before and looked half way decent when they went into the mercantile store. They bought a few more groceries and then set out again. They had ridden two more days when they came to another town. Here Frank pulled his horse up in front of a church.

As he helped her down off her horse he said. "Lizzy will you marry me?"

"Yes!"

So they went into the little Church and with the preacher's wife as a witness they were married.

It was two more days before they dared to double across country and join the wagon train. It had made good time and Sarah was glad to see Lizzy made it. Frank had sent three Conestoga wagons. So he and Lizzy drove and lived in one. Sarah and the other driver now known as John Henry drove and lived in the other two. And they had timed it just right. Sarah said that someone had checked the wagon train for them two days before and then turned and gone back the way they came. So maybe they had made it free and clear.

Sarah and John Henry were black. Lizzy took this for granted. All the workers at her house had been black. They were freed slaves. But come to find out Frank had to pay extra to let them drive his wagons and join the train. They had had to drive all the way in the back of the train eating the dust of all the other wagons. This they had endured without complaint. They were as excited as Lizzy and Frank to be going to a new land. The man that had driven the other wagon had a family and when Frank and Lizzy joined the train he returned to his wagon and family. He had big sons who had taken their turns driving their wagon and Frank's.

Their trip had started near Albany, New York. They had joined the wagon train just before they entered into Pennsylvania. They followed a wagon trail that went into the northern edge of Virginia as that is where many of the families were headed. At several stops they would lose a family or two. Lizzy had made friends with some of the women on the train and was sorry to see them go. But they were making their way same as Lizzy. When they reached Virginia the wagon master called a meeting. Standing in front of the few wagons left he told them that the next part of the journey would be the worst. He again told them about Indian raids and there would be no military help, as they were not supposed to be going into the territories. They were camped close to Marietta, Virginia and he told them that if they were not up to the troubles here would be the place to stop. Although later the Northwest Territory would be divided up into the states of Ohio, Indiana, Illinois, Michigan and Wisconsin, they were wild country at this time. So the wagon boss told them they would start out in the morning.

"If you are continuing you need to get extra supplies bought." He advised them.

In the morning several families had decided to stay and they stood by their wagons and waved as Lizzy and Frank and the rest rode by. Now the real adventure was going to begin.

Staying to the northern side of the Ohio River they crossed several tributaries. Some were not so deep but others had the horses swimming and the wagons floating across. They were out several more days when Lizzy came in with firewood and started the fire with help from Sarah to cook supper. Franklin laughed at her.

"Madame, did you even bring a dress with you?"

Lizzy was standing in front of him in her boots and riding pants. "I did bring one but I am not putting it on until I am in my new house."

"So I will hold you to that and we will have a party for you to wear it to." Frank hugged her up close and smiled over her head.

The trip had not been without many troubles. Wagon wheels broke. Horses and mules had to have their feet cleaned often. One man broke his leg and one young woman had a baby. These were all taken care of without the aid of any doctor. One wagon had caught on fire when one of their little ones played with a branch from the fire. But it only burned the cover and they were able to continue on but it sure looked bad. And as before as they went along more settlers stopped and claimed their land. They had been out a little over a month when the wagon master called a meeting again.

"On the other side of this river is a small town. That is where I get off. They are looking for settlers so if you are a mind to they would like to have you. The rest of you I have enjoyed working for you and God Speed."

Sure enough the following day, when they had crossed the river and rode into town the people were friendly and happy to see more settlers. Lizzy and Sara spent the day buying supplies while Frank and John Henry saw to a new wagon wheel and new leather goods for the horses and mules. When they left at day break the next day it was just their three wagons. One of the sons of the man who had driven the wagon before Frank and Lizzy joined up came up to their wagon and ask Frank if he would consider taking him on and him going with them. Frank was happy to have him and he soon drove the back wagon and Sarah moved in with John Henry. The new member of their group was a big muscular lad named James Walker. He told them he was eighteen years old but later Frank told Lizzy he doubted he was a day over sixteen. But he had his families' blessing to go with them and after lots of hugs and handshakes they began again.

That night sitting around the fire it was John that asked the question they all wondered but hadn't asked. "So where are we going Mr. Farnsworth?"

"John Henry, first of all I am Frank, not Mr. Farnsworth. We are now in this together. And we are going about another week or two."

"Won't that throw us into Indian Territory?" Lizzy joined in.

"Yes it will. But by my calculations it should be some of the best country to raise our horses."

He went to the wagon and they could hear him rummaging around. He return with a map and they all huddled around and watched him trace where they had come and where they were going.

"I think we will try for here. He made a tap with his finger and they all tried to figure out how he decided on that place."

The wagons that had left originally each had a horse tied to it. They were Franklin's seed stock and they all had to be exercised and feed each day. Quickly that job fell to Lizzy and she loved it. She was able to race across the prairie with wind in her hair. And with a different horse each day it was a new adventure each time. Some days she would drive the wagon and Frank would ride the horses. Some days James would take a turn. He quickly became a good horseman.

He also rode ahead to find water and a camping spot. Soon he was also tracking food for the camp. And it was only about a week out that he came back in and announced that there was wagon tracks ahead of them.

"They are ahead but not by much I could see their dust. We should catch them tonight or tomorrow."

Sure enough, about noon the next day, they had caught up with four wagons with families in them. The families with all their belongings and children made Lizzy think of her family at home. She had been so excited by all the new adventures she had not spent much time thinking about them. She wonder now as she sat on her wagon seat if they were angry and did they spend much time looking for her. She knew in her heart that she did not want to cause them pain, but she also knew that they would have never accepted Franklin because he had no title. She decided that when she had time and a way to send it, she would write them, especially her Father, a long letter trying to explain why she did not want the life they envisioned for her.

Lizzy climbed down from the wagon and Sarah and her went over to meet the new families.

Where are you going was always the first question and then where did you come from?

The new families were not sure where they were heading but had decided they had not found it yet. They were mostly from Pennsylvania. So it was soon decided that it is better to have more than less so they all joined up. That night Frank took out his map and showed the others where they were going and they decided that it looked like a fine place. The next day they all set off with a common goal now. It would only be another couple of weeks now, Frank had assured her and they would be at their new home.

And it was. A couple of weeks later when they came upon a fine valley and Frank drew his wagons to a halt. He stepped down and lifted Lizzy down from the wagon seat.

"Here will be our new home."

The others soon joined them and then said goodbye and all set off in other directions to pick out their own places. They all promised to visit soon as they were settled. That left John, James, Sarah, Frank and Lizzy to start their new lives together.

It was the next morning that the sickness started. Lizzy ran away from the camp site to throw up. Soon as it was over she was ok, but the next morning the same thing. Sarah followed her out of the camp the second morning. She laughed at Sarah and asked,

"When is the little one coming?" Sarah laughed.

"What little one?"

"Why the one in your belly."

Lizzy stared at her like she had seen and heard a ghost. "What do you mean? You think I am pregnant?"

"No, I knows that you are." Sarah laughed again.

"I can't be right now. I won't be any use to helping do anything."

"Sure you can, up to a point. The throwing up will go away in a few weeks and you will be right as rain." Sarah was still laughing as she returned to camp.

When Lizzy returned to the campfire they were all looking at her like she had the plague.

"What are all of you staring at? Haven't you seen a pregnant woman before?"

Frank quickly took her in his arms and hugged her tight. ""Wow, what a great way to begin our new life."

They had arrived at their valley in July. The first order of business was the house. Although Frank asked Lizzy what things she wanted in a house the plans were mostly his. He did incorporate as many conveniences for Lizzy as he could think of. Sarah added some good ideas about the kitchen and a nursery for the baby. Soon as he had it marked off on the ground the other men began cutting timber and hauling it to the building site. While it was being built they continued to live out of the wagons and cook and eat around the campfire. And Lizzy continued to be sick. She was about 4 months along when the pains started and by the next day she had lost the baby. Sarah did everything she knew to do but it was not to be. Lizzy grieved for a few days but then fell whole hardily into the building of the house and barn. She got back to exercising the horses after a while and when she was out riding she felt the best. A few of the nearby families came by to visit and then they all came to help one day raising the roofs of the house and barn. It was fun having them all there. The women had cooked and brought food and they all sat around eating and visiting about their families and their futures in the new place.

A few days later Lizzy and the others returned the favor by going to help put up a barn for one of the families. They had chosen a flat piece of ground near a stream. While she was there the women told her that a new man had come by and was proposing to build a store and livery to start a town. Lizzy was so excited. She couldn't wait to tell Frank. A beginning of a town! What an idea. And sure enough in a few weeks they were helping the young man build his store and livery barn. In a few weeks a mule train brought four wagon loads of goods for the store and leather goods for the livery. One of the new families (who had not built a house yet) decided to build their house on the edge of where the grocery store was. So it was the first house for a family built in Rockwood. And the building out of rock and wood had been the idea for the name of the town. Soon the town grew and became what the men had found when she first met them the day she needed her wagon unloaded. That seemed a long time ago.

The colt nuzzled her and she got up to walk with it back into the barn and poured out it some feed. She then got a bucket and carried water from the stream for his water trough. "You realize that you are getting big enough to eat and drink with the rest of the horses like a big boy don't you?" She had not heard John join them and she laughed when he replied

"Yes mam, I had a feeling that I was getting big enough to join the others."

Lizzy without thinking gave John a hug and they both stood there looking at the colt and sharing a moment of understanding what the colt meant to them both.

FOURTEEN

John and the others had chosen the site of their homestead to include behind the house and barns a box canyon. A box canyon was one that had three sides made of cliffs and only one way out. And they had made good use of it by building a fence across it to keep the mares in. The mares had plenty of room to graze and good water. The water came out of the side of one of the cliffs and provided a waterfall and a continual source of water. At the bottom of the waterfall was a large rock bottom pool that the men used for bathing. When Lizzy and Gertie came along they had to kind of make a taking turn calendar so they would not be there at the same time. After the pool the water again feel down another fall about a 15 foot fall. It then gathered strength and rushed down the valley and watered the whole area. Although it would be less in the hot months it never dried up. And in the spring the melting snow made it a rushing river and the falls were very noisy. It rushed for a while and then it would make a big pool and then rush on down to the next rocky dam would hold it up for a while until it spilled over and ran down some more. All these pools in the stream had large trout. And when the bears awoke in the spring they were seen fishing for the trout not far from the house.

Henry was the first to mention the coming out of the bears. "We can say that old winter is really behind us. I counted three bears fishing down the valley this morning. We had better be on our toes. They are hungry and we had better be looking out for them. We had better think about what to do with Magi too. They will try to get him for sure."

They all nodded in agreement but no one wanted to be the one to say that he had to go to the pasture with the mares. The mares would protect him from the bears alright, but they knew how attached Lizzy had come to the colt and didn't know how to proceed.

It was a few nights later that Red was the one to sound the alarm. He was racing around in his pen and making an awful racket. John was the first one to him and saw the big black bear on the side of the barn trying to dig under the side to get to the colt. He quickly ran back to the house for a gun and was joined by the others. But by the time he came back out to the barn the bear was gone. In the morning light they could see where he had walked up and down the side of the barn. Not only did he smell the colt he could smell the pigs and chickens—any of these would have made him a nice supper.

Mike said, "He will be back now that he know where the stock is. I guess we should take turns staying up at night until we get him. Let's leave this one shotgun in the barn anyway just in case he were to come and we are out here, not in the house."

So that afternoon Mike made some hangers on the side of the tack room and hung the shotgun on that wall. Below on a shelf they put a box of shells for the gun.

As the days and weeks wore on more bears were seen along the water of the valley. And it would be Lizzy that would have to tangle with them. Gertie and she had gone down to the water's edge to carry water to a big pot they were boiling water in to do the laundry. It took about 10 trips to fill the pot and about that many more to fill a tub with cold water for rinsing. Lizzy had told Gertie to go ahead and start the wash and she would continue to carry the water for the rinse tub. As she started back to the stream Magi came along to offer help or just get in the way as usual. Lizzy had carried another couple of buckets full for the rinse when she heard the colt cry out. When she turned to see the bear had managed to get a hold of the colt on the back. Lizzy ran for the shotgun. She grabbed some extra shells and put them in her pocket. When she got back outside the colt had somehow gotten away and was heading for her with the bear right behind him. For a while Lizzy could not shoot as the colt was in the way. Closer and closer they came. Lizzy realized she would have to let the colt pass her and then would only have a small bit of time to get the bear right behind him. Sure enough the colt ran passed toward the barn and Lizzy shot the bear not once but twice and it landed about 10 feet in front of her. She quickly reloaded the double barrel and waited to see if the bear was dead. While all this was going on Gertie had run to the horse pens yelling for the men. They had all gotten there in time to see the big black fall at Lizzy's feet. They gathered around and one went over and kicked at the bear. Dead was all he said. They all looked at Lizzy in amazement.

"I guess he won't bother us anymore."

Then they remember the colt and all hurried to the barn. The colt was in the back of its stall still shaking from fright. Lizzy had put the shotgun back on its rack and then they parted a way for her to go to the colt. It had some back slash marks on its back and hips. Quickly they got water together and salve to doctor the cuts. Fresh bedding was put in the stall and feed and water.

"Little one you will not be going out to play for a few days it's for sure."

When they came back out of the barn, Eb was already working to gut the bear. He was then skinned and dressed. After cleaning him out, they tied him up on a rafter of the barn and cut the carcass into pieces. Gertie then instructed them on trimming the fat off and it was put in a big bucket by itself. The leaner meat was then cut up and salted and covered with salt sack and put in the meat cellar. The fat would be rendered another day.

Gertie and Lizzy had washing to finish today. They were soon back at work and the men had gone back to working on the fence they were building. The white or light colored clothes were washed first with the lye soap that Gertie had made the winter before from the fat on some of the hides. Then they were rinsed and hung on the clothes line that had been repaired after the colt tore it down before. This would include the sheets and tablecloths also. Henry had spent some of the cold winter evenings carving clothes pins for the girls for when they did laundry. Next the shirts and dresses were washed and rinsed and hung to dry and last the breeches were done. The rinse water would be changed often but the hot wash water would do for all the washing. Since the sheets were washed first, they dried first and soon as they dried the next basket of clothes were hung and dried. Most times the breeches had to hang out overnight and up into the next day to get dry. This got the next bear.

Just about dark Lizzy and Gertie took in all the clothes that were dry, leaving the breeches on the line. Now the line stretched between three sets of posts. The middle posts were to keep the line from swaying down and the clothes getting on the ground. The breeches were hung on the end farthest from the house. Jo was the first one up this time. He heard a great commotion coming from the clothes line. The bear thought that the clothes were something to eat and had gotten all tangled up in the breeches and clothesline and couldn't get free. Soon everyone was out and one shot from Jo's rifle did the second bear in. But it was not in time to save the breeches. Only a couple of pair were saved. The others were just strips of denim. Sadly most of them were Mike's.

"How come all of my pants were in one place?" He wanted to know.

"That is just the luck of the draw." Jo told him as all the others laughed.

It was still cold enough at night that the bear would keep until the morning. In the morning the same procedure of skinning and cutting up the meat took most of the day. Gertie told them she was tired of putting up bear meat and would they refrain from shooting any more bears for a few days. They all laughed again.

FIFTEEN

So their lives all continued on. Together they had made each one a home and they were happy with their companions. Eb had trapped all winter and had a wagon load of hides to sell. They all decided the snow should be melted enough for them to make a trip to town. Jo and Henry decided to stay behind and see about things. Gertie and Eb rode on the wagon and the rest went horseback. Gertie put her fingers on her nose and declared to Eb that something stunk around them. Laughing they all took off. Same as before it was two nights out before they came to town. They felt like it was safe to take John with them. He had grown a lot and was sporting a full beard when they went to town.

Rockwood had not changed much since they were there before. There were a few more houses built around the edge and a new boarding house and saloon on the other side of town. Lizzy took Gertie under her arm and they went into the hotel. We will have two rooms and a bath right now. And send the girl up to press our dresses.

"Ms. Farnsworth?" the man at the hotel desk.

"Yes, it's Ms. Farnsworth and I want that room right now."

"Yes Mam. Here are your keys."

"Oh Lizzy I can stay at the boarding house. I am not used to staying at a fine hotel like this." Gertie said.

"You will not! You are my guest and we are going to do the town up right."

Lizzy had carried them each a dress in her saddle bags (since on the wagon they would have stunk). Soon they both had had nice baths in a fancy claw footed tub and the girl had ironed their dresses. She also stayed around to dry and fix their hair.

When they came out on the street the men hardly recognized them. Mike and the boys also had had haircuts, shaves and baths. Eb was always the one that made the most difference in his appearance when they cleaned up. They all looked really good!

Holding out his arm to Gertie he said, would you ladies like to join us for lunch?

"Yes we would" laughed Gertie.

Eb stepped up to take Lizzy's arm, so off they went. The new saloon had a restaurant beside it and in they went to eat. They could hardly eat for looking around at all the people. It had been nearly a year since they had been to town and they tried not to stare but they did. And they discussed quietly what so and so was doing and Lizzy and Gertie watched what they were wearing. A few people came by the table and visited with Lizzy and were introduced to the others. Among them was the man who had bought Lizzy's place. Carlisle Woods had made himself comfortable at the next table and started carrying on conversation like he had been invited into their lunch. He bragged to Lizzy how he had only kept her property for a short time. He had made a profit on it to a Thomas Harold Claire Esq., the new lawyer in town. He had a wife and three daughters, Nancy, Elizabeth, and Winifred.

As he turned he called out to a man standing at the door.

"Over her Mr. Claire I want you to meet some folks. This is the lady that used to own your property."

Lizzy took the man's hand in a handshake and then introduced everyone at the table, being careful to only address John by his first name.

"They moved farther west of here and run a horse farm."

After pleasantries were addressed, John noticed the girls at the door first.

"Oh, here is my family. Have them come over and join us." Carlisle told him

So again all the introductions were made and the girls and their Mother took seats at the table next to John. He tried not to stare but he thought Nancy Claire was the most beautiful girl he had ever met. And he nearly died when she spoke to him.

"So you raise horses do you? "She smiled up at him.

John stuttered out a yes. The others around the table were enjoying every minute of this episode.

"I like to ride although I am not very good at it yet; although I rode a lot on the wagon train coming out here. We came from Pennsylvania. Where did you come from?"

There was an intake of breathe as his companions realized John would have to come up with something quick to answer this one.

"I came out west from Virginia."

"Oh, you had to come a long way too." She smiled and John smiled back.

"How long will you be in town?" It was the mother's turn to ask the questions.

"We will be here another day or two." Lizzy answered.

"We would then like for you to come out to the house tomorrow night for dinner. Could you do that? We don't have company very often you know."

Lizzy turned to look at the rest of them and it was decided. They would join the lawyer and his family for dinner the next night. This would throw them an extra night staying over but as they walked away from the restaurant down the side of the street, they decided they earned it. And they teased John about going to see Miss Nancy. And of course John took it good natured but blushed a crimson red.

The luncheon went well and afternoon ran on as they all visited about the state of the country and the Indians. Mr. Claire was sure that the Indian Territory would legally be opened for settlement soon. The government just couldn't keep all this land and its resources in the hands of an ignorant race like the Indians. He drone on and on about the resources that the land held and how it would make the country progress. At time his wife had to interrupt and they would talk about other things as when she asked about where they lived now and how they liked living in the wilderness.

Through all this John remained silent. Mike and Lizzy carried most of the conversation. But as he ate lunch he was seated right across from Nancy and on several occasions he caught her looking directly into his eyes. And on more than one of these occasions she smiled the sweetest smile he had ever seen.

When they had adjourned into the parlor again, John and the rest of the kids went out to sit on the porch. They all wanted to know about their horses and John of course had to tell them about the bears' episodes and the things the colt, Magi, had gotten into. The others laughed a lot and were at ease with him. He did not realize that he had missed visiting with young people. All the others of his new family were older and didn't cut up much. He found out that Nancy was about his age and then two brothers and two sisters were born after her. The boys seemed very educated and John soon found out that they attended boarding school back east and were just home on holiday. The girls had a tutor here at the house, but he was on holiday and had gone to visit some of his friends. When John mentioned that one of the things that he missed about being out in the wilderness was not being able to get his hands on many books, immediately they all escorted him into their study. Every wall was lined with books. John felt like he was back at The Manor. Mr. Claire heard them and joined them. When they told him about John needing books to read he immediately started picking out books from the library for him to take home with him.

He told the servant standing nearby to produce something to put them in and soon he had a whole packet of books ready for John to take with him.

"You can bring them back when you return. You were planning to return were you not?"

Again John felt the blush coming to his face.

"Yessir I would like to return if it is ok with you."

"It is fine with me. We have enjoyed having all of you very much. Please come back soon."

John took his packet of books back down the hall to the parlor. The rest were standing and saying their goodbyes to the Lady of the house and then in turn to Mr. Claire. As they were going outside John found Nancy right beside him and she managed to catch his hand and squeeze it. John felt a warm glow go through his entire body.

"Read in a hurry John so you will come back soon." She smiled again.

"I will and I am sure that I can come back soon even if I have not read all the books."

The ride back to town was in nearly darkness. They had eaten late so no one was interested in going out for supper. Lizzy invited them to her room (it was the only one with a sitting area) and she had

had sandwiches and drinks arranged from the hotel. They sat around eating and discussing Mr. Claire's attitude about the government. They had not ever even mentioned it at their place, but now it was an item of interest.

"Do you really think they could send the military to throw us off our land and give it back to the Indians?" Henry asked.

"We will just have to watch and see and in the meantime we had better get a surveyor of some kind to come out and survey what we are presently calling ours." Lizzy said. "Tomorrow before we leave I will instruct our lawyer to find someone and send him out. That way we will at least have a legal paper with our legal claim to the land."

Turning to John, Lizzy grinned. "Those children seemed to take to you John, especially that Nancy. And didn't I hear Mr. Claire say you could come back anytime? You better watch out he will have you as his son-in-law before you know it."

They all joined in laughter and Eb who was sitting next to John pounded him on his back.

They then all drifted off to their rooms. They had decided on an early start in the morning.

As much as they all enjoyed coming to town they were eager to get back "home". They were up and by daybreak they had all the supplies loaded and were on their way. They made good time and the morning of the third day they arrived back home. Henry was the first out the door.

"What happened to ya? We expected you yesterday?" Mike spoke up.

"We would have been here yesterday but John here had some courting to do."

"I did not!" John replied rather loudly.

The others in turn said yes he had been the reason they had not come back. And they all were still picking on him as they unloaded everything and put the supplies away.

Jo had some stew made and they all sat around the big table with a bowl and told Jo and Henry about their trip. Of course to make John uncomfortable each one had to add something about a certain Miss Claire. John took it in stride and grinned about it a lot.

He was eager to go to his room and read all the books in a hurry and then he could go back. What was he thinking? He had work to do and horses to see about. He didn't have time for books or a certain Miss Claire. But as he sat there daydreaming he could feel her little hand in his as he was leaving.

"Are you coming or are you staying here with Miss Claire?" Mike laughed.

They all laughed again and John hurried out to the barn.

While they had been gone Henry and Jo had brought to the barn two of the mares that they thought were nearly ready to foal. Their bellies were big as barrels and both had milk dripping a little out of their tits. That was a sure sign that they were nearly ready. But they would not be the first to foal. Mares have been foaling by themselves since the beginning of time and one took her freedom to heart and had her foal by herself out in the pasture. Henry found it the next day when he went out to check on the horses. He patiently told the mare that the reason they took the mares and foals to the barn area was to protect them from bears and mountain lions. He returned to the house and recruited John and Mike to help him move the mare to the water lot close to the barn. The little one was about three days old and could already run and keep up with its mother as she trotted into the new pen. All of the others came over to the pen to look the new one over. It was a filly and they all said that Lizzy should name it. While she was watching it, it went into the shadow its mother was making and lay down. Lizzy chuckled and said she would call her Shadow.

That night at the table it was decided that they would take turns staying up at night checking on the babies to keep them safe. John volunteered to take the first night shift. Before dark he rode out to the other mares to see if any other one needed to come up closer to the barn. After deciding there were none needing him he headed back to the barn and pens. He had pulled his chair over by the big door of the barn and put a lantern by him on a table. Then he took out his books and began to read. He was thrilled to have books again! Until he started reading he didn't know how much he had missed them. But at the same time all the times at The Manor came flooding up on him. He wondered if they had ever gotten any of his letters and if they were alright. Then his mind wandered over to think about his family. He was not getting much reading done. And then the books reminded him of Nancy Claire. And even though he took the ribbing from his friends graciously, he knew in his heart they were right. He was very interested in Nancy Claire and fully intended to go back and see her when they got back to town. But he also realized that that might be months and she might go off with someone else. His book fell off his lap and he quickly gathered it up. After setting it on the table he walked out to check on the horses again. They were bedded down and nothing was moving about. So he went back to his book and this time was able to read without his thoughts wandering. The night passed uneventful and when it was daylight he went into have breakfast. Gertie already had the fire going and coffee made.

"Now you realize that you don't have to wait on us old folks for you to go back to town to see that little ole gal. We all knowed that you are sweet on her and you don't need to tarry around or some other moon struck lad will come along and snatch her up. And I am sure that she likes you too; and ain't neither one of you getting any younger. I just thought I would just give you that Motherly advice."

Gertie then returned to her bread making and John sat drinking his coffee. Lizzy had heard the conversation from her room as she was dressing. She decided that if they didn't need supplies, in a few days she would make some excuse to help John go back to town.

Each of the others in some of their down time thought about the same thing. They all wished the best for John and wanted to help anyway they could. It was Henry that brought it up again.

"I think it is time that we started on your own house John. You decide where you want it and we will start cutting the lumber."

"What do I need a house for?"

"You dumb ox, for your bride."

"What bride?"

"You are going to marry that Claire girl in town aren't you?"

"I don't know. I haven't seen her but the once and I haven't even talked to her much. And her Daddy might not like me and I have no money."

Eb cut in. "If those were the reasons for not marrying then none would ever get married.

Let's go find a place for you a house."

Out the door they all tromped after breakfast, even Gertie and Lizzy. They felt like they needed a woman's opinion on this also. After picking a few places and discarding them, John found one just down the valley a little ways and back in the trees a little. He blushed when he said for some privacy. The others agreed it was a great place and then they returned to the big house to draw some plans and then decide on what lumber they needed. John's first house drawing was quickly discarded as too little. And of course Henry's was too big. In between they drew up something with a nice kitchen and cellar and a sitting room and a large bedroom.

It was Eb again that added, "It will need two bedrooms one for them and one for the little one. And we should build it like we did this one so we can add another story on the top.

"What little one?" It was John again.

They all laughed until they cried. Then decided they might should go to work and check on the mares and then they could start on the house for John.

It only took a couple of weeks and a new cabin was on the edge of the trees back well back from the water so when the spring rains and flooding would not reach the cabin.

Henry stood back looking at it. "John you better go get that gal to say she will come live in this fine house."

And others at the house agreed when they went in for lunch. They had already made up a list of supplies he would have to get while he was in town.

Lizzy decided she was going with him. She used the excuse of having to take care of some business, but had made up her mind to help John get Missy Nancy Claire to come out to live with them. And since he had no experience in this area she decided she would take care of that part.

It was an enjoyable trip and the weather held and they made good time. They arrived in their usual three days. Immediately on coming into town, Lizzy made John go to the barber a bath and she went and bought him new clothes. John assured her that he would do all of this in good time.

But Lizzy insisted that he needed to look good, Miss Nancy might even at that moment be in town with her family, he didn't know.

So he was now all cleaned up and looking good. They had taken rooms at the hotel and now Lizzy turned to John.

"Get on out to her house and ask her Dad for her."

"Just like that?"

"Yes, just like that. We are not going to get any work out of you until this is settled."

So John went to the livery and brushed Red until he shown. He then saddled him up and Lizzy saw him go down the main street from her hotel window. He looked good!

Dogs barked as he rode up to the house and soon the whole family was out on the porch. Mr. Claire came down the steps and welcomed John. After he had tied Red to the hitchin' post, John quickly took off his hat and spoke a hello to the whole group. Mrs. Claire ushered them all inside. Mr. Claire was immediately interested in how the foaling was going. And John was soon describing all the new foals and their personalities. He blushed when he realized that he had taken over the whole conversation. All this time Miss Nancy had sat very primly in a side chair with her hands folded in her lap. She smiled at John when he looked at her and he thought he was going to die. Mrs. Claire had excused herself and brought in snacks and drinks. She asked about Lizzy and the rest of his group, as she called it, because it was not exactly a family. John told them that Lizzy was in town seeing about the supplies and wanted to invite them to come to town and eat dinner at the hotel that very evening. Mr. Claire quickly answered yes to the offer for all of them. So John visited a little while longer and then said that he must go help Lizzy and was looking forward to seeing them at dinner. A time was arranged and then he was back on Red and back to town. He had not even spoken directly to Nancy! Well he didn't know much about this courting stuff. But Lizzy did and she was preparing for the dinner with the hotel manager. After she told him how she wanted dinner to go and what food, she was ready to go to the mercantile for their supply order. She remembered to buy each one of the others some little something. There was material for work shirts and each one of them got new breeches. She picked out some pretty print materials for Gertie and her new better dresses. And a little lace to go with it. She splurged on some stick candy and extra sugar treats. And as a last minute thing she bought material for sheets and curtains for the new cabin. John found her in the store.

"Well how did it go?"

"Ok we just visited."

"And they are coming tonight?"

"Yes."

"Ok I have everything done except the list for the blacksmith and some leather and rope that Mike wanted so you take that list and get it ready. Tell them we will load up in the morning to go back."

So John went and gave the blacksmith his list and then walked around the main street a little, but his mind was on Nancy. She was still just as beautiful as when he first saw her. And he had caught her smiling at him more than once. He even found himself whistling as he walked along. And whistling was what helped Lizzy find him after she had settled up with the store. She had walked outside on the porch of the store and saw him directly across just walking along whistling. She smiled to herself. She remembered that feeling a long time ago.

John thought that it took a long time for the afternoon to go by. Since he did not drink he couldn't go hang out in the saloon and there was not much else to do. So finally he just went to his room and took a nap. When he awoke he carefully did his toiletry and then was ready to go downstairs to dinner. Lizzy was waiting in the lobby. The Claire's had not arrived yet.

"What are you thinking dear?" It was Claire's Mother standing at her bedroom door.

"He didn't even speak directly to me. Oh, Mom do you think he doesn't like me? I really thought he did when he was here before."

Mrs. Claire quickly covered the space between the door and her daughter and took her into her arms for a hug.

"It took your Dad six months to speak to me."

"I am not waiting that long. I am ready to speak to him and him to me."

She drew back. "And if he doesn't ask me to marry him, I will ask him!"

Mrs. Claire laughed out loud.

"You just might have to do that, as I don't think John Dunn has had much experience in the asking area." She was still laughing when she left the room.

Claire finished her preparations to go and then went downstairs to join the others. She loved her family very much, but she had also realized that she loved John Dunn the minute she had seen him first. And she was sure that he liked her also. So what was his hold up? She must have some time to speak to him alone tonight. Maybe they could take a walk after supper or something.

225

They were a little late for dinner but not too much. Lizzy and the proprietor lead them into an adjoining room from the main dining area. There the table was already set and a nice young lady was there to wait on them. Lizzy called out where each on was to sit and of course that meant John next to Nancy. Mr. and Mrs. Claire were on Lizzy's right and left so they could visit and the kids were on the side with their mother. That left John at the other end with Nancy on his right. Lizzy realized she had not had a lesson on etiquette of eating with John but knew he would watch her and follow suit. A nice wine was passed around the table and the younger children had lemonade in the same glasses as the adults wine glasses so they did not feel left out.

The conversation was easy as Lizzy asked the Claires' about their crops. She included the younger children by asking them about school and their hobbies. The meal was served and then dessert. After dessert over coffee, Lizzy asked John if he and Claire would like to be excused to take a walk. John stuttered a quite yes and then they were out on the wooden sidewalk. The only lights were the ones coming out of the stores still open and the saloons. They walk a short way and then found chairs in front of one of the closed stores.

They at first just talked about everything except each other, weather, horses, and family and on and on. Nancy thought she was going to yell at John. We did not come out here to talk about my family or the gosh darn weather and we only have a little time! Then all of a sudden they looked right at each other and John blurted out.

"'I came to town this time to ask your Father if I can come around and see you. But I really wanted to ask you if you would like me to come see you. Or if you would just like to marry me. I don't have much, just some land and some horses, but I have already built a cabin and Lizzy made some curtains and stuff and we would really like for you to come be part of our family such as it is. And I love you."

Then he stopped. He realized he had said more than Lizzy had told him to say. He was supposed to get the permission to court Nancy and after a time of visiting and getting to know each other then he would ask about marrying her. So what did he do? He just blabbed out the whole plan in one swoop. And when he looked right at her she looked like a scared deer in a light. That did it. She probably never wanted to marry him anyway. But just as he was thinking all this, she moved closer to him and lifted her face to him and said

"Yes to everything. Yes to marrying you, and yes to going to live in the cabin and yes I love you too."

She then allowed him a short little kiss, but right on the mouth.

Then she jumped up and grabbing his hand said.

"Hurry we must go tell my parents."

"Aren't I supposed to ask you Father's permission and all that?"

"Maybe but we are going to skip that part. Since I know that he likes you and I like you so that is all that matters."

So they went back into the dining room, where Lizzy and the couple were still drinking coffee and visiting. To John it had been a lifetime, but it had only been a little while. The adults were only on their third cup of coffee.

Nancy walked right up to her Father and said, "Father John Dunn wants to marry me and I want to marry him. That is ok isn't it?"

Lizzy thought she was going to laugh out loud. Mrs. Claire had to put her handkerchief up to her mouth to keep from giggling. The look on her husband's face was so funny.

He was trying to be very proper as he said, "Young man this is quite sudden isn't it? Aren't you suppose to ask for her hand and then there is the courtship time?"

Nancy spoke up. "I told him that I didn't need all that courting that we could just skip that part if it was ok with you."

Mr. Claire then turned to his wife for some support on this crazy turn of events. But she was no help. She was refusing to look directly at him.

"Mr. Claire," she finally said. "We are all waiting for your answer."

"Answer to what?"

"About the getting married part without the courting part."

Mr. Claire stood up, nearly knocking over his chair. Pulling up to his full height he stuck out his hand to John. "Welcome to our Family John. So looks like we are going to have to plan a wedding."

Nancy was so happy she just hugged John right in front of everyone. John nearly died.

Mrs. Claire had come around the table and hugged him also and then Lizzy stood up and said,

"I purpose a toast." So they had some real liquor brought and they all had a toast and drink.

"To the new couple. And to a new country for them to live in."

The other kids were watching all the doings but were tired and just wanted their beds. So not too long later the Claire's were loading up to take the short ride back to their house. Before joining them on the seat, Nancy turned to John and had another short kiss and then he helped her up on the seat. Lizzy then spoke up.

"We will come by your house tomorrow when we had loaded our supplies and then will head home. Maybe you can try to figure out a date for a wedding before we go."

And then they were gone out into the night. John turned to Lizzy to make sure all this was not a dream.

"I can't believe that I am getting married."

"I know isn't it a kick? Let's have another drink before we go up."

So they went in and had another drink and with a small hug from Lizzy they went up the stairs to their rooms.

The next morning John was up early with the others loading their supplies and then they all set out to go by the Claire's on their way home. By the time they rode up to the house the whole family was out on the porch. They all stepped down and joined the family in the house.

Nancy had smiled her little extra smile at John and they sat together at the table.

Mr. Claire laughed.

"This is not a funeral. You too look like you are about to be hanged."

All the others joined in razing the two of them.

"We have to decide on a day to have this wedding party. Is that right Mrs. Claire?"

"Yes we need to decide on a day." Mrs. Claire agreed.

"Ok, How about a month from now? We will want to have it on Saturday so everyone can come and join us on their days off. We will have the service of course at the church in town and then have the dinner and reception here." Mr. Clare announced.

John and Nancy had sat just nodding as on and on Mr. Claire went about the wedding plans. It was very apparent to John he was not needed for any of these decisions and he was certainly glad. He really knew nothing about people getting married.

Lizzy had remained quiet while Mr. Claire named off all the things to be done.

She then quietly started.

"Who is going to pay for what? We need to pay our part and we need an amount so we can get our part together. And what food and other things do we need to help provide.

How many people are we expecting for this affair? Are we going to send invitations or is just everyone in town invited?"

Mr. Claire looked a little perplexed at her. "We figured that we would have to pay for everything."

Lizzy frowned and a furrow came across her brow.

"I have you know that we will pay our share and we let you know right now that we are able to do that without any due hurt to any of us. We may look like a rough bunch, but we are all the family John has and we have the money to provide anything that he needs."

"Oh I did not intend to insult you. Yes, we will certainly include you in the preparations and help with money to pay for it. As you know we are quite conservative so we will try to keep the cost down as much as possible. How about we get the wedding done and then we can itemize the cost and share it any way you see fit."

So it was decided that Saturday the 15th of May 1840, John and Nancy Claire would be married.

Then Mrs. Claire handed around pie and coffee and they visited for a while. John and Nancy had excused themselves and went outside for a walk.

"I did not know that weddings caused so much commotion." John admitted.

"I know, but my parents have missed being able to have parties like they did before and I think they are making up all at one time at my wedding. You don't mind do you?"

"Oh no, it is ok as long as that is what you want."

"I just want to be married to you." Nancy smiled her sweetest smile.

"Me too."

A warm kiss by the barn and the couple rejoined the others who were waiting on the porch for them to get started on their trip back home. After hugs and handshakes all around they were on their way back down the trail.

As soon as they were out of sight, Nancy ran to her room and there her mother found her sobbing. "My dear what is the matter with you?"

"I already miss him so much. I just wanted to run out and get on his horse with him and ride home with him."

"That will happen soon."

"Oh yes in a whole month." Nancy pouted.

"You will be so busy this month will go by in a hurry."

She took Nancy in her arms and hugged her tight.

"And then you can live with him the rest of your life, like your dad and me."

SIXTEEN

And they were busy that month. Nancy did not know there was so much planning for a wedding. Lists were made, marked off and more lists made. They began with a trip to town to see the preacher. He was put out because John had not come with them. Mr. Claire explained that they had a large horse herd and they had to get back so the Indians would not steal them. So the preacher relented. And the date for the wedding was entered into his date book and the time. They would have the service at 10:00 that morning. Then they would go out to their house, where there would be a blessing of the new couple and food and then the reception. They would have to get the marriage license the day before at the clerk's office in the court office.

Nancy had to ask a couple of girlfriends she had met to be her bridesmaids and then they had to get material and dresses made. Nancy had already tried on her Mother's wedding dress and with a few alterations it would be great! And she really wanted to wear it! Mr. Claire was fitted for a new suite and Mrs. Claire would make herself a new dress.

Supplies for food were ordered at the mercantile and barrels of beer from the saloon.

Invitations were made and carried around town. Of course the Claire's knew that everyone in town would come anyway. Invitations were also mailed to family and friends back home knowing full well they could not come but would enjoy the announcement anyway.

Since there would only be a few wild flowers decorations would mostly be ribbons tied on everything. The reception would take place in the barn so it had to be cleaned out and the floor washed and swept dry. Several new tables and chairs had to be made to sit around the sides of the barn.

The bridesmaids came out several days in a row and they all sewed the dresses. Then they spent one whole day making the ribbons to tie on for decoration.

The week before the wedding was spent with cooking. The men would cook the meat the day before. Bread, vegetables, and desserts would be made a day or two before and be ready to be warmed the day of the wedding.

One night Nancy put her head down on the table and before she knew she was sound asleep. Her mother awoke her and sent her to bed.

John was not so lucky to be so busy and it seemed the month dragged on forever. He went through the motions of doing his work but it seemed to take twice as long as before.

He also had to put up with lots of jokes from the rest of the bunch.

It was just a few days before the wedding when John realized he had no suit to wear.

"Lizzy! He came barging into the house.

"I don't have a suit to wear for the wedding!"

"It is a fine time for you to decide that."

The others had eased into the living room and were all standing around grinning at each other. Mike spoke up. "I guess you will just have to wear your best shirt".

Jo chimed in. "It don't have too many holes in it".

John looked from one to the other. "I can't wear that wore out thing!"

While he was pacing up and down he did not see Lizzy ease into her room. "Then I guess you will have to wear this." She held up a beautiful suit. "This is from all of us. We had it made a while back."

"How did you know that I would be getting married?"

"We just guessed and we were right. Go in now and try it own".

So John took the suit and new shirt to his room and came out all smiles. Lizzy turned him around and around and then announced it all good. Unknown to him the others had all had new coats made and they would all look pretty sharp at the wedding.

"We have one other problem". Mike said.

"What is that?" John asked.

"You have not designated a best man."

"Let me see," John rubbed his chin and looked around the room. "I think I will ask Henry, oh no I think Eb, no maybe Jo because he knows about weddings, but then there is Mike. I think I will have all of you".

"Can you do that?" Mike asks Lizzy.

"Yes you can have as many as you want far as I know".

So it was decided that they would all stand up for John.

Gertie and Lizzy had been busy getting their dresses made for the occasion. They also were packing boxes with food they would take to help with the food.

The few days before the wedding they all packed up and decided everyone would go. Jo did not think that was a good idea but they didn't want anyone left behind. So everything was loaded on the wagon and they were off to town. It was still cool at night but the days warmed up and they were all in a great mood as off they went.

They arrived in town on the third day. A little earlier than usual as they had pushed themselves to hurry up for some reason. They stabled the horses and took their rooms at the hotel. They sat down to lunch when Mr. Claire came in. He joined them and he said that he thought they should just call the whole thing off. John's face fell nearly down in his plate. Mr. Claire could not stand it.

"But my Nancy would kill me and her mother would help her after all the work that they have put into this shindig." Everyone laughed and they enjoyed the meal.

Next day Claire and her family came to town and they along with John and Mike went to the court office and signed for the marriage license. The clerk reminded them that it was not good until signed by a clergy or Judge.

Back out on the street, John thought he and Claire could spend the day together. He had nothing planned to do. But Claire's mother had plenty for them to do to finish all the work. So they parted and Nancy went home. Lizzy and Gertie took the wagon and joined them to help with last minute cooking and other things that had to be done at the last minute. They then took the decorations for the church back with them and decorated the church that evening. The ribbons and candles looked really pretty!

Wedding day dawned bright and clear. Some clouds the day before made them worry that it would rain but the weather stayed great! John and the boys were off to the barber shop for baths and shaves, while Gertie and Lizzy had bathed in their tubs in their rooms. After they were all dressed, they then all gathered in the lobby looking pretty "dressed up".

There was a flurry of excitement at the Claire's house. Soon they were all packed and in the wagons for town. They would dress in their fancy clothes at the church. They arrived in good time and dresses were exchanged for fancy ones. Hair was redone from the ride to town and ribbons tied in it.

Mr. Claire dropped in. "I hate to tell you but I didn't see John and his bunch anywhere in town. Maybe he got cold feet and went home." He couldn't stand it when Nancy collapsed into a chair and began to cry.

"Oh, no I am just kidding. I just spoke with them at the hotel. Stop crying. Everything is alright."

Mrs. Claire came up to him. "You should be ashamed of yourself". She playfully hit him on the shoulder. "Get out of here and don't cause any more trouble."

The little church was the proud owner of a foot pedal organ and an old lady that played it terribly, but it made a noise anyway. And the congregation could boast they had an organ and an organist. She sat down in her best dress and a large hat that made her nearly disappear under it.

With gusto she played a couple of songs if that is what you could call them songs. Two young men, that happened to be the preachers kids, came down the aisle and lighted the candles around the alter. Lizzy and Gertie were seated on the groom's side and Mrs. Claire and the rest of the kids on the bride's side of the pews. The groom and groomsman then took their place by the preacher at the front of the church. With a loud chord, the organist began to play the wedding march. The bridesmaids came down the aisle and took their places. Two little flower girls followed throwing wild flowers out of baskets.

John thought he was going to faint or throw up, he didn't know which. This was more pomp and circumstance than he had ever encountered in his whole life. Then he looked up and there came what looked like an angel coming down the aisle.

Nancy too was holding on tight to her Father. She was not use to being in the limelight like this ever. He turned to her and smiled to her and patted her hand. "It will be over soon."

This helped some of Nancy's nerves a little.

After the service John or Nancy could never tell you much about the service. It was some preaching and then the rings and I do's and then they were in a buggy on the way to Nancy's house.

The ring for Nancy had been provided by all people, Eb. Eb had caught John in the barn just the two of them and said, "I have the rings from my first wife. I would like you to have them. You haven't bought any have you?"

John said, "Ring, I had forgotten all about one. "Yes I would love to have them. Are you sure you want us to have them?"

"Yes but don't be going making a big deal about where they come from".

Then Eb had walked away. John looked down then at the rings expecting a small diamond solitaire and then a wedding band. Instead he was looking at a large diamond cut stone with two diamonds on each side. The wedding band was four diamonds across all the same size. It was beautiful but very expensive. John would always wonder where he got it but would never ask.

John and Claire would be instructed to drive around town and then very slowly back to her home so everyone could get there before them. And they did. Lots of hugging and kissing in the buggy and giggling went on. They could not figure out why everything was so funny but it was. Claire told him over and over how beautiful the ring was and how much she loved him. John looked right into her eyes and professed his love.

Then they were at the ranch and everyone was there. John was whisked off to the barn for beer as Nancy was hurried into the house to change clothes. Her mother with tears told her what a beautiful bride she was and then helped her out of the wedding dress to be worn by her sister in later years.

John was then rounded up and the two of them were announced by her Father to the crowd in the barn area. "I give you Mr. and Mrs. John Dunn." Hurrahs and clapping from everyone started the party. Toasts to the bride and groom were given and the wedding cake cut and pieces handed around.

And what a grand party it was. BBQ beef and pork with all kinds of vegetables and salads and desserts of pie and cakes were served. The tables had been covered with salt sack tablecloths and candles were on every one. Some men from the community had made up a band and guitars and fiddles and one harpsichord played by an old woman made merry music way into the night.

John and Nancy tried to speak to everyone there. As the night wore on John took Nancy aside, "Can we leave now?"

"I think so. Let me ask my Mother." Nancy approached her mother and pulling her aside,

"Can we go now?"

"Yes, she laughed, "the sooner you leave the sooner all these people will go and we can go to bed, I am exhausted."

So John and Nancy bid everyone a thank-you and without their driver, climbed on the buggy and made their way back to town to spend the night at the hotel.

Soon after people began to drift away back to their own homes. After that it was just the Claire's and John's bunch left sitting around the tables. Mrs. Claire had just returned from tucking in the younger siblings and she also joined them.

"I want to propose a toast". Mr. Claire. "To all our new friends and family".

He was joined by all the others in clinking their glasses together.

Mike and the others stayed a while longer and after offering to come back in the morning to help clean up and being soundly told no, they could do it, started back to town.

The sun came up very early seemed like to Mike and the rest. But they were soon downstairs and planning their day. They wanted to start back soon as possible, but didn't want to hurry the newlyweds. But to their surprise the newlyweds were already up and sitting down to eat. They had already fed the horses and had hitched them to the wagons. They were parked outside waiting for their journey.

Nancy had come west in a wagon, but it was like a bedroom. It was a large covered wagon with her bed that she shared with her sister. It had a chest for their clothes, a rug on the floor to keep them warm and dry and her dresses and shoes had their own place. This was not the case when she set out with John Dunn. He had told her to wake up before it was even light. They had dressed with backs to each other still very aware of each other. Then it was down for some breakfast and then he had her out to the livery to help saddle the horses and get the mules harnessed to the wagon. She had never even saddle her own horse and John was amazed when she was not able to get the saddle on her horses' back. He patiently showed her how, since she was so short and small, that she would have to learn to put the off side of the saddle on the saddle seat and then literally throw the saddle on the horses' back. It was the third attempt before she didn't drop it from the weight of it or threw it clear over the horses back to the other side in the dirt. John did not offer to help her. He knew she had to learn to saddle her horse herself. It might mean her life in the back country. That did not keep him from feeling sorry for her and when she finally got it right, smiled at her in approval. He then showed her how to pull the cinch and get the tension just right, to keep the saddle on, but without hurting the horses' back.

Then she just stood there.

"What are you waiting for to get aboard?" John asked.

"Aren't you going to give me your hand?" She replied.

"What do you need my hand for?"

"So I can get aboard".

"Do you think every time you are going to ride this horse I am going to be there to help you get on? Find something to stand on and get your horse close enough to get up on him."

She was not liking this adventure too much so far. She soon found a barrel to stand on and after a few times her horse stood close enough for her to get mounted.

As she turned around to go out of the barn, John called to her. "What about these horses for the others?"

"I have to drive the wagon, you take these horses." John handed her the lead ropes to each of the other's horses, after he had tied a couple of them to the back of the wagon. The ropes pulled on Nancy and would have burned her hands had she not pulled on her gloves as she had left their room. They then proceeded down the street and stopped and tied the extra horses to the horse rail in front of the hotel. They then loaded their things out of the hotel room. She had been appalled when John told her that she had to restrict her clothes to one chest as that was all the room in the wagon that they had. He explained that the rest of the wagon had to be used for their supplies for the next few months. She had told the hotel man to store the rest of her things and her family would pick them up later. She would never know how her mother had cried when her Father had brought the rest of the things back to the house. Her mother would wonder how her little girl would manage without all her conveniences she had always known.

While the others were getting their packs on their horses, Lizzy and Gertie had driven the wagon down to the mercantile and got all the supplies loaded. Gertie laughed when Lizzie bought candy for the new little one.

Lizzie asked Nancy if she wanted to ride on the wagon but she quickly told them she would ride her horse. They all grinned at each other. They knew she had only ridden a few hours at a time. Not all day like they would be doing to get back as soon as possible. They had been gone too long as it was. In the back of each one's mind they knew that the possibility was very real that there would be nothing there when they got back. They had heard in town about many settlers to the north of their valley had been having a lot of trouble with the Indians. There had been several farms burned out and one wagon train had been completely destroyed and the women and children taken prisoners. The military did little to stop most of the damage. They had been told to just keep the settlers out of the Indian Territories. The government had told the settlers to not settle in the Indian country. The country was too vast and the settlers were determined to have their own country to live in. So the military was actually restricted to reacting to episodes as they happened. Mike had been told by one military man that everyone should just go back East. The military man like so many others did not realize that many of the settlers like their bunch had nothing to go back to. This was their home and this was their family now.

Nancy began to wiggle in her saddle long before lunch. She could hardly walk when she slid down to the ground at lunch. Lizzie and Gertie soon had a lunch together on the back of the wagon and they all ate. When they had cleaned up Lizzie did not ask but told Nancy to take a turn on the wagon. Her horse was tied to the back of the wagon and Nancy climbed in the back after passing on riding on the wagon seat. They had not gone far when Gertie punched Lizzie to look back in the wagon. There was Nancy curled up on a salt sack sound asleep. Later when John rode by he asked where Nancy was. They made a shhhhh motion with their fingers to their lips and let him look inside the wagon. He looked in and then grinned and rode away. When Nancy woke up, she at first could not remember where she was. Then rubbing the sleep out of her eyes she climbed to the front of the wagon behind the seat where Lizzie and Gertie were. They then invited her to join them on the seat. She scrambled up on the seat between them.

"I am so sorry I fell asleep."

"That is ok I guess you didn't get much sleep last night and you were up early." Gertie replied.

The boys all repressed laughter when John decided it was time to stop for the day. They usually rode until dark but understood that this was a special trip. Finding a small stream to camp by, each one soon had their horses unsaddled and tied to the out rope. The out rope was tied between two trees and then each horse was tied to that rope. It gave them a little room to graze but not get away. John looked over at the wagon where Nancy's horse was still tied. She was busy helping get the supper cooked, so he went over and took care of her horse. She saw him and rushed over.

"Oh I forgot to take care of my horse."

"Well you are busy with supper so I will do it".

When supper was finished and things washed and put away. Everyone drifted off to where each made their own bed and lay down for the night. John had shown Nancy that they would move a little away on the other side of the wagon for their bed. When he just threw a blanket on the ground and one for cover Nancy was amazed.

"Aren't we going to change into our nightclothes?" she asked.

"No on the trail you sleep in your clothes, you might have to get up in a hurry and not have time to get another suit of clothes on."

Nancy then looked around and then quickly removed her petticoats and John looked at her and said that she might be more comfortable if she took off that thing cinching up your middle. So with his help the "cinching thing around her middle came off". And except for a few special occasions she never wore it again. She had never felt so liberated!

The trip was like a great adventure for Nancy. She had never been anywhere without her family and could not believe what things she had failed to learn from her mother; Like how to make a fire and how to cook and certainly her father never taught her to drive a wagon and team, but all of these she was learning. Since they had been away too long everyone was hurrying with everything to get back as soon as possible. Since they all knew what to do and how to do it, Nancy was sort of left out. They did not mean to ignore her but they had things to do to stay on the trail. And they did make good time. The weather was good and they made home on the third day. It was about the middle of the morning when they pulled over the last mountain and Nancy had her first look at the valley and the houses that were to be her new home. She was horseback, riding along with John when they crested the last and John pulled up so Nancy could take it all in.

"Mrs. Dunn this is your new home."

Nancy thought that it was the most beautiful place she had ever seen. They quickly rode with the others into the wagon yard. Everyone put their horses up and started unloading the supplies. When that was done everyone looked at John and Nancy.

"Aren't you going to take her to see her new house?" Mike offered.

"Oh yes. Nancy come on our house is over here". John said blushing.

They walked a little ways down the stream then turned up into the trees where the cabin that John had built stood. Nancy was surprised that it was so little. She guessed that she would be moving into a large house like the one she had come from. But when John opened the door and picked her up and carried her across the threshold, Nancy would not have cared if it had been a tent.

Inside after some smooching, John showed her around. Nancy was surprised to find everything all fixed up. There were curtains on the windows and quilts on the bed. Everything was scrubbed and polished.

"Tomorrow we will go down and get some of the supplies for us." John assured her.

But when she went to look in the cupboards they were all filled everything they would need. After more looking around they found the cooler had meat and potatoes and homemade jellies.

On the table was a note. It read: "We hope you have everything you need, if not tell us and we will help you get it. We also hope you will want to live with us forever. And be happy with John." At the bottom each of the others had signed their names.

They then had walked outside on the porch just in time to hear Lizzy ring the dinner bell.

Without thinking John had Nancy by the hand and started down the path to the big house.

"Aren't we going to eat at our house?" Nancy inquired.

"Not tonight, Lizzy said that you could begin cooking tomorrow or when you wanted to."

So down the hill they went and joined the others in a fine supper. Nancy looked around at her new family and to herself wondered if she would ever be able to cook for all of them.

SEVENTEEN

Since it was May it was time to start haltering the new colts born during the winter. Since they were not old enough to wean (although some weaned them this early) the mare and colt were brought in together. This also made the colt more secure having its mother at the ready. The colts followed their mare down the crowd chute and when the Mother was let out the end, the colt was held up by the gate. This allowed the hands to place a rope halter over his head and let the lead rope fall free. The colt was then let out into a larger pen with its mare. As the mare or the colt itself stepped on the loose lead rope it brought the colt to a halt. The colt soon learned this and realized that a pull on the lead rope meant it would stop. This action was repeated as each mare and colt was placed in the crowd chute and the halters put on. The Ranch had had a good year and there were 28 colts to handle. They brought in the older half and would work with the next group in about a month. In the evenings the same exercise was repeated in reverse. The mare and colt were herded into the chute only this time the halter was removed. While the colt was in the chute, the cowboys were able to let him feel them rubbing his back and sides and hear their voices. Each had taken their pick and only worked with their chosen colts. That way the colt learned that particular man's voice and feel. By the end of the week they were not very scared although very leery of the other cowboys still. The second week most would enter the chute without their mother knowing that she would be in the pen on the other side. The ones that were still not going in continued to have their mother lead them. John was amazed that the wild mares that they had picked up from the old stallion learned quickly and maybe sooner than the others. These mares were haltered the same as the colts and rubbed so they also learned to trust the cowboys.

In the mornings after John had been fed and Nancy had straightened out her house she would walk up the stream to the big house. The very first day she was amazed to see Lizzy in her pants and her hat on heading out to the barn. Nancy didn't even own any pants. Lizzy was tickled when Nancy wanted to follow her to the barn.

"You can come but not in that dress. First you will get it all dirty and second you and that hat will scared the horses. Don't you have any pants?"

"No I have never had any."

"Let's see if I have a pair in my trunk."

Back in the house Lizzy took out a couple of pair of worn pants and when Nancy tried them on they were a little big but a belt hitched them up and her man's shirt covered up all the bunching at the waist. That just left her shoes, but there were no boots so the shoes would have to do.

"Those are not your good shoes are they?"

"On no I have several more pair."

"Ok but try to stay out of the manure or they will be ruined. And remind me the next time we go to town to buy you some boots."

So with hitched up britches and long hanging out shirt and shoes and no girlie hat she followed Lizzy to the barn.

John was busy with one of the colts and had his back turned to the opening of the barn into the stalls. But Mike and Henry saw her and nearly died to laugh out loud. They both turned back to their work but watched out the corner of their eyes to be watching when John saw her. When John turned the colt he saw her and Lizzy. It was his undoing. While he was staring at Nancy he had taken his eyes off the colt and it turned its butt to him and kicked him squarely on the side of his leg. Mike and Henry could contain themselves no more and laughed heartily out loud. Lizzy too joined in and soon Eb and Jo joined in the merriment. Nancy could not figure out what they were all so tickled about. John quickly tied the colt and came over to where the others had gathered.

"What is the matter? Are you hurt?" Nancy said.

"Yes of course I am hurt the darn fool kicked me." Then looking Nancy up and down he said "those clothes don't fit very well, they must be someone else's. Didn't you bring your own?"

"I didn't have any to bring." John was at a loss and quickly looked to Lizzy for an explanation.

"John, ladies in town don't wear pants. They wear dresses all the time."

John still did not get it. "Why don't they?"

"Because most of them don't even come to the barn except for someone to saddle a horse so they can go ride it and then someone else puts it away and they don't get dirty." Eb explained.

They had all forgotten that Nancy was still standing there in her too big pants and shirt.

But they soon knew it when she put her hands to her face and started to cry and then turned and fled to the big house, changing into her clothes and running back to her house.

John had stood there for a while and finally Mike spoke up. "I think you had better go home and tell your wife that she looks great in too big pants and that she can come to the barn anytime she wants to."

"Why doesn't she know she can come down here? I just was not expecting her in work clothes."

"That is what you go and tell her I think". Mike shook his head.

The others nodded in agreement and John left. Then followed another round of belly laughs with Lizzy joining in.

"He has a lot to learn doesn't he?" Jo nodded as he talked.

"Yes, but that is part of the fun." Henry answered.

They all wandered back to their work with their colts and would have like to have been a fly on the wall in the new little cabin when John tried to explain his reaction to her coming to the barn. When John reached the house, Nancy was sitting on her bed still sniffling from crying.

"Nancy we did not mean to make fun of you. We were just took back for a minute." John stood at the end of the bed with his hat in his hands.

"No you thought I looked like an idiot. And your friend thinks I am a spoiled little city girl."

"The problem with all of us here is that we have been just us for so long we say just what we are thinking without thinking about how anyone will take it."

"Well it wasn't very nice."

"No it probably wasn't, but it was not spoken to hurt you. He was just trying to explain to stupid me how you have been raised."

"I want to fit in and Lizzy loaned me the only clothes that she had that wasn't a dress. Why didn't you tell me to get some pants and boots in town?"

"Again I didn't know and we will get some soon as we can. But right now you will have to wear what we have and now if you please, would you put the pants back on and join us at the barn? I have work to do and we need to get the colts broke."

With a hug and kiss they walked back to the big house and again Nancy put on the too big pants and big shirt, and with her shoes followed John back to the barn. She had been to the barn at their house before and knew a little about horses. But Mike was right, there was always a stable hand to saddle her horse and hold his hands laced for her little foot to be in to hoist her up on her horse. And when she came back that same stable hand lifted he down and did all the work of taking care of her horse. Here she learned, would be very different. John did not offer to help her and she learned to take care of herself. And she knew that if she complained that her alternative would be staying at the house in her dress.

The first few days she didn't do much but watch as each man worked with his colt. Then one day Mike told her to come out to the chute and watch closer. She then was able to touch the colts and let them smell of her. Some didn't mind but others, used to the smell of the working men, snorted at her and shied away. But they were soon used to her also.

The change in the men was noticed by Lizzy. They had toned down their cussing and yelling when Nancy was around. This made Lizzy smile. She remembered the same thing going on when Franklin and her first married. All the men except John did this. John was just John, anytime and around anyone. More than once he had pushed Nancy out of the way with no apology and Lizzy started to speak up, but decided to let them work that out.

As spring turned into early summer, Nancy had learned to turn the soil for planting the garden. She could lead her two colts around by their halter. Her cooking had improved with help from Gertie at the big house. Her first few attempts John had eaten without making too much of a frown. But when he went back to work he stopped by the big house and asked Gertie if she could help out on the food cooking. She had laughed and invited him in, where he sat down and had lunch. They were both busy visiting and unaware that they had been joined by Nancy. She quietly sat down next to John at the table and then asked Gertie,

"Could I have the same as John is having?" So that had been the start of cooking school.

EIGHTEEN

Gertie, Lizzy, and Nancy would join John and Mike on the trip. Everyone made their lists and they started out early one morning. John, Mike, and Nancy were horseback and Gertie and Lizzy took turns driving the team that pulled the wagon. They had started out right at sunrise after a good breakfast at the big house. They had not gone buy a mile or two when Nancy turned her horse off the trail and dismounted. They all heard her throwing up. John turned to Lizzy

"Do I need to go see about her?"

"No I don't think so, but you can ask about her when she comes back."

When Nancy rejoined them they started off again.

"Are you alright?"

"Yes, I am fine; I guess I have a little bug. That is all."

Soon the horseback riders were a little ways away from the wagon.

Lizzy turned to Gertie, "Do you think she knows?"

"I have no idea, but we will see and maybe her Mother will tell her when we get to their house.

"I told John she needed to stay with her folks while we are there not in town with us."

So they moved on along and with good weather and no problems they arrived at the Claire's place the next day. All of the family came running out to see them. There were hugs all around. They then settled at the big table and Mrs. Claire brought out some lunch and they had a good visit. Mr. Claire was very interested in what they had been doing with the horses. Nancy told them how she had learned to halter her colts. Her Mother had to ask her twice about being at the barn with the men.

"I am going to do everything everyone else does and do my part to help out. I can also cook for all the hands now too. Miss Gertie has taught me how. And I helped put in the garden and when it is ready she will teach me how to put all the stuff up in the cellar."

Mr. Claire smiled at his daughter so excited about her new life, but her Mother was very concerned about the callous' she had observed without remark, on Nancy's hands.

That afternoon everyone loaded up to go to town except Nancy. John looked over at the others trying to figure out what he was supposed to do, stay or go with them. Nancy came over to his horse and whispered, "I think I will stay here and visit my folks. You go on ahead with the others, I will be fine."

The next morning Nancy's mother heard her before she saw her out by the barn throwing up again.

"I guess I have caught a bug. I have been sick since we left. But it is strange because it is just in the morning."

"No it is not strange, most pregnant women just throw up in the morning but some all day long, and you must be one of the lucky ones." Nancy took one look at her mother and then they were both hugging each other.

"Does John know?" her Mother asked.

"I don't know he hasn't said anything to me."

"Have you said anything to him about it?"

"No, but I just thought I had a bug."

"Now we will get ourselves together and go to town to see Dr. Lambert and make sure you are ok."

So Mr. Claire was told to hitch up the buggy, they were going to town.

"We just went to town before they came, why do we need to go again?" Mr. Claire inquired.

After a stern look from Mrs. Claire, he soon had the buggy hitched and pulled around the front of the house. Nancy and her mother and the kids rode in the back and one of the boys in the front with Mr. Claire. They had just come into town when they met John.

"Hi, I didn't think you would come to town today," he spoke to Nancy. He helped her down from the buggy and then she said, "I have to go to the doctor and you have to come with me."

"Are you still sick?"

"Yes."

So Mrs. Claire poked Mr. Claire and told him to proceed to the mercantile store. And Nancy and John proceeded into the Dr.'s office. Dr. Lambert was standing in his office and motioned them into his office. He had been taking care of the Claire family ever since they arrived from back east.

"Come in, come in. What can I do for you two?"

"I believe I am pregnant."

John turned to her in disbelief. He had not thought a lot about having a family. He had just thought it would just be the two of them for quite a while. Without thinking what he was saying, he turned to the dr. "Can she really be pregnant already?"

Dr. Lambert chuckled, "Yes, she can already be pregnant. Let's go in here and see."

John excused himself to the waiting room. While he paced up and down, he thought about a baby. A BABY! Wow, he hadn't thought about that and how were they going to take care of it. He certainly didn't know anything much about them and Nancy was just now getting the hang of cooking.

He looked up as they came into the room. Dr. Lambert came over to shake his hand.

"It is still really early but I would bet she is pregnant. You don't work her too hard and come back in a month or two and then we will know for sure. But if I was a wagering man I would bet on this one."

So out the door and down the street they went. First they told Gertie and Lizzy that they met on the street and then down to the mercantile to tell the rest of them. Lots of handshakes and hugs went with the news.

Gertie always the practical one, announced to the grocer they needed baby material for making blankets and clothes. Mrs. Claire chimed in and told him they would need some material for Nancy new clothes.

"You don't realize that in a few weeks you won't be able to wear a thing."

Lizzy had pulled John aside and told him that they needed to buy her some boots. So they had taken Nancy by the hand and a trip was made to the boot maker. With their luck he had a pair on hand that fit and Nancy was delighted with them.

That night they all gathered at the hotel restaurant and again enjoyed eating and visiting. It was mostly Nancy telling them all the new things she had learned to do. Her mother cringed at some of them, but her father just smiled and was very proud.

Later in the evening, Mr. Claire drew Lizzy aside.

"How are the kids doing?" he asked.

"Fine as far as I can tell." Lizzy answered.

"I mean do they need anything?"

"I know what you mean and no they don't want for anything and I am able to see that they don't need anything and that includes money!"

"Oh I am sorry I didn't mean to be putting anyone down. I just needed you to know that I will help anyway I can. I figured that I couldn't ask John without hurting his feelings."

"Ok, I understand. So if I ever think that they need something I will tell you."

The next morning the supplies were loaded and they had started out when Nancy's Father caught up with them.

"I just thought I would ride along with you for a while." Nancy knew that something was not right about that since they had spent the evening before together.

"How are the colts doing?" he asked.

John spoke up, "They are growing fast. Most of them are ready to be weaned and are all halter broke."

"And I broke my own colt. His name is Warhorse. He belongs to one of the mustang mares and is three colors, white, black and brown." Nancy chimed in.

"You have to be careful now doing those things since the baby is coming."

"I am Dad."

"When you get ready to sell some of the colts, I believe that I want two or three of them." Mr. Claire said as he rode along.

"We would like for you to have them, but we are not selling any this year. Maybe next year. We were thinking about bringing them to town and having a horse sale." John told him.

"That seems like a good idea. Not only will you make some money but people will get to know that you are raising them."

While they were talking about the horse trade Mr. Claire's impression of the man that his daughter had married had gone up considerably. He had his doubts when she picked him out, thinking that he might have to support both of them, but after getting to know him and his companions, he had changed his mind. And he could tell that Nancy was still enamored with the whole idea so he was also happy.

He rode another mile or two with them and then bid them goodbye and turned south as they turned north to their mountain home. He was still concerned about how they were going to get along since they were not going to sell any colts this year. How would they buy supplies and pay for things for the baby? He turned a little east and headed back in town. He tied up at Lawyer Burke's office and walked inside.

"Come in Claire, how are you?"

"I am just fine. I just came from seeing my daughter and her new family off."

"How are they doing?"

"I am going to be a new grandfather."

"That's great I guess. But I realize that you did not come in here to discuss your new grandkid."

"Yes I do want something. I know you can't give out any information that someone tells you in here but I just need to know, uh, if you can tell me, uh, what do you think they do for money? They all seem a disjointed lot and none look too wealthy."

Lawyer Burke laughed a jolly belly laugh. "I can't tell you anything, but I can tell you that you have nothing to worry about you daughter being taken care of."

Mr. Claire started to speak again.

"No, we can't discuss this anymore." Lawyer Burke held up his hand.

"In that case I better get back to my rat-killing at the ranch." Mr. Claire mounted his horse and rode away. Lawyer Burke stood on the sidewalk and chuckled to himself.

"No, Mr. Claire you don't have to worry about your daughter, that Ms. Lizzy has more money than they will spend in their lifetime."

An old cowboy walked by on the wooden sidewalk. "Are you talking to yourself these days?"

"It seems I am", lawyer Burke did not realize that he had been talking aloud to himself.

It was that evening when they made camp and no one would let Nancy help carry wood or water or actually anything. So when they all sat around the campfire she started,

"Ok all of you. Yes, I am pregnant but I am not an invalid. From now on I will tell you when I need help or am not able to do something by myself. I promise not to overdo anything, but you must stop smothering me right now!"

Sheepish grins went all around their little circle. They were all delighted at the prospect of a little one around. And they knew that it would be hard not to pamper their "little momma". So they would spend her pregnancy trying to help her without her knowing it, and Nancy would spend her pregnancy seeing them pamper her, but acting like she didn't know it.

Of course when they were returned to the place the "helping" continued, especially the men.

Each in their own way now realized that this was now their family and had the feeling that they were to become grandfathers to the new baby. Gertie and Lizzy too could hardly wait to be "Granny" to a little one.

NINETEEN

Summer found them all busy working in the garden to put up the food needed for winter. Nancy especially liked the days when Gertie and Lizzy would gather up baskets and the three of them would wander out into the woods nearby and pick the wonderful wild plums. Gertie said it made the best preserves in the world. By July, Nancy could pick many a basket of fruit. She then learned from Gertie how to boil them with sugar and put pectin in them and ladle them into the jars. The candle wax was then poured on the top of the jelly to form a tight seal when it hardened. When the jars cooled enough they were lovingly set on the shelves made for them in the storage cooler. Nancy took a jar home with her and the next morning fed John the wonderful stuff with his breakfast.

"I am quite impressed young lady with your expertise in jelly making." John told her. He had pulled her down in his lap and she laid her head down on his chest.

"I have a few more surprises left too."

"Ah you do now. And what would that be?"

"Since you do not remember the exact date of your birthday we have decided that it is this Saturday and we are going to have a party. And I am going to invite everyone up to our house and I am going to cook."

"Don't you need some help, with the baby and all?"

"I am pregnant, not helpless as I have told you before."

That afternoon Nancy walked up the hill to the big house. She then announced to Gertie and Lizzy her plans to have a birthday party for John. This invitation was received with great to-do.

Instantly the two of them began to plan for the party. It was a little while before they realized that she was having the party not them.

"Oh dear! We assumed you meant for us to help you." Gertie smiled at her.

"Uh, we will be glad to help in any way that we can, you just tell us what we need to do". It was Lizzy that had quickly smoothed over the obvious. Gertie and she knew Nancy did not know how to cook for all of them or whatever to cook. But they would be as discreet as they could and help her without her knowing it.

It was Gertie that then ask, "What are you planning to have?"

"Oh, I thought we would have cake and punch."

Gertie did not dare look at Lizzy as she was having a hard time keeping a straight face.

"And what time of day will we have this party?"

"Tea time is four o'clock so I guess that will be a good time for the birthday party."

"That sounds like a perfect time." Gertie could not stand it one more instant. She excused herself and went out on the porch with a bowl of green beans to snap. Sitting there with the beans in her lap she snickered to herself. She could just see all of them dressing up in the middle of the day and going down to the little house and having cake and punch.

In a little while the others had come from the barn for a glass of cool water and rest. Nancy then announced that on Saturday they were all invited to their house at 4:00 for cake and punch in honor of John's birthday. She then took the supplies that she had come to get and went back down the stream to her house. While they watched her walk away it was Eb that spoke first.

"Does she think we are going to bath and put on town clothes and go down there for a party in the middle of the day?

"Yes that is exactly what she thinks and that is exactly what all of you are going to do." Lizzy eyed each one of them in turn. As they returned to their work she could hear them muttering as they walked along.

That night at the supper table the party came up again.

"Are we supposed to rustle up a present?" Mike asked.

They all looked at Lizzy with one gaze.

"Yes I guess we are."

The next day found each one trying to figure out what kind of present that they could come up with by Saturday. John thought they were all acting funny, because when he would come upon one of them they would put whatever they were doing away or try to direct him to another side of the barn to look at something else.

Friday when Nancy came down for supplies Gertie quietly ask her if she needed any help with the cake making.

"No I have everything I need and my mother sent some recipes so I will use one of them."

"If you decide you need me just call out and I will come help you . . . . and no one has to know that I helped you." Nancy looked at her in surprise and then with a great grin she quickly went up to her and gave her a big hug.

"I am so blessed to have all of you to see about me."

Early Saturday morning Nancy fixed John's breakfast and then shoved him out of the house.

"Do not come back until just enough time to dress and have the party. Don't even come for lunch as I am decorating the house."

So after he had made sure she had plenty of water and logs for the fire he went on up to the barn and started working, doing his chores and getting a lot of ribbing from the others about being older.

Gertie and Lizzy were as tense as cats. "Do you really think she knows how to fix the fire for the cake not to burn?" Gertie asked.

"Do you think she has enough of her ingredients? Maybe we should just go down and ask if she needs any help?"

"No, we were told to come at four and that is what we are going to do."

Meanwhile Nancy had bought some colored paper in town when they were there last. She had cut out some designs and made placemats. She sat the table with her best dishes that her Mother had sent with her. She had a large Hope Chest of things when she married that she had made starting when she was about 10 years old. Today she realized that she missed her mom, especially when the baby started kicking and moving around. Maybe she should go home and have the baby. That is what John wanted her to do. But she wanted him to be there and she knew he could not be gone for a month. No she would have the baby here and Gertie and Lizzy would help her.

Unknown to Gertie and Lizzy, making a cake was about the only thing that Nancy did know how to cook. And she was quite pleased with herself when she slid the layers out of their pans and stacked each one with icing in the middle of each layer. She knew that the sugar used for the icing was a real indulgence and they might get a little low before their next trip to town, but it was for a good cause.

The clock that she had brought with them, an old mantle clock handed down from her grandparent's gonged three o'clock before she was ready. Quickly she ran in her room and washed up and put on a good dress. Then she came back in the big room and surveyed her work.

She was quite pleased with herself! It looked so festive! When John came she made him clean up and dress outside so he could not see inside until the others came. With a few little touches here and there she was ready for the party.

The others had been busy too. They had all bathed and dressed in Sunday-go-to-Meeting clothes and then with their gifts marched together down the draw to the little cabin. They laughed when they saw John out on the porch.

"I have been banned from the house until all of yawl got here."

About that time, Nancy hearing them arrive, came to the door and announced that they could come in. Although it was afternoon and there was plenty of light, the table was set with two candelabras with tall candles lighted.

"Wow, I never seen anything so pretty!" It was Jo to speak first.

"I feel like we are in a big city with all the lights," Mike answered.

They settled down at the table and the cake with four little birthday candles was brought out. The candles were lit and blown out and John was told to make his wish. They then all had cake on real china plates and the punch was served from a large bowl with tiny cups with tiny handles. The grown men's hands had trouble holding the tiny cups and mostly just cupped the little things in their big hands to drink. They had several servings as the tiny cups full were little more than one drink themselves. Gertie congratulated Nancy on a wonderfully cooked cake and said that she would have to share her recipe with her. This made Nancy smile a lot. When she passed by John's chair again, he gathered her up in a hug and the rest all applauded. Then it was time for gifts. They were of course all handmade and hurriedly done since they had only a few days but were all gratefully acknowledged.

Gertie had made food for supper and after the party everyone went back and changed back into work clothes and did their night chores. Then they all gathered at the big house for supper.

Nancy was again told how wonderful the party was and they would have to do it again next year.

TWENTY

It was a couple of days later when Eb was running his trap line. He had made nearly all his traps. When he went to get the beaver out of the last one something caught his vision out the left side. It was just a movement but he felt the hair stand up on his back. He knew better than to turn and look but he knew he was being watched and he also knew it was probably Indians. He finished resetting his trap, even braving a little song that they could hear. He didn't want to show any fear and wanted them to think he did not know they were there.

There were five of them; one seemed to be the leader, riding a big paint stallion. He was magnificent in full buckskin clothes and moccasins and he had more feathers than the others.

The others were also in buckskin shirts and breeches but they were an odd lot, all sizes and ages.

Eb slowly loaded the last beaver on the extra mule and began his trip back home. He was undecided what to do. He couldn't go to the house and expose the women and he couldn't go to the horse pens where everyone else was as then the Indians would find out about the horses if they didn't already know. He had seen them just now and realized they were just a hunting party. So they don't think I have a home. Well, we will just go a little hunting ourselves.

He climbed a little higher on the side of the mountain where he could get a better look at them below. They seemed to be deciding if they were going to waste time on an old trapper or continue on their way for food. They would like to have the pelts, but luckily Eb had them covered up so they could not really tell how many he had. Eb eased on a little more heading away from where the home place was. He did not hurry; again he wanted them to think he didn't have any idea they were anywhere around. As he climbed a little higher he found he had walked into a cave entrance. Quickly he led the two mules inside the cave and then picked up some branches and retraced his way and then made tracks going back down the mountain. Then he went back and covered all his tracks to the cave. He then checked his rifle and his pistol to make sure they were loaded and ready. He then sat down a little back of the cave and waited. It would be dark soon and he knew they were tracking him now. He could hear their horses breaking the brush and then heard them turn to the new track away from the cave. He hoped they didn't decide to come in the cave for the night. But he waited until it was good and dark and then heard them no more. Finally he allowed himself to ease out of the cave to have a look. Quite a ways and down to the right of him he could see their campfire. He was fortunate, it was moonlit night but with some clouds. He returned to the cave and unloaded the pelts back in the cave. With his lead rope in one hand and his gun in the other started back down the mountain. Turning and twisting, he changed his tracks many times, all the time hoping that the mules would not bray as they got close to the barn. Finally he could see John's lights on in the little cabin.

Eb called out and when John came to the door, he quickly told him they had to have a confab as Eb called it. Getting a lantern, John and Nancy followed him up the stream to the big house. Nancy went inside while John and Eb went to get the rest of the group. Lizzie and Gertie quickly made coffee and set out a few sweets. They did not question Nancy as she had already told them she knew nothing. Soon all of them were gathered around the table.

"The Injuns are here. I was trapping about 7 miles west of here when I ran into a hunting party. They tracked me for some time but then bedded down and I hid in a cave and left my sled there. So even if they haven't followed me here they will soon find my tracks. Hopefully they will think I went somewhere else. I covered my tracks as best I could. But they will now find us eventually."

There was silence all around the table. Nancy was the first to speak. "We must send someone to Fort Negal and ask the troops to come."

"We can't do that," Mike turned to her. "We are in Indian Territory and they are not supposed to come in here unless there is a reason. We have no reason to give them except we saw some Indians."

"Well, first things first. We have to make a guard every night. Nancy and John have to move in the big house. I will take this watch. John you and Nancy stay here tonight and then go get your things in the morning. The rest of you get some sleep we may need it later on." Henry spoke up.

John put Nancy to bed in his old bedroom and then went back out to the main room. Gertie had gone back with Jo to their house attached to the barn.

"We knew they would come. We just thought since we had been here four years that they had missed us some way." Lizzy was still drinking coffee at the table.

"Yes I guess that I thought that also. I had not prepared Nancy at all for this and now we have the baby on the way." John sighed.

They heard footsteps on the porch and John reached for his gun. They both grinned when Mike came in. "Is there any of that coffee left? And why was the door open?"

John and Lizzy looked at each other sheepishly. They certainly were not prepared for an Indian encounter. After Mike drank his coffee he went back into the night. It was middle summer now and the nights were balmy. He stretched out his big frame in one of the porch chairs. When he felt the night getting colder he raised himself up and made another round of the place. He first made the barn and the horse pens out back. Then he circled and went around Jo and Gertie's cabin. Then he crossed over the yard and circled the big house. John who was still awake saw his reflection in the window when he passed by. Feeling safe with him watching, he turned over and hugged up his wife and baby and went back to sleep.

The next morning early, John hitched up one of the wagons and he and Nancy went to their house and got clothes and supplies.

"How long will we have to stay?" Nancy asked.

"We have no idea. They may not come at all. But my bet is that they have already found Eb's tracks or the pelts and will begin looking for us."

Gertie had a good question for all of them. "What about the smoke from the chimney when I cook?"

It was Eb who spoke up. "We can't go hungry while we wait, and if they are close enough to see the smoke they already know we are here. And we don't know maybe they are scared of us or maybe they are friendly tribe." He was trying to water down everyone else's fear especially Nancy's. She looked like a spooked raccoon in a lantern light.

After the men left to do chores she approached Lizzy. "Aren't you scared to death? I am and I don't know what to do if they come."

"Oh dear. We have totally ignored you. Let me help you out. If the Indians come and the alarm sounds you will run into my room, open the trunk take the trays outs and climb in and do not come out until we tell you to. I will go and clean it out right now."

Gertie who was listening to this conversation thought she was going to burst out laughing.

She knew good and well that if the Indians came, she and Lizzy would be using their rifles just like the men and standing their ground. But as she considered this she decided that the trunk might just be the safest place for Nancy and the baby.

It was the third day when Nancy decided to get out of the house. So she started to the barn to see the horses. She had barely stepped inside the barn when she felt someone put their hand over her mouth and pull her down to the ground. Quickly she was pushed to a corner and with gestures she was shown to keep her mouth shut. The Indian was tall and lean. He wore buckskin clothes and had a rifle. Looking around she saw no one else and she wondered why he had not killed her already.

Soon she heard John coming into the barn whistling. She wanted to cry out but was so afraid that she was speechless. The Indian turned and saw John and about the same time they both covered the distance between them and bear hugged each other. "Talking Wolf, you old devil, what are you doing here?"

Nancy had nearly fainted when she saw the two of them going to each other. She was sure that it would be a fight to the death. They both now turned to her. Talking Wolf hurried over to help her up.

"I am sorry missy; I did not mean to scare you. I just saw that you all were staking out the place so I didn't want to get shot by someone who didn't know me."

"Nancy this is Talking Wolf a friend of Eb's and ours."

"Are you by yourself?" John asked.

"No I have a few braves with me. They are waiting for my signal. Let me call them in."

He stepped out into the opening from the barn and raised his gun in the air. Almost immediately it seemed to Nancy a group of men, tall and well buckskinned joined them. They did not speak they just watched.

Gertie had come out on the porch and realized everything was alright. She returned to the kitchen putting her gun back on its rack and started fixing food.

John had called to the others and they all went over and sat on the big wide porch of the big house. Mike and Eb and John told stories of their time with Talking Wolf. When Gertie offered food the Indians refused. Instead Talking Wolf asked for some meat and the other braves took it off to build a camp and cook it.

"So tell us how come you are way out here?" Mike asked.

"The government made all of us move over into what is known now as the Indian Territory. Supposedly all you white folks have moved out of here too. So why are you still here?"

"First we homesteaded this land and it is ours. And we have already spent all our time and effort to build this place before the president decided to give it back to you."

"Yes," Talking Wolf replies. "We saw lots of settlers east of here in a small town."

"That is where my family lives." Nancy finally spoke.

Talking Wolf looked sadly at John and then rose up. "Are you going to show me some of those blooded horses or not?"

They had rounded the barn and started to the horse pens when John asked him.

"Something is the matter, what is it?"

"That town had a bad time with a band of Indians. Most of the settlers moved into town after their houses and barns were burned out. Many were killed and they are even having trouble getting supplies into the town, so they are getting desperate. John, I believe that you and your family are in a bad place. You better gather your family and horses and get out of here. There is no one to help you."

"We have to go to town and see about Nancy's family first. Then when we bring them we will see what we can do about here."

"You cannot go to town without someone with you. I will go with you to get your family. I will leave the braves here to guard your family until we get back."

Nancy had a fit to go with John to get her family. "I can help my family pack and do a lot of things."

"You don't need to put you or our baby in danger. We do not know what the dangers are yet. You will move into the big house and stay there until we get back. Now get your things together right now. We will leave at first light in the morning. Mike and Henry will go with me and Talking Wolf, the others and Talking Wolf's braves will stay her and guard the place and you."

When she started to protest again, he pulled her to him and kissed her really hard.

"I will not have you putting yourself and the baby in harm's way. And neither would your family want you to. I will bring them back in a few days. In the meantime get what supplies you have here in the wagon and your clothes and let's go down."

Gertie and Lizzy were busy getting food together for the trip and getting food prepared for all the braves and the men left. Nancy joined in but everyone knew she wanted to go with John to get her family.

Talking Wolf reminded Gertie that the braves did not want to eat with them. Just furnish them with some supplies and they will cook for themselves. They will not ask for more unless they do not get any meat staying so close to the house.

Early the next morning they were all busy getting everything loaded and John and the others off on their trip. They took a wagon and all rode their horses except whoever was driving the wagon and that horse was tied to the back. When they changed drivers that one took up his horse and the other driver's horse was tied to the wagon. Soon as it was light they were ready to go.

John hugged Nancy and told her to be careful and they would be back at least by the end of the week. And then they were off. The others left stood and watched until they could no longer see them and then turned away.

Eb was the first to speak, "We best get all the work done up before anything else happens."

John and Lizzy had decided the best thing to do was to move all the horses into pens closer to the house. So Jo and Eb and Lizzy along with a couple of braves went out and spent the day moving the horses into fenced pastures behind the house. This also meant getting feed cut and stacked up nearby to feed them while they were penned up. Extra water was pumped up to the barn and barrels of water carried to fill the water troughs. Eb told Jo as they dipped the buckets and filled the troughs, "I didn't know horses could drink so much water."

The women were busy too. They made up extra bread and cooked extra meat in case they could not have a fire in the next few days. Although they were still scared of the braves, they came and went silently and they would see them making their rounds of the house and barns seemingly on a schedule although Gertie knew that they did not have a clock. The braves communicated with them mostly with sign language and grunts. But the braves were very patient and smiled a lot.

They had set up their camp behind the barn. They believed that if an attack was made they would be coming from the front of the house. So the Indian braves felt they could attack them from a place of hiding. Gertie was also amazed that they were so clean. They washed all the time. She could see them cleaning their clothes and themselves in the water. She offered them some soap but they couldn't seem to figure out what it was for. They would take it down to the water with them but she never saw them use it and then they would take it back to their camp.

One day Lizzy noticed that the brave that was helping them with the horses was scratching and scratching. "Let me see your arm." she said.

She slowly pulled his arm toward her and raised up his sleeve. A violent red rash ran up his arm. Pulling him along she took him to the porch and motioning for him to sit down in one of the chairs Mike had made. She went inside and called out to Gertie.

"Bring me some ointment; one of the braves had gotten into some poison ivy."

So they took the ointment out and with not too much resistance they put the ointment on the rash. The ointment immediately started to cool the rash and soon had stopped most of the itching.

Since they had no way to convey how to put more ointment on, the women decided that they would just hunt him up later in the day and put some more on him. With gestures though they were able to convey that he was not to wash it off. So nearly supper time they both had walked out to the barn and found the brave and using a spoon they smeared more medicine on the arm.

Then the next day or two they took turns getting the ointment put on him.

Unknown to them his arm and the magic medicine had produced quite a bit of ribbing from the other braves. But they were happy when the rash was gone and he was not itching, as it had kept some of them awake as he scratched during the night.

It took John and Mike and Talking Wolf the same three days to get to town even though they had left with first light and would travel into the dark at night. They went straight to the Claire's place and found no one there. So they immediately went to town. The town was crowded. People were everywhere. There were many camps with wagons on the outskirts as they rode in and then people were bustling up and down the boardwalks. John and them tied their horses and went into the saloon. Talking Wolf had stayed at the Claire's place. Not knowing what to expect the reaction to an Indian might be. He knew the settlers knew there were good Indians and bad Indians, but they couldn't tell which was which just by looking at them. And some settlers, after having bad experiences with the bad ones, just disliked all Indians. John had left him some food and they decided that they would pick him up on their way back.

In the saloon, John, Mike and Henry soon had everyone wanting to know where they had come from and had they had Indian trouble. With everyone talking at once it was bedlam. They were soon rescued by Lizzy's lawyer who recognized them. He steered them across the street to his office.

"What are you boys doing here? Haven't you heard the Indians are taking us over?"

"Yes we heard and we have come to get Nancy's family out of here. Have you seen them? We went by their place but no one was home."

The lawyer downed his head, "Theirs was one of the first ones hit. Only their son survived. He had come to town for supplies. When he returned home they were all dead, scattered out all over the yard from the house to the barn. "J.D. came riding in like a banshee and the law went out with him and they tracked them a ways but then lost them in the water a few miles upstream. I believe everyone in the territory came to their funerals."

After talking a drink of what he had offered to them he continued. "I have all their legal papers. And JD had enough money to bury them all. I believe that he is camping on the north side of town with some of his friends. Everyone around had come into town. They sent for the military but they will not come. They claim that this is now Indian Territory and we were supposed to have moved out."

John sat there staring straight ahead. He was thinking about how he was going to help Nancy when she heard that her family had been all killed. He turned to Mike who was talking

"Let's go find J.D. and then we will decide what to do next."

They saw J.D. before he saw them. They rode upon him before he knew it and then he turned and John was down off his horse and they were in a big bear hug.

"I wasn't there to help them." J.D. cried out.

"There was nothing you could have done. They were outnumbered." Mike had joined the group.

"We are here now and you are to come home with us." John still held him by the arm.

They all stayed together in one room that night, with J.D. having nightmares most of the night.

The next morning they were again in the lawyer's office.

"The government was earlier buying back the land from the settlers. So I propose to buy the Claire property at land value and then when the government agent comes I will hopefully get my money back. Mr. Claire was always good to me. This is the least that I can do."

While they waited for the paperwork to be finished, Mike had suggested that they fill the wagon with any supplies that they thought they would need. He also had thought to try and buy extra clothes especially pants for all the men. All over town they saw people that they knew living in town and abandoning their farms and ranches. So they were not surprised the next day to find a crowd gathered around a man standing in the back of a wagon. They moseyed over to hear what he was talking about.

"So we have decided to put together a wagon train and head south toward Louisiana and Texas. Since we know most of you just have what you have brought to town, we propose to leave one week from today. That gives all of you time to go home and get your things together, take care of your property selling or whatever you plan to do and then meet at the North end of town one week from today. We will all throw our livestock together and herd them along with us. Are there any questions?"

From the back of the crowd, a tall man asked, "What about the Indians?"

"We will just have to pray that our large number will discourage them. Otherwise we will just have to stand and fight. No one is telling you this will be easy. But many of us have decided that we do not want to go back East so we will push southward."

As John, Mike and J.D. walked away, John was the first to put words to thoughts. "We need to join this group and get out of here too. We are sitting ducks out there where we are and soon as the Indians decide to take the horses we are done."

"I agree," said Mike. "So we need to get this show on the road." They quickly went back to talk to the man that was talking out of the wagon.

"We believe that we would want to follow along with your wagon train. But we already live south of here so we would have to catch up with you when you came that way. Would it bother you that we have a big herd of mares and a couple of stallions? We realize that they might be a big draw for the Indians. And we have a band of friendly Indians that live with us. They would be valuable in tracking and watching for Indians. But with what these people have been through they might not want them around."

The wagon boss, as he would soon be called, stared right through all three of them.

"We would appreciate the Indian help. We all have had good Indians at some time. But they would not be able to associate with the train and would have to stay apart some way."

"We believe that would not be a problem. They will help us wrangle the horses and stay away from camp. We haven't asked them if they want to join us yet but we have one of them just out of town. Would you like to meet him?"

They rode North out of town but not to J.D.'s place and were soon joined by Talking Wolf.

The wagon boss was impressed with the tall well-built man that shook his hand. He also was surprised and impressed when he spoke proper English and had great manners.

Talking Wolf replied when questioned, "I believe that my band would consider moving south with you. Maybe not all the way but we are needing to move from where we are. All around us are tribes that are raiding and have no desire to live in peace."

"How many of you are there?"

"Besides the braves at your house we have about 20 women and children. But we can follow along with the horses and not bother anyone. The braves and I could track and watch out for other Indians. We also would know which ones were friendly and ones that are not."

After shaking hands, Talking Wolf faded almost like a ghost back into the woods. He would join John and the others when they started home the next day.

Back in town a trip to the lawyers' office and a trip to the bank for some money and a letter of credit for the rest of the sale of the land completed their tasks for the day.

"I would like to go back out to the farm would the two of you go with me?" JD spoke.

John and Mike quickly agreed and the three of them rode out to what was left of the farm buildings. One corner of the barn was all that was left standing. All the rest of the buildings were just piles of ashes. They rode up to a small hill in the back and JD showed them where his family was buried. After spending a short time there, JD gave a whoop and started back down the hill at a lope. The other followed with guns drawn. When they arrived at the house and rode around the corner of the barn, there was JD down on his knees holding a spotted calf and next to him a large black and white milk cow. They looked away when he stared up at them with tears running down his face.

"We can take her with us can't we?"

John smiled, "Yes. We certainly can."

So slipping a rope around the cow's neck they started back to town. The calf trotted along the side of her mother. When they reached town they put her in a pen by the livery. They then went to the hotel and had supper and fell into their beds and with JD on the couch in the room. JD only woke once during the night and then slept the rest of the night.

The next morning they gathered all the livestock and then they tethered them to the back of the wagon. Mike climbed up on the wagon seat, JD and John were leading three horses each that they had found while coming back from JD's. The baby calf trotted along by its Mother.

They camped by a stream that night and by daybreak were back on the move. They had not gone long when a tall Indian joined them.

"I was wondering where you were." John patted him on the back.

"I have been tracking you since yesterday, but there were others along the trail so I decided that it would be best to lay back."

It was after dark when they rode in the yard after the three days to get there and everyone came out with lanterns to help them. Nancy was the first to realize that the extra rider was JD.

"Where are the rest of them? Did they not come?" She asked.

JD had pulled her to him and hugged her up to him. "About a week ago the Indians attacked the farm. I was in town getting supplies and I found them when I got back. They are all gone."

Nancy began to cry and then it became a wail and she collapsed to the ground. John quickly scooped her up and carried her into the house and laid her on the sofa. Lizzy lay a cold wet rag on her forehead and washed her face. She soon recovered. JD standing by then moved a chair and sat down next to her.

"Tell me everything." Nancy whispered.

"There is really not much to tell. A few months ago an Indian agent from Washington came to town and then went out to meet with the Indians. With an interpreter told them that all the settlers had to move and the Indians would have their country back. Then he came to town and called a town hall meeting. He told all the settlers that they had to move back across a line and he showed them where the line is on a map. When the settlers told him that they were not going to move and this was their home now and he could not make them move. They had paid good money for their land and it already had buildings and pens and lots of labor had gone into their places. The Agent then told them that if they were not out of the territory by the first of the year the military was going to come and move them out. After he left the church, where the meeting had been had, everyone began to talk at once. Finally the preacher called the group to some kind of quiet.

Father stood up. "I don't think that the government has the right to make us move. But the lawyers and I will make a trip to

Washington and see what the status of this mess it. I agreed that it doesn't seem right, but no telling what has happened to cause this."

He left the next day and was gone about two weeks. A judge and several lawyers and two other ranchers went with him. When they returned we could not believe what they said. The Indian Agent was right; the government said that the land belonged to the Indians by a treaty.

It was made to move all the Indians out of the land where the settlers to the East were living.

"Mother and Father now faced a dilemma. They had sold everything they had to come to the new land. They had put down roots here and raised a family. What were they to do? Where would they go? They talked late into the night. I saw their candle alit long into the night. The next day a decision was made. We were going to come here to be with you all. But it would take us a few days to get everything together and start out. I was given the list and sent to town for supplies. It took me most of the day since I had a lot of errands. I had to get supplies from the mercantile. I bought another wagon and team. I had to go by the lawyer's office with a letter from Dad. Mr. Gainsby caught me and asked what we were going to do. I had to tell him that we were pulling out and would come here to Nancy and John's. He began to shout and called me and my family coward's and how could we abandon our community. His ranting drew a crowd and I just stood there not knowing what to say or do. We just were trying to do the best we could for us and you all had invited us to come before now. So when I could I faded back out of the crowd and finding the young man that I had hired to bring the new wagon and me in the old wagon we headed back to the ranch. The sun was just setting when we drove over the hill and looked down and saw the smoke. I quickly jumped on my horse that I had tied to the back of the wagon and galloped down to the yard. I found Mother first and then the other kids in the front yard. Dad and the other two hands were dead behind the barn, killed where they had been working. The hand came down in the wagon. He found me on my knees in the barn, screaming and screaming. I could not stop! He finally slapped me hard on the side of my face. Then I cried until I couldn't breathe anymore. We moved all the bodies over by what was left of the barn. We built a fire and sat by it all night. The next morning we carefully loaded them in the back of the wagon and covered them with my blanket from my pack and made our way back to town. We stopped at the Sheriff's office and then he directed us to the funeral parlor. After we unloaded them and made arrangements I went to the church and told the preacher. By then everyone in town heard what had happened. We decided to have the funerals the next morning. I had to buy new clothes since mine had burned. We had the funeral and then we went out to the hill behind the house. It took a lot of men to carry the coffins up the last part of the walk. Some men had come out the morning and dug the graves. The preacher said some words, something about the hereafter. And I just sat down near them and one by one everyone left. It was after dark before I touched each grave and said goodbye and then went to town. I got a room at the hotel. When he asked me for how many nights I told him I had no idea. I had no idea about what I was going to do, except come out here. Then the next day John showed up and here I am. And I am so glad to see all of you."

Nancy had sat up during his recounting of the events and he now moved over on the sofa and took her in his arms.

"I am so sorry I couldn't do anything."

"It is not your fault and if you had been there you would probably be dead now too. And I am glad you are here with us."

Gertie brought out food and they all took their places around the table. Lizzy took Nancy's hand and Nancy took JD's and then one by one they took each person besides them. She prayed.

"God this is the biggest mess we have been in so far. Please give us guidance as we go forth to find our new place. Help us grieve and then let us help each other. Help us in the new land and bring us safely there." "Amen" was the chorus from all of them.

John didn't realize how hungry he was. Everyone was waiting for John to tell them what they were going to do.

"While we were in town, the people were organizing a wagon train to carry them south and west, either Louisiana or Texas. I hope you all are not mad but I signed us all up. Talking Wolf assured us after going out and listening to the wind, that the settlers that are still there are in dire straits. The Indians will hit there after a big pow-wow that is coming up in about a month. So what do you think?"

"Gertie and I are in if you will let us go with you." Jo spoke.

Then Eb "I don't have anywhere else to go but with you."

Then Lizzy stood up all 5 ft. of her and said, "Where this family goes I go."

Mike joined in. "So right now what we all need is some sleep and then tomorrow we will start getting ourselves together. We only have about a week to do everything."

When Nancy and John had gone to their room, Nancy began to cry again. John helped her out of her clothes and held her the rest of the night. The next morning she looked really bad, eyes red and her hair needed putting up. When she decided John could comb her hair, he balked. He eased himself out of the room and rounded up Gertie.

"Could you please fix her hair up a little it is going everywhere and I don't know how to do it."

Gertie eased into the bedroom and without a word began brushing her long beautiful dark hair. Nancy sat staring straight ahead. She was so distraught. She did not want to live. What was there to live for? Her Mother would never see her new baby. Her Father would never ride his favorite horse again. Thinking about her siblings lying dead with no one to help them, it was too much. She began to cry again and then it was a river. Gertie had stepped to the side of her and Nancy buried her face in her apron and hung on to her like if she held tight enough all the pain would go away. It was a while before she realized that it was real pain. And she evidently had wet her pants. She drew back from Gertie and screamed

"It's the baby!"

"Can you walk?" Gertie asked.

"Yes"

Let's get you over to the bed. Now get out of your clothes if you can. Where is your nightgown? Nancy motioned to a chair nearby. Quickly they got her out of her clothes and into the nightgown. Gertie then after placing extra bedding on the bed eased her down onto the bed.

"Stay here I will be right back."

Gertie hurried to the porch and called Lizzy.

"Nancy has gone into labor. Start boiling water and get some more sheets and towels."

Lizzy jumped up and began ringing the dinner bell. The bell was used for meals, but also for safety. Hearing the bell all the hands thought that the Indians were here already, they were soon on the porch. They could see nothing the matter until John heard Nancy screaming. He bolted into the house with the others at his heel. Lizzy turned everyone by John back.

"What is happening? We are not to have this baby for another month."

Lizzy touched him on the arm. "Many times when pregnant women become over worked their nerves start the birthing process. So that is what has happened to Nancy."

"Can we stop the contractions or something?"

"No her water has broken so we are having baby soon."

John walked over to the bed and bent over and gave Nancy a kiss, but she didn't seem to respond much. Looking back at Lizzy with a question on his face,

"She doesn't seem to know much does she?"

"No and she won't for a while now. Why don't you go out and sit with the men and I will call you if we need you."

John reluctantly let go of Nancy's hand and eased out of the room and went back out on the porch. He slumped down in the closest chair.

"How is she doing?" Eb had taken the chair next to John.

"I don't know, she didn't talk much. But they said that her water has broken, so we will have baby whether it is time or not. But it is still really early. I guess the shock of losing her family did it to her."

Nancy was very healthy pregnant woman. All those months of agonizing about being so big and fat had mostly been growing a big baby. So when hours later when he was born he was a big weight and not a little bitty thing. When he came out he gave a lusty yell and opened two big blue eyes to look around at this new world he had come to visit. Lizzy quickly cleaned him up and wrapped him in a clean baby blanket and then called John to come see. John came almost tiptoeing into the room. Lizzy dumped the baby in his lap as he sat down in a rocker nearby.

Then Gertie and her proceeded to massage the afterbirth out and then clean everything up. With new gown and clean bed Nancy smiled at the sight of the new baby and his Father.

"Now you can give it back to its Mother."

Quickly John obeyed, handing the baby down to its Mother and giving both of them a kiss on their foreheads. He then told them he loved them and out the door he went.

Out on the porch he proclaimed the birth of the baby.

"What is it a boy or girl?"

"I don't know, they didn't tell me."

John went back into the house to the little bedroom. Looking down again at the baby who was by now nursing, he asked, "Could you tell me if it's a boy or girl?"

"It's a boy." Nancy said.

John never said anything to her and out the door again he went.

"It is a boy!"

Eb had gone in the meantime to his bunk place and brought out a bottle of spirits and

Gertie brought glasses and they all had a drink to the new baby.

"What is his name?" Jo wanted to know.

"Henry, unless she has changed her mind again." They had spent many times in the last few months trying to think of a name. They had tried and discarded a lot of them. But they both like Henry in the process of elimination.

"Henry Dunn, has a nice ring to it." Mike answered.

They all stood around for quite a while, every man knowing he should just go to work as there was nothing more to be done here. Gertie had already started the fire under the big kettle outside to do the washing. Lizzy was fixing food for supper. Gertie was the one to realize why they were all standing around like fools. She then marched over to them all and said, "Come inside. You aren't going to get anything done until you see him." And leading the way they all marched into the tiny bedroom taking up all the space. Nancy smiled all at of them and they thought she looked just like an angel. Gertie stooped down and took up the baby. She then gave it to Mike and he held it just for a moment before it was handed to the next one and around the bed it went, each holding him like a glass doll that might break. He was then returned to his Mother and all but John went out to do the evening chores. He sat by the bed holding the baby and rocking him.

"Are you still going to call him Henry?" Nancy asked.

"Yes if that is alright with you."

"Yes Henry it is!"

John had just met his son but already did not want to put him down, but knew he needed to go help at the barn. So he soon leaned over and gave him back to his mother. With a kiss he was gone again.

After supper the question on everyone's mind was when Nancy could travel. They had discussed it quite at length when they noticed Nancy and the baby standing by them.

"We will not change our plans. I believe that we were going to leave in four days from tomorrow and four days from tomorrow I will be able to ride in the wagon."

Gertie started to object but Lizzy put her hand on her arm and nodded a no to her.

Lizzy had risen from her place and moved over to Nancy. "That is four days that you young lady are going to stay in bed." So Lizzy and Nancy returned to the bedroom.

John turned to Gertie, "She can't travel that soon can she?"

"Of course she can. But we will have to take it slower than we planned. So tomorrow we will get everything together and we will leave on time to meet up with the wagon train."

And to that end, everyone began the next morning to get everything together to move all of them and a new baby to a new place. The horses were culled and only the very best were chosen to go on the trip. The others were turned out to go and join the old black stallion. Some stayed around the pens a day or two but then finally grazed off. John and Lizzy were sorry to see them go, but were encouraged in the thought that the old stallion would pick them up and he would keep them fed.

The morning of the leaving they were all up before sunrise and with breakfast cooked and eaten they all stood together in the yard of the big house and Lizzy said a prayer for them a safe trip. Then mounting their horses and wagons they turned southeast to join up with the wagon train.

Part Three

INDIANA INDIAN TERRITORY TO TEXAS

ONE

Jim Ryan was the "wagon boss". His main job was to keep the wagons moving. This also meant he had to have trackers that could watch for Indians and could find water. Both were about the same in importance. He was very pleased when he was joined by John Dunn at the signing up for the wagon train. He could tell by looking at him he would be an asset to the train. He wondered some for a young man to have a whole group of people joining him. He had mentioned seven people and one on the way. The one on the way was the one he worried the most about. He had made this trip several times before and had to bury several babies. He was happy that other women would be there to help with the little one.

The last day of signing up was a good one. He now had twenty-seven wagons and several buckboards. He had signed on a cook, the trackers and two other men to help keep the wagon train moving. Each wagon owner paid a set amount and extra for livestock. They could bring as many people as they could pile in the wagons, and many had too many. But they were whole families and none could be left behind.

He had a printed sheet that outlined the rules for the wagon train.
Wagon Train Rules by Jim Ryan
Each group will be responsible for their own water and food.
Each group will be responsible for taking their turn at night watch.
Each group will be responsible for keeping their wagon and animals up with the wagon train.
If a group is unable to keep up or continue they will be on their own to return to where ever they came from. The wagon train cannot spare any men to go back with them.

In the event of Indian trouble, each group will take part in helping defend the wagon train. So each group must have guns and ammo for each person over 14 years old.

Fighting and getting drunk will not be tolerated.

If a member of the group has a special talent that will lend to the moving of the wagon train such as smithy or doctoring please let the wagon master know.

Wagon Boss makes all decisions and they are final.

It was a clear day when John and his group started on their journey. Their part of the train included two wagons, a flat wagon for supplies and feed. Besides the people there were the chickens, two pigs, one milk cow and the horses. After culling all they could stand, John and Lizzy had decided on 14 mares and Red for their breeding stock. They felt like they could manage this many and maybe keep the Indians off of them. The wagon boss was not really pleased with all the horses but it seemed to him that they had enough men see about them. And a new born baby was a worry for him. But he had had them born on the trail with him so at least this one was already here.

Their departure was to be no later than 9:00 am sharp. And looking at his pocket watch, he raised his hand right on time and the first wagon started out. Although it would be a lot dirtier near the back, John and the others decided that they wanted to be close to the livestock and horses. If it became unbearable they would move the women and the babies up some or let the livestock move back some.

To Nancy sitting by John on the wagon seat with their new born son, this was the trip of a lifetime. Gertie had come up on her side of the wagon and slipped her what looked like a large pillow. "Sit on this, until you get to feeling better."

When Nancy had gone from the east to Indiana Territory it was just like a vacation with her family. This trip was to be an adventure into unknown perils and she was excited. The others too in their own way found this a grand adventure. Jo and Gertie, who had joined this group out of dire circumstances, now thanked the Lord they were able to join this adventure. Mike and Henry took the first turn driving the horses and livestock with other men. And good ole Eb drove the flatbed wagon with his mule trailing behind.

John drove the wagon the first day to teach Nancy how to handle the team. When the baby slept in its bed made in the wagon, Nancy would take the reins and learn to steer it behind the wagon in front of it. One time she had to pull out of the line when without warning the wagon in front of her stopped dead still. But they were soon going again and she was able to get her rig back in line. Their wagon was pulled by 6 horses. This was two more than most but their wagon was large and heavy and it put two more horses to go with them. Jo had spent a lot of his time teaching the horses to draw the wagons. Jo and Gertie would share driving with Lizzy. Their wagon only had 4 horses and Eb's wagon was pulled by six mules.

The first day they did not get very far. The wagon boss called the night halt in the middle of the afternoon. When he rode back to John's group he explained that this would be the time for finding wood for fires and hunting. It also gave the train time to learn to circle the wagons and watch for Indian attack.

Mike and Henry went off to hunt. Jo and Eb went to watch the livestock. Gertie and Lizzy started a fire when John brought in some wood. He had gone back and brought back two or three more trips gathering wood. He then took their ax and cut up the wood. What they would not use that night he planned to bundle and then tie on the side of the wagon. That way when they didn't have a way to get wood, he would have some.

It was not long before Mike and Henry were back with a couple of deer. One had large antlers that Henry wanted to make knife handles. They soon had the deer hung up in a nearby tree and cut up. Gertie helped them salt the meat and wrap it the salt sacks and packed into a barrel. While they were busy doing this Lizzy and Nancy were making supper and the cooking meat smelled great. Although it did not feel like they were doing any work, the men found that they were really hungry. To go with the meat, they had beans (cooked the day before they left) and onion and rice. While they still had coals left from the fire more beans were put in the hanging pot to cook and be ready for the next night.

Soon, if Nancy was busy, there was one of the hands to rock little Henry. Many nights around the fire, Henry would fall asleep in one of the group's lap. He soon learned the sight and smell of each of them and would hold his little hands out to any of them to take him to entertain him. And they readily, almost as a game, would try to be the first to get to his bed to get him. Even old Eb would hold him and rock and sing to him.

The second day out Mike took the reins of Nancy's wagon and John took his turn riding drag as the livestock wrangling job was known as. John introduced himself to the others riding that day and they had plenty of time to visit and get to know each other. A few times some of the cattle would try to drift away and had to be turned back but mostly it was just moseying along. Wagon trains did not travel very fast. Not only did they have to stay together but if one wagon had a problem all stopped to try and get them going again. Broken wheels, lame horses or mules pulling the wagons were common occurrences that brought the train to a halt.

Nancy found the first few weeks very trying. She was very happy with the pillow on the wagon bench. She was very concerned when she continued to bleed a great deal. This was sapping her strength. She was too shy to speak to anyone even John about it. They had been out a couple of weeks when Talking Wolf rode up next to her as she drove it in the line. He had never come up to her except if John was there and he never talked to her.

"My woman says you need to chew this every day for a while." He leaned over and placed some kind of plant stems in her lap. Then he turned and rode away. Nancy gathered up the greens and placed them in the wagon. When John came later to take a turn driving the wagon, he noticed the green plants.

"What are these?

"I don't know. Talking Wolf brought them to me from his woman. She says for me to chew some every day for a while."

"What are they supposed to be for?"

"I don't know."

"Well don't chew them until I ask Talking Wolf about them."

Later in the day John approached Talking Wolf.

"What are those plants you took to Nancy for?"

"My woman says she is sick. Too much blood. And the plants will stop the blood."

John turned Red and loped back the wagon. Climbing up on the wagon seat and taking the reins from her he asked,

"Are you still bleeding from the baby?"

Turning her head away she whispered, "Yes I am."

"Why haven't you told someone?"

"I didn't know how long I would have it."

"The plants are for the bleeding. And they are not poisonous or anything. Indians know a lot about medicine that we don't know."

Talking Wolf's woman had noticed how tired and pale Nancy continued to be. She had produced the plants and told Talking Wolf to take them to the little woman.

So Nancy chewed a little of the plant each day. It was not very good and the stringy shreds got stuck in her teeth. But she continued chewing it like a religion. Occasionally she would see the Indian lady at a watering hole. The Indian lady never moved towards her or spoke, she would just make eye contact and nod and then be gone. But her word was good. In about a week the blood flow lessened and then stopped. Nancy never knew if it was the plant or the timing but she would believe that it was the plant.

Day after day they trudged along. There were still a lot of trees so there was plenty of wood for the fire and fresh water in the streams that they crossed. The Wagon Boss Ryan assured them that when they had traveled out to the west there would be less trees and little water. But for now that was no problem.

It was a couple of weeks before they saw the first Indians that were not with them. John saw them on the horizon to the trains right. He informed the others riding drag with him and then loped up to the middle of the train where Ryan was.

"I see them. If they are going to do anything it will be probably during the night. Tell the others to slowly move their livestock and you bring up your horses closer. When we circle the wagons tonight we will move the livestock into the circle. And be sure that every wagon is pulled as close as possible to the next one, leaving as little clear space as possible. I will tell the front part of the wagons and you tell each one on your way back to the end. It is early and we need to keep going another hour or two if we can and we can always hope they go away. And ask your Indian who they are."

John turned his horse and rode back to the next wagon. He repeated Ryan's instructions to each of the wagons. Men that had been driving wagons soon were horseback and women took over driving the wagons. Guns in the saddle holsters of each one were checked and made sure that they were loaded.

When John got to his wagon, Lizzy had already left Gertie and come up to take the reins from Nancy. Nancy knew this meant something different even before John told them what was up and pointed out the Indians riding along on the horizon. She could see them in between trees as they rode along.

Her question of whether they were good or bad made John chuckle.

"I am going to go ask Talking Wolf that same thing right now". He then turned and rode to the back of the train where the horses were trailing. Mike and Eb rode up with Talking Wolf.

"Miss Nancy wants to know if they are good or bad." John turned his head toward the Indians.

"Not too bad. Just a hunting party that had picked up our track. They are not too many and they follow along trying to figure out how mean we are. I don't think they will bother us."

"Just in case we will move the livestock inside the circle and what about you families?"

Talking Wolf looked sternly at John and replied "We will be better off by ourselves. But if you need some of us will fight them off."

That afternoon Nancy saw the wagons in front of them began to slow and then begin a large circle. Lizzy pulled the big hitch to a halt and Mike appeared and pulled the lead horse out of the line and alongside the wagon in front of them. He then unhitched them and led them over to their wagon side and tied them off. Since they had not chosen to wait and find a place to stop near water, the horse hitch would just get a bucket of water from one of the barrels that had been filled at the last watering hole. Leaving one end of the oval made by the circling, the livestock was eased into the oval and tied to each family's wagons. John was glad that their horses were gentle and did not act up as they tied them each one to one of the wagons. They were then watered. The wagon boss had advised for no fires to be built so supper would have to be cold. Nancy helped Lizzy and Gertie get out some cold beans and meat to feed their group. Gertie as usual had thought of this happening and had some left over biscuits and some jelly for their dessert. Little Henry was fed early and put to bed to try and keep him very quiet. Although he was basically been a good baby, he was very vocal when his needs were not met very soon.

The other settlers and their families were used to wandering around the camp and visiting at night and Nancy found the unusual quiet disturbing and the night was very dark. John and her had sat at the back of the wagon for a while and visited and then Henry and the others came by and they decided on shifts to help patrol the train. They then went over to where some other men were and they discussed with them and the wagon boss how they would patrol. John had gone with the others to talk to them so Nancy had snuggled down in the bed with the baby, but she was certainly not asleep. John had loaded her rifle and placed it at the side of the opening of the wagon. Thank goodness he had taken the time to show her how to use it.

It was a couple of hours before she was awakened by the first gunfire and was surprised to see Lizzy crawling into the wagon with her.

"What is happening?" Nancy asked as she quickly pulled on her boots.

"I really don't know but figure we were better off here together." Lizzy replied.

"Should we get out of the wagon?" Nancy continued.

"No John said to stay in here that way he could find us in the dark."

"Lizzy are you scared?"

"You would be a raving fool not to be."

John appeared and told them that he had moved the Indian families near their wagon.

"Do they need to get in here with us?" Nancy quickly asked.

"No and they wouldn't come in anyway. I just needed you to know they are here so you don't shoot them. And the gun shot was a young man on the other side thought he saw something in the brush but I think he was just over anxious. Do you two need anything?"

"No we are fine."

"I will get back to patrolling then."

Sunshine and Henry wiggling made Nancy wake up and sit straight up. She then looked over and saw Lizzy grinning at her.

"Did I sleep all night?"

"Most of it."

"Oh I am so sorry!!"

"You didn't miss anything that I heard."

John came by to tell them that they would be leaving soon so get the bunch fed. But still no fire so breakfast was cold meat again. Soon as everyone was ready the lead wagon started out and the train continued. The hunting party could still be seen on the horizon and through breaks in the trees. The train continued on for two more days of being on high alert. On the fourth day Talking Wolf came up to John and told him that they were gone. John quickly loped to the front of the train and told Ryan what he had said.

"We are very pleased with that news. We will stop early today at the next water and everyone can cook and eat. As you go back tell each wagon what we have planned."

So John stopped and told each family they would be able to make a fire soon and then he rode back to tell the men herding the livestock and Eb was the happiest of them. He was getting mighty hungry.

So earlier than usual they stopped and made camp. Fires were soon going and food cooking smells filled the air. The horses and livestock were herded to the stream and let fill their bellies with the water that they had not had much of the last few days. People wandered around and visited and little Henry was passed around in laps until he fell sound asleep in Gertie's lap.

It was several days later that Talking Wolf reined up next to Nancy's wagon.

"You need to talk to brother. He goes out in the brush at night and cries a lot."

Nancy slowed her wagon a little to talk to Talking Wolf, but as always he was already gone like the wind. When she finally picked him out he was way back of the last wagon. She didn't really know what to make of what he said. She knew that she hadn't seen much of J.D. but she just thought it was because he was helping with seeing about the hunting party.

That night when they were serving supper and he came to fill his plate she quietly said, "I need to talk to you."

"Ok talk"

"No not now later, just you and me."

After supper was finished and the women had washed up and put the pans away, J.D. came by Nancy and John's wagon. Nancy had already mentioned to John that she needed to have some time with her brother. So she slipped out of the wagon leaving John to watch little Henry. She stepped up and took her brother by the arm and they began to walk a ways away from the wagons.

"I haven't seen much of you lately. And it feels like you are avoiding me for some reason. Want to tell me why?"

They had found a large rock and had sat down next to each other.

"I have not been avoiding you. It is just that we have been very busy."

"That is not exactly right I don't think. I hear you have been going off by yourself a lot. And I am pretty sure I know why. You need to realize that I do not hold you responsible for not being able to help our family. I couldn't help them either being so far out here. But you must know that if either of us had been there, we would have been killed also. But for some reason God left the two of us and we are together and I need you."

Nancy then hugged him up to her and could barely hear him when he whispered, "I need you too."

He then stood up and pulled her into a hug and then walked back to the wagon and just as Talking Wolf was gone.

John was still up when she came back into the wagon.

"Is he all right?"

"I think he will be but it is just going to take time I guess."

"I am really glad I have you, John Dunn to lean on. I hadn't really realized he didn't have anyone but me now."

TWO

The next few weeks were more boredom for Nancy than anything else. The wagon train woke in the mornings, fed livestock, made breakfast and ate, cleaned up and then hitching up teams they would set out. This was the same nearly every day. So quickly Nancy began visiting the other families when they were stopped. She learned that Sarah and Tim had the wagon next to theirs in line in front of them and John and Lea were behind them. A Brother Sims held the church services on Sundays. John Dunn had met John behind them while taking care of the livestock. They started visiting and soon were cooking and eating together. They had one little girl named Lilly. Lilly was nearly four and was fascinated with Henry. She would come up to Nancy and beg to hold him. Nancy would patiently let her climb up on her wagon seat and put Henry in her lap. She would keep a good hold on him, as he was nearly big as Lilly.

Soon it was summer and hot and humid. Some days they would be able to cool off at a nearby stream but most days it was just hot. John and the others stayed busy trying to keep the livestock with water. He tried to let Red rest and ride one of the mares every few days, but the others said that they spent all day trying to keep him from going to John. So he finally gave up and just rode him all the time. Red was a full grown stallion now and with the warm weather he had shed all his winter hair and shined in the sunlight. Some days he had to be admonished around other people's horses but John was good about keeping him reined in.

John too had made a few friends; especially the wagon boss. Ryan had learned right away that he could depend on John and his friends for just about anything. They kept the train going along with others and the livestock moving. Ryan was especially pleased with the way that they had handled themselves when the Indians were spotted. And Ryan learned to depend on Talking Wolf. He had been very apprehensive about bringing them along but now a few weeks out he had to admit they were some of the best trackers he had rode with. And Rabbit Feather could nose out a water hole with the best of them. Some of the other train families did not like the idea of them coming along but after the "Indian Incident" and seeing how they helped out, the bias eased mostly. But not all, as they would learn later.

It all started after they had come upon a burning wagon. There were three men and two women lying there and they had been shot with arrows. One of the men had been scalped. John and Mike rode out with Ryan and then refused to let anyone else come near it. John loped back to his wagon and took out a shovel. Nancy wanted to ask but she could tell by the look on John's face it was not good. So she sat without asking on the wagon seat.

After they had buried the bodies the others from the train gathered around to have a funeral.

They had an elder in the wagon that everyone called Brother Dave. He led the service. John had found some papers in one of the men's pocket that identified him with a last name of Bruster.

Brother Dave went with the Bruster name asking God for their souls to be taken up to heaven. Then someone started Rock of Ages and when they had sung all the verses that anyone knew each family went back to their wagons. Quickly wagon boss Ryan got the train going again. Knowing that the sooner they were somewhere else besides here the better. So the train continued to their regular stopping time and then circled the wagons and made camp.

That night after supper John could hear some loud talking a few wagons up from theirs. John told Nancy he better go see what was going on. Ryan and other men had gathered around Mr. Michael Johanson's fire and it was him that was doing the talking.

"And we don't know if those Indians that travel with us won't turn and kill us the same as those we buried today." Mr. Johanson spouted out. "I say we get rid of them right now."

There was some murmuring from others in the crowd. Others had heard the loud talking and had come up to where they were.

"We do not even know what tribe did that today." John walked up in the firelight. "And Talking Wolf and his family have not caused any trouble here."

"That does not mean they won't in the future." Johanson continued. He was a pompous man and had brought help of every kind on the trip to see to all his needs. He did not drive the wagon and he had a cook for his meals. Most of the people on the train tried to avoid him as he was a very disagreeable person.

"All these savages are just alike. You can't tell one from the other."

It was Ryan's turn to speak. He held his hand up to quiet the ones who had started talking around the fire. "I will decide who will ride with us and who will be dismissed. One thing I will not tolerate is someone causing trouble by getting everyone all scared and riled up." He stared right at Mr. Johanson. "Until something happens to show me otherwise Talking Wolf and his family stay. Now go back to your fires and get some rest we have a long day tomorrow."

As they all dispersed back to their own fires, Ryan pulled John aside.

"Did Talking Wolf know those arrows that I gave you?"

"No he said that he didn't recognize them. He said they maybe just a small group that has been sent away from a main tribe for doing something wrong. But he said they would watch carefully for them while they are scouting."

"That's good. And John we better watch Johanson as he seems to be a trouble maker and

I don't need any of his mouth." Ryan added before turning and riding away.

Johanson was watched by everyone on the train. About twice a week he was dressed by his man helper to dress in a full riding habit. From a very clean and brushed hat down to boots so polished you could nearly see yourself in them. He would have on a ruffled white shirt covered with a vest and riding breeches. John and Nancy's group would snicker behind their bandannas when he rode by. When he was properly dressed the man helper would entwine his big hands and Johanson would step into them to be lifted up so he could mount his horse. The horse was a big bay, proud cut gelding. He would dance around for a while as he was not rode enough to keep him very quiet, as Johanson did not take part in any herding of the livestock or riding at night to keep guard. That had been made very clear at the beginning of the trail. He told Ryan that he was a paying customer and he had not brought any livestock and he would just take care of his own. He of course did not take care of anything the man helper did all the work. Not only did he take care of the gelding and the team that pulled the wagon, he did everything else. He cooked and drove the wagon. Every day he washed Johanson's clothes and his sheets. The sheets were washed in the mornings before they started out and hung inside the wagon to be dry by the end of the day. Johanson insisted on being one of the first wagons so he would not have to ride in the dust of the others. So of course he was not one of the favorites on the drive. Most people just ignored him.

Nancy made sure to speak to the man helper. She soon learned that his name was George. And he didn't know his last name. She would engage him some times by the creeks where they would stop to gather water. John and the rest of the group would help him with his horses when he needed help. At night after all his work for Johanson was finished, they would invite him over to their campfire. George little by little told his story.

"I was born on the plantation that Mister Johanson was also born. We was born just a few weeks apart and when we was about four I was brought to the big house to play with Master Johanson. I stayed there the rest of my life. My parents were sold off and I never saw them again. I was fed in the kitchen with the other help and had a small cot in the attic. All my life I was to take care of Master Johanson. So as we went along, he learned what to wear and I learned how to bath and dress him. When he had lessons, I would sit in the back of the room. I was not taught but I listened and learned a lot of things. Enough that when we went off to advanced school I could remember stuff to get him passed."

"Are you a free man?" Mike spoke up from the other side of the fire.

"No sir, I ain't. I haven't seen any use for being freed." George shook his head.

"I don't figure I am going to do anything else but see about Master Johanson until he dies. I wouldn't know how to do anything else."

Eb then ask the question that everyone really wanted to know. "What is the story of old Johanson? Why are you all out here on a wagon train instead back at that Plantation?"

"We are going to Texas where his family has bought a ranch. Master Johanson you see is the middle son and so he don't inherit anything like the oldest. The oldest gets everything. So about a year ago his Father died and the brother who inherited everything said he could go into the military or he could come to Texas. Master was sure he didn't want anyone telling him how to do so he chose to come on this here wagon train." George then faded into the night as he could hear Master calling him.

"What are you doing over there with those people? You know we don't need to have anything to do with people that are beneath us." Johanson was yelling out the back of his wagon. And of course half the camp heard him.

George did not answer. He just crawled under the wagon on his pallet. As he lay there he thought about what they had said and he wondered about being free. He drifted off to sleep to dream of being free and especially free of Master Johanson.

In a few days they would reach Nashville, Tennessee. Just the thought of a real city excited everyone on the wagon. Men and women both sat down and checked their monies and then made their lists; some longer than others. Nancy, Gertie and Libby worked on the food and clothes needs. One of the wagons covers needed patching so they would have to try to buy some canvas. All of them by now need new shirts and dresses. Although they had to sew everything by hand they had plenty of time when someone else was taking their turn driving the team. And Little Henry had outgrown all of his clothes!

The men checked every halter, bridle and hackamore. Each one went over his saddle to see if it needed a new girt. Some would even need a new sole on their boots. And the horses would need to be seen by the farrier to see if their shoes were loose. Only the riding horses were shod. All of the families were doing this same type of lists.

Except for Johanson. He had told George that day that he would need a new wardrobe and new boots and a new hat. George tried to explain to him that he didn't think they would have time to have clothes and boots made.

Wagon Boss Ryan called a meeting when they stopped the next night. All of the people gathered round so they could hear and children who were running and playing were hushed.

"In a few days we will reach Natchez. My rules only apply to this wagon train. What you do in town is none of my business. But I am here to tell you that with or without you we will be pulling out of here 10 days from today. So get everything you have to do done and be ready to go on that day. I will be taking role the night before so you should be in your wagon and in the circle by dark."

The fact that they were going to stop and actually go into a town of some size made the everyday chores a little lighter. Lilly, Gertie and Nancy were part of that excitement. They could not keep from asking each other what are you going to wear, or what are you going to buy, or do you think they have this or that. Many discussions were repetitious but it was fun. The men on the other hand were very serious about what the wagons and horses needed. They never mentioned clothing except Eb, who needed his well-worn boots resoled. His boots had been the subject of conversation a night or two ago when Mike asked John and Henry about them.

"Do we have the money to buy him a new pair. The sides are so run over he is basically walking on the ground."

"Yes, but they would have to have a pair on hand as we don't have time to have a pair made." Henry advised. "And you would have to convince him to have a new pair."

This made them all laugh. But the conversation was cut short when Eb appeared. They all could not help looking down at his awful boots. Eb caught on quick. "Now you don't be considering me getting any new boots. These are just fine. Just need new soles on the bottom."

With knowing looks they all went their own ways John laughed out loud as he turned Red toward their wagon. Nancy was out helping get the supper fixed as they had stopped for the night.

"Howdy ladies. Are you all ready for the big day tomorrow?"

All three turned a little red as he had interrupted a ladies only conversation on the items for the buying spree. Lilly answered him with, "Yessir we have a list big enough to buy out the town."

Gertie helped with "We might need another wagon to haul it all."

And Nancy quietly added "I just would like a bath in a real tub. I might soak in it all day."

Nancy pushed the hair back out of her face and smiled at John. John remembered the first day he had seen her and he moved over and gave her a hug.

"And where is the prince of peace. Asleep?"

"Oh no he has gone calling on the neighbors." Lilly spoke up.

"Little Miss Ellie came over and ask to take him with them to play. I was a little reluctant but her Mother said that she would watch them careful. They are just two wagons ahead of us. They seem like great people." Nancy hurriedly told John.

"I think I will go and get him. It is my turn to play with him." John said as he started toward the other wagon.

When he arrived at the Morgan's wagon he quickly introduced himself to Mary and Kevin Morgan. He had seen Kevin and spoke to him several times but had never been formally introduced. While visiting with them around the corner of the wagon came a wonderful young lady about twelve with the brightest red hair he had ever seen. As he tried not to stare Little Henry held out his hands and struggled to go to John.

"He must know you as he want go to nobody else around here. My name is Kerry. What's yours?"

"John Dunn and yes this young man knows his Daddy quiet well. And thank you for playing for him this afternoon."

"It was fun but I don't think I would want to keep him all the time like Nancy does."

"I better get him back for some supper." John tried to not laugh out loud as he turned and went back to Nancy and the others. But when he told her what Kerry had told her he laughed heartily.

The next day the wagon train pulled out as usual but then stopped at a creek about 2 miles from the town that claimed to be the start of the Natchez Trace. The Natchez Trace linked the Cumberland, Tennessee, and Mississippi Rivers. It was created and used for centuries by the Indians and then late by the explorers, traders, and emigrants going west.

All that Nancy and the girls needed to know was that it was a town. They all had decided to ride their horses into town and then later in the week bring in the wagons to load up on supplies. They went to the nicest hotel that they found and checked in. Nancy at once at the proprietor if he could arrange for her to have a bath in her room.

His eyebrows went up but he assured her he could manage it for her. All of their rooms took up one whole floor of the hotel. Only Lizzy had a room to herself so it was designated the bathtub room. Lizzy was first in the tub. She had not complained to the others on the trip but her old bones were bothering her some especially on the long days riding on the wagon seat. So she spent a long time in the bathtub brought up earlier and filled with hot water. Hot water who would have thought it could be such a luxury. After she soaked a while she dressed and went next door and got Nancy and Little Henry. They were soon both in the tub and splashing and laughing. After his bath Lizzy brought a towel and motioned to Nancy to continue enjoying the bath while she dried and dressed him. Then they settled down in a nearby rocking chair and he was soon asleep. Nancy too dozed in the tub. She never wanted to get out. But she knew that Gertie would enjoy the bath the same as them. So she got out and dressed and tiptoed to the door and to the next room to get Gertie to come for her bath. Lizzy and Nancy and Little Henry went to Nancy's room to give Gertie some privacy.

While all this was going on the men had all gone down to the bath house. Taking turns they bathed, dressed in clean clothes, and cleanly shaven they came back to the hotel to pick up the women of the group. Lunch was taken in the restaurant in the hotel and then they all went out on the wooden sidewalk to check out the town. The town was Nashborough before later being named Nashville. It was constructed as a Fort and several years were spent bringing settlers to the area. So it still had the fort feeling to it. There were lots of military men on the streets and one side of town was saloons and other businesses. Mike, Henry and Eb left the group to attend these businesses. Gertie and Jo excused themselves. Lizzy took Little Henry in her arms and told them to pick him up when they came up.

John and Nancy enjoyed an evening walking and sitting out on the porch of the hotel. When they passed a space between two buildings John saw a man lying on the ground. He told Nancy to stay in the light. He stepped cautiously up to the body, thinking that it was probably a drunk sleeping it off. He eased up closer and felt of the man and called out to him to wake up. Getting no response he put his hand down and felt of the man he was ice cold. John had seen dead men before now and quickly pulled his hand away and hurried back to the street. Taking Nancy by the arm he turned her around and headed back to their hotel.

"I need you to go to our room and stay there. I have to go find some law. I believe our drunk has passed on." John told her.

Nancy did not question his instructions but went to Lizzy's room instead of their own and explaining to Lizzy what was up they settled down to wait on John to come back.

John in the meantime had reentered the street and hurried down the street. It took him a few minutes to find the Sheriff's Office. It was lit up inside as they had quite a bit of customers this night. Going in John walked up to the first man with a badge.

"I think there is a dead man down the street in an alley on the left side."

The deputy looked right at him and ask "Is it anyone that you know?"

"No I am not from here and I do not think I know him, but it was very dark."

"Why were you in a dark alley?"

John then explained that Nancy and him were walking and saw the man lying there.

"Ok we will go check on him. Probably just some drunk passed out."

"I don't think so. He is really cold." John insisted.

The deputy then instructed him to leave his name and where they were staying with the man sitting at an old roll top desk nearby.

"They will call you if they need anything else." The office clerk told him.

John then turned and left. Going straight back to his hotel. He heard Little Henry before he got to their room and turned and knocked on Lizzy's door. Opening the door Lizzy and Nancy were full of questions. What did they say? What did they do? Who was the man?

"Whoa. All they did was listened to my story and ask where I was staying. Then I left."

John picked up Little Henry and Nancy went to their room. Nancy put Little Henry to bed on a pallet on the floor. John was sitting out on the balcony of their room and Nancy joined him in the other wicker chair.

"I have a bad feeling about that man. I don't know what it is or if it is anything but it is just a troubling thing."

"We can't do anything about it tonight. But you can go down in the morning and see what happened." Nancy held out her hand and they went in and went to bed. But John could not sleep and later Nancy again saw him out on the balcony. She went back to sleep and he was already gone when she got up the next day.

John had gone early back to the Sheriff's Office. One of the same officers was still there. John inquired about the man in the alley.

"Oh he was dead alright. Some Indian had hacked him in the back with a tomahawk. Probably one of that bunch that came in with that wagon train a few days back. The Sheriff has ridden out to the train to talk to them."

John tried not to run out of the office. But soon as he was down the street a ways he hurried to the hotel. Taking the stairs two at a time, he was soon banging on everyone's doors. Mike, Henry and Eb were up first and told to meet him in his room. Gertie and Jo and Lizzy soon followed. Nancy was up with Little Henry. They all gathered in the tiny room.

"We have a major problem. A man was killed with a tomahawk in an alley last night. Nancy and I were walking by and saw him lying there. When I checked on him he was ice cold so he had been there a while. So I went and told the Sheriff's Office. Today they tell me that the Sheriff thinks it is an Indian that came in with a wagon train a few days back. That's us and it is Talking Wolf's family. So we need to get out there and see what is going on."

"Let's go." Mike started to the door.

Turning to Nancy and the others he told them to pack and be ready to leave if they need to when he came back.

"Jo come with us and bring the buckboard back in and Gertie, you all get all the supplies bought and carried to the wagons. We may have to leave without the train."

The men followed John to the livery. They all caught their horses and saddled them while John paid the livery man. They eased down the street not trying to look like they were in a hurry. Then when they were out of the edge of town they let their horses out and made good time to the wagons.

When they reached the wagons John first checked with the outriders and made sure the livestock and horses were ok. He then asked them to get them gathered up a little closer to the wagons.

In the meantime the others had fanned out among the wagons and heard that the Sheriff's men had been there but had left tracking Talking Wolf and his family. But they had lost the trail and come back. Then they looked all through the wagons and then had gone.

"When did Talking Wolf leave?"

"Some time during the night." one of the outriders offered. "It was like one minute they were here and the next they were gone. There was no sign that they were ever here. You could not even tell they had ever had a fire."

Mike, John and the others then went over to their wagon.

Eb spoke first. "Talking Wolf knew something was up so he moved. We all know they didn't have anything to do with this."

All the group nodded in agreement.

"But of course the Sheriff will think that they are guilty, that is the reason they took off." Mike added.

And he was right. It was not long before the Sheriff and three deputies rode up. "Looks like we were right. That bunch of Indians that you had riding with you have lit out."

"Those Indians did not kill that man. We have been around them for several years now and they would not do that. First of all they did not even go to town." John spoke up as he walked out from the others."

"We will see. But someone has to pay for killing that old man. And I don't know any white men with tomahawks." The Sheriff and the deputies turned their horses and loped away back to town.

"What do we do now? Try to find Talking Wolf and straighten this out or what? Henry looked around at the others. "We know they didn't do it."

Mike was standing by his horse kicking dirt. "I believe the best thing we can do until the wagon train leaves next week is find out who did this." He then swung into his saddle and sat waiting on the others.

The others joined him in their saddles and John was the one to speak. "We will ride out like we are checking the horses. When we are out of sight, Eb you cut off from us and see if you can find Talking Wolf. Do not bring him back, tell him to stay away and then find us further down the trail. Eb then cut back and find us. We will either still be here or you know that we will be following the Natchez Trail. We will go back to town and try to act normal and wait for the train to leave out."

So they rode out to check on the livestock, stopping to visit with the outriders for the day. When they were by a stand of trees, Eb quietly slipped away. John was always amazed how he could disappear just like a ghost.

After staying a reasonable amount of time they all went back to town. They returned their horses to the livery and then went to find the others. They helped with the shopping and loading of the buck board. It took two trips to take all the supplies back to the wagons. Then several days of packing and storing the supplies. But as they worked they all were thinking about Eb and Talking Wolf but no one spoke

Nancy wanted to talk about it. She was really upset about them thinking that their friends had done this horrible thing. But John assured her that the best way to handle it was to not talk and just do a lot of listening. They had all decided on ways to try and find the killer. One of the ways was for the men to hang out in the saloons and the women to go to church. The women got the worse of it. Talk had quickly gotten around town that those were the Dunn's Indians and if the Indians were not here then the Dunn's should have to pay for the murder. Most of the people who had made their acquaintance before now did not speak as they met them on the street.

It was the third day of the affair when Mike came rushing up to John's room. It's that fancy pants from the wagon train stirring up the town about the Indians. He is holding court over at the Fancy Saloon and talking to anyone who will listen. John quickly got up and going down stairs he turned to the right and soon (followed by Mike and Henry) walked into the Fancy. Sure enough Johanson was standing by the bar and spouting off his mouth.

"And they need to get a posse together and go after those murdering Indians." Seeing John he turned his venom at John. "And this is the man that brought those murders into your town and killed one of you citizens."

John had never been one to start a fight, but he could not stop himself, he walked right up to Johanson and hit him solidly in the mouth. Johanson fell back clinging to the bar and then slide down to the floor.

John then turned to the patrons of the saloon. "I have known this Indian family for several years and not only have they lived with us they have fought against other Indians that have attacked us and this very wagon train. On their own accord they did not come into your town to get supplies that they needed. We bought them for them. They did not want to disturb your town. And now you want to accuse them of this horrible murder. Maybe you all did not know that you can buy tomahawks from any Indian dealer. Maybe that is where you need to be looking, not at innocent men who have done you no harm."

Johanson had come around and struggled to get up. The other patrons that had been listening to him had faded away.

"I hear you spreading that filth against Talking Wolf again I will be back and I will beat you to a pulp." John threw Johanson's fancy hat off the bar onto him and left the saloon. Outside on the sidewalk Wagon Master Ryan fell into step with John.

"You know this is not over."

"Yes, I know that but it cost me a good friend and I don't like it."

"I know that Talking Wolf and his bunch had nothing to do with this but you know that they cannot come back to the train."

John nodded in agreement. "I know that but I am going to make it my primary business to find out who here owns a tomahawk and I bet it is not an Indian."

Nancy of course wanted to know what had happened at the saloon. John just told her that he didn't think Johanson would be running his mouth about the Indians around him anymore.

The next day John, Mike and Jo made the rounds of the saloons again; trying to get someone to tell them who would kill someone with a tomahawk. No one would talk to them. It was two days later when Mike pulled John to one side of the sidewalk. "I have a little hint on the murderer. I was out with a certain lady of the night and she said that a certain young tough was bragging that it wasn't any Indian that rolled the guy in the dark." It did not take long for them to find him the next night in one of the lesser of the establishments. John could smell him before he got close to him. Mike and John eased up to the bar. John offered to buy him a drink and the young man quickly accepted. It was Mike that spoke to him from his other side.

"I hear that you do some trading with the Indians. I might be interested in a little action in that area."

The man drained his drink and turned to Mike. "What do you have in mind?"

"I hear that they will trade hides and other things for barrels of whiskey. I might know where we can get the whiskey." John looking over the young man's back could hardly keep from laughing out loud.

"I have a wagon load of trade goods at my camp just outside of town, we might could make a deal. Meet me just west of here about middle of the day tomorrow and we would see if we can make a deal. Just make sure you are not some of those Indian Government people. They don't want us giving the Indians any drinks."

"I will be there tomorrow." Mike told him and left the saloon. John stayed a while longer and then moved out on the sidewalk. He could see Mike about half a block away and moved down to him.

"I intend to take that sheriff with us one way or another. We may have to go with him on our tale but he has to go with us. I bet we find another tomahawk just like the one that killed that man." John said.

The next morning found Mike and John ready to ride at noon. John stopped by the Sheriff's office and spoke to the sheriff. He explained that he had some new information about the murder and he needed to come with them just in case the information panned out. The Sheriff at first just blew him off.

"You just tell me what you think you know and I will tell you if I think your information is worth riding out with you."

"I can't tell you anything until we get there. And you might bring a deputy or two." John looked right at the sheriff.

"Ok, I don't have anything else to do."

The sheriff called to a couple of his deputies and they all rode out together. When they had gone a couple of miles they could see a fire and camp with three big wagons with tarps on them.

A big man came out to greet them. "Ho, sheriff what brings you out here? Step down and have some coffee."

They all stepped down and he handed cups all around before filling them with the hottest coffee John had ever tasted.

"This here guy thinks you have some information about the murder by that Indian the other day in town. How long have you all been here?" the sheriff sipped his coffee as he sat squatted by the fire.

The old man waited a minute before replying. "We been here about a week but we haven't been uh to town much. We just got some supplies and are headed out to do a little trading."

"Who is we? Who is traveling with you?" The Sheriff stood up.

"Just a couple of men who drive the wagons, an old cook and my nephew."

"Where is your nephew now?" John was anxious to see the kid.

"I am right here." The kid from the night before came out behind one of the wagons with a rifle in his hand. He was still holding it down by his side but John knew that it wouldn't take much time or effort to raise it up and shoot them.

The old man was looking at him mean. "What do you need that gun for? Put it away."

"Is this the man you wanted me to talk to? The sheriff had turned to John.

"Yes, he told us that he had trinkets and stuff to trade to the Indians." John said.

"Is that right? You know you are not to be trading with the Indians right now."

The Sheriff had moved his hand to his gun holster.

"We also might be interested in what are in these wagons under this tarp." It was Mike who had eased around behind the kid and had his rifle to his back. "I don't think it is all the right trading stuff. He had taken the kids' gun and then moved back to the wagon behind him. He then grabbed the corner of the wagon tarp and threw it back. The Sheriff and John moved over and were surprised to find crates in the wagon. They all knew what were in the crates—guns!

Mike had found a pry bar and jumped up in the wagon and opened on of the crates. Sure enough they were full of rifles. In the meantime one of the other deputies had uncovered another wagon and called out.

"Well, lookee here! Isn't this just like the tomahawk that we found on that man's back in town?" He held up two tomahawks. The Sheriff had eased his gun out of its holster and now had it on the old man and the nephew.

"What did you do?" The old man bellowed at the kid. "I ought to kill you."

"I didn't mean to kill him. I just was going to steal his money but I guess I hit him too hard and down he went." the kid acknowledged. "And that fancy man told me where to find the drunk."

"What fancy man told you that?" the sheriff asked.

The kid turned to John and said, "You know that fancy man that came in with your wagon train. He said that if I used the tomahawk they would think an Indian did it and they wouldn't be looking for us."

The Sheriff asked John if he knew who he was talking about.

"I sure do and I know where he is." John jumped and caught his stirrup and sat up in his saddle and turned to go back to town. Mike had ridden up next to him.

"We need to let the law take care of this." He quietly told John.

The deputies and the Sheriff tied the kid's hands together and throwing him on his horse they all rode back to town. When they reached the edge of town it was John that opened the conversation.

"What can you do about Johanson telling that kid to kill that man?" John asked.

"It makes him just as guilty as the one who done it, but the problem will be proving it. It will be the kid's word against Johanson. And by the looks of him he can afford a good lawyer to get him out of this." The Sheriff turned into the hitchin' post in front of his office and after giving his deputies instructions to put the prisoner in the front cell, he turned to John and told him to pick Johanson out for him. They proceeded down the street and they tied their horses in front of the saloon where Johanson had been in. The Sheriff went in first and then John and Mike. Johanson with his usual swagger held out his hand to shake with the Sheriff.

"Did you get that Indian that shot that poor man?" Johanson asked him in a loud voice.

The Sheriff took another step closer to Johanson and took his hand but he then clamped a pair of handcuffs on them."

"I have found the killer". The Sheriff was talking in a loud voice so all could hear him. And it was quiet enough for everyone to hear as soon as the handcuffs had come out they were all watching with great interest. "And it wasn't no Indian. It was the kid with the traders out the edge of town. And his story is that this man here put him up to it. So Johanson you are coming in too until we can sort this all out."

"You don't think you can take me in on the word of some worthless trader's kid! I won't have it. Take these cuffs off me right now! Do you know who I am?" Johanson was trying to get the cuffs undone.

"I don't care who you are. I am taking you in as an accomplice until we figure this out." The Sheriff then grabbed him by the arm and pushed him out on the sidewalk. He then turned and pushed him down the street to the sheriff's office. Johanson was heard yelling at him all the way down the street and all the patrons of the saloon looked like a parade as they followed them. Others out of other saloons and people on the street joined in the crowd.

John wanted terribly to join in the crowd but as usual, but calm Mike had motioned him to his horse and they rode back to their hotel room. The others had seen the commotion from their balcony and wanted to know all the details. They had been joined by the Wagon Master who had been in the lobby when they came in and had been invited by Mike to come upstairs. They recapped all of the events that had happened that day. Turning to Wagon boss Ryan it was Mike who questioned him.

"What happens to him now? We are set to leave in a couple of days. And there will not be a circuit judge here they said for months."

Ryan stood up and announced, "I am not waiting around for him. He got his self into this mess and he can get himself out of it. We will leave as planned."

Mike remembered Johanson's hired man George. "We have to go out and tell George and see what he wants to do about this. I will go."

George had been in town to buy supplies but was not invited to party with Johanson, so he had returned to their wagon out near the other wagons. It did not take Mike long to find him. He recounted to him what had happened and asked him if he wanted to go back to town and see about Johanson.

"I guess I have to but I really can't do anything for him I don't think." George hung his head.

"I should have told you before, but he had killed a man and that is the reason that his Father sent him out here."

Mike soon relayed George's confession about the reason for Johanson being on their wagon train to the others and to the wagon boss. They all decided that they would ask George to join them as a free man and partner in their adventure. They did not have time to tell him. As Mike was the herder for the horses that day he was looking in their wagon for something when he heard a pistol click behind him. And then he heard Johanson telling him to turn around.

"You and your no good buddies think you can get me thrown in jail do you? It didn't take long for my money to talk me out of this mess. And now I am going to kill all of you."

"Like it did the time before this?" Mike looked right at Johanson. "Yes, we know all about why you are out here on this wagon train."

"That tattling George, I will teach him a lesson too." Johanson growled.

"I don't think you are going to teach any of us anything." Eb had eased up and put the end of the barrel of his shotgun to the side of Johanson's face. "And I don't think the sheriff will let you out now as you threatened to kill Mike and now George. I think you may be in jail for a long time."

Johanson had dropped his gun on the ground and Mike hurriedly picked it up. They tied Johanson's hands and threw him on his saddle and then them all three headed back to town. Mike leading Johanson's horse and Eb covering Johanson with his shotgun. It did not take them long and it did not take long to gather a crowd as they rode through the edge of town to the Sheriff's office located in the middle of town. Nancy heard the crowd and called to John and they all looked out the window and then hurried down to see what Mike and Eb were up to.

Mike roughly threw Johanson down off his horse and then grabbed him up by the arm and half dragged him into the office, passing the Sheriff on the sidewalk. Throwing him into a chair he turned to the Sheriff.

"This no good piece of cow turd came out to the wagon train and pulled a gun on me and threatened to kill me."

"I did not! It is just his word against mine." Johanson shouted and started to stand up.

"You seem to forget the rest of the story," Eb spoke up. "The part about where I heard you not only threaten Mike but poor George too."

"None of you can do anything about what I will do to George. He belongs to me and has since I was born." Johanson tried to get up but Mike pushed him back into the chair.

"I believe," Mike said, "That George has a piece of paper that makes him a free man. So you can't do anything to him".

"He isn't any free man. He was given to me by my father!" Johanson was yelling again.

"Your Father signed the papers and told George he was free and anytime he wanted to he could leave you. He has stayed with you all these years because you were completely unable to take care of yourself." Mike continued.

One of the deputies lifted Johanson up and as he was walking him to a cell, Johanson was still yelling that they could not lock him up, his name was Johanson and he would kill them all.

The Sheriff then turned to Mike and Eb and asked them to repeat their story. They recounted what had happened and the Sheriff wrote out a short statement and they signed it.

"What will happen to him now. He is nuts." Eb inquired.

"He will be in here until we get a circuit judge out here. And that may be several months. I don't send for one very often. And it may be next year before I request one." the old Sheriff smiled.

"We are leaving tomorrow and can't stay around here." Mike had realized what the Sheriff was telling them.

"I will keep him long as I can, and then try to get the judge to lock him up on you all's statement. If I can't do that, you should have a big enough lead on him so he can't find you.

What about the colored that was riding with him.?"

"We will take him with us." Eb spoke up. "And the wagon and supplies that he came with. We will look at the two of them as partners and he is taking his part."

"Ok by me. I don't think this here prisoner needs a wagon and team." the Sheriff stood and shook hands with Mike and Eb and wished them a good trip to where ever they were heading.

Back out on the street Mike and Eb were surrounded by the onlookers, everyone wanting to know what was happening.

Eb raised his hand and said," You will have to talk to the Sheriff."

Mike had eased over by John and told him they all needed to pack and get to their wagons.

So John and Nancy hurried back to the hotel and getting Gertie and Lizzy they were soon packed, and the wagon and horses were gathered from the livery. Bills were paid and then they all set out to the wagon train. Many others of the train were already at the camp and waved and talked to them as they set out. John quickly found Wagon Boss Ryan.

"They have arrested Johanson again so we have asked George to join the train. I hope that is ok?"

"It is ok with me. Will he be taking all of Johanson's things?"

"I don't know yet but when we find him we will see. We are going to look for him now."

John and Mike found George a few miles away on the bank of a small stream. He had been crying. They told him everything that had happened.

"I guess Mister Johanson is in jail again."

"Yes, and for a long time." Mike told him.

"The Sheriff gave you all of Johanson's things. Johanson threatened to get you so we thought you might want to come with us. We can help you get away from him for good." John had gotten down off his horse and went to stand in front of him. He then held out his hand and helped him up.

"What do you say? Want to come to Texas with us? John said.

When George stood upright he grabbed John in a big bear hug. "Nobody done cared anything about me like you all".

When they returned to the wagon train George went to Johanson's wagon and began going through the things in it. He summoned John and everyone over with him.

"I am goin' to make a pile of everything I don't want here." He made a motion around an area. "And I want all of you to see if you want it. Then what you do not want I want everyone else on the train to see if they need the things." He motioned to wagons.

Quickly he had divided the clothes, bathtub, chair and all the other things that Johanson had had to have on the trip. Since he was about Johanson's size he kept some of the clothes and the boots. Next out came the fancy bed. He kept the bedclothes as he thought he might need the blankets. He kept only a few pans and silverware putting the others in the going pile. Soon the going pile was larger than the keeping pile. So he quickly put the things that he wanted back into the wagon.

Wagon Boss Ryan was standing nearby watching like all the others. George turned to him

"Are you sure I can comes with you?

"I am sure you can come with us. So get in line along with John's wagons and you will be fine."

"What about paying for the trip?"

"Mr. Johanson had paid up front for the trip so we will count that as your payment."

Nancy, Lizzy and Gertie had watched from the side while he had divided up all the things. So when he told them to get what they wanted they dived right in. They took the pans, silver, china and then Gertie took all the fancy clothes that George did not want. She had told Nancy and Lizzy she could cut them up and use them for other things. John then realized that Johanson's horse was still in town.

"Do you want Johanson's horse?" He asked George.

"No sir. I do not want that mean ole' thing. I just need the wagon's team."

John smiled and said, "If you need a horse to ride later on we have plenty."

The ladies took their loot to their wagons and packed it with the other things. Then they made supper and they were all happy to invite George to join them. And they had not even had time to ask Eb if he found Talking Wolf.

When they were all finished eating and sitting around the fire Eb started telling them about his trip. "I thought I picked up their trail about ten miles out. I tracked them for a couple of days and then lost it in a running stream. I decided I would follow the stream for a while and see if anything turned up. Nothing could I find that even mentioned that they had passed this way. About the fifth day I awoke during the night with a blade to my throat. I was tied and then carried on my mule away some direction, as they had my eyes covered, and then pulled down and thrown to the ground. Then I heard them ride away. I struggled enough to get the blindfold off and it was beginning to get light. When I sat up to look around Talking Wolf was sitting right in front of me. I had never heard a thing! He quickly untied me and gave me a big bear hug."

"I am so glad to see you are alright old man." Talking Wolf began.

"Why in the tar nation did you have them grab me up and carry me off like a sack of potatoes?" Eb asked him.

"Ho! I did not carry you off or anything. That was some other ones. I don't know why they dumped you here or why they did not take the mule but I am glad that they decided to put you down."

"What do you mean? Your braves did not pick me up?"

"No, I have been tracking you since you left the wagon train. I could not figure out why you would leave John and the others. So I decided to follow you. During the night I was not very far from you when I see these men dressed like braves, but not, come in and take you off. Since they had not harmed you I just followed along to see what was up. When I saw them dump you and ride away I came to see if you were alright. Now I go to see what they are doing." Talking Wolf had stood up. "By the way what are you doing out here?"

"I am looking for you. They found that a white kid killed that guy and we wanted you back on the train with us." Eb grinned. "We have gotten attached to you."

"We cannot come now. I go to see what these men are up to. I will come visit when you are back on the trail." And then he vanished into the brush and Eb could neither see nor hear him. Eb quickly mounted his mule and going back gathered up his camp and came back.

"Wonder what some white men were dressed like Indians wanted with Eb?" Nancy asked and then looked around the camp fire.

"Up to no good that is for sure." Jo told her.

"I think when we start tomorrow we better watch extra close and we will put out extra guards. Tomorrow I will talk to the Wagon Boss about them." Then John stretched and stood up and started to his wagon.

THREE

Next morning John was up early and found the Wagon Boss drinking coffee with some of the leading wagons. John explained to all of the men standing around and Ryan what had happened to Eb. They mostly just shook their heads about the whole mess.

One of the older men quietly said "There are just some men born bad and they just cause trouble for all of us. I told my wife that Talking Wolf and his little band would be blamed and that they would be found innocent. These others trying to be Indians, now that is bad for Talking Wolf and the other Indians that are just trying to get along." Others standing around agreed by shaking their heads.

Ryan then spoke up, "We will just have to be more watchful. I will put out extra pickets at night and I suspect you will do that for the livestock John."

"Yes we are prepared to have extra men on the livestock. But since we don't have Talking Wolf and the braves we are plenty thin on help."

"How about you and I go back into town and see if we can rustle up a few more men." Ryan asked.

"Yes I think we might find a few drovers that would like a little extra money. And I can pay them a little along with their board." John replied.

So Ryan and John, after stopping by to tell Nancy, rode back into town and started looking at likely candidates. They separated and Ryan went up the street. John started looking the other way. Some were passed over because they just looked bad. But farther down the street he ran into a couple of brothers looking for work. They said that they had farm experience and John liked the looks of them.

"We will feed you and have horses for you to ride. When we get to Texas we will give you money to get back." John offered them.

"I don't think we will be wanting to come back. We don't have anything to come back to. Our parents have died and we owed the bank and they came and claimed it about two weeks ago. So what you see is what we have."

John asked, "Do you have a saddle? Or any more clothes?"

The taller one sheepishly looked down and muttered "No on both counts."

"We will have to get that taken care of. First though my wife will have a fit if I bring you to the wagon train smelling like you do." John stepped down off his horse and tied it to the hitchin rail. He then guided the two young men that were named Guthrie and Samson Hunter, into the mercantile store and holding clothes up to each they bought two shirts and pants, underwear and socks. John also thought to buy some more supplies as looking at these two they needed a little fatting up. They bought second hand boots at the boot store as that is all he had. After baths and shaves and haircuts they looked completely different. The livery was next for two saddles and one wagon and team. John had thought about buying another one earlier in the week but with all the excitement he had forgotten. Guthrie, the older, climbed in the wagon and took up the reins and guided the team as though he had been doing it all his life (which he had). John chuckled to himself as he led them back out of town to the wagon train.

When they arrived, Ryan rode up and introduced the two cowboys he was able to round up, but he had not brushed them up much. After John herded his two with their wagon over to the end of the line to join the others, Nancy was the first to make them welcome and then the others came over.

Gertie with no problem said "When was the last time the two of you ate?"

She quickly went to her wagon and brought out some food that was left over from their breakfast. She sat it down on the back of their wagon and motioned for them to get down and eat.

They tried to be polite but the truth was they had not eaten in a couple of days and the food was so good. Guthrie had even turned to Samson and told him not to be such a pig. Through the mouths of food, they told the group that Guthrie was nearly twenty and Samson would be fourteen in the fall some time.

Jo came in from his round with the livestock and took the boys out to the horses to catch them each one. They didn't ride very well but managed to stay on. He left them to Mike and Eb and drove the wagon back to get in line.

The wagon boss had told everyone they would leave after lunch and just travel a short distance to get everyone lined out. That also left time that morning for any of the families to go back to town if they needed some last minute supplies that they had forgotten. When all the wagons were lined up again the Wagon Boss called them to start out again. The Natchez Trace wound from Nashville, Tennessee to Natchez, Mississippi. It was a well-worn two rutted road used by previous settlers and at the beginning a trail for the Indians moving back and forth following the hunts. They only went until right before dark and circled the wagons for the night. Fires were easily built as there was plenty of wood. When supper was taken care of, families strolled around the circle and visited each other. They exchanged stories of what they had seen and down in town. The women talked about what they had bought for dresses and shirts.

Guthrie and Samson had come in and ate and then quickly returned to work bedding down the livestock. They had been assigned to ride the first shift with Henry and were excited. They were going to be real cowboys! Henry on the other hand just had to turn away and laugh at them trying to ride in the dark. You could hear them occasionally ride into some brush. They had not gotten accustomed to seeing in the dark. But Henry liked them and had taken them more or less under his wing. He also had learned more about them. Their Father was a drunk and couldn't keep a steady job, and of course they had little to nothing to eat. They quit school and went to work soon as they were big enough. They lived with daily beatings from a rampaging alcoholic and a scared to death Mother. Their only sister ran away with the first trader that came by and they never heard of her again. And they had been just taking any job that came along so they had learned a lot of different trades.

It began to rain the next day after they had started up after eating lunch. The wagon train did not always stop for lunch. But the clouds were gathering and turning dark when Ryan motioned for the wagons to go ahead and circle. Quickly everyone circled and unhitched their teams and had just enough time to gather their children and wives into the wagons. They quickly pulled the canvas closed in front behind the wagon seat and close the back near the tailgate. Nancy and Little Henry did just like everyone else. Just in time as the rain came down in sheets and the wind began to blow and rock the wagon. Little Henry took it all in cuddled into his mother's lap with his favorite blanket pulled snug around them. It was several hours later when John showed up, pulling the canvas back from the wagon seat.

"Are you both ok?" He asked as he laughed at them all covered up against the storm.

"I guess we are not going anywhere anytime soon." He was covered from head to foot in his slicker and his hat was turning the rain off of him.

"I better get back and see what else I can do." He was then off into the night.

He had just ridden up to Boss Ryan who was calling to him. "John we have a big problem. The Nelson's can't find their oldest boy. He was out running by the train when we were caught in the storm. Now no one can find him. I have ridden the whole train thinking that he might have jumped in with someone else but no one has him."

"I will ride back where we first started circling and look for him. And I will get my men to start looking for him." And John loped away. The wind was still blowing but now as bad as before. By the time he reached the out riders the rain had let up to just a slow steady rain. But he still had to yell for the riders to hear him. He explained that the young man was missing and they decided on who should go where to look. They rode all night but by daylight no one had found him. John had to tell Nancy that he didn't think there was anything they could do.

Wagon Boss Ryan was torn. He knew that they needed to get the wagons going again, but wanted to continue looking for the boy. So he decided that they would stay one more day and night and maybe if the boy was caught in the storm, with good weather he could find them. The parents were beside themself with worry. So the morning was spent again with everyone horseback looking and calling for the boy. Gertie had taken Little Henry in with her and Nancy and Lizzy joined the others horseback to help look for him.

Although it was a sad day, Nancy did not realize how long it had been since she had ridden and found herself enjoying the ride. Lizzy and Nancy were riding back from where they had been before the storm when they heard the moaning. It was the kid. He had found shelter in a washout under the roots of a large tree on the edge of the stream they had watered that day before. Nancy quickly jumped down from her horse and ran to him. She soon had him on her horse and riding back behind her, they loped back to the train. She reined up near the parent's wagon and called out. As the parents hurried out the boy jumped down off Nancy's horse and was caught up in hugs from both parents. It was the Father who remembered and turned to thank Nancy.

"It was nothing. We are raising a boy and couldn't imagine how we would live without him." Nancy had stepped back up on her horse and Lizzy and her rode away leaving the family to hear the story of how the youngster had been left and then caught in the storm.

They were soon back at their wagons and realized they had sunshine so they better get everything that was wet out in the sunshine to dry out. All along the line others were doing the same. Clothes and bed clothes were hung out to dry everywhere. Nancy, Gertie and Lizzy joined in this continuous clothes line. Some had found small trees and stripped them and driving them in the ground they had stretched a rope from there to a corner of the wagon and had a clothesline. A good breeze soon had the clothes dry. They were then gathered in and folded and put away until they were needed.

FOUR

It was well into the winter when they realized that it was nearly Christmas. Christmas! The last one was such a cheerful occasion that Nancy again wanted this one to be. Someone came up with a calendar of sorts they had been keeping and decided that Christmas would be a couple of weeks on Saturday. As they had gone along the Natchez Trace there were many places that they passed where a family or group would be selling merchandise on the side of the path. These were called "stands" usually with the family or group name in front as in Joslin's Stand or Gordon's Stand. These continued all the way to Natchez, Mississippi. Some were only a few miles apart and others farther. They all carried a variety of items for sale. Mostly food products, milk and eggs were plentiful. But some made trips to the town nearby and had a variety of wares, pants and material might be found in one place. Pots and wagon wheels might be found at the next one.

As Nancy, Lizzy, and Gertie caught the Christmas "bug" they began scouring each of the stands for items to make for Christmas and things to use for decorations. Without houses and not enough room for them all to meet in one of the wagons, it was decided that the clothesline would be put in use again. Berries found along the road were strung for a tree. Nancy had bought candy at one of the last stands. It would have to do for their gifts to the group. Jo had found some Indians that had shells from the coast and he traded with them. Then he helped Gertie make them into jewelry of a sort for Nancy and Lizzy. Although they had money on the trip, John had made sure that they rarely spent any of it. He told them that he didn't want anyone to know they had any more than the others traveling with them so they would not be robbed.

Christmas was the next morning when they pulled into their circle near Toscomby's Stand Christmas Eve. The girls were happy to find that they had eggs and sugar so they could make Christmas goodies. And so soon as they had bought their ingredients they were back at the wagon cooking like crazy! John had come in and relieved Nancy of Little Henry so she was free to help. As she looked around the wagon circle others were doing the same things, cooking and getting their decorations up. The whole wagon train had a festive air about it. Not long into the afternoon when all the chores were done they could hear a fiddle and guitar begin to play Christmas carols. Soon most of them drifted over to join in singing. It felt good to sing the old songs from each one's childhood and thoughts of home.

Nancy too thought about home. Her home with her family that were no more and her new life with the family she had now. She whispered a little prayer to God, thanking him for her new life and asking for his blessing in this Christmas season. She had walked a little ways away from the singers and turned to see J.D. standing to the side too. She quietly moved to stand by him and he gladly took the hug she offered him. They stood there for a while just holding to each other and holding on to their past lives. Then J.D. pulled something out of his pocket. It was a locket with their parents' pictures in it. He handed it to Nancy and then simply walked away. She started to call out to him, but knew he had gone away so she would not see him cry. But she hurried over to her wagon and she cried and cried. John found her there and took her into his big arms and held her until she could cry no more.

Christmas morning they all stood around the fire drinking hot coffee and eating Gertie's wonderful Christmas cinnamon rolls. They all exchanged gifts and little Henry received the most. After a while Boss Ryan came by and wished them all Merry Christmas. He then reminded them that they need to get an early start in the morning. So after eating Christmas dinner and resting a while they men were soon back to work and taking time to mend tack and see about all the wagons. In the evening after all their chores were done they ate again and soon everyone drifted to their own wagons and the camp was quiet again as they knew they had to get up early the next day.

It seemed really early when Nancy heard the others getting breakfast together. She quickly dressed and easing out of the wagon to not wake little Henry she soon joined them. The fire glowed in the still dark of morning. But by the time that they had cooked and the men had eaten the sun was coming up. Gertie, Lizzy and Nancy finished cleaning up and put out the fire. The men were back with their teams and they were hitched up to the wagons and then they were ready for the new day. It was coming winter and they could feel it in the air. The mornings like today were a little wetter and cooler. Nancy could hear little Henry wiggling around in the back of the wagon. He was beginning to crawl and she had to learn quickly that he could get into a lot of stuff. So she had moved many things up higher than his reach was. He still amazed her sometimes when he could find things to get into.

It was not long after they had lined up and pulled out that John had appeared. Nancy had learned quickly how to manage her team and so John had time to help others and see to the horses and livestock. She knew something was wrong when she looked straight at him.

"What is the matter?"

"Keep this under your hat, but we have lost a couple of horses. Someone took them during the night."

"Do you mean Indians?"

"Maybe."

"What do you mean maybe?"

"The horse thieves rode horses that were shod. Most Indians in this part of the country do not put shoes on their horses. Eb and Mike have gone off to see if they can pick up a track."

"Whose horses did they steal?"

"One mare of ours and a big bay gelding of the Moore's. They are up at the front of the train."

"Have you told Boss Ryan we have a thief?"

"Not yet we decided we would like to catch them before everyone knows. So don't say anything, but keep your eyes open to anything different around here." He then turned and rode back to the back of the train and the livestock.

When they took a break, Lizzy came up to Nancy's wagon.

"What do you think about the thieves?"

"Makes me nervous."

"Me too. I don't like the idea of someone around that we can't trust. I believe we better get all our good stuff put in some hidey hole in our wagons. And you start watching the little one real close. We have no idea who or what these rogues are so we need to keep a good watch out."

Lizzy went back and crawled up on her wagon seat. She was more worried than she let on. She knew people on the train were aware that they were not as poor as the rest of them and she felt uneasy about that. She realized that they were traveling on the "trace" and there were a lot of unsavory characters at nearly every stop they had made lately so it could be any of them.

When Eb and Mike didn't show up the third day, John and the others began to worry. That night around the camp fire they discussed what to do. Henry opened with "We could send someone else to see what the matter is. They may be in jail or something like before."

John said, "That leaves us one less to help with the stock. Let's give them another day or two and then decide."

As he walked away from the fire, he could see a figure moving past their wagon. John eased over their wagon trace and found himself face to face with one of the men from the front of the wagon train. John did not know his name but called out to him anyway.

"How are you this beautiful night?" The man had jumped when he was spoken too.

"Ok I guess."

"Been out to check on the livestock?" John grinned in the dark. He knew the man had no livestock and had no business on this end of the train.

"Uh, yes. And just taking a walk."

"I suggest that you walk somewhere else after this, as my bunch is not used to strangers snooping around after dark."

"I was not snooping around." The man bristled.

"I believe it looks like you were and I intend to discuss it with the Wagon Boss in the morning." The man shuffled off into the night and John joined the others by the fire. The brothers were getting ready to go out on their shift.

"I believe I will ride out with you for a while." John said.

Nancy made a face at him and when he walked by her he said, "I will be right back."

Following the brothers, John turned to look back at the wagon train in its circle. He was trying to figure out how the man came completely around the circle without being seen.

"You alright Mr. John?" one brother said.

"Yes, I just need you two boys to be very aware of your surroundings. I caught a man snooping around our wagon and camp. I would like to know what he is up to."

"We will watch everything for you."

And watch everything they did. Everywhere John looked the next few days, one of them was around. He saw them riding with the Wagon Boss at the head of the train all the way back to the drag of livestock. He even saw one of them driving a widow's wagon up near the front of the train. It was a couple of days before they were together again.

"Well, I see you have been all over the place the last few days. Even driving Widow Martin's team for her."

"Yessir we have been around trying to find out about the snooper. And we have found out a lot of stuff. You see Widow Martin drives right next to the family and camps next to them at night. She says that he is a sorry drunk and beats his kids, drunk or sober. If it is alright with you I thought I might ask the oldest one to ride drag with us. He seems to get the worst of it they say. He doesn't have a horse but thought we might find one for him. He looks about fifteen or so." said Guthrie.

John readily agreed and the next day met Carlos Smith. He was a little on the chubby side but seemed to know his way around riding and seeing to the stock.

"Sir I want to thank you for letting me ride with the livestock." Carlos rode up to John the next day.

"Riding in that wagon getting a little old is it?" John smiled at him.

"Oh yes. I will be glad when we get somewhere and have a real house and farm for the kids and my mom." Carlos turned away as he said this.

"We will help you when you get to where you want to start that farm." John patted him on the shoulder and rode back to his wagon.

The next day John was pulled down from his back off his horse to the ground. He looked up and he was looking right at Carlos' dad and realized it was the man that was snooping around their trailer. John was soon on his feet and asking the man what he thought he was doing.

"I am going to teach you not to meddle in another man's business. Especially mine. My boy does not need a job or your money. So you leave him alone. If you don't I will beat the thunder out of you." The man smelled of liquor and staggered a little as he tried to talk tough to John.

"I did not intend to meddle in your affairs, but the boy is having a good time being away from you all day and he is not hurting anything. Why do you not want him to make a few dollars of his own?"

"Well, he will not be riding for you anymore because I don't want him to. He can help his Mother drive the wagon not be off with your bunch. Leave us alone." And he turned and staggered back to his end of the wagon train.

John was met by Mike when he went out to help with the livestock.

"You better come see this." He said in a very serious voice.

They loped a while back to about half of the drag. John saw Carlos and rode up to him. He was not prepared for what he saw. Carlos' eyes were swollen nearly shut, his shirt was ripped nearly off and blue bruises showed through the rips.

"Mike go get Ryan right now". John stepped down off his horse and lifted Carlos gently to the ground. He did not have to ask him what had happened to him.

Carlos said, "He said that I couldn't help you anymore with the drag. And I told him he couldn't tell me what to do anymore. I told him I was tired of him beating on me and my mom and he could just take his drunken self somewhere else as we didn't want him anymore. He then came at me and we fought like two wild animals. My mom was screaming and the kids were crying. I didn't mean to cause so much trouble, but when I came in last night he had broken her nose and she had bled all over her clothes and I just had had enough of him."

John held the young man in his arms and rocked him like he did little Henry. "I will not let that man hurt you or your mom any more. I swear that to you."

Boss Ryan and Mike soon came riding up. John and Carlos had remounted their horses.

Ryan asked him what had happened and Carlos told his story again.

"We have a decision to make here. By the rules I am to kick the wagon off the train, but I can't see kicking off the women and her children. I guess the other choice is to take him to the nearest sheriff office and see if they can do something with him."

"You can't kick them off. He will eventually kill one or all of them in one of his rages." Mike growled.

"Ok we will take him to the nearest sheriff office we find but it will be a few days so I guess we will put him under arrest. Mike come help me get him and tie him up somewhere."

John added, "Bring the women and children and their wagon back here next to us and we can see about them till we can get them somewhere. And check his pockets for any money. They are going to need it for grub now instead of booze."

Mike and Ryan found the old man passed out in the back of his wagon. They eased up and before the drunk knew it they had him down and his hands tied behind him. He had awaken yelling and screaming that they could not do that to him. Then he had started in on the women telling her he would beat her to a pulp for letting them sneak up on him like that.

After telling the women to get out of line and wait for John's wagons and then get back in line, Mike then helped drag the drunk to a supply wagon farther up the train. There he was thrown not too gently into the back and tied to the hooks on the side of the wagon. He could hardly move around but the shouting continued.

Ryan, after mounting his horse, rode up next to the wagon. "If I hear one more sound out of you, you will walk the rest of the way tied to the back of this wagon."

The drunk looked at Ryan and realized that he meant every word of what he had said. So he wiggled around and made himself as comfortable as he could and was soon passed out again. The driver of the wagon would complain to Ryan that he could snore louder than a mule braying.

Mike had in the meantime gone back and helped the women get in line behind Lizzy. He had noticed three other little dark headed children peeking out from the wagon back. When he found John again he told him that he didn't know when the last time they had eaten. This information was soon sent to Gertie and she said that she would fix extra for them that night. So when the time came and they stopped for the night. Gertie started a big supper for all of them. She then went over to the wagon and introduced herself to the women. She found out that she was called Angie for Angeline and there was Carmen, Delores and Christopher beside Carlos. Gertie soon had them gathered up and over to their campfire and introductions were made to everyone. When the food was finished and the children gobbled up their food it was Angie's turn to explain that they had not had much to eat.

"We just came through a stand yesterday. Did you not get any food there?" Nancy asked.

The rest of the group looked like they had swallowed a frog.

"The man went to town but all he bought was whiskey and did not bring any food." Angie lowered her head and hugged one of the children up.

"Oh I am so sorry I didn't mean to hurt your feelings." Nancy hurried over and hugged the woman and child. "Everything is now going to be alright. We will see that you and these children are taken care of until we get to where you are going. Where are you going?"

"I don't rightly know. I don't think he ever told us. We just sold the little farm that we had and joined the wagon train." Angie sobbed.

Later on in the evening, Ryan came by the camp. He was smiling from ear to ear. "Mr. Smetana has decided that being quiet in the back of the wagon is better than walking behind it. Also here is the money out of his pockets. It is not much, but here is a little collection that others on the train gave me as I came a long."

He had walked over to Angie and handed her the money. Angie began to cry.

"This is more money that I have seen in a long time. I will not spend it foolishly."

Carlos had stood back away from the rest of the group unable to figure out why these people would be so kind to them. But he was sure enjoying the food and the men had been very nice to him on the drag. That night when the little family went to sleep in their wagon they slept like they had not in years. They all felt safe and not hungry. It was a great day!

You would have thought it was some kind of holiday that night. What had happened was little Henry had taken his first step from Eb to Mike and they all were excited. What a miracle the baby's first step. Soon as John and Nancy took him they set him down and sure enough he took two steps before sitting down on his butt. Nancy had seen him pulling up in the wagon and trying to get things he shouldn't but this was certainly his first independent steps.

Later she saw John over by the wagon and noticed a somber look on his face.

"What's up with you?".

"I was just thinking about soon he will be a young man and then gone."

"I think we will have him quite a few years before then." Nancy replied as he hugged her up to him.

Next day the women's topic of conversation was the new little family attached to them.

"They sure need some fatting up; I don't think they have eaten very well." Gertie started out as she stirred something in the big pot over the fire.

Lizzie added." I think those rags we washed were their own clothes as they are all we have seen them in.

The night before they had stopped near a clear running stream and Lizzy and Gertie herded the little ones down and used lots of soap washing them until they were red and their hair shown in the afternoon sun. Then they proceeded to put some of their shirts on them and washed their raggedy clothes and hung what was left of them to dry.

"Lizzy we have to get some clothes on these little ones the next stand that has any." Gertie said.

"I agree. Even if we have to just get some material and make them something." Lizzy smiled.

"I had forgotten. I have the clothes from Johansson still in the boxes in my wagon. We can see if any of them fit them. Some of the shirts Carlos should be able to wear." So they went to Gertie's wagon and she dragged the box to the back of the wagon. Opening it up they looked at several of the items. As they were going through the box, Angie, as she was now known, came up.

"We are looking at some clothes that someone had when they left the wagon train and thought there might be something for you and yours to wear or that we could sew into something for you." Gertie said stepping down out of the wagon.

Angie looked puzzled. "I don't rightly understand why you all are doing all this for me."

"Each of us of this group has our own story. And we have all come together because of these problems, just like you and yours. As long as we have enough for all of us we pull together and are now one family even though we are not blood kin." It was Lizzie that had come up to join them.

"So let's go through this stuff and see what we can use." Gertie began going through the boxes. Nancy soon had Angie up next to them holding things up to her to see if anything could be made to fit her. Several of the jackets fit really well and although the pants were a little big they thought that they would wait until she had some more meat on her bones' before taking them in. When Carlos came in he was subjected to trying on some shirts and they even had him put on one of the ties. He took the teasing in good humor. But they noticed that when he took the shirts to his wagon he left the ties in the box. The women laughed the next day when Carlos came for breakfast in the same shirt they had given him the first day he had come to work.

"Are you going to wear that same shirt the rest of your life?" Eb poked him as he came by.

"I learned right quick that Ms. Lizzie and the other don't let you go dirty anymore."

Carlos blushed beet red. "I am sorry Ms. Lizzie. It is just that I have never had but one shirt and haven't gotten the hang of changing all the time."

"You will learn not for us but for some young lady that will come along." Lizzie had joined the conversation to rib him also.

The next few days each woman had some piece of Johansson's clothes to reconstruct. Nancy had quickly decided to dress little Carmen. Soon she had cut up some shirts and made her some smocks. She also was fitted with a couple of pairs of pants with a draw string to keep them on. While fitting them on her, Nancy remember Lizzie loaning her breeches when she first came out with John. She chuckled to herself about the story.

Shoes and boots would have to wait until they found a stand that might have some. Nancy couldn't figure out how they were so healthy having gone through the winter with no shoes.

The wagon passed through Toscomby's Stand in Tennessee and then they were in Mississippi. As luck would have it, the Tennessee did not cause them too much trouble and they circled their wagons near Buzzard's Roost Stand. Eb came in late in the afternoon with a silly smile on his face.

"Guess what I have for supper?" he asked.

Lizzie was game. "What do you have for supper? Some ole wild thing for us to cook?"

He had gone back to his horse and brought out a salt sack and gave it to Lizzie. She peered inside and Gertie had come over. Lizzie quickly gave the sack to Gertie.

"Wow! I have not seen catfish for years now. She quickly went over to their table and with Eb's help they quickly had the fish filleted and cut up. She then dipped each piece in corn meal and spices and set them aside for supper. She then cut up onions and potatoes for fries.

When Mike came from the stand he had found a place to get the kids some shoes and socks. He then quickly found Angie and he took them all back to town for fittings.

That is what started the whole mess.

Soon as they had left Gertie started, "They make a great looking pair."

Lizzie added, "Too bad she already has that drunk for a husband."

"Isn't that the truth?" Gertie kicked the dirt with her boot.

Nancy came up with little Henry. He immediately put his hands out for Lizzie to take him. She happily took him on to her lap and began to play with him.

"We were just pondering on what a great looking couple Mike and Angie would make if she wasn't stuck with that drunk." Gertie brought Nancy up on what they were visiting about.

"She is not stuck with him anymore. At least for a while. John and Henry and wagon boss Ryan found a deputy sheriff in town that was happy to lock him up and then will take him to Memphis on the next stagecoach. So he is gone. Wagon Boss Ryan and the men all wrote out a statement and gave it to them and he was sure that would be enough to jail him for quite a while. The Deputy said that the judge that he would be judged by was a 't-totaler' and threw the book at drunks. They also said that he was yelling and hollering for something to drink when they left him in the lock up place."

Unknown to Nancy and the others this yelling and hollering would cause a lot of problems for Mike and Angie and the little ones. Mike was unaware John and the others had taken the drunk to town and turned him over. This stand was only made up of the ferry that they came over on and then a saloon, merchandise store and a few shacks. One of these shacks served the area as the jail. So Mike and Angie had to pass right past the yelling and could see him with his head out the small window. The kids immediately saw him and cringed in the back of the wagon. He called out to Angie and called her all kinds of names and then changed to crying and pleading before Mike could get them on down the road. Soon as they were away from the spectacle the children came up to the wagon seat and hugged up to Mike and Angie. Mike told them that they did not have to worry about that mean old man anymore. He would keep him away.

Mike hurried on down the main road and then turned off and headed about a mile out in the country. There they stopped in front of a nice looking tiny clapboard house with a few flowers growing in the garden. They could hear banging in the barn so Mike drove the wagon past the house and stepped down and walked into the barn. When his eyes adjusted to the shadowed inside there stood a giant man working over a table.

"Come in and don't just stand there." He man motioned to a chair near him.

"What can I do for you?"

Mike quickly told a short version of why the children didn't have any shoes. The cobbler had already heard the drunk yelling when he went into town.

"Let's see those little feet then." He said as he followed Mike out to the wagon.

He made the little ones comfortable with him even though he towered over them.

Soon he had Christopher up on his shoulders and the girls by the hand and they all reentered the barn. Angie and Mike followed.

Setting Christopher down on a table he went to some shelves farther back in the barn. He came back with a shiny pair of black boots and some socks. He deftly put on the socks and helped Christopher stand down and pull the boots on. They were just his size! Then he went back to shelves and had to dig around a little but came out with some lace up shoes for each one.

"They will be a little big but they will grow into them soon." He smiled as he straightened up. "What do you think?"

Mike quickly said that they would take all of them. "How much do I owe you?

"Not a cent. I didn't pay for them. So I can just pass them along." He shook Mike's hand and walked with them back out to the wagon. They all smiled to themselves but said nothing as the children tried walking in their new shoes and boots.

FIVE

After Lizzie said grace they all filled their plates with the wonderful fried catfish and potatoes cooked with onions. Left over red beans and cornbread rounded out the wonderful meal. Wagon Boss Ryan had been invited and readily came to eat fish.

After eating the fish and potatoes everyone sat around laughing and playing with the kids. Mike asked Angie to take a walk with him. The night was light as it was a full moon.

"We are so grateful to you and your friends for what all the things you have done for us." Angie told Mike.

"We could not leave you and the little ones in the straits you were in." Mike smiled.

"Do you have family somewhere?" Angie quietly asked. "Oh I am sorry I didn't mean to pry like that."

"It's alright. And no I don't have any family. Unless you count this bunch that I am riding with here. We have been together for a few years now and they feel like family." Mike did not tell her about the Indian raid that had caused him to join this little group. He was not able to share that yet.

"I have something I need you all to know but I am pretty ashamed of it." Angie had stopped and faced Mike squarely. "I am not married to the drunk although the kids are his. But not Carlos he belongs to someone else. He just uses the Smetana name like the rest. Martin is the drunks name and he took Carlos and me in when we didn't have anywhere to go. He said that we didn't need any old piece of paper to make us a couple. The kids have no birth certificates either. I born them by myself and no papers were made for them. Martin Grimes is his name and I have always just used my name for me and the kids. Smetana is my family name."

Mike looked down at her. "Now none of that matters to any of us. We just want you and the kids to be alright. But when we get to a town we will see about making birth records at a court house for them."

They walked back to where the others stood visiting around the embers of the fire. Soon they all drifted back to their wagons for the night. Mike walked with Angie and the kids back to their wagons. He had carried the youngest that had gone to sleep in Gertie's lap. Angie and the others crawled into the wagon and Mike carefully handed the little one up to her.

"See you tomorrow", Mike said in a husky voice.

"Ok." Angie smiled and turned to tend to the beds.

The next few days found Mike and Angie and the kids visiting and spending time together.

Of course that was all that the women needed.

"Do you think they will get together?" Gertie asked as they prepared supper when they stopped the next night.

"If he don't he is a fool." Lizzie added as she pointed her knife at Angie's wagon.

"But we don't really know too much about her, maybe she has a bad history somewhere." Gertie frowned.

Lizzie looked at her and replied. "So now we are choosing our friends by what we know about them?"

Gertie laughed, "You didn't know anything about us did you and took us in.?"

"I have a good feeling about her myself." Lizzie continued peeling the potatoes.

"Who are we talking about now?" Nancy and Little Henry had come to help.

"We were just musing about Mike and Miss Angie. What do you think? Lizzie asked.

"I think that Mike will decide without our input." Nancy said as she put Little Henry down. He was walking pretty good now, but they still had to watch him to not fall into the open fire.

The next stand had some posters nailed up on the front of posts and some taped on windows announcing a camp meeting complete with singers. Camp meetings were religious meetings usually held out in the country and led by some evangelist. They mostly did not have a distinct religion but Methodists and Baptists were the usual fair. This one advertised for each family to pack a lunch and come for the day. John's group instantly decided to take advantage of this. The camp meeting was to be held about a week's ride at another stand. Other families also decided they wanted to do this so Wagon Boss Ryan decided that they would just make near there their nightly stop. So a few of days later found them camping along a stream that was just about five miles from the encampment. The women had been busy cooking the two nights to have picnic meals. They also had taken out their best dresses and shirts for the men so they would look good. Eb had cleaned out his buckboard and fixed some seats inside the back of the wagon for everyone to sit on and ride to the revival. The men rode horseback and the ladies and children rode with Eb when they started out the next morning. The meeting was to begin about four o'clock and would last into the night.

They soon found the encampment and picked out a spot close and also near the spring that was running to the south of the meeting place. With the wagons circled, each family took care of their horses and mules and the outriders drove the rest of the livestock across the stream downstream and up the bank on the other side to get them away from all of the commotion. John and the others made up them a schedule for night watches that let everyone enjoy some of the evening. Some like Eb offered to do extra duty. He had carefully explained to John that he did not relish listening to somebody telling him how to live. John made sure that Mike was off to take Angie and the kids to the meeting. Then he rode out to find Guthrie and Samson. They were still across the stream with the horses.

"You boys need to get cleaned up and make sure that you show up for the sermon." John had to work at keeping a smile off his face. He had explicit orders from Nancy and the other women that they had an obligation to see that the boys made it to church.

"If you don't mind sir we just as soon stay here with the horses." Guthrie spoke up. "We never had any religious training and we wouldn't know exactly what to do."

"Miss Nancy said you were to come clean up and go with here so I suggest you go get cleaned up and then find Miss Nancy and go with her."

Samson replied for both of them. "If Miss Nancy said we were to go we better get going."

After they loped off to get cleaned up, Eb and John had a great laugh.

"Did you see their faces when you told them Miss Nancy told them to come? I believe that they would do anything for her." Eb was still chuckling when he turned his horse and headed back to see about the livestock on the other side of the stream.

Henry was already riding slowly around the stock keeping them in a group, but loose enough to graze the afternoon. They certainly needed the time to eat. On the trail they ate only what was available and that was not always much. Here on the side of the stream they had found a good meadow with considerable grazing and the woods around helped keep them in a group. Eb soon found him as he was quietly talking to the herd.

"So you are not going to the meeting either?" Eb asked as he rode up.

"No it doesn't seem to be my cup of tea." Henry answered. "I have a little trouble with the hell fire and damnation parts especially after what I saw those Indians do. I don't think I am the best person in the world but I do believe that I am on the side of the good ones most of the time."

Eb was shaking his head and agreeing with Henry. They rode around the livestock and stopped and visited with others from the train that were taking their turns. About half way around they met up with Wagon Boss Ryan and they visited a while. Then they continued around the outer edge of the livestock pushing a few that were straying a little out of where they wanted most of them to stay. When it neared dusk and dark most of the cattle and mules would bed down. The horses wouldn't stray far from where they had been rounded up to.

Back at the camp, Nancy and Lizzie had joined Gertie and Angie to help get supper fixed. They had decided that they would just set the food out and everyone could eat when they wanted to. To keep the flies off each dish was covered with a dishcloth. Spoons and ladles were set out by the dishes. Beans were warmed over the coals of the fire. Then they all went off to get dressed and by 4:00 that afternoon they were all dressed and made a small parade over to where the preaching would be held. Nancy had brought an old blanket and made a pallet for the little one and Angie's kids. Angie's kids had become great babysitters and this evening was no exception as they sat down next to little Henry and began playing with him.

Jo had moved his wagon close enough that they could all sit or lean on it for chairs as there was no seating for the day. First the preacher introduced himself and the crowd became quiet except for a baby now and then. After his introduction a couple of songs that everyone knew were sung. Some that did not know the songs just hummed. Then the preacher began telling a few stories and then proceeded to what Henry had described as the 'hell fire and damnation part'. Then when he had them all stirred up good they were told to come to the front of the wagon that he was standing in and profess their sins and be saved. The ones that came forward were then herded down to the stream and dunked in the water that 'that washed away all their sins'.

As Nancy and most of the rest had already had this dunking when they were younger they did not take part in this. But to their surprise they saw Samson go down to the stream and be baptized. They were so proud of their kid!!!

After this was over they all drifted back to their wagon and everyone had supper. When Samson came by they all made over him with hugs and back slapping. He was pretty embarrassed over all the attention but loved every minute of it. After a while they could hear a fiddle and guitar or two playing music so they went over again and joined in. With Angie's kids watching little Henry, John asked Nancy to dance. He took her in his arms and away they danced. They would come back after each dance to check on the kids and to their surprise when about the second dance was over Jo had them all in the back of his buckboard sound asleep.

They ask Jo if he wanted them to watch them so he could dance with Gertie.

"I ain't learned to dance and I don't think I will do that now." he told them.

So away they went and joined in the dancing circles. Mike and Angie came by dancing together, and Lizzie had been dancing with the Wagon Boss Ryan. They saw Gertie standing just inside the circle and clapping looked like she was really enjoying the music.

The people playing the instruments changed occasionally and then some would sing some song they remember from where they came. So they heard a variety of songs and tunes. When late into the night they were tired and all headed back to the wagons. It was a moonlight night so when John had seen Nancy and little Henry in their wagon he told her he would make one circle and see if everything was alright with the livestock and then come back.

SIX

John eased Red across the stream and up the bank on the other side. He could hear someone soothing the stock but it was not Henry. By now he knew his voice by heart and he did not hear it. He continued around the bedded down livestock and a few horses that were still milling about.

He had seen several cowboys and none of them said they had seen Henry or Eb since before dark. John was beginning to be uneasy about them not being here. But he could not call out as it would rouse the stock. He had never gotten used to Eb being able to ride his mule right up behind him as he did now.

"Damn you Eb you nearly got shot." He had turned his horse to ride next to the mule.

"Shh we have company and I don't think we invited them." Eb whispered to John.

"Where is Henry?" John whispered back.

"He is circling the stock and telling the outriders to have their guns ready and keep their eyes open." Eb said as he turned into some thicker woods on the edge of the clearing.

"Are they Indians?" John wanted to know.

"No, their horses are shod. There are four or five of them. They haven't done anything yet but they have been nearby since before dark." Eb answered.

All of John's group had been on the watch as they had heard that around the stands were always some no good thieves and rustlers. So far they had not encountered any real threats until tonight.

"Where are they now?" John held Red up.

"They are on the off side from the stream."

Henry then joined them. He was not as quiet as Eb but was pretty good.

"They are still on the other side. They are just sitting there talking. I didn't get close enough to hear it all but they did say some more would be joining them at daybreak."

John quickly told the two of them to stay on the lookout. He would ride back to the wagons and get more help and alert the other. He then turned Red and back across the stream he went. He quickly found Wagon Boss Ryan and told him what was up. Ryan said he would alert the others and send help. John told him that they needed to join up on this side of the stream and then go as a group across. John then quickly went to his wagon and told Nancy what was going on.

"Get your shotgun where you can get to it quickly. We do not know what is happening here. I will send the others to stay with you."

John then went to each wagon of their group and sent Gertie, Jo and Lizzie to stay with Nancy. He then found Mike and Mike quickly saddled his horse and they took Angie and the kids to Nancy's wagon. Jo and Lizzie both brought their guns and one took the front and one at the back of the wagon.

Mike and John then returned with Samson and Guthrie to the streams bank and joined Ryan and others that he had gathered up. They made about 20 guns altogether.

"Now men these characters haven't done anything wrong yet. We are just going to be watching and waiting to see what they are up to. So no shooting unless your life is in danger." Ryan told them.

Ryan then sent them two or three at a time across the stream with instructions to just join in circling the livestock. He also had told them to pair up and ride together. Since the moon was still out he told them to ride in the shadows at the edge of the meadow and try not to spook the stock. Mike took Guthrie and John took Samson as their pairs. Ryan had paired off with a good shot from the front of the train named Clark. As they circled the stock, on the off side from the stream they could see a fire in the woods a ways back. They rode all night and waited but nothing happened. In the morning Eb was back and said they were gone.

"Got up, stomped out their fire, and faded back into the woods." Eb announced. "Shall I go after them?"

Ryan spoke," No I think we will just get on with our schedule but we will be watching. We will also set out more night watchmen."

SEVEN

Although they hadn't slept much, Gertie and the others were up and had breakfast going when John, Mike and the others came in. They quickly ate and then hitched up the wagons and within the hour they were on their way again. They had arrived in Natchez Mississippi about sundown. They all took turns going to town and getting cleaned up.

Nancy and John took their turn at going to town and spending one night at a hotel. Again they treated themselves to baths and new bought clothes. Little Henry had outgrown nearly everything that he had so material had to be bought to sew new clothes for him also. As before Lizzie, Gertie and Angie joined Nancy with lists in hand to buy supplies. Angie insisted that she and the kids go back to the wagon train, but was overruled and they joined Lizzie in her room at the hotel.

That evening as they all sat around the hotel restaurant the first to speak was John.

"Ok we have made it this far. Let's talk about what each of you think we should do next. I know that we had started out for Texas but I hear around town that there is a lot of good land between here and the Texas border. That would mean that we were still in the United States. With Texas just starting out we don't have any idea what the future will be there."

Lizzie jumped in, "I am still for going to Texas. It will be a complete start over for all of us. And I am game to join a new country and see what we can help it become."

Several others nodded in agreement.

Mike then spoke up. "We will have to travel farther into Texas. I heard today that the border especially around Nacogdoches is plenty wild. And of course the farther into Texas we go we will have to contend with Indians. And we still have to cross the Mississippi and get across Louisiana. But I am for going ahead."

Eb and the others spoke for going to Texas also. So John spread a map on the table and they all gathered round. Each looking and listening, they soon again made a plan on how to proceed to Texas. They also all agreed that they wanted to get their stuff together and get back on the trail as soon as they could.

Next morning Lizzie and John went down to the livery and traded their teams for fresh ones. They also bought new tack, bridles and hitch lines. The livery man was very interested in where they were heading out to.

"We are going to Texas."

"I hear it is mighty rough people between here and there. You all better be good with a gun."

When they had moved out of the hearing of the livery man, John was the first to speak. "Lizzie are we making a mistake not staying where it is a little more livable?"

"I believe we are able to take care of ourselves. And we have learned a lot making the trip so far. I think we go ahead."

They meet up with the rest of their party. Everyone had taken turns coming in to town and getting their supplies. Now they loaded the buckboard and headed back out to what was left of the wagon train. John was surprised to see four or five wagons still here. When he rode up several families came out to meet him.

"We five families would like to join you going to Texas. Do you think we could?"

John turned around and looked at his group, they all nodded yes. They had met this little group on the trail and they were nice and hardworking people.

"We planned on leaving in the morning can you be ready to go by then?"

The speaker of the group nodded in agreement.

"We need to have all your names so we can rightly help take care of all of us."

That night they had circled their little band of travelers and with a big fire, they all ate together and sat around visiting, getting to know each other's families.

Early the next morning each wagon driver heard a familiar call as Wagon Boss Ryan, now just Jim called for the wagons to move out. They circled downtown Natchez and then made their way down to the wharf. Ryan had made arrangements for the ferry the day before and it was standing by to take them across the Mississippi. The wagons with the families were taken first. It was slow going as the ferry could only carry three wagons at a time. After them came the buckboards. When the ferry got back to the Mississippi side it was fitted with board slats and the livestock were herded on the ferry. Each man handled four or five horses with their lead ropes. It took many trips to get them all across. The very last group was the cattle and the pigs. And when they were nearly across for the last time one of the pigs pushed under the bottom slat and dove into the water. Everyone figure that was the last of the pig. But to their astonishment, the pig swam to the bank and stood there looking at everyone like I am waiting on you. The men laughed as they unloaded the last load. Ryan and John had paid the ferryman in advance and so with a wave they too joined the others.

Although John knew that with the extra families they would travel slower, he had discussed the fact with the others that the extra guns might come in handy if they needed them. Two of the families were pulling their wagons with oxen so they traveled slower. But in a pinch the oxen were great pullers up hills and out of mud holes.

As soon as they reached the Louisiana side of the Mississippi they were surprised to find a good wagon yard. Seems they were not the only ones going "west". They decided to camp on the backside of the wagon yard but not in it. They had plenty of hands now to take care of the livestock as the additional families had nearly grown sons that quickly joined the others as wranglers. The five additional families were named Fowlkes, Sanderson, Riley, Davidson, and Younger. Each family consisted of husband, wife and children except for the Riley couple. They had no children and he was a doctor/dentist. John was delighted to have them. Ms. Riley was a school teacher, something they sorely needed with their train.

That night they had a meeting and made sure everyone had made the crossing ok. They then worked on a schedule of night riding and caring for the livestock. During the meeting something spooked the pigs and they ran right under one of the tables and dislodge some of the food. They were soon shooed out and they picked up what was left and then ate. They also decided that the wagons would take turns in the line. Each day they would start with the next wagon in line so everyone took a turn.

That afternoon they had all checked their supplies one last time and had gone into the wagon yard to buy what they had forgotten. The next morning, as the sun came up, they sat out westward. Ryan had without votes, stepped back into the lead man for the wagon train. They soon found themselves in a different part of the country. First the going was very slow as there was only one road as such and to get off of it was your own peril in the swampy sides. The other problem was finding a proper place to stop that was not swamp and had a little dry area. It takes a lot of ground for about 15 wagons as they were now to stop for the night. As they passed other wagons going east they both had to squeeze by each trying to stay out of the ditch of water on the sides. They had figured a week to get to Alexandria and it looked like it would take every minute of that. It started raining the day they sat out and continued off and on for three days. They did not make camp, each family just eating and sleeping in their wagons. Gertie did her best with hardtack and biscuits with jelly that she had put up, but would be glad to have a fire so she could cook proper. The destination of Alexandria was decided when they had learned that there they could find someone who had trailed to Texas and could tell them the best place to start looking for a place for them to get some land. After a week of the biggest mosquitoes, being wet, cold food and just plain misery they arrived at the wagon yard in Alexandria. Finally the rain had stopped and the sun came out. They quickly found a place to park their wagons and a farmer that let them board their livestock a few miles away. Continuing the schedule, the men and boys took their turns going out to stay with the livestock. Gertie and the girls quickly got a fire started and began cooking. While the cooking was progressing they busied themselves with trying to wash clothes and get them hung out to dry. Nancy looking around, laughed and said,

"Well we look just like everyone else here!" Lizzie and Gertrude joined in the laughter. John had ridden up and immediately asked what was so funny.

"All of us are wet and feeling very ugly until we looked around and everyone else looks just like us." Nancy told him.

Little Henry was the biggest problem that Nancy had immediately. He was walking everywhere now and having to stay in the wagon did not suit him. He had started a wailing soon as everyone else was out and working. It was too muddy for him to get out and Nancy had work to do.

"Can't you at least see to Little Henry?" Nancy went over and handed Little Henry up to John on his horse. John started to protest but looking over at Lizzie he saw her shake her head no, so he turned and rode up the wagons to see Ryan.

The clothes washing continued the next day. When one of the Hunter brothers came in to eat lunch he had a tale to tell. He had ridden up to a stream to water his horse. Just as he came close to the bank, the bank moved. It was an alligator, a very big alligator. It quickly had slide into the water. Samson laughed as he told them that he guessed the horse would have to get water somewhere else.

The water was a problem for the ladies too. Very little clean and clear water was available. Most of the streams around were muddy. So they had found a man that hauled clean water. John protested that the price was too high, but the man had a monopoly on clean water so they paid. All their water barrels were filled up and all the clothes were washed. Samson Hunter and his brother came in during the second day and brought their clothes and Eb's and using the used water they washed and hung them out to dry on a make shift line they put up running across Eb's buckboard.

"Wow," Gertie called out. "You guys are going to make wonderful wives one of these days."

The brothers had taken up with Eb on the trail and helped him anyway they could. And old Eb seemed to really like someone taking care of them.

That night as everyone gathered around the center fire area, it was decided that they would spend another day or two until they all dried out. Ryan also had news. He had found a scout to take them into Texas. Called "Scout" and looking every bit the part, his name was Walker Livingston. He had experience and Ryan and John had checked out his references in the town. Each family had to pay part of his salary, feed him and his horse and go when he said go and stop when he said stop. Not quite a wagon boss but near it, everyone understood that Ryan still was the boss.

Walter stood nearly five feet and five inches. He had dark hair and eyes and had a dark complexion. His English was broken with words of creole and French. He wore a small hat, a bandana around his neck. His breeches were khaki and tucked into tall topped boots. His shirt was a faded silk shirt. He cut quite a sight.

Gertie stepped up and said, "We will take care of feeding you with our men. My name is Gertie and this is my man Jo."

Others stepped up and introduced themselves and shook his hand. Then they all drifted back to their own campfires.

The next morning the wagon train started out. They now were used to how to follow in line the wagon in front of them. They had not traveled long until one of the wagons near the front of the train slipped off the wagon trail and into the muck. This was when one of the new families became the savior of the whole trip. Their team that pulled their wagon was big Belgium geldings. When the wagon went off into the muck, the man simply pulled his team off his wagon took them back to the wagon in the muck and hitched them to the other team and with little commands the big sorrels put their chests to the harness and pulled the other team and wagon out and back on the trail. All of the people standing watching clapped and hollered at the ease the big horses did their job. The man working them was embarrassed by all the attention and quickly eased his team back into their harness and he climbed back onto his wagon seat next to his wife. Ryan came by and thanked him again the man just smiled and said,

"Don't you think we need to get going again?"

Ryan chuckled to himself and rode to the front of the wagon and yell for them to get going again.

After this the family named Davidson was one of the most known in the wagon train. Mainly they were known as the owner of the big team that had to pull someone out of the muck nearly every day. Mr. Davidson always just unhitched his team and quietly went where ever they were needed and when he was done he just quietly returned to his wagon. He hardly stayed long enough for the people he had pulled out could thank him. John soon learned that he had been a farmer not far from Nancy's family and had been burned out by the Indians. They only thing they had was the clothes on their backs and this brace of Belgium horses. Some of their Church people had gotten them some clothes together and he had borrowed money for the wagon and they had set out for a new life.

Nancy was not too pleased with John these days. The weather was hot and hotter. It was either humid or raining. There was very little place to let Little Henry down to run and play so he was cranky and on top of that he was teething. And the bugs! Nancy complained to John that the wagon was full of every creeping creature made. Every bug either bite you or made you nearly hurt yourself trying to get away from it. The only saving grace had been the salve that had come from Talking Wolf's wife. Nancy was determined to have her tell her how to make the stuff. It didn't smell too good so she was not sure she wanted to know what it was, but it certainly took care of the itching and the bites. Nearly every day when John came in for supper she would ask him if he had seen Talking Wolf and the answer would always be no.

EIGHT

The wagon train did not make as good time as when they were on the Natchez Trace. But they plugged along each day bringing them closer and closer to Texas. If it was raining they still drove in the rain and they did not even stop and circle the wagons at night. When Ryan called a halt each little family just crawled into their wagons pulled down the front and back flaps and went to bed; everyone except Little Henry who was not ready for bed. Both Nancy and John took turns telling him stories until he would fall asleep. When the weather was good Gertie and Jo, or Lizzy or the Smetana's would volunteer to take Little Henry in their wagon to give Nancy a rest. Henry was fond of all of them but really like playing in Angie's wagon with the kids.

Angie and Mike continued to be together a lot. Lizzy had even asked Nancy, "Why don't they get married?"

"I don't know and I am not going to ask. I guess they will when they decide to."

But that night she was still thinking about it and told John. "We all want to know why Mike has not asked Angie to marry him."

John laughed at her.

"Well hon if you want to know the answer to that you will have to ask Mike or Angie as I don't rightly know the answer to that."

As they had traveled along there had been questions about George the freed slave. Some people were downright ugly to him. And some questioned him having his own wagon and team and nice clothes. To people that mattered to John he explained how he had joined them. To others Mike or John simply told them to mind their own business. But a few times it had gotten plenty heated. So when they had had one of the run-ins with someone on the trail, George had pulled John aside and asked him if he didn't think it might be better if they just said that

George was his slave. Then people would assume that his wagon and things belong to John and they would not be so upset about a black having things.

"We'll talk it over and we'll see." John had told him.

That night around the campfire, John told everyone that George had a problem and needed their help. The others quickly gathered closer and George looked around at his adopted family and began to speak.

"You all have been very good to me and I would never want to cause any of you any problems. But we are going into more country where there are people who don't think there should be free blacks. So to stay out of trouble I thought I should just say I belonged to one of you."

Now George thought he was talking about John owning him. But before he could say that, Lizzy spoke up.

"I would be very glad to claim you as my hired hand Mr. George." Everyone laughed and clapped.

"Now all of you have to remember that George and his stuff belong to me." Lizzy had stepped around the fire and taken George's hand in a handshake.

"So is it a deal Mr. George?"

"Yes mam as of now I belongs to you."

So the next day quietly everyone made a point to speak to each family and tell them that Mr. George had come from Indiana with Lizzy and was hers.

But in a few days Lizzy had to gripe at the campfire to Mr. George. "Just because you belong to me you do not have to wait on me hand and foot. I was doing for myself before I got you and I can take care of myself thank you."

Later John asked Nancy about Lizzy and Mr. George. Nancy giggled when she told John that Mr. George had been doing all Lizzy's chores even taking care of her team of horses and gathering her wood and water.

Clampton was a welcome sight for the travelers. Nancy especially was tired of the bugs, rain, and moldy everything. So when they pulled into Clampton she was the first one in the back of their wagon and was completely taking everything out.

"What may I ask are you doing? John ventured to ask.

"I am cleaning out everything."

Having learned better than to further this conversation, John simply asked, "What do you want me to do to help?"

Soon Nancy had handed out to John all their bedding and clothes. When Eb came by he started to ask what they were doing. With a motion like he was cutting off his head he was quickly silenced.

"I just came by to ask if I could help in any way." Eb ventured to Nancy.

"Yes get some wood and water so I can wash all this stuff."

Behind Nancy's back John just nodded to Eb. Eb quickly grabbed the buckets and loaded them into his buck board. He then proceeded down the trail to the Red River and filled the water buckets and on the way back gathered wood for the fire. He did not have the heart to tell Miss Nancy that when they left here there would be many more days of bugs and rain.

As the fire heated the water, the clothes and bed linens were washed and rinsed and hung to dry. The others had followed suit, Gertie, Lizzy, and Angie soon had their laundry hanging out. The weather was co-operating and soon the laundry was dry. Nancy busied herself remaking their nest and re-packing their clothes. When John came back by she looked like a wreck but he said nothing.

NINE

That night when they had finished supper John called a meeting. "We plan on leaving day after tomorrow for Natchitoches. So get everything done tomorrow that you need done and supplies bought in town. Let me remind you that when we leave Natchitoches we will be in a no man's land. It is wild country. It is also without government as it has been disputed between France, Spain and finally the US for the border between Louisiana and Texas. The Spanish said that the border was Arroyo Hondo and US claimed it was the Sabine River. Even though the Sabine River is the official border it is still wild country with little law enforcement. So we must be very vigilant, watching for thieves and especially rustlers. When you are in town men refurbish your ammo along with your supplies as we do not know what we will encounter. Any questions?"

The next day found all the group together again in the town. They took the opportunity for baths, shaves and shopping. Especially shopping was done for Little Henry. They could not keep him in clothes, he was growing so fast. After a great lunch of Cajun food at the hotel's restaurant they returned to camp. As some of them took the opportunity for a nap or siesta John and Mike rode out to check on the horses and livestock. It was Mike that spoke first. "When we leave out tomorrow morning I think I will ride near Angie's wagon if that is ok with you."

John's reply was swift, "I was thinking the same thing for myself. I really don't know what we are getting into here. So let's also make sure that we have all our wagons together in the line and I think at the very back. What do you think?"

"We need one outrider with each wagon if we have the people. The women can drive the wagons and the men can be on horseback along

346

the line. We will have to cut out some horses for some of them as some only have their wagon teams."

"Ok," John agreed. "I will hunt Ryan and then go along the wagons and tell everyone how we plan to travel. We need to practice this for the trip along no man's land and this is as good a time as any."

Sunrise the next day found the wagon train ready to move out. And when it did it was a different configuration than before. Each wagon now had an outrider, mostly the man of the family. The wife or older child was driving the team. And within reach was a shotgun or rifle for whoever knew how to use it. John was sorry he had caused them to be so afraid but he also wanted the people on the trail that they met to know that they were "loaded for bear". Just maybe it would keep the bad guys from thinking they were an easy mark.

As he turned back and came up next to their wagon he noticed how tired Nancy looked today. Had she been looking that tired before? He decided to ask Lizzy when he rode back to check on her.

He realized that it had been a long and tedious trip. He also allowed himself to worry about what was coming up. He worried about him having asked her and their son to come on this trip and whether he should have just found a job in one of the cities that they had passed. He was very talented with his hands and he was a good wrangler. Should he have stopped somewhere and settled down instead of dragging all these people out here to whatever lay ahead?

Mike was talking to him, "Earth to John." Embarrassed John reined up and to look at his dear friend. "What's up?"

"What's up is that you are away off somewhere." Mike grinned.

"Just thinking that I hope we made the right choice to come all the way out here instead of going back east."

"I don't think that anyone here was roped and tied and dragged along to come out here with you. We all decided together and yes we all knew it would be dangerous but we will stick together and we will build a new life in Texas."

As Nancy herded her team along the trail, she had the same worries. Had they done the right thing bringing Little Henry way out here in this forsaken place? She had taken a good look at herself in a full length mirror that they had seen in one of the stores. Her hair did not have the shine it used to have. She had not lost all the "baby fat" from having Henry. Her complexion that used to be almost like cream now was ruddy from the sun and wind. She also wondered if John had noticed she didn't look too good anymore. He had not said anything but she wondered. It took about two weeks to lumber into Natchitoches. They had seen less wagon train but lots of wagons carrying supplies. The bull haulers were a loud and unkempt bunch. They quickly found that the wagon train did not want to visit with them and they then camped away from the train.

Natchitoches had a wagon yard and they decided to use it. They also rented a corral and put the livestock in it and started a rotation of riders to watch the pens. Since they had store up supplies in Alexandria the only thing most of them needed was water. Eb and some other hands filled everyone's water barrels. John encouraged everyone to stay with the train.

That afternoon he went into town with Ryan and Mike. They rode the length of town and then turned in at a lawyer's office. They stepped up on the wooden sidewalk after they had tied their horses to the rail outside. Inside an elderly, white headed gentlemen stood up to shake hands with them.

"What can I do for you fellers today?" he had quickly sized up these as not your usual run of the mill cowboys.

"We need to talk to someone about a couple of things. One is how dangerous is to cross dead man's land and then we need to know who to see when we get to Texas about settling there. Can you help us with either of these or do you know someone that can?" John had spoken first.

"I am the one who can help you with the first question. There is little law here or the trip across no man's land. If you have plenty of guns and look like you could put up a pretty good fight you will probably make it ok. Those hooligans out there are not very brave, mostly just picking on people they can take advantage of. As to the second one, I believe that you will have to arrive in Texas and then go to the nearest settlement to ask for directions on how to get the land."

John and Ryan returned to the camp and relayed what they had learned to the group that had been called together. Ryan was first to speak. "I believe that we are able to take care of ourselves so I favor pushing on into Texas and then finding a lawyer to tell us what to do when we get there." He then spread out a map on the common table and they all gathered round.

"We are told to go across this wild man land as quickly as possible. So I suggest that we take the Sabine trail here and get to Texas as soon as we can. We were shown this trail and where the easiest place to cross the Sabine River." He traced the route with his big fingers. "If we go across the Sabine here we would then just be about a week to the post at Natchitoches."

TEN

The first two days were miserable. It had rained and rained. They were all wet and depressed. Samson had drawn the job of being Miss Nancy's outrider. He liked riding with her as she would talk to him a lot. After lunch break they were again in conversation when a rider he did not know rode up and said John Dunn had said he take over his shift and he was to report back to the drag. So Samson relayed that information to Nancy and turned and loped to the back of the wagon train. It was Gertie that first noticed that Nancy's wagon was drifting along and not staying in the trail. Jo had come up to get a bite to eat when she told him to go up and see what the deal with Nancy's wagon was. It was not unusual for someone to go to sleep while they were driving or in Nancy's case they just figured she had stepped back into the wagon to see about Little Henry. So she was quite surprised when Jo showed back up with Little Henry and passed him up to her.

"What is the deal? Is Nancy sick?" Gertie asked him.

"I don't know because she is not there." Jo said.

"What do you mean she is not there?"

"I mean she ain't in that wagon." He then turned and went back to Nancy's wagon and grabbing the lead on the first horse in her pair and led the wagon out of the line. Ryan had come up to see what the trouble was and was very surprised when Jo related that Nancy was not in the wagon and had left Little Henry in the wagon by himself. Ryan then loped back to the drag and was hollering for John Dunn to come quick. John reacted by passing Ryan on the way to their wagon. When he saw no one in the wagon he turned to Jo and Ryan.

"Where are Nancy and Little Henry?"

"Well Little Henry is in our wagon with Gertie. And I don't rightly know where Miss Nancy is." Jo answered.

"What do you mean you don't know where she is?"

"Gertie called to me and we seen your wagon going off the trail and I rode up to see if Nancy needed any help and she wasn't there so I picked out Little Henry and took him back to our wagon and then went back and pulled your wagon out of the line. And that is all we know."

"Where is Samson he was supposed to be Nancy's out rider?" John yelled at Jo.

"I didn't see him when I came up." Jo told them.

Ryan quickly told John that he had seen him when he came to get John. He was riding on the other side of the drag. John quickly turned and lite out to the back of the wagon train. Jo and Ryan rode right behind him. He soon saw Samson and rode up to him.

"Samson where is Miss Nancy?"

"I don't know sir. She was in her wagon when that rider came up and relieved me and told me that you wanted me to come back and help with the drag."

"What rider?"

"I didn't know him sir but I don't know all the new families.

"What did he look like?" John demanded.

"It was raining sir. He had his hat pulled down low and he was wearing a slicker."

"What exactly did he say?"

"He just said that you said he was taking my place and you said for me to fall back to the drag."

Mike, Henry and Eb had come up to see what all the yelling was about.

"Nancy is missing. A strange rider came up and sent Samson back here. They left Little Henry in the wagon. Now we know that Nancy would not leave Henry like that. So I assume someone has taken her."

Mike jumped in. "We will find her John."

"Yes we will and we will leave right now." Eb had pulled his mule up to the group. "We still have a few hours of daylight left."

John turned to Ryan. "Can we circle the wagons for the rest of the day in case she needs to come back here?"

"Of course we can." Ryan said and turned and started back to the wagon.

"Eb you and Henry go with me. Mike you stay here and help keep the wagon train together."

"Do you want some more men to go with you?" Mike added.

"No that might just be what they want. They might be thinking they will draw us off and then attack the whole wagon train. The train will need all the hands if that happens; besides the three of us can move faster than a bunch of us." John turned away from the drag and back to the train.

Ryan had started the circling of the wagons and explained to each wagon family what was going on. He waved at John when he saw him ride up to Jo's wagon. John took only a minute to tell Jo and Gertie and Lizzie that the three of them were going to look for sign of Nancy and her kidnapper.

The three of them rode back to where they supposed that the man had taken Nancy but they soon realized the wagons following her had wiped out the tracks they would have left. Then they began moving out away hoping to catch the track of something. Eb had only moved about a hundred yards when he saw a partial print in the side of a cutback. With it continuing to rain off and on he realized that tracking would be very difficult. This print had just managed to set back under an outcropping when he saw it.

He called to the others and they soon joined him. On his prompting they began again to circle around where the print was. They did not have any idea that this was the person they were looking for or someone else.

They soon came to a stream and with Eb and his mule going down the stream Henry and John took the bank on both sides. They followed it away from the direction of the wagon train but after several hours they found nothing. They turned around again and fanned out going back.

It was Eb who spoke up the next time they were together. "Ok boys we need to go back and get properly geared up. We do not know how long or far they have gone. But I know that if we on a few days out we are going to need more than we have."

"I hate to go back without anything." John said with his head down.

"We cannot help that. We need supplies and I need ammo." Henry added.

"Ok we will turn back but we need to get going early in the morning." John said.

It was still misty rain when they entered the camp. The other families could tell they had not found Nancy. Ryan rode up and offered to help them get supplies together.

"We know how to do this." Eb quickly told him.

John had ridden over to Gertie and taken Little Henry in his arms. He turned away from everyone else so they would not see his tears. He hugged him tight until Little Henry protested and he realized he was squashing him.

"He has already had his supper." Gertie found them. "Do you want me to bed him down with us?"

"Yes because we are going to leave at first light." John gave Little Henry a quick kiss and handed him over to her.

While he was seeing to Little Henry, Eb and Henry had caught a couple of pack mules from the remuda. With everyone helping supplies were packed. Food and blankets, ammo and extra clothes were packed and then wrapped in a tarp and placed on the pack mules and ropes tied the pack to the mules' backs. The three of them then took time to eat supper that Lizzie had warmed up for them. Although all of the three knew they would not sleep they went to their wagons to rest and wait for the sun to come up.

John lay down but he could not sleep. He remembered when he was single and slept like a log. He knew that he had become used to having Nancy and Henry in bed with him. He didn't know when he finally dosed. It didn't seem very long. Eb was banging on the side of his wagon. He quickly dressed and taking his guns and saddle bags climbed out. Henry already had Red saddled and ready to go. Eb had insisted that they bring along an extra horse in case they need it. So when they left out Eb and John led the two mules and Henry led the extra mount.

As they filed by the others stood quietly waving them goodbye, except for Lizzie who was ending her prayer with "thy will be done". John, too not very religious, now prayed for God to please help him find his wife.

Ryan had decided with John the night before that the train could not stay out here with no security. They would give them one more day and then they would continue on the trail. John had agreed with him.

"When we find Nancy we will catch up."

John let Eb take the lead as they again went back to where Nancy was taken. At least today it was not raining yet. Again they began circling the area looking for any tracks. None were to be found. The next circle around Eb turned off in a northwestern direction.

"Did you find something?" It was Henry who asked as they rode up to him.

"No but this is the direction that I would go if it were me, and I am tired of riding around in this damn circle and not finding anything." Eb had not stopped to visit with the other two. He sat straight up on his mule and John and Henry fell in behind him.

They had traveled most of the day when they again came to a stream of running water. They all three stepped down off their horses and let them and their packs drink. The three of them drank as well and filled their canteens. Eb then insisted that they press on. He had turned his mule into the stream and again they followed their routine of him in the water and John and Henry on the sides. They only went about a hundred yards down when Henry, on the west bank called out.

"I have a track."

John quickly crossed over the stream and joined Eb who had come up out of the water. Sure enough, there on the river bank were horse tracks and a slide where they had slipped as they came up out of the water. Eb was quickly off his mule and following the track into the woods.

"There are three of them and one is carrying two riders. One of the other ones' horse is missing a shoe on the left rear. See how the ones print is deeper than the other two." Eb pointed out what he was showing them.

"The problem is they had a good couple of so days on us. These tracks have filled with water and dried out. But we are on the right trail." He stepped back onto the big mule and began slowly tracking by walking slowly and hanging off the side of the mule's neck watching the sign. John was impatient. He wanted to ride fast as they could go, but knowing that Eb knew best he held himself in check. Eb had instructed them to follow right behind him so they would not walk over any tracks to either side of him.

They had again entered the woods. But to their surprise they were not following a fairly worn deer trail. Eb was going a little faster to John's delight. They had gone about a hundred yards when Eb held up his hand and signal for the others to be quiet, by placing his fingers on his mouth. He then gave Henry his mule's reins and slipped into the woods.

After what seemed eternity Eb was back and motioned the quiet sign again but urged them forward. They rode only a short time when they came out on a clearing. Even from the edge of the woods they could see that someone had camped here. As they drew closer to where the fire was, they could see where they had cooked and slept. John was really happy to see that you could continue to see evidence of four people so he felt Nancy was still alive.

It was late evening when they had found the camp. After a short discussion they decided they might go on for a while; actually at John's insistence. At nearly the last of the sun's light Eb called for a halt.

"We will not build a fire tonight. Just get something to eat and get some sleep. We will be up early in the morning."

So as was Eb's custom his mule was not unsaddled. The others were tied out on a long line that way they could graze. Then they all ate a little of their left over food and rolled up in their blankets. John decided he was getting old or soft as the ground was sure hard and cold tonight. He had trouble at first going to sleep as all he could do was think about his little family. But when sleep did happen he again slept like a log. By the time the others woke him up they had already packed the mules and saddled the horses.

"Why didn't you wake me up?" John asked as he scrambled to get his bedroll rolled up and tied on the back of his horse. As he was getting up on his horse Henry leaned over and gave him a biscuit and meat with a cup of coffee. He was hungry and the coffee tasted great!

"I thought we were not building a fire?" He looked over at Eb, who was grinning.

"White man build big fire and sit way back. Indian build little fire and sit up close. So we built little fire and sat up close for breakfast." Eb chuckled as he turned up the trail again.

As they progressed the woods thickened. Although they tried to be as quiet as they could to John it sounded like a herd going through the woods, what with horses and mules stumbling and making their way up the slopes they were going on now.

After about a mile, Eb motioned for Henry to take his mule and pack mule again. He motioned for them to get off the trail into the woods and be quiet. With his hands he motioned that he would go ahead alone and they were to wait here. He had pulled his rifle out of its scabbard on his saddle and before they could say anything he was gone and they could not see or hear him again.

For a while they just sat on their horse, but then when Eb did not come back they both stepped down and tied their mounts and packs to nearby trees. Finding a fallen log they sat down. For a long time neither one spoke.

"You never get over the loss you know."

"I think she is still out there somewhere." John said as he looked out into the woods.

"If she is Eb will find her and bring her back." Henry added. Then they stayed silent both absorbed in their own thoughts. Henry's thoughts were more gruesome than John's. He knew that by now Nancy may not be the beautiful lady John married and he also knew that no telling what horrible things they had done to her.

John guessed he dozed a little when he felt the blade of a knife at his throat and heard the holder of that knife,

"You get lazy white boy! Letting an Indian sneak up on your like that."

Henry was already on his feet and hugging everyone around him. Talking Wolf had also gathered John up in a big bear hug.

"What are you two and I see Eb doing in these woods? Talking Wolf asked as he motioned to Eb's mule and pack.

"We are looking for Miss Nancy. About a week ago now during a rain storm someone took her right off her wagon seat in broad daylight. We have been looking for them ever since."

"What about Little Henry?" Talking Wolf asked, as he knew Nancy would not be without him.

"They left him."

"We have tracked them to a camp last night and down this deer trail. One is carrying two people and one has lost a shoe on his horse's back hoof." Henry offered.

Talking Wolf then told them they would help find Miss Nancy but they would have to be careful. In this part of the country the white men and the Mexicans, did not like any Indians. So if they came to a town or farm they would hide and join them later. In the meantime he would send Sitting Grass to find Eb and help him track and would tell Eb where they were.

Talking Wolf then carried them deeper in the woods. About half a mile he stopped and the ten braves with him hurriedly built a camp. It was getting nearly dark so a small fire was built and rabbits that they had killed earlier were roasted for supper. Several of the braves then took all the horses and mules back to the stream to water and then brought them back and tied them to the long line. John and Henry were amazed at how fast they did everything. And it seemed they never talked aloud. Two of the braves had built a lean to for John and Henry.

Then to their amazement in perfectly good English he said,

"It will rain on you before morning." And then he disappeared into the night.

Not only was it a good lean—to, it was piled with leaves so it made a great bed! And with the company helping stand watch John and Henry slept. They slept until someone snoring woke them up. And turning over there was Eb. And just as the brave had predicted a light rain started before dawn. When the sun peeked over the mountain they arose to get their day started. To their amazement, their breakfast was cooked, horses saddled, packs on the mules and the braves standing around waiting for them to say go.

As they ate their wonderful breakfast Eb told them what he had found. "We are about a day behind now. They are in no hurry. And by the looks of their tracks and camps they are not aware that someone is following them."

Talking Wolf stood up. "My braves and I will go get Miss Nancy. That way if anything happens they will just say that some Indians stole her."

John started to protest, when Eb put his hand on his arm. "I believe that is a good idea. We will wait close by but out of sight until you get her."

John again wanted to protest. He wanted with all his being to go into their camp and kill them all. Eb knew this was what he was thinking and looking at Henry he said.

"After you get her and have them tied up we will come get them and take them to the nearest town to a sheriff."

Talking Wolf then told Sitting Grass to stay with the white men, and the others silently like they had never been there disappeared. Talking Wolf shook all three men's hands and he took disappeared. Sitting Grass squatted down by the fire.

John was the first to speak. "Aren't we going to follow them?"

"Yes." Sitting Grass continued to sit.

"Well let's go." Henry said.

"Not time yet." Sitting Grass answered.

"When will be the right time?" Eb then joined in.

"When the sun is right we will follow." Sitting Grass smiled.

ELEVEN

Nancy knew that John would come for her. After the shock of having the stinking awful man pull her out of the wagon seat and assure her that he would kill the kid if she made a sound, Nancy began trying to remember every tree or rock that would help her get away. She found none and by the end of the week she could not imagine why John was not coming to get her. Then it dawned on her. It had been raining very hard when the one had pulled her from the wagon seat so there would be no track for them to follow. But she just knew they were out there looking.

They had traveled three days, when one night one of the other ones decided to have his way with her. As he held her down she just knew she was done for. Then the first man pulled the other one off of her.

"You know what the boss said. We was to bring her to him like a lady and that is what we are going to do. Now get away from her. You are alright mam?"

"Yes, I am not hurt. But I heard you say that you were taking me to your boss. What is his name?

"We are not to tell you his name. But he acted like you all had met before."

As they continued on their way there were no more incidents. Her captors were decidedly afraid of whomever "boss" was. She was provided with a slicker to keep the rain off and had a good bedroll for the night. They fed her well and to her amazement let her have private woman time. This made her wonder why, since didn't they think she would try to run away? Then she realized they figured that she had no place to run to.

Nancy had been able to keep up with the days they had been traveling and this was day ten. She had called a halt and told them that she had to be excused. She had decided that day to run away. So when she went into the woods out of their site she began to run. She hadn't run far before she was cut and scratched by the tree limbs and vines. She stumbled and fell several times, but got up and continued to run. She had stopped behind a large tree to get her breath and look to see if they were coming looking for her, when a large hand covered her mouth. She nearly died. She just figured the three had found her. But when she turned around, she saw a large brave. She had already figured out it was not one of the three, as he did not smell like the others. The brave in sign language told her not to yell for help and to follow him. He had bound her hands together at the wrist and had a length of rope tied to the hand rope that he held. Motioning again for her to follow he started off in a trot. Nancy had trouble keeping up and fell several times. When she did he was careful to help her up, but was very insistent that they keep moving. They waded down a stream and then came out on the other side. The brave took the time to use some brush to sweep their tracks and then cover them with brush where they had come up the bank. Then he hit a trot again. They were now on a deer trail and the going was a little easier. Nancy wondered how long and far they were going to keep this pace up. After about a mile she had pulled on the rope and with gestures told him she had to rest just a minute. The brave smiled at her gesturing.

"You would not make a very good translator." the brave spoke to her in perfect English.

"Wait, why have you not spoken to me before?" Nancy asked.

"Because I didn't have anything to say. But we do not have time to talk. Those bad men have already begun looking for you and we have to get far away from here."

"First who are you and why are you helping me?"

"You fed us in the Indiana Territory. So we have come to get you."

He didn't elaborate and turned and started out again tugging on her rope when she slowed down too much. They had traveled for several hours before he stopped and listened. She was petrified! She just knew the bad guys were coming to get her again. And she could just imagine what would happen this time. They had come close to an opening in the woods. She looked everyway the brave was looking but could see no one. The brave then motion for them to continue on the trail. When it was nearly dark, he told her they would make camp here. They moved away from the trail and he found a large log and told her to rest beside it. He reached inside a pouch that he carried and brought out some dried meat. Nancy was hungry and chewed the meat readily. He also had a canvas pouch that had water in it. She drank until he took it away from her.

"You drink like a pig. What if we need some for tomorrow?"

"Where are we going?" Nancy asked.

"We are going where we need to go. Then someone will come and get you to take you somewhere else. Now go to sleep we will only rest for a while."

It seemed only a little while until the brave shook her awake. "We go now."

Up she got and he again took the end of the rope and the trot began again. Every bone in Nancy's body ached and she was so tired. Her hair was hanging down everywhere and it was hard to see where she was going. The brave stopped her and taking a piece of vine from a tree limb, he patiently braided her hair and tied it with the vine. Then he nodded and turned back to the trail. They had traveled for another couple of days. Nancy could no longer keep up with the days. They would trot and walk and rest and then go again. For a few hours in the night he would let her lay down but then he would be up and going again.

She had a million questions for him. But he had hushed her and nodded no to her talking so she had remained quiet. She was so tired and she had begun to think that the brave was nearly as bad as the first men. At least they had a horse for her to ride, this brave just kept dragging her along forever. And she wondered if it would ever end.

And then it did. It was so sudden that she barely noticed when they ran into a camp. There were braves everywhere and a campfire. They were laughing and patting the brave that had brought her back. Evidently they were very proud of him for dragging her into their camp!

He had turned back to her and said. "I am going to take your rope off now. You are safe here with us. We will not let those bad guys come here and get you. Now you must eat and rest." He took her over to the camp fire and filled her a plate of food. It was some kind of fish and some wild vegetables.

"Do not eat too much or you will be sick." the brave that seemed to be the cook said.

After she ate and had excused herself she was shown a bedroll and she fell on it with joy. She thought she should not sleep but keep watch but it was only a short time and she was sound asleep. When the sun came up and shine on her face she opened her eyes to see about 10 braves sitting around her looking at her. She rose up and saw her brave just a few steps away.

"What are they looking at?" She asked.

"They have a bet on when you will wake up. Now they will have to pay up." he laughed.

Nancy had been too tired the night before to notice the horses on the long line. But after her breakfast she was delighted to have one of the braves help her up on a pinto mare. The braves nodded in great admiration as she sat on the mare and rode along just like them. They had already made their bets on how long she would last before she fell off.

They traveled quickly now. They did not stop even for lunch. They acted like they had some place to be and didn't have time to visit. At the middle of the afternoon, they had stopped to listen. Everyone was perfectly still and quiet. Nancy realized as she looked around she could hardly see them, their horses and clothes blended so well into the trees.

Then he was there. He was not John, but when he came up behind her and pulled her down off her horse, she was again scared to death. Then she realized it was Talking Wolf, hugging her and she hugged him back.

"Are you ok?"

"I knew someone would come find me. I had no idea it would be you, but I am glad it is you and that is the reason that the brave said that I had fed him once."

"Yes, he was with us on the trail from your first home. He was very proud to be chosen to go steal you from the bad men."

"John and I will do something special for him."

"No, he wouldn't like that. He is already known around the campfire and that is enough."

"Where is John? I know he is looking for me. Have you seen him?"

"Of course. That is the reason we are here. We are making it look like Indians took you so we can go and find the bad guys and see what they are up to."

"I can tell you what they are up to. One of them said they were taking me to a "boss man". But they never did say where or who he was."

"We will meet up with John in a couple of days and then you can go home."

"I will be glad. And how is Little Henry?"

"They said that he drove the wagon very well." And they both laughed.

Good to his word one of the braves came in and said that sign said that John was only one day behind them.

John was indeed just behind them and nearly crazy with the way that the brave had taken them. His zigzags through the forest nearly drove him crazy! He wanted to gallop fast as Red could go but the brave held him back. And John had enough sense to know that Talking Wolf was doing the right thing. So he held his tongue and endured the daily slogging along when he wanted to run. He just hoped that Talking Wolf had found Nancy and she was ok. He worried about the things that could have happened to her. But he was determined that she would know that whatever had happened to her, she would still be his love. He did not realize that he had been dreaming when the brave that was leading them was kicking his boots.

"Get up. Word has come that we get the woman today."

"What are you talking about? Who came and where is she?" John asked as he jumped up and made up his bedroll. He looked around for the others and they were all standing around already packed and saddled including Red. "Why didn't you wake me up sooner?"

Eb laughed as he handed John Red's reins. "We knew you needed the rest. And the brave said that Nancy was ok so we let you sleep a while."

John jumped for his stirrup and mounted. Sitting Grass turned his horse and started through the trees, up the side of the mountain and they all followed. They rode hard for about four hours and then rested. John did not want to stop but he knew the horses needed the rest. When they started out again it was only about an hour when they passed some braves along the way. John knew they were look outs.

They joined behind John and the others. Sitting Grass made one more turn and came out right into a camp. John could not get off his horse fast enough and then there was Nancy.

He scooped her up in his arms and then gave her a big kissed. He didn't think she had looked more beautiful, even though she was filthy and her clothes had never seen such bad days.

"Are you alright?". John asked.

"Yes, I am fine."

And then they kissed again. That is when the braves could stand it no longer. The bet had been one or two kisses. And then the pay offs started. John looked at Nancy with a question in his eyes.

"I will explain it to you later." Nancy assured him.

After supper cooked by the braves, Eb, Henry, and Talking Wolf sat by the fire for a while. They speculated on who the kidnappers were and what they wanted. Nancy and John snuggled in the lean-to that the braves had made for her the nights before. Soon the men all settled down for the night. Without any directions, some of the braves took first watch and then others would trade with them during the night.

Morning light awakened Nancy and John. John looked around. There was no one there. He quickly pulled on his boots and clothes. He wanted to let Nancy sleep but knew they needed to get back to the wagon train soon as they could.

"Wake up sleepy head."

"I am awake." She said and snuggled farther down in her bedroll.

"Oh no get up we have to get going."

"Wow they are finally awake." it was Eb stirring something in a skillet and it smelled so good.

"Where are the rest of them?" He pointed around the camp.

"Henry is fishing and I am building a fire and everyone else has left. Talking Wolf said the track was pretty easy to read so they were going to go back to following the bad guys to see where they would lead them."

By the time that Nancy and John were dressed and up and about, Henry was back with some fish and Eb soon fried it with some potatoes. Although Nancy had not missed any meals, she ate with relish. She was so blessed to again be with her family. While they were finishing up and getting their pack mules loaded, Sitting Grass came into the camp. First he just stood there looking around and then spoke.

"I am to tell you where the wagon train is."

He then squatted on the ground and drew a map showing where he had left the wagon train three days before. After eating breakfast and thanking Eb for it, he stood and remounted his horse and turned and like the others just disappeared into the woods.

"I will never figure out how they just disappear like that." Nancy commented.

"It is quite a knack they have there." Henry answered.

"I guess we better get on the road if we are going to catch this wagon train anytime soon." Eb replied.

They were all packed and on the trail in a short time. They rode at a steady pace but now did not have to ride hard. They stopped for cold lunch that Eb had packed that morning. Then they were on their way again. They made better time than they knew the wagon train was going. Even with that it was the fifth day before they could see the train in the distance. Nancy wanted to go at a gallop to her baby, but rode at the same snail pace as the others. Finally she could stand it no more. She kicked her mount into a lope and was soon at the remuda. The cowboys saw her and all gave her a yell as she went by.

Lizzie was the first to see her coming. She had Little Henry in her lap while she drove her wagon. She pointed out his mother to him and he gave a cry out to her. John got to the wagon first jumping down from Red he grabbed up Little Henry and swung him in the air. Then after a short hug turned and relinquished him to his mother. Nancy hugged and kissed on his until he protested. Then they both laughed. The wagon train had stopped and everyone came over to welcome her back. They all wanted to hear her story but were polite enough to know that the little family needed time with just each other. Samson was driving John and Nancy's wagon and quickly got down and after Henry took their horses, John and Nancy and Little Henry settled down on the wagon seat. Looking around he called out,

"We still have a lot of daylight. Boss Ryan get this wagon train going!"

TWELVE

Everyone on the train returned to their wagons and the train was soon on its way again. Unknown to them they had but a few miles to go to the Sabine River and after they crossed that, they would be in Texas. The Sabine River crossing would wait until the next day. The wagons pulled into a wagon yard on the East Bank and John and Ryan went ahead and checked out the crossing for the next day.

That night when fires were lit and supper over, people drifted over to John and Nancy's campsite. Nancy knew they all wanted to hear her story so she had them gather around and she told the story of her kidnapping and rescue. She had decided to tell it to them all at a time so she wouldn't have to retell it a dozen times to each one. One or two of the women in her audience sniffed back tears as they imagined what an ordeal it had been for her.

After they had all drifted back to their own camps, John and Nancy's little group gathered together for Lizzie to pray.

"Lord, we just thank you today for the return of our Nancy. We knew you would find her and bring her home. Amen."

They too then dispersed and John, Nancy and Little Henry crawled into their wagon. They for a long time just lay in their bed snuggling. It was such a blessing to all be back together.

The next morning breakfast was quickly eaten. The wagon train had made several river crossings by now and each one knew what to do. They soon lined up and one by one the wagons drove off into the Sabine River. When the first wagon reached the far bank and pulled up on the trail, the man of the family stood up in his wagon seat and yelled to the others

"Welcome to Texas!"

Each wagon and family in turn drove across accompanied with out-riders in case they had any trouble. Only one wagon got bogged down and had to have some cowboys help pull and push them out the other bank. John had taken the reins from Nancy and steered their wagon across without any trouble. He then gave the wagon reins back to her and mounting Red, returned across the river to help get all the livestock across. A few horses and cows had to be herded with a little more persuasion than the others, but before lunch they were all safely across.

The wagon train then circled and set up camp for the night after traveling only a few miles. John and Ryan had gone ahead and soon found a settlement. They inquired at the general store for a lawyer and were given the name of a man down the street. But they assured them that he would not be in until the next day. They returned to the wagon train and told the gathering that they would return to talk to him the next day.

As they had promised, John, Ryan and a few other men returned to the settlement to find the lawyer. They had no trouble finding his shingle hanging out in front of his door. It read Frank Dubose Esq. They entered and found a large heavily bearded man sitting at his desk.

"Come in gentlemen." he gestured to chairs.

After they all were settled Ryan was the first to speak.

"We have a wagon train a few miles out of town. We need to know how to apply for citizens of Texas and then how to go about getting land for each of our families."

"I am afraid you will have to travel some more to do both things. Most of the land around here is already taken up. Your best bet will be to continue to Fort Nacogdoches and see the judge at the Fort there. But I do have a copy of the rules for settlers here somewhere." He rummaged through a couple of drawers and then came up with a sheet of paper.

NEW SETTLERS FOR THE REPUBLIC OF TEXAS

The new settler is required within six years to pay a nominal sum to the state for his land. For each sitio of pastureland he will pay $30; for each labor of unirrigable land $2.50; and for each labor which was irrigable he will pay $3.50. The government required no part of it to be paid until the end of four years. At the close of the fourth year one-third of the amount was due; at the end of the fifth year, another third; and when the sixth year closed, the last payment was to be made to the state. To acquire a title to his land the colonist had to occupy or cultivate it.

Fourth Class Headright

Issued to those who arrived between January 1, 1840 and January 1, 1842.

The amounts issued were the same as for third class headrights, plus the requirement of cultivation of 10 acres.

Signed by the Representatives of the State of Texas.

After reading the document and handing it around to the others from the train they returned to the wagon train. They all gathered in a group in the middle of the camp to hear Ryan read the paper to all of them. Ryan then told them that they would be going to Fort Nacogdoches the next day to see a Judge who would advise them of where land was available for them to try and settle on.

"The lawyer did say that we may still have to travel some more to find land as most of it right around here is already taken up. So be prepared to make a few more miles to find our place."

Each family drifted back to their campfires. And John's little band of friends gathered together.

"I don't know about the rest of you but I am anxious and ready to find us a new home." Mike stood next to Angie and the kids.

"Oh I can hardly wait!" Nancy clapped her hands. "It will be a joy to be in a house again with more than one room."

"Who said the new house would have more than one room?" John teased her.

Somewhere near them they could hear a fiddle and guitar and they drifted over and joined in the dancing and festivity. They were all so glad to nearly be to their destination.

The next day John and Ryan and a few others met and went to town to see the Judge. They were very disappointed when he told them there were no more land grants in this area. He had a couple of places, but they were really just small farms. He took out a letter and told them he had received this the day before. It was a notice of land grant for Beale and Grant Land Company. It was farther west and another month or two of traveling. He showed them on a map where they were located. I am instructed to stand in for this Grant and can sign your people up on it.

"We will have to go back and ask everyone else what they want to do." John told him.

That night around the campfire the meeting centered around the move farther west. John did not mince words when he told them there would be no settlement and it would not be very protected by any soldiers. He did tell them about the couple of farms here and two families decided to stay and they pulled out to go get their map and land from the Judge.

The others although disappointed and tired, got up early and begin their trek again.

THIRTEEN

The going on the wagon trail was still slow. The area they were traveling through was piney woods. The tall pines stood straight up and offered lots of shade. Some places they hung over the trail completely cutting out the light of the sun. But the sun was welcome when it shone. The days were getting shorter as the autumn set in. John worried that they would not have enough time to build much of a house before winter set in. They crossed the Brazos River the first of November after traveling another couple of months and then entered the Beale and Grant Land Grant. The Judge had filed the papers the day they met with him and shown them on a map the country that they had purchased. It lay to the west about two weeks more of traveling.

"We will reach our grant land tomorrow. We now have to decide who will live where. I suggest that we build a common area first for the winter. Then by the spring we can have all gone around and found where we want to settle. John has suggested that we use a draw system to decide who gets what. Each family will put their name in the hat and on turns they will draw out a number. That number will decide in what order you get to pick out your land." Ryan pointed to the map.

John had put the numbers in his hat. Each family sent a representative up to the table and drew out a number, and then the number was recorded in their wagon train book. Although John's group had decided they wanted to be next to each other, they each took a number individually. They had also made sure that the brothers drew two claims. John and Lizzie had spoken to George the night before and with his permission they did not put a number in the hat for him. They all agreed it might cause a lot of trouble for him. So it was to be that George would live with and take care of Lizzie on her claim.

The entries on the wagon train book read like this:

1. Guthrie Hunter
2. John Luther Fowlkes
3. Angelina Smetana
4. John Dunn
5. Satterwhite Clayton Sanderson
6. Nancy Dunn
7. Jo Berkhalter
8. Mike Collins
9. Dr. Mike Riley
10. Bertha Riley
11. Lizzie Farnsworth
12. J.D. Claire
13. James Carl Ryan
14. Cole Manny Younger
15. Chrouler Davidson
16. Ebenezer Jack McWilliams
17. Henry Richards Roberts
18. Gertrude Berkhalter
19. Samson Hunter

Each person came up then and affixed their signature by their name. A few like the Hunter brothers just made their mark as they had no formal education. Later this list would be revised to include number in household and children's names and occupation of the land grant holder and where their survey was but that was in the future. This was a great start now.

The next day they all rode horseback out from their camp and decided on a clearing with a small hill to the back for their main place that would become their meeting place. For the immediate future it would hold all these families in a stockade type of closed in area for protection. This started the very next day with the men falling trees and using horses pulled them into a common place. The men had to adjust their ideas on a stockade. They did not have the big pine trees that they were used to using for lumber. They had left the piney woods and come to a country with scrub and small trees. The trees were something called liveoaks and they were pretty scrawny compared to what they had left in East Texas. But they would make do. They were then stripped of their branches. The trees then looked like tall fence posts. Holes were dug and each tree was put in the ground and dirt tamped down around it to make it stay upright. They next tree was sunk in a hole and then lashed to the next one. It was slow going but soon it began to look like something. They had carefully measured each of the wagons and built the stockade so that all the wagons could be pulled inside. This would be their homes until spring could bring them surveyed land and their own houses. The front of the stockade was set aside for pens for the livestock and shed built to shelter them out of the same tall posts.

The first bad weather came in December. For the settlers used to the northern winters it was barely a bump, but it brought cold and a few days of rain. It also proved that they had picked a great place for their stockade. The rain ran off down the hillside and it only took about a day when the sun shown for the land to dry. As had been their habit since they had started on this trip to Texas, the friends moved their wagons together on one side of the stockade. Here they continued to build their communal fire and the women all pitched in to cook for the men of the group. As time went on Henry as usual built furniture for the group. They had no house to put it in but it was nice to have chairs for a change around the big table he had provided on the trail.

Nancy had told her tale of the kidnapping several times. But soon the other families tired of asking about it and it was dropped to Nancy's joy. Most of the time she didn't think about it much. For a few weeks after John had brought her home she had nightmares that woke everyone up but they were getting less and less. The biggest problem she had now was with John. He had treated her like a glass doll ever since they came home. After she had told him about what the awful man tried to do to her and how dirty she felt he had hardly even hugged her. Today she had decided to tell him about her feelings.

"Lizzy would you watch little Henry for a while? I think I want to ride out and see the new baby colts."

"Sure I will be glad to have the company. You just go ahead."

Nancy went out to the horse pen and caught her mare. Samson appeared out of nowhere and saddled the mare for her. Nancy protested that she could saddle her own horse but he ignored her. Then he held his hands for Nancy to step in and lifted her up to her saddle.

"You really don't have to wait on me, Samson."

"I know mam but I want to. I feel bad that I let that bad guy take you from the wagon that day."

"Oh Samson. Do not feel bad. You didn't know what they were going to do. Now I don't want you to worry about it anymore. I don't."

Samson smiled and waved at her as she cantered out to find John. It did not take long before she could hear the axes that the men were using to cut down the trees. She rode up and slipped down off her horse before John saw here. When he saw her he hurried over to her.

"Are you alright. Is something the matter?"

"I am fine. I just wanted to ride for a while. I was getting a little closed in at the wagon. Can you ride with me for a minute?"

"Of course I can." He laid his ax down on a log and hollered out to Mike the closest person and told him he was going to go ride with his wife. He just smiled at the two of them. He was so glad to see that they were getting back to normal.

As John and Nancy rode by a running stream, they reined in and leading their horses sat down on a fallen log.

"I need to talk to you." Nancy started.

John started to answer but she placed her fingers over his lips.

"Ever since we got back from the woods, you have not been very affectionate. I think you think about what that man tried to do to me. I want you to know that I need you to touch me and make love to me just like we used to. That bad man thing is over and he is gone and I am trying to forget the whole thing, but I need you to forget about it too."

"You are right. I haven't been holding you afraid that you wouldn't want me to yet. But I want to."

Nancy reached over and took his hands and put them around her. John quickly hugged her up tight.

"I was so afraid that I would not get you back. I don't think I could live without you."

"I thought about you and little Henry too. I am so lucky to have both of you."

They didn't realize how long they had been gone. They soon were back on their horses and returning back to the stockade.

FOURTEEN

The decision on which family got what pick of the land had been decided long before they reached the place they put up the stockade. When the additional new families joined the wagon train they were made aware that John Dunn and his group, then Wagon Boss Ryan would get first pick when they finally reached their destination. Then each of the new families would get a choice by lottery. So the first to ride out and find a new place for a home was John and Nancy and their group. After the stockade was finished they chose a day and Gertie packed a lunch and they started out. Nancy rode her mare so Lizzie rode with little Henry in the back of Gertie and Jo's wagon. They rest rode. They had decided the night before that they did not want to be right on top of the stockade but they realized it was a good idea to be close enough they could ride for help if they needed it. With the horses they would need a good water supply. So they wandered around for a while before they crossed a wide running stream. It had a rock bottom and the water ran clear down it. They crossed easily and soon came upon a clearing backed up by a good size hill. When Jo brought the wagon to a halt with a whoa they all knew they were home again. They sat and ate lunch and each one had a say in the choice of a place for them to live. The strange thing about the discussion was it did not include any talk of any of them living away from each other. The discussion centered on where the barn would be, Gertie and Jo's house, the big house with room for Lizzie, John and Nancy a house, and a bunkhouse for the rest of them. There was some embarrassment when they realized they had not talked about Angie and her family who were in the wagon. Nancy was the first to bring it up.

"Angie do you want to live here with us for now and then when you decide you can have a place of your own nearby?"

"I was hoping you would invite us to stay close by all of you. We will do everything to help out and Carlos can help with the livestock. I can cook and clean and sew." Angie blushed as she realized she was talking more than usual.

John spoke up.

"We always intended you to stay with us until you can have a place of your own. We will survey off your land when we do ours, but for you and the kids' safety you will live here until you feel like moving out."

"Until she moves out she can have some rooms in the big house." Lizzie spoke up.

So it was decided that this was the place and they talked about getting their survey done so they could start building on the houses and the barn. The women talked about houses and the men talked about barn and pens. They hung around long as they dared and then headed back to their stockade.

"Well did you find a place?" Ryan asked soon as they arrived back.

"We sure did." John replied. "We need to get the map out and start figuring out where each ones land is located on it."

The next morning found John showing Ryan where they had chosen their homestead.

John told his group that they each needed to go out and decide where they wanted their land to be. They had already decided that each ones land would radiate out from a center point like a pie. That way they could all live together and share the land, but each would have their part surveyed and registered in each ones individual names. So the next few weeks each one, usually with two or three others rode out and decided where their country would be. Using the contract that they had obtained from the Republic of Texas the map slowly evolved. After that Ryan decided on his place and it was added to the map. Then each of the other families drew their lots from the lottery and went out in search of their new places.

As each family decided where they wanted to live it was registered on the communal map. They soon contacted a surveyor who would come and drive the stakes for the division of the land. Some families like Dr. and Bertha Riley, the doctor and teacher, requested and were given their land, but remained near the stockade to build their house. Here the Dr. would have his practice and the teacher could envision a school house and a church. Chrouler Davidson, the blacksmith, too decided to build nearby to open his business. The Fowlkes family decided to open a store. They realized it would take a while to get supplies for the store but they could build the building in the meantime. The rest decided to move a way out of town. None were as far as John and Nancy, but John wanted lots of land for the horses. And they had the advantage when it came to having men to keep them safe.

They had heard of the Indians continuing raid around this area of Texas. In fact some of the cavalry had come by one day and had stopped to visit. John could tell that the officer in charge of this company thought they were all crazy for coming out here to live. He had told them, over some of Gertie's lunch that he could not wait to get back to civilization. He then recounted some of their latest Indian raids north and west of where they were.

That night still in their wagon, John again asked Nancy,

"Are you sure we are doing the right thing? You know we could go back to where there are roads and shops and a school for little Henry."

Nancy took his big hand in hers.

"We are doing the right thing. If we had been going to go to a city we would have gone back East when we started out. We knew what this was going to be like when we started. And I want to make Texas our new home. I know we will have to be careful with the Indian threat, but we know how to do that too."

John had loaned Samson and Guthrie out to the surveyor. John had insisted on him platting what would become the town so people could help those folks get going with their houses. After that he rode out with them nearly every day to see exactly where his country would be. It seemed to take forever, but they could not build until they had the survey completed. But it did not keep them from setting up a camp and build pens and the day finally came when they took the horses to their new home. The hands all went out and stayed at the camp with the horses. They took turns coming to town every few days.

The map soon had surveys for one street and three buildings for the town. Lizzie had decided to have the houses and barns on her land. So they were surveyed in a circle and that land was subtracted from her acres. Then the surveyor started with John and Nancy and then the others until all of their country was surveyed. Ryan then decided to join next to Mike on the outside.

Then the other families connected on between the group and where the town would be. Each of the town families then had their land surveyed on the opposite side of the stockade.

It was springtime before the surveying for John and the others was done. They then immediately moved their wagons out to the temporary camp. On their way they met two old Mexican men with two mules packed with their things. They invited them to join them for lunch. As they sat around talking the first man named Javier Gomez asked them how they were going to build their houses and barns.

Quickly Mike spoke up, "We will build them like before I guess with wood from the liveoaks trees."

"They will not last very long like that. You need to build your buildings with rock and adobe so they will last."

Both of the Mexican men spoke English, taught by the padres in the Catholic schools.

"So do you know how to build with the rock and adobe?" Eb asked.

"Yes we do. But it will take some work that you do not know how to do. So we will stay and show you how to make the stone buildings."

Of course, the barn was built first. And it did not take as long as their other one did. They knew from the other one in Indian Territory what worked and what did not. They also made a few changes that they had discovered they needed before. The bunkhouse was added on to one side of the barn. On the opposite side they quickly built Gertie and Jo's house. They wanted to make it bigger than the one they had had before, but Gertie liked her little house so they made it the same as before. They did add a nice porch for them to sit out on in the evening. John insisted that their house be last so the big house was built next. It also was on the order of the one they had before with some minor changes. It had the living area, kitchen and dining area and Lizzie's apartment on the bottom floor. This one would be two stories with three bedrooms upstairs so when they all had to come to one place and for now would house Angie and her small children. Carlos would live in the bunkhouse with the men.

Each building was built with stone from the surrounding outcropping on the hills and the adobe mud came from the nearby stream bank. The Mexican men taught them how to chip away at the limestone to make rectangle bricks. The adobe was made out of mud and water. This was poured into forms made out of cedar logs. They were then set out in the heat to dry. When they dried they would be banged out of the forms and used. The adobe also was used to fill the cracks in the stone blocks. The Mexican men worked tirelessly. Their days went from sunup to sundown. The men had trouble keeping up the pace with them. From the corner stones to the finished roofs, they labored in the heat of the sun, not seeming to be bothered by the sun; while Mike, Henry and John sweated and tired long before they would quit in the evening.

They had a party when the big house was finished in late summer. They invited to other families from the wagon train out to help them celebrate. It was a bbq with all the fixings. Some other wagon train had come by and so there was a lot to talk about. Dr. Riley had brought out some newspapers that they had left. Lizzie and Nancy could not wait to read them!

Then the next week it was John and Nancy's turn to have a house. They had moved in with Lizzie to finally get out of the wagon but they were ready to have a place of their own.

This time they chose to build a little ways back of the others. It again would be near where the stream came down out of the hills. It would look down on the others and the valley below. This house was bigger than their other one too. It would have three bedrooms; one for them, one for little Henry and one for the next child. The next child had not happened and Nancy was beginning to worry about it. John did not seem to worry about it at all. He was perfectly happy with Nancy and little Henry.

FIFTEEN

Now that the houses and the barn were finished, it was time to get back to raising livestock. They had gathered quite a herd of horses and cattle on their trip south. Red had done a good job of breeding his mares. And to their surprise one day, a longhorn bull appeared with their twelve cows. John had not had a bull on the trip since he was afraid they would hurt someone especially when they had to herd them into the circle of wagons away from the Indians. But now he needed a bull and to ride out and find one was a small miracle. He was brown and white, sort of spotted, and had a long set of horns extending out from his head. By the time John found him with the cows, he had already taken possession of them and was not too glad to see John and Henry.

"Whoa! What do we have here?" Mike said aloud.

The bull had moved around between them and the cows. He shook his big horns with a side to side motion of his head. Then he pawed the dirt with his front hooves. He threw dirt up on both of his sides. As John and Henry eased around him, but not too close he seemed to lose some of his steam. The bull seemed to be trying to decide if they were friend or foe. When he felt they were not a threat he turned back and joined the cows.

"I just had been thinking about looking for a bull. Seems God thought we needed one. But I worry that he might carry the cows off with him. We will watch and see what he does. In the meantime we will let him breed the cows." John said.

When they returned to the barn and was unsaddling, Nancy came in with Little Henry. They had been out finding eggs and then putting the hens up in their pen for the night.

"Guess what we saw!" John said as he lifted Little Henry up on his shoulders.

"A big longhorn bull was running with the cows. And he is spotted brown and white with big horns. In the spring we will have little longhorn calves."

They stopped off at the big house for supper and Little Henry went running in telling everyone that they were going to have baby caves soon. John and Mike then took turns describing the big bull to the group.

"We will have to ride careful around him until he gets used to us. And we will have to take turns keeping a watch every day to see that he doesn't take off with the cows." Mike added.

The next day nearly everyone rode out to see the bull. They all heeded Mike and Johns warning to not get close and bother him. But they had to see the magnificent horns.

Lizzie was back riding nearly every day to see about the horses. They had several colts born on the trail and they were now old enough to start their training. So she picked one out and with Samson's ready rope they brought him into the pens at the barn. He was plenty spooked about the whole affair. But Samson soon had him at ease. Lizzie gently taught Samson and the colt what to do and how to go about getting to know one another.

Gertie and Angie and the younger children decided to go in the buckboard to pick berries that they had seen along the edge of a draw that ran into the bigger stream by their homestead. They had carried baskets and with the children's help they soon had four baskets full of wild plums. These they would make jellies and jams for the winter. They had carried a picnic lunch and the children had a great time wading in the stream. The sky began to cloud up and they decided to head back to the ranch house. They were about half way there, with the houses and barn in sight, when they heard the first whoop! They knew immediately it was the sounds of Indians and they soon saw them come out of the brush. Gertie yelled at the team. Angie quickly made the children lay down flat in the wagon bed. When she turned around Gertie handed her the 30-30 rifle they had put under the seat of the wagon. Turning as best she could, Angie started shooting. They had turned the little corner going into the ranch and headed for the barn. Gertie ran the team into the barn. By then the others had come out shooting. Mike had caught the team and hurried Gertie and Angie and the kids up to the loft of the barn. He then had run over and shut the barn doors. Gertie hurried over to the hayloft doors and began firing out the opening.

"Stop firing. Stop firing. They are all gone!" Jo was yelling at her.

Mike then came back in and helped them down the ladder. Holding Angie a little longer than needed he then helped the others down. They all then went into the big house for a sit down. Gertie's hair was sticking out all over and the children began to laugh.

"We don't think we will go pick berries by ourselves anymore." Gertie told the rest of them in a serious tone.

"I think that is a great idea!" John chimed in. "They will not go far as they will come back for their dead. We need to get out there and see if we can tell what tribe they are."

Eb rose up and went to the door. "I will go but some of you might cover me if they see me. They will think I am doing something bad to their dead. They are plenty superstitious."

Samson and Guthrie quickly followed him out with their rifles. The others took up a look out on the front porch. Eb was only gone a few minutes and then back with an arrow he had taken out of the handmade pouch on the braves back. The Indians called it a quiver.

"I believe we have been attacked by a part of the Comanches. Comanches are a group of Indians made up of several members of other tribes that have banded together to kill or drive out the white men. Now that they know we are here we will have to be extra careful. First thing I think we need to do is to build some kind of fence across the front here so we can open and shut a gate. This will at least slow them down where they cannot come right at us." Eb settled down in a chair. Samson spoke up asking if they would kill them when they came back for their dead and was met with a resounding no from everyone. Only if they attack us do we kill them was the main theme of agreement around the room.

Just as Eb had figured the Indians reappeared during the moonlit night. He and the brothers were standing guard by the side of the house. The braves quickly carried their dead away. They hardly made a sound. Eb then had the brothers stand watch the rest of the night but the braves did not return.

"I agree we need some kind of fence so we will begin that today." John said.

In the country where they had decided to homestead there were not tall pine trees. There were scrubby cedar trees and mesquite. So the fence would have to be made from crooked small logs from the cedars. Soon the women could hear their axes working and soon they could see a fence like the stockade in town going up across the front of the houses and barns. For some reason this little barricade made them all feel better. Before now they had not worried too much about the Indians as they had not seen them. But today was very real and they had seen them up close and the fear was now there.

SIXTEEN

After supper Mike sought out Angie. "Wow that was plenty close today! You did a good job shooting.

"Gertie did the best job getting us into the barn. I thought we were going to go straight through the other side." She laughed quietly.

Mike spoke next, "I was really scared for you. I don't think I would like it if anything happened to you." He took her in his arms and kissed her tenderly. "Have you thought about my proposal in a while?"

"Yes I have. And I have decided I will marry you."

"Well darn it. When were you going to tell me?" Mike stepped back.

"I think I decided when we were racing along in front of those Indians." She answered.

"And if the Indians had not come along would you have said yes?"

"We may never know."

Hand in hand they walked back to the big house and told everyone. There were hugs and back slapping. Everyone had been wondering when they would finally tie the knot.

It took the better part of the rest of the week to get the fence and gate up. Henry had decided that they should have a real entrance so he had cut out a post to go across the top of the fence. The problem now was that they had no name to put on it. So that night at supper that was the discussion.

"I don't have a name to hang over the gate. Does anyone have any idea what we are going to call this place?"

Since no one had worried about a name they decided to let everyone have a few days to think about a name for their spread.

The next day found Nancy and Angie doing the laundry on the side of the big house. They had built a fire and the kettles were filled with water. As the clothes were placed in the boiling water they added lye soap to one. Using a long stick they would stir the clothes to agitate the soap. The other kettle was filled with cold water from the stream. John and Mike had carried the water in buckets up to them. When Nancy and Angie decided the clothes were clean they were lifted from the boiling kettle to the cold one and then pulled out one at a time and hung on the nearby clothesline. They had done this a lot of times by now and worked together as a great team. The work was hot and both women sweated and their hair was mostly down from handling the clothes going back and forth.

Just as Nancy was hanging up the last pair of Levis, Angie ran to the house. Nancy looked down the row of clothes and there stood a big brave. By that time Angie was coming off the porch with the rifle that hung over the door of the big house. Nancy yelled at her,

"No Angie he is a friend!"

At that time the brave walked closer and said,

"Ho, John's woman." Then he gestured with two fingers from his eyes to Nancy. She immediately copied the I see you sign. She then motioned him to follow her up on the porch.

"Go get John from the barn," she told Angie.

John heard Angie before he came out of the barn.

"It's an Indian on the porch with Miss Nancy." She yelled.

John quickly grabbed the gun they had put in the saddle shed after the round with the Indians. He crept around the edge and up on the porch of the house. He then walked quietly around to the front of the house. There was Nancy and the Indian sitting with their backs to him. They were drinking lemonade and eating cookies. They were talking and gesturing and sometimes he heard Nancy laugh. He then walked around them to face them.

"Ho, John Dunn. Long time no see you." Sitting Grass laughed aloud.

"Ho Sitting Grass I see you." John then shook hands with Sitting Grass.

"What brings you to see us?"

"Talking Wolf says "the boss' name is Johansson. And he lives about a hundred miles East and North of here. And do you want him to kill him?"

Nancy looked at John with a pale panicked look on her face.

"No we don't want you to kill him. Does he know where we live?"

"I do not know that but I am sure they are looking still for your woman."

"We will be on the lookout for them. And we will pass the word in town to look out for him too."

"Where are you camping now as a tribe?"

"We are a few miles down this river from you. We know that you had Indians come up on your family the other day and so now we watch over you. You don't seem to be able to see about yourselves very good."

John laughed. "When can you come eat with us?"

"We will come the next full moon to eat with you. I will want pie."

Nancy then was the one to laugh. As they were talking the others had come up on the porch and Nancy quickly introduced them all around. She then coaxed Angie out of the house to meet an Indian that was not trying to kill her.

Sitting Grass then turned to John.

"The fence is good but it will not save you if you do not put it all around. I came in over the mountain at the back and you did not see or hear me."

"We wondered about that. So we will have more fence when you come back."

Sitting Grass then rose up out of his chair. Turning to Nancy he again motioned the I see you sign and then loped off out the front gate. In less than ten minutes he was gone, melting into the landscape and they could no longer be seen.

"I am glad to see him, but I worry about them. Other settlers will not realize they are the good ones and might shoot them. Also we know that the soldiers will not hesitate to kill them." Nancy pondered aloud.

"I will speak to the next officer that comes around and explain that they are no harm to anyone." John replied.

Everyone then went back to what work they were doing and Nancy and Angie finished the laundry washing and hanging out to dry.

SEVENTEEN

Talking Wolf knew that his little band's days were numbered. They could not continue to hide all the time. He had watched the soldiers ride into John's place. They did the same thing every time. They would ride through the gate and the lead man would dismount and go up on the porch. He never went inside. Nancy or whoever was home would greet him. They would offer him something to drink. John or one of the men would talk to him for a little while. The other soldiers never got off their horses. When the lead one was through talking and getting a drink, he would remount and they would all go away again. Talking Wolf had watched them several times now. With this information he had decided on the plan to move to the back of John's property and then he felt they would be safe for the time being.

The next day they circled John's house and then disappeared into the brush behind it. Mike saw them and soon John and him joined Talking Wolf. John and Talking Wolf shook hands and then gave each other a bear hug.

"How are you and your family? Talking Wolf asked.

"We are all very well. Nancy worries about you. I told her that I would speak to the soldiers and tell them you are not any trouble."

"You must not do that. The soldiers were sent here to kill all the Indians they could find and they are doing their best to do that. We will just stay hidden when they come."

"Ok I will tell everyone not to tell anyone that you are here."

"We will move back about a half mile and can then see the horses and your house and help keep watch for soldiers and bad Indians."

Nancy watched from her front porch, as she sat picking beans, and wondered how they would be able to keep the bad Indians off and the soldiers off Talking Wolf's little family.